Earth Walker

Book Three in the Fire & Ice Series

By

Karen Payton Holt

Think 'Twilight' meets 'Game of Thrones', with a dark twist, and you are in the right mindset to enter the world of Fire & Ice.

AVAILABLE NOW:

Fire & Ice Prequel: Death of Connor Sanderson

Available in Paperback on Amazon
ISBN 978-1-9831113-4-1

Paperback and Hardback available in bookstores:
A5 Paperback ISBN 978-1-9996614-8-9
Hardback ISBN 978-1-9996614-9-6
FREE on Amazon Kindle Unlimited

BOOK ONE in the Series:

Fire & Ice: Awakening

Available in Paperback on Amazon
ISBN 978-1-9806710-4-6

Paperback and Hardback available in bookstores:
A5 Paperback ISBN 978-1-9996614-0-3
Hardback ISBN 978-1-9996614-1-0
FREE on Amazon Kindle Unlimited

BOOK TWO in the Series:

Fire & Ice: Survival

Available in Paperback on Amazon
ISBN 978-1-9830806-5-4

Paperback and Hardback available in bookstores:
A5 Paperback ISBN 978-1-9996614-2-7
Hardback ISBN 978-1-9996614-3-4
FREE on Amazon Kindle Unlimited

This is **BOOK THREE** in the series:

Fire & Ice: Earth Walker

Available in Paperback on Amazon
ISBN 978-1-7181294-5-0

Paperback and Hardback available in bookstores:
A5 Paperback ISBN 978-1-9996614-4-1
Hardback ISBN 978-1-9996614-5-8
FREE on Amazon Kindle Unlimited

Watch This Space,

TWO upcoming releases are:

BOOK FOUR: Heart of Stone

BOOK FIVE: Invasion

For the latest news on the publishing dates visit my websites:

karenpaytonholt.com

Karen Payton Holt on Facebook.

karenpaytonholt on Instagram

@karenpaytonholt on TWITTER.

Our epic journey continues, and I hope you enjoy Book Three in the Fire & Ice Series: Earth Walker

Please share your thoughts and feelings in reviews – this is my fourth novel and I welcome your support.

I dedicate this novel to two people who believed in me.

They drove me forward, and, at times, gave me a much-needed kick up the posterior.

This is for my mum, Sylvia, and my friend of forty years, Steve.

And as the journey continues, and, at times I feel like giving up,

thank you to my family members and friends who want me to succeed

and for buying the books – you know who you are.

Chapter 1

Lying on a bed in the cavern, Doctor Connor opened his eyes and watched the darkness billow like ink floating in water. Rebekah lay snuggled into his side, her warm thigh draped over his stomach. Holding her while she slept continued to be an interesting challenge to Connor's vampire senses. Blood would always register as food, on a primitive level.

Connor eased Rebekah's head from his shoulder without waking her and settled her cheek onto the pillow. He rolled out of bed, quickly gaining his feet and, in a blur of movement, pulled on black pants and a shirt and scraped back his black hair.

He glanced across the darkened chamber at the girl watching him from the doorway. It was like looking into a mirror. Her slate-gray eyes glinted in the gloom. The contrast of her cobalt-tinted black hair and milk-white skin never failed to entrance him. He committed each facet to memory, knowing that another month would see her grow three inches taller and, seemingly, become a decade older in maturity.

I've got this, Seren. Stay here with your Mama. Connor frowned until he saw his daughter nod, and knew she had reached inside his mind and read his thoughts.

He smiled then, as she crossed the room and threw herself at him with force which would have knocked a human father off his feet. She hugged him briefly around the waist before climbing up onto the bed, laying down on top of the covers, and cuddling into a stirring Rebekah.

Okay, Papa.

Rebekah's heart rate quickened as sleep fell away and her eyes opened. The instant of awareness racing through her body delighted Connor. He watched, enthralled, as perspiration scattered diamond-hued dewdrops over her skin.

"Hey, honey," he murmured in appreciation.

Sitting up in the bed, taking in Connor's fully dressed state and the flint-like glitter in his eyes, she knew better than to delay him with questions.

"Stay safe," she said, her determined gaze filling in the rest.

"You too, and stay together, okay?" Satisfied, in a seamless movement, Connor collected a vial of human blood from a wooden chest, flipped open the lid, and downed the contents. He shouldered aside the canvas curtain in the doorway and left. Breaking into an easy run, he accelerated along the underground tunnel and, in moments, was moving faster than the human eye could see.

The distance between him and the sleeping cavern rushed from dozens into hundreds of feet within seconds. But, with crystal clarity Connor still heard Rebekah's sleepy voice asking Seren what was going on. He picked out the rustling noise of bedclothes being thrown back and the sound of cotton brushing over skin as Rebekah hurriedly dressed in her noisy human fashion.

With a rueful smile, Connor fitted pictures to the fading sounds. It would take her only seconds to pull her feathered blonde hair into a ponytail, rub her hands over her face, and burst into action.

He and Rebekah had enjoyed almost two years of tentative peace since Seren's birth, but, only last night, Connor had made the discovery that some vampires inside the London hive were openly challenging Principal Julian in court. As Connor's closest ally, Julian used his position as best he could, but was finding it increasingly difficult to persuade the hive that the answers to Seren's hybrid birth were *still* unknown.

Initially, the failure of early trials of the hybrid breeding program made the hive members more tolerant. But, the council's assurances that Doctor Connor was making progress became less convincing as a year passed by and now, the second was well underway.

Connor *was* making progress, but not in the direction the hive hoped for. Every round of tests took him closer to discovering a blood substitute which would enable vampires to survive on animal blood alone. That was where Connor's heart lay, in liberating human kind from being held captive on vampire controlled farms.

As things stood, a vital daily dose of human blood remained the only way to hydrate the vampire brain. It unlocked the brainstem and allowed the three separate cells known as the brain centers — or, as Connor saw them, the trio of personalities in control of vampire compulsions – to feed and rehydrate, preventing vampire dementia.

It was inevitable the feelings of unrest within the hive would erupt into rebellion.

Connor rushed towards the surface, wondering what scale of threat lay in wait.

Every few feet, the light from a bulkhead lamp illuminated the tunnel. Their dim electric glow flickered like strobe lights across Connor's retina. On the final approach to the hidden entrance of the eco-shelter, electric lights changed to the flames of torches mounted in sconces. Connor could also smell the meadow grass and the dew in the air which humans would never detect.

Although they faded with every powerful stride he took, Connor's preternatural senses picked out the noise of human footfalls deep underground. Their rhythm laced enticingly with the wet shushing sound of racing heart chambers. He knew that when he returned, Rebekah and Seren, and the other humans would be locked inside the panic room. They would be safe.

He raced his shadow along the smoothly carved tunnel. His attention shifted back to the challenge ahead.

The black and white movie of the vision Seren placed inside his mind replayed. When she had laid her palm on his forehead, her images had exploded like a phosphorous flare, imprinting in his occipital lobe as if they were his own.

The fragmented impressions of the vampire attack became Connor's driving force. He already knew what he and Anthony would face, in a matter of minutes. He hurtled through the shelter's claustrophobic passageways. The vial of human blood he had swallowed tingled through muscle and sinew fibers. He hit top speed and knew a moment of satisfaction. Being at the peak of human physical fitness when turned, he had become a vampire of formidable force. *If Seren is right, Anthony and I will need everything we've got.*

The torch flames guttered in his wake as Connor swept by and slipped out from behind the blackout curtain. He let the flap fall shut, trapping the dancing rays of light inside the passageway behind him. Having the perfect vision of a supernatural being, the plunge into pitch-black barely registered. On the final bend, he skimmed up the wall like a toboggan and burst from the black maw of the tunnel mouth into the dark, moonless night.

Connor barreled across the field, compressing the air ahead of him and driving it forward. Collecting the soundwaves which bounced back, he looked for the dips in their resonance which would tell him how many vampires were moving through the woods.

Seren saw six, and her visions have never yet been wrong.

Connor frowned, oblivious to the frost forming on his cheekbones as the icy air dragged at the marble-white perfection of his skin. *Seren's visions are coming closer together, as though keeping pace with her accelerated physical growth.*

Seren had left babyhood behind in mere weeks, and now, not quite two years later, she was as tall as a teenager. Human years no longer had any meaning.

Cupping his hand, Connor hooted like a tawny owl, copying a trick Greg and Seth used when out on reconnaissance. Humans could still teach vampires something, it seemed. Tawny owls were no longer seen in this part of Kent.

Both men were Royal Marines. Greg, who was the largest mountain of human muscle Connor had ever seen, and the more-wiry Seth, were a reassuring presence in the eco-shelter. *Of course, neither can survive a vampire attack, but they'd cause one hell of a diversion trying to save the others.*

Connor surged forward. *Let's get this done.* He heard Anthony's answering owl-call just as a black figure darted into his path.

Instinctively, Connor leapt up, grabbed a tree branch, and drove his legs forwards. His boots hit the approaching vampire squarely in the chest.

The force launched the vampire backwards. He slammed into the dirt, his shoulders carving a trench in the woodland floor before he ground to a halt.

Letting go of the branch, Connor followed through, both his feet landing heavily on top of the prone figure. Reluctant excitement filled his mouth with saliva at the vibration traveling up through his thighs when the vampire's ribcage collapsed.

Without pausing, Connor set off between the trees. Snagging his shirt on the bark, he cut a path through the wood. He tracked another fast-moving black shape, honing in on the intent white face flitting through the thick picket of trees.

Connor closed in on his quarry. Coming up behind his victim at speed, he grabbed a handful of the vampire's hair and rammed his face into the trunk of a solid English oak. The vampire's cheekbones crumbled, and a shower of crushed bark clattered to the ground. Connor jerked the head back until the stricken vampire's spine snapped. He let the body fall to the floor, resisted the urge to look down into the cavity of what used to be a face, and took off after intruder number three.

They're disorganized. They're not guardsmen. The thought left a bad taste in his mouth. Though he had no choice, this felt like execution, not combat. But there was no room for sentiment. A sickening crack rang through the woods, and Connor had no doubt that Anthony was finding them just as easy to dispatch.

He circled back through the undergrowth at a slower, more measured pace. Even though he drew a blank, every instinct told him they were not yet done.

He stopped and listened to the silence, closing his eyes and waiting for a misplaced breeze or an unfamiliar noise. Taking in a vampire breath, he washed the damp, earth-scented atmosphere over his palette. His lip curled at the decaying blood clot aroma that hit the back of his throat.

He's nearby. So, it's a game of nerves. Who will blink first?

Connor froze. The sound of mud squelching under foot gave him the bearing he needed. In a lightning-fast move, he dropped down, scooped up a stone, and, slicing his arm upward in the accelerating arc of a discus throw, bounced it from a tree trunk. He felt a spike of satisfaction when he heard bone shatter and the stone buried itself in the eye socket of the vampire creeping up behind.

Connor cut off the splutter of surprise with an explosive uppercut. He drove the heel of his hand up under the vampire's chin, shattering the vertebrae in his neck. The third body thudded to the ground.

Another shadow moved, and Connor whipped around. He stopped in mid action and smiled when a disheveled Anthony moved silently forward, running his hands through rust-brown hair and shuffling his broad shoulders to tidy his coat.

"Three?" asked Anthony. He surveyed the tattered undergrowth and the fallen vampire at Connor's feet.

They would not move the bodies because the vampires were well inside the twenty-mile exclusion zone around the human habitat – their deaths were sanctioned by the council, although, for how much longer, Connor could not be sure.

"You know, every one we kill eases the load on the human farm facility. Fewer vampires to feed is a good thing." Anthony smirked, but his brown eyes glittered with regret. "Pity they don't listen to the council. Setting foot in these woods is a declaration of war. You'd hope they would fear that."

Connor took a deep breath. "Things are spiraling out of control. The storm clouds are gathering, and Seren feels it, too. She knew this was happening." He grinned, touching his forehead as if it bore the imprint of her palm. The jolt of her anxiety had been like the discharge of a Taser gun. "And, she certainly knows how to get her old man moving, that's for sure."

"And is she still growing as fast?"

Anthony's expression was wistful. As Connor's surgical assistant at the hospital, he had witnessed the harrowing moments leading up to Seren's birth, but he rarely ventured inside the human eco-shelter.

He had come a long way in the decades under Connor's tutelage, but he remained a vampire who struggled for control around injured humans. Rebekah's labor had turned out well, and Connor had forgiven Anthony for adding to the ordeal. However, Anthony was having a hard time forgiving himself. In vampire terms, two years of guilt was a drop in the ocean of eternity.

During Seren's birth, to filter the compelling aroma of blood, beneath his face mask, Anthony had packed his sinuses and throat with surgical gauze before setting foot in the operating theater. But, when Connor needed his help to perform Rebekah's emergency C-section, the river of fresh blood flowing from the incision had flipped Anthony's vampire senses into feral feeding mode.

Connor could easily recall the moment Anthony tore his mask away, snarling. Shredded wound dressings had spilled from his mouth like from the pouches of a rabid hamster. His brown eyes had pleaded for help. He had wanted Connor to stop him. *So, how could I not forgive him? He tried.* Connor had physically ejected Anthony, leaving Julian to lock the mortified vampire in a cadaver drawer.

"She's growing as fast as ever. C'mon, Anthony, let's get back," said Connor, quickly veiling a sympathetic glance.

At an easy run, they reached the edge of the woodland within seconds. Connor came to a halt, gazing out over the oil-black expanse of darkened meadow. Still on alert, he scented the air. The tightness in his chest eased when he found nothing amiss. The rolling hills of the Kent countryside provided the perfect camouflage, and the entrance to the labyrinth of caverns was disguised as a natural fissure in the scarred terrain. *Although, it no longer matters because the location is not secret. We passed from secrecy to standing guard when I saved Rebekah's life.*

Anthony stood beside Connor and nudged him with an elbow as he said, "Connor, you know, we have to head into London and tell Julian about the attack. He has to sanction the killings."

Connor nodded thoughtfully. "We've been lucky to have held the hive at bay for so long. In the last few months Seren's appetite for blood has become insatiable. I'm sure the woods will run out of rabbits. It will be a good thing when she moves a little higher up the food chain." He chuckled drily. "I think it's her survival instinct. She senses danger, and the more she feeds, the faster she grows. In the animal kingdom, babies are vulnerable, and her hormones are providing her with the solution."

"But she is well?"

"Everything about her is thriving. Her psychic powers are growing, too. Her connection to me, at any rate. She walks her thoughts through my head so clearly that I'm beginning to feel lonely if she's not there."

"And how is Rebekah bearing up?"

"Oh..." Connor smiled. He recalled the sounds of Rebekah hurriedly pulling on clothes as he was leaving. He rewound to the night before, when he had become lost in the delights of removing them.

Seren took human sleep only once in a blue moon, or so it seemed. The downside of their psychic connection proved to be keeping her out of his head. Not allowing her to see through his eyes was not always easy.

Last night, when Seren fell off a precipice into unconsciousness, Connor's mind had turned to love, his fingertips tingling at the anticipation of touching the velvet of Rebekah's skin.

Rebekah always knew when she had his undivided attention. The predatory smile when he looked at her and the carefully measured stride as he closed the distance between them sent shivers down her spine. And, slipping his hands around her waist and over the satin skin of her delicate ribcage, Connor felt them, too. Stroking up inside her shirt, he had drank in her scent and kissed her. *Practice makes perfect.* And he was still working on that.

When touching Rebekah, he always sank into revival sleep, unlocking the cell door in his brain and releasing the chilled-out mellow persona which reduced vampire stress levels. And, as though he waded through molasses-thickened air, he could measure the movement of every muscle. There were times when he became too eager and bruises blossomed beneath her skin, but, even though regret tightened his body, her sighs of pleasure would chase the doubts away.

Those moments took him back to the heady, addictive days when he first stumbled across her. He ruefully acknowledged he was still hooked.

"Okay, judging by your face, Rebekah is doing just fine." Anthony lifted a get-a-room eyebrow, and his chuckle drew an answering one from Connor.

Connor glanced at the navy, star-littered sky. "I have two hours before dawn." Slicing a look at Anthony's amused profile, he said gruffly, "I'll go and put Rebekah's mind at rest, and meet you at the council buildings in an hour."

Anthony nodded and melted into the shadows, his gentle laughter drifting on the breeze.

Breaking into a run, Connor retraced his path over the rutted acres of potholed meadow. Inside the hillside, he ducked behind the thick sackcloth curtain. His skin tingled as the torch flames spat, licking out to taste the condensation pluming from his ice-cold skin.

Connor bypassed the large meeting cavern and entered the more modest dining chamber, with its orderly array of wooden tables and chairs. The kitchen appeared deserted. But, running his fingers over the polished steel counter, he detected heat from where metal trays of hot food had rested upon it. *Not like Oscar.*

Oscar usually sluiced the steel surface with crushed ice after cleaning the kitchen. It made it impossible to calculate when it was last used, even with a vampire's ability to measure heat down to the tenth of a degree. It told Connor that the half-dozen humans had rushed into hiding. *In this instance, I agree. Speed was more important.*

Just as Connor expected, Greg stepped out from the shadows.

With some concentration, Connor could hear Seth's depressed heart rate coming from the deep recess beside the larder cupboard. The beta blockers and pheromone suppressant spray the humans used worked well, but the Marines were a tag-team and never far apart.

"Is it all clear?" asked Greg, relaxing the grip on his blacksmith's mallet and coming down from red alert to careful amber.

Connor nodded. "For now, but I have to report to the council. I think they should all stay in there, until I get back, at least. I'll just say 'hi' to Rebekah."

His combat gear creaked as Greg rested a hip on to the kitchen counter. "Sure thing," he said lightly, "she'll climb the walls if you don't."

Greg's straight-faced delivery drew a snort of amusement from the shadows. "So will *he*," muttered Seth.

"Hey, give a guy a break," Connor said ruefully, turning away and silently crossing the tiled floor of the kitchen.

He pulled aside the wooden shutter which obscured the entrance to the converted walk-in refrigerator which served as the panic room. Plastic pipes cut through the packed clay soil overhead, letting in air from the meadow above. The rubber-seal on the door contained the adrenalin-soaked odor of human trepidation and deadened the delightful sounds of thundering human hearts, making it almost impossible, even for vampire senses, to zero in on those inside.

Squeezing the steel trigger on the handle of the door, feeling the metal creak in his grasp, Connor carefully pulled it open.

Battery-powered lights cast a warm glow over the biscuit-colored padding on the walls. Five faces turned sharply in his direction, looking up from where they huddled on the cushioned floor. Oscar and Evie were holding hands and, a foot or so away, Rebekah sat sandwiched between Seren and Leizle.

Catching sight of him, the group relaxed, the stiff lines of anxiety in their bodies melting. Leizle waved a hand in greeting, directing a hopeful glance over Connor's shoulder. When she realized he was alone, her smile of welcome dimmed. *Julian has been away too long.* Connor resolved to remedy the situation when he got back to London.

His attention turned to Rebekah and the beaming smile lighting up her face, and, for a moment, Connor forgot to move. As he predicted, her blond hair was pulled back into a ponytail. Her determined warm, brown gaze dominated her delicate features.

"Hi, Honey, I'm home," Connor said gently.

Lifting her hand from Rebekah's arm, Seren wriggled woolen gloved fingers at him, and he smiled.

She also wore a fleecy jacket, not for her own warmth but because she was trying not to chill her mother. Her eyes met Connor's, and he nodded minutely. *You were right.*

He felt her light touch gathering his unspoken words, and her gray eyes shone with satisfaction.

"Hey," Rebekah grumbled.

His smile twitched as, helping Rebekah to her feet, he leisurely kissed her and murmured, "I just dropped in to say, 'hi'." Leaning back, he stared down into her earnest face. "I have to report back to Julian. Stay in here 'til I get back?"

"Of course," Rebekah answered.

"So meek and mild." He chuckled, and Rebekah jabbed him in the ribs and hurt her hand.

As his cold touch covered her fingers, soothing the throbbing, he felt it tingling through his palm in a dull echo. Glancing over Rebekah's head and raising an eyebrow, he said innocently, "Hello, Oscar. I see you are well prepared."

Oscar pretended to bristle. "You'll thank me one day, lad."

The survival kit the older man had packed contained enough food, flasks of soup, and water to last two weeks. Connor was grateful for his attention to detail.

Oscar had been the chef in the eco-community for seventeen years, ever since the pandemic wiped out most of the human race. The big bear of a man had looked out for the shocked and confused six-year-old Rebekah, took her into his heart as a surrogate daughter and watched her grow into a headstrong young woman. After the birth, his fiercely protective nature instantly expanded to take in Seren and, strangely, Connor.

Of the six humans still under Connor's protection, Oscar was the only one who dared to slap him on the back and call him 'lad'. Connor found endless amusement in that.

Reaching down to ruffle the coal-black strands of Seren's hair, Connor said, "Be good, Squirt." Straightening once more, he framed Rebekah's face between his palms and kissed her. "I'll be back soon." His hands lingered on her warm cheeks as he stepped back and reluctantly turned away.

He was almost out of the door when he registered Leizle's crestfallen features and paused. "You know, things are tense right now, Leizle. But, I'll tell Julian to get his ass over here, if he knows what's good for him."

And with that, he was gone.

Connor cut through the Kent countryside, taking a direct route through the town humans used to call Swanley. From there, he headed northwest into London, crossing the River Thames at Vauxhall Bridge and tracking the perimeter of Hyde Park.

The council building loomed as a pale gray ice-castle, the carved quartz of the facade glittering like frost in the pre-dawn light. Anthony was not waiting outside, so Connor took the sixteen steps up from the sidewalk in one leap, pushed open the twelve-foot tall solid oak door as if it was made of card, and headed down the walnut paneled corridors.

Connor followed the sound of vampire voices, and his annoyance bit deep as the stream of sound, like that of a babbling brook, separated into two protagonists. *Great! Supervisor Matthew.*

Gripping the handle of a door marked 'Courtroom', he arranged an expression of faint amusement on his face designed to irritate the supervisor, and entered.

The vampire gallery was full. But, instead of the disinterested silent throng Connor had faced for decades, their impatience swept like a Mexican wave across the room as they turned expectantly in his direction. Seren's birth had been a stone tossed into the pond of vampire complacency, and the ripples were becoming a tidal wave of intolerance. True, Councilor Serge had been banished to the Scotland Hive, but support for the hybrid breeding project was gathering momentum even in his absence, along with the expectation that Connor should provide answers.

"Doctor Connor." Supervisor Matthew had found a target for his gripes.

Taking his time to survey the court before looking the supervisor up and down, Connor almost smiled as Matthew shrank. "Supervisor?"

"Principal Julian has ordered one rest-day per week for humans over the age of forty? He..." Matthew shot an apology in Julian's direction. "*Principal* Julian tells me this is on your recommendation?"

Connor glanced up at where the three council jurors were seated on their elevated dais, and lifted an eyebrow at Julian before answering. "It's a long-term view. It makes the rations tight, true, but ten humans have died in the last two years and their autopsies revealed that seven were avoidable. Their immune systems were shot. A day of rest, and amino acids and vitamin supplements, will reap long-term rewards. Even allowing for a rest day, the blood harvest will be sufficient." Connor delivered his opinion in one hit. Knowing Matthew would be dying to jump in, he denied him the chance.

"But for how much longer? Humans die, even well-cared for ones, so what happens when the rations are not enough?" Supervisor Matthew dragged his eyes over the stiff faces in the gallery. "I find it hard to believe you still have no news on how you fathered the hybrid child."

"My blood substitute research is at a crucial stage. It *will* pay off, and it will be a faster and more immediate solution than a hybrid breeding program."

"That may be so, but Councilor Serge was right." Matthew glared at Connor. "Hybrids *are* possible, and if *you* can't tell us how you achieved it, then perhaps the child should be moved to the farm where *we* can test her."

Over my dead body. Connor reined in his anger, allowing the cell door inside his brain to rattle as the compulsion to descend into grave sleep and tear Matthew limb from limb burned a hole in his gut.

Julian shot a decisive glance at Connor's glazed features. He banged his gavel on the bench, shattering the concentration of every vampire in the court. "This court will decide when Doctor Connor's efforts to produce a blood substitute are no longer needed. And Doctor Connor *has* revealed the secret of the hybrid birth."

Connor's eyes darted around to bore into Julian's face at the same moment as Supervisor Matthew exclaimed, "What?"

"You heard me. Doctor Connor has shared his findings with me. And over the next few weeks, *your* task is to complete a health check on human females of child bearing age, and increase their calorie, vitamin, and mineral intake in preparation. The hybrid trials will begin when they are passed fit by Doctor Connor and Surgical Assistant Anthony."

Absorbing the impact of Matthew's stunned glance, Connor clamped his mouth shut and hid behind a calm expression. *What the hell is Julian playing at? We can't tell Matthew that humans need to be cooled until hypothermia sets in, and vampires be boiled in hot water. I've no idea at what point Rebekah and I were at the same temperature and conception occurred. This is no better than Russian roulette.*

"Why now, Principal Julian? Why are you revealing this now?" said Matthew.

"Serendipity, Supervisor. You wanted answers, and I have them. You should be happy."

Supervisor Matthew's jaw snapped shut, and the vampires in the gallery shuffled in their seats.

"Clear the courtroom. And Supervisor, I suggest you get back to the farm and appoint a team of interns who can be trusted to compile the breeding data."

Julian rose from his ornately carved throne. His sweeping green gaze passed over each stunned face before he strode from the room, towing Jurors Marius and Alexander in his wake.

Connor resembled a Christian standing in the pit at the arena, except that *he* exuded all the power and drew every eye. Shoving a hand through his hair and settling his steady eye on Matthew, he said quietly, "Well, don't just stand there."

Exiting through the same door he had entered, Connor closed it behind him. His casual demeanor evaporated as he moved along the corridor and rapped his knuckles on the door of Julian's private chambers.

"Come."

Connor burst into the room. "What the hell are you playing at? Telling Matthew the hybrid breeding trials are going to happen? Are you mad?" He began circling the chamber at an unrelenting pace.

"You are the one who's mad if you believe anything less would distract them," said Julian. He crossed to his mantelpiece and picked up the polished pebble Leizle had always used as a signal whenever she visited his house in Richmond. When the humans were still a secret, she would move it along the shelf to alert him to her presence, before she hid in the soundproofed room at the back of the house. To him, her warmed chestnut aroma always tainted the atmosphere in any case, but she found comfort in their routine.

Julian smiled at the memory, weighed the stone in his hand, and then threw it at Connor's head. "Stop pacing. You're driving me nuts."

Connor scrubbed his fingers over the point of contact on his scalp, even though it did not hurt, and scowled.

"We bought two years breathing space, Connor. But the attack last night proves time is running out. Although Anthony says the attackers were not guardsmen, they *were* frustrated hive workers. The reality of immortality having a shelf life is hitting home. It's just the beginning. You must reconsider moving Rebekah and Seren." Now that Connor stood anchored in one place, Julian approached and laid a heavy hand on his shoulder.

"But I'm close to splicing simian blood cells with perfluorocarbons. Think of it, Julian. Vampires would have no reason to keep humans in captivity if PFCs can unlock the vampire brainstem and allow animal blood in." *Unless they prefer the taste of human blood, of course.* Nothing matched the exhilaration of the real thing, but he would fight that battle when the time came.

"Well, until you have succeeded, shouldn't you send Rebekah and Seren away so that no one knows where they are? I would say goodbye to Leizle to save her, if she was in danger."

"You would send Leizle out into the unknown? I doubt it," scoffed Connor. "Where is this safe place you suggest? There's nowhere that is not in the backyard of a vampire hive. It's better if they stay near London. At least they know London. They have a fighting chance here."

"You're right. Nothing is certain."

Connor frowned. "One more week. If I have nothing to bring to the council by then, I'll take Seren and Rebekah and go. But I won't send them out without me."

Julian nodded slowly. "Very well." Slapping Connor on the shoulder, Julian changed tack. "And where in the woods are these bodies? I'll order Captain Gerrard to have them carried through Hyde Park before delivering them to Storage Facility Eight for internment. Perhaps they'll act as a warning."

Knowing Anthony was back on point in the woods, Connor delayed his return to the eco-shelter to make a flying visit to the vampire hospital. He supervised the blood deliveries to the dispensary from the human farm and stopped by his laboratory to collect his greatcoat. It was barely seven a.m., and the weak winter sunshine could easily be avoided, but it was his one sentimental item of clothing.

The emaciated Hungarian refugee – a casualty of the Soviet invasion of his country – had parted with it eagerly when, instead of being the Angel of Death he imagined, Connor, despite his fierce white features, had heralded salvation. Connor had long ago made the choice to use his hunger as a form of retribution, killing only those who deserved death and filing them away in the clear conscience drawer. The bemused refugee benefited from Connor's expertise as an Army Field Surgeon. After three weeks of being cared for and fed, both intravenously and by mouth, the Hungarian went on his way. He gave the greatcoat to Connor, along with his thanks.

The high-buttoned collar of thick serge fabric covered Connor's face up to the cheekbones. He pulled on leather gloves, strode down the corridor, and took a shortcut out of the hospital through the mortuary.

He nodded to Isaac, the attendant, as he walked into the clinical cold room where the walls were filled with cadaver drawers. The red metal tags hanging from the sealed hatches rattled violently. Connor raised a brow as the screech of razor sharp nails punctuated the unseen feral convulsions of vampires in grave sleep. It was a graphic reminder of the potential carnage that, in the days when humans outnumbered vampires hundreds of thousands to one, went unnoticed.

Given a choice, vampires were lone hunters. In decades gone by, if an occasional vampire lapse gave rise to the birth of a serial killer rumor, making a footprint in the sands of human consciousness, the horror was easily swept away by pushing a human scapegoat into the limelight. *And humans have such short memories.*

The red metal discs on the occupied lockers continued to jangle loudly.

"You are busy tonight," Connor said.

Isaac stepped up to locate an empty drawer for his new arrival, but Connor raised a hand.

"At ease, Isaac, I'm just passing through."

Jerking his chin in farewell, Connor shouldered his way through the steel door marked 'fire exit', skimmed down the steps, and hit the sidewalk at an easy jog. He shot a glance at the gray cloud-cluttered sky and smiled, knowing he would still risk the direct route to the eco-shelter across the open fields. He tucked his chin deeper into the high collar of his coat, and the raven-wing sweep of his thick hair fell forward, easily shading his face.

This time, when he opened the door of the panic room, no one was startled to see him. Seren was the first one to leap up. She hurtled across the floor, and Connor laughed as he easily spun her around, even though her childlike proportions had changed to long-limbed adolescence. A frown flitted across his face at the surprising force of her grip on his shoulders as he set her down beside him.

"Is it safe, Papa?"

Connor glanced at Seth who idly swung a mace from loose fingertips, and nodded as he replied, "Yes, Squirt, it's safe, but hang with Seth and Greg for a bit while your Mama gets some sleep, okay?"

Seth shouldered his weapon and took a chewed twig from between his lips to say, "Greg's hiding somewhere out there. How long do you think it will take to find him?"

Seren raised her chin, delicately scented the air, and grinned. "About four minutes, tops."

"Hey," said Seth. "Give the guy a break, he'll have no ego left. Let's pretend, hmm?"

Connor chuckled as the pair disappeared.

Smiling weakly, Rebekah walked over to him, the blueish smudges beneath her eyes making her protests futile as she said, "I'm fine. I just need some fresh air, walk a bit."

Connor shook his head and held up a finger. "Doctor's orders, sleep," he muttered, and then vanished.

By the time Rebekah had crossed her arms and tapped her foot twice, he was back, his arms filled with a padded bedding roll, a sleeping bag, and a pillow.

"You're so bossy."

"Yep."

Leizle, Oscar and Evie had disappeared into the kitchen, and the clinking of china made the inside of Rebekah's mouth feel like sandpaper. "I need a drink."

"Oscar will bring you some tea. I need to talk to you."

"Okaaay," she said slowly.

Drawing her down to sit beside him on the cushioned floor, with his arm draped around her shoulders, Connor said, "You know there was a surprise attack today? Well, things have reached crisis point, and Julian had to lie to the council, or rather, tell the truth, and say that we know the secret of Seren's birth."

Rebekah jerked forward. "He did what?"

"He had no choice. Honey, think about it. It's beginning to look like I'm a complete idiot if, after all this time, I still had nothing. Matthew wants to run tests on Seren at the farm, and the reasons to refuse are slim. No, he was right."

Rebekah subsided back into his embrace, about to speak again when they heard footsteps. Oscar brought a tray of tea, laid with two cups, and Connor grinned.

"Good manners costs nothing. A thank you will do, lad," Oscar grumbled.

As his bear-like frame disappeared from view, Connor laughed gently.

"He hates not offering you food and drink." Rebekah tried for reproach. "Be nice."

"I *am* nice." Connor's brows climbed to innocent surprise, and Rebekah frowned harder.

"So, this thing with Julian. What happens now? Shall I take Seren and run?"

"You're kidding." His surprise was real this time.

Her thoughtful tone gained enthusiasm. "I've survived in dug outs before. I've been on survival training missions with Greg. Seren and I could hide out in the woods for months."

A growl rumbling in Connor's throat cut her short. "Rebekah, promise me, no running."

When her chin dropped from its mutinous angle and she nodded, he continued. "Seren has not yet developed her vampire sleeps. What are you going to do if she goes into grave sleep and tears your throat out?"

Rebekah spluttered in protest.

"Don't argue, Rebekah." His gray eyes were bleak. "I know better than you on this, trust me. The young of a species are weak, and it seems Seren's faster growth rate is a solution to that. She's already far stronger than you can imagine."

"But she will stop growing? Ageing?"

"She will reach maturity, and then, when her bone marrow and human cell multiplication process ends, she will stop and remain at that age." Connor's words rang with conviction as he entertained the alternative without voicing it. *Maybe she'll race past that point into rapid old age. No, her growth will stop.*

"So, what's the plan?"

"We give it another week, two at most, and then we leave together."

Rebekah smiled. "I can live with that."

"If, in the meantime, I can offer the hive vampire immortality in a bottle, then it will ease their fear, and take the pressure off finding a breeding solution, both human *and* hybrid. Then, maybe we will stay." Connor took Rebekah's hand in his. "There are no guarantees out there. We could be leaping out of the frying pan and into the fire, but I don't believe we have a choice. At least we will face it together, as a family."

"You could always turn me," Rebekah said quietly. "It has the added advantage that Seren couldn't hurt me, then."

Connor's cold finger lifted her chin, and he lost himself in the wonder of her face. If only she could see what he saw. The brown of her eyes was an entrancing blend, ranging from darkest chocolate to the glossy finish of beaten bronze. The moisture on her warm living skin scattered glittering fragments over its surface. And, more than that, the nectar of her blood pulsing beneath his fingertip, flushing her cheeks as he gazed at her now, gave her emotions a delightful aroma as dopamine and pheromones rampaged through her system.

"I will turn you when the time is right. I promise." Connor kissed her lips and, rolling onto his back, he drew Rebekah with him and tucked her into his side. "Get some sleep."

If the time is ever right, thought Connor. Resting his head on a raised arm, he locked his muscles down tight and endured the blade of thirst cutting a path down into his chest as Rebekah slid her thigh over his stomach and snuggled in closer.

For the hours she slept, he lay staring at the sound-proofed ceiling without blinking. He was in hell, and he wouldn't have missed it for the world.

Chapter 2

Julian idly inspected the plush pile of the bronze-toned carpet, looking for evidence of the bald spots he expected to soon mark the surface. *Connor's pacing plays havoc on my furnishings.* He replaced the toffee-veined pebble he had bounced from Connor's skull. The copper threads running through it were a tangible reminder, not only of Leizle's presence in his life, but of the fiery chestnut tones of her hair. *Finding time to visit the eco-shelter is impossible, and as for a moment alone, forget it.*

Resting an elbow on the mantelpiece and a boot on the wrought-iron hearth guard, Julian checked his watch. As he reviewed his exchange with Connor, the relaxed posture solidified to stiffness. The deep green tint in his eyes dimmed with regret. His last movement was to mirror Connor's gesture of frustration and stab his fingers through the straw-colored strands of his hair, disturbing immaculate to a mess of gold.

In the semi-darkness, the thick brocade curtains billowed in the breeze from an open sash window. Despite the wintery evening chill, Julian always blasted the room with fresh air after spending time in the musty atmosphere of the courtroom. On a damp rainy autumn day, the closely packed vampires smelled like damp hounds. The odor thickened as their clothes dried out during the hours of the court listings. Julian breathed as little as possible, but he was still often left feeling suffocated.

There's nothing quite like a breath of fresh air to blow away the cobwebs.

The arrivals he waited for were announced with a brisk knock on the door.

"Come in." Julian reanimated smoothly, restoring his hair, tie, and jacket to order in a flowing movement.

Marius appeared first. He had shed his juror's garb and a black Edwardian-cut jacket molded to his wide shoulders. In an updated twist on his 18th century Georgian roots, he wore well-cut long pants rather than knee length knickerbockers. No longer wearing a hat was as far along the road of 'dressing down' as he would travel.

His strong jaw naturally lived at an angle which suggested he detected an unpleasant odor in the air, and his effortless efficient gestures blurred the edges of his silhouette when he moved.

Stepping aside, Marius ushered Juror Alexander forward with a somber inclination of his head.

Like a chess piece from an opposing set, Alexander wore clothes of a warm-brown hue, which lacked drama. His youth ran like a seam through his movements, and enthusiasm colored his body language. His eyes skimmed the world, rather than studied it, and his inclination to question rather than wait gave the council an extra dimension. In explaining his reasons to Alexander, Julian often plumbed new depths in his own perceptions.

The intricate footwork of good manners between the two occupied Julian's attention. He absorbed the austere formal air of his companions and prepared for some fancy footwork of his own.

Marius closed the door and announced blandly, "Supervisor Matthew was certainly gunning for Doctor Connor in there."

Alexander stopped in the center of the room. "The supervisor certainly got more than he bargained for in the end."

"*Do* you know the answers to the hybrid birth, Julian?" asked Marius, sinking smoothly into an armchair.

Julian loosened his shirt collar, shrugged out of his black principal's robe, and turned to face Marius. "Of course not. I was just buying Doctor Connor time."

"Time for what? To run?" asked Marius with a stiff smile.

Julian's hollow laughter filled the room. "England is too small a space to hide in, and they'd never get off the island, so, no," he murmured. He turned away to hang his robe and closed the wardrobe door. Frowning, he tidied his shirt cuffs. "Doctor Connor is serious about finding solutions for the hive. You know that, Marius."

Alexander swept a pale-fingered hand through hair the color of wet sand. "So, Doctor Connor is less interested in giving us answers and rather more in providing solutions," the younger vampire said heavily.

"You want answers, Alexander. But, have you considered that sometimes there are none?"

"I know you have known Doctor Connor a long time," said Alexander slowly, "but, after so many breeding failures we had admitted defeat. The hybrid child's birth came out of the blue." Looking at Julian, he smiled deprecatingly. "I've never been good at waiting, but you are right, I know Doctor Connor will work out how, all in good time."

"Even with Councilor Serge banished to Scotland, the tide is turning. I think the child may be in danger," said Marius, flatly.

Julian inspected the blank expression on the elder juror's face. "Her name is Seren. Let us not forget that, first and foremost, she is a person."

"That is what worries me. In my experience, innocents suffer."

Julian knew Marius had seen terrible things. It may have been more than a hundred and fifty years ago, but whenever he spoke of the hundreds of women and children buried beneath the city walls in Mandalay, sacrificed to sanctify and protect the city, his own body became as still and lifeless. Julian had not thought of Marius as an ally at the start of all this, but he became one, just by going along with the idea that a talented doctor like Connor had not yet got to the heart of their problem.

Marius resembled the human concept of a vampire. A sleek cap of black hair set off his arresting bone structure, and his eyes were dead – and yet the black pools stirred with currents which seemed to draw the very thoughts from your head. *Yes, Marius knows I'm lying, but he has chosen his side.*

"You're right, Marius, and Serge may be in exile, but he certainly is not keeping quiet. I understand tales of Seren's birth are rife between London and Inverness. Even hundreds of miles away, he is still a thorn in our flesh."

"Councilor Serge is due a visit. Perhaps I should make the trip this time? He does not fear me. If he is spreading malicious gossip, he will be more likely to let something slip," said Alexander.

"You may well be right. And if he is stirring up rebellion, Principal Tavish is a hardliner, and a decade in solitary confinement will curb Serge's enthusiasm." It occurred to Julian that crossing swords with Serge would be a valuable exercise for the younger vampire.

"The next court session is not for another week, perhaps I should go now? It would be useful to find out what Councilor Serge is up to before Supervisor Matthew begins to suspect the female health checks for the breeding program are a ploy to buy time."

"The Loch Glascarnoch Hive will certainly be an experience for you." At Alexander's curious expression, Julian said, "I can't imagine Serge is enjoying the Highlands of Scotland. Surviving in the coldest place in Britain is no problem for us, but looking out for humans on the farm is an endless task. I'm surprised he has found time to make mischief, but it does look that way."

Alexander glanced at his watch. "Shall I set off at dusk?"

By eight p.m., Alexander was in the north of England about to report to the keeper of a fort in Hadrian's Wall. The wall, improved by vampire hand to a height of sixty feet, cut across the country from the mouth of the River Tyne on one shore, to the Solway Firth on the other. The deep ditches and mounds along its length remained, but were no obstacle to vampires. Alexander headed towards the turret which marked the location of a vampire guard station, oblivious of the needle-sharp impact of icy rain falling from the night sky.

As he drew near, a vampire wearing a thick gray woolen cape appeared from within a black chasm carved into the stone. "Halt."

Alexander obeyed the barked command and recited his unique identification number. "LHJ496056."

"A juror? You're a long way from London. Where are you headed?"

"To the Highlands, to see Principal Tavish."

The guard's impassive face twitched as he searched for the appropriate tone to address a London juror. "Juror. Ah. Sir, if you've a yen to hunt on your way through, some bear cubs have just been released into the park. Principal Tavish would be obliged if you let them be. We want them to grow a wee bit."

Alexander smiled. "I'm on a flying visit, but thank you for your hospitality."

The vampire grunted in satisfaction and beckoned a black gloved hand in welcome. He retreated out of the moonlight, and the oil thick shadow oozing over him melted his gray cloak into black.

Alexander followed him into the cold cavernous archway and faced a portcullis gate.

"So, this is Hadrian's Wall?"

"Aye. And about ninety miles north of here is Antonine Wall. The safari park covers the glens and heathland between the two." The vampire smiled proudly. "Best stock of pumas, tigers and grizzlies north of London, I'd say, sir."

"Who could have guessed that human fascination for zoos and safari parks would prove so useful?" said Alexander, filling the seconds it took his companion to grind a metal key in a lock and open an iron barred gate.

With the twist of a wrist, the vampire rotated a pitted-iron wheel and the portcullis spikes disappeared into the stone arch overhead. Alexander stepped forward into a rectangular chamber paved in slick, worn flagstones. *I wonder how many have passed through here in the two thousand years since it was built by the Romans.*

Faced by yet another grid of riveted iron rods, Alexander glanced over his shoulder as he waited for the gate behind him to hit the ground with a dull clang. The feeling of being incarcerated was a little unnerving, and Alexander's colorful imagination flirted with the idea that if the vampire guard wished it, he could be held here indefinitely. *If I was human, of course.*

The gate in front of him whisked upwards, the frame grinding along rusted runners, and Alexander stepped out into the moonlight. The terrain was as wild and untamed as he had expected.

Hadrian's Wall did not mark the border between England and Scotland, although it was a widely held misconception. All Alexander knew was that a mile or so north the ground became soft underfoot, covered with thick moss and peat bogs. Heather sprang in stiff bristled clumps between the pale rocks littering the hillsides, tinting the vista in bursts of lilac and cream. Every few miles through the Lowlands of Scotland, Alexander zeroed in on the rumbling growl of a distant big cat – a puma or tiger. The instinctive tightening in his gut flooded his mouth with venom, but he dismissed the urge to hunt. He was more interested in getting to the Highlands.

I wonder what Councilor Serge will have to say? Alexander smothered the inner voice which hoped he would hear something he could use. The hybrid child, Seren, he reminded himself, was a ray of hope. When Connor had risked everything, stood before the council, and declared he had fathered a child, Alexander had embraced excitement for the first time in decades. But, the child was almost two years old now, and Alexander's excitement had hardened to frustration.

Thinking about Serge, Alexander's nostrils flared as he recalled the stench of unwashed dead skin which clung to the councilor like a toxic cloud. *Is this a fool's errand?* Serge's jealousy was toxic, too, and he remained obsessed with condemning Doctor Connor to a life sentence in Storage Facility Eight. *It must be hard being a vampire saddled with a human body seventy years old.*

It was rumored that Serge had believed being 'turned' would restore his youth and vigor. Instead, he faced an eternity of old age. At their last fateful encounter, Doctor Connor tore Serge's arm from his shoulder. *It is no wonder he's causing trouble here in the Highlands.*

"Are his threats empty, or has he discovered something?" Alexander muttered, his words snatched away by the bitter breeze whipping at his hair and stiffening his clothes with crystals of ice. *Something to force Connor's hand and make him share his findings, that's all I want.* Alexander was sure Julian, and Marius, for that matter, were not going to force the issue.

Just as the vampire guard had said, the Antonine Wall interrupted Alexander's progress in the foothills of the Highlands.

Alexander was tempted to scale the wall to the ramparts, and drop down onto the ground beyond. But, in the end, good sense prevailed, and he endured another set of iron gates and supplied his unique identity number. If he hoped to receive a human blood allocation from the Loch Glascarnoch Hive, it would not do to flout protocol.

Traveling north, Alexander did not fancy getting his feet wet, and skimming around the long finger-shaped bodies of water called 'lochs' became a pinball machine trajectory which helped ease some of the tension. Heading east to Inverness, he paused to take stock. The larger Loch Ness, famed for having a mysterious sea monster lurking in its depths, blocked his path.

Looking at his watch, he calculated, that even with the detour around the loch, he would be in Loch Glascarnoch within the hour. *Okay, I have a mountain or two to climb, but still...*

Alexander shifted his shoulders in a bring-it-on gesture and exploded into a fast run. An avalanche of chalk-colored rocks tumbled in his wake, and the moss-covered stones which crumbled in his hands stained his stone-white palms green as he scaled the steeper inclines at a steady, untiring pace. He stopped breathing as human habits were driven out and vampire instincts rampaged through muscle and sinew. The effortless coordination felt exhilarating.

Standing on the summit of the last mountain, Alexander surveyed the rugged landscape.

Stars punched pinpricks of light into the black sky. The crust of snow beneath his boots was repeated as gray frosting on every peak on the horizon. Below, the oil-black pool of Loch Glascarnoch glistened in the moonlight. At one end of the loch the footings of an impressive fortress formed a dam, and Alexander knew instinctively that Principal Tavish would be found inside.

Beyond the dam, as if God had tossed a necklace of glowing diamonds onto the ground, a row of floodlights circled the acres of a scrubland compound. An enormous steel-colored siphoning shed sat in the center, like the body of a spider – its asphalt-gray legs extending to create the pathways between the moss-stained slate roofs of the human dormitory blocks.

The three well-spaced perimeter fences enclosing the human farm were a familiar design, repeated from the London Hive. If it ain't broke, don't fix it, thought Alexander. He wondered if one vampire had been the architect of all. Vicious barbs of razor wire crowned the fences for the protection of both species. Vampire wardens crawled like ants just inside the outer perimeter, keeping thirsty vampires out and exhausted siphoned-to-the-point-of-collapse humans safely inside.

Alexander could not see any vampire dwellings. *Perhaps all they all live inside the fortress.*

Choosing the steepest slope, Alexander set off to free run down the mountain side, tearing a hole in the tough bark of each pine tree in the forest he grabbed onto. They created a windbreak for the humans on the farm, softening the arctic winds to merely bitter cold.

Within minutes, Alexander was scaling the smooth granite face of the dam using the footholds of strategically placed metal pegs. When he vaulted over the capstones on the wall, a guard stopped him in his tracks, pressing the point of a knife into the base of his sternum.

A leather gauntlet smothered the hilt of the weapon, but Alexander had seen the vampire draw the blade from a sheath beneath his armpit. *A short blade.*

Alexander stared at the scowling hard features of the vampire and reined in the instinct to defend himself. His plans had not included having the serrated edge of a Scottish dagger buried in his innards. Raising his hands, he rattled off his ident number.

The guard still glared. "I apologize, *juror*, we were not expecting you." He did not sound sorry, and the pinpoint pressure of metal, poised to slip the blade up under Alexander's ribcage and gut him, prevented him moving.

"I'm here on urgent business. Principal Julian sent me."

The guard took a slow step backward. Still brandishing the dagger, he said, "Follow me."

Falling into step behind, Alexander scraped his hands through matted hair. The smell of mulch and mud filled his nostrils and he realized that in his tattered state he did not look like a juror. Staring at the broad back of the vampire who now strode along the granite walled passageway, he decided Tavish's guard was right to challenge him.

As they drew near to the main hall, Alexander's escort swelled to four vampires, who boxed him in. The group marched along the ancient flagstone-paved corridors.

Stopping when the leading guards blocked his path, Alexander peered through the gap between the broad shoulders. The battered oak door to the principal's chamber bore the scars of ax blows and the rivets in the planks of wood were dented. Even the remote hives had their share of conflict, it seemed.

With a clenched fist, one guardsman hammered three times on the door and earned a sharp retort.

"Enter."

His escorts – in a shifting flow of muscle – corralled Alexander into the room and retreated to line up against the wall behind. He swallowed hard. A glint of steel had reminded him that at least one guard still held an unsheathed dagger, and he was now out of sight. *Is it pointed at my back?*

Principal Tavish approached with a heavy stride. Stopping in front of the young juror, he rubbed a hand over a thick russet beard. His eyes gleamed in the candlelight as they raked over Alexander's grimy appearance.

"Aye, laddie?"

Alexander dipped his chin respectfully. "Principal Tavish, I'm here on London Hive business to speak with Councilor Serge." Tugging a leather pouch from inside the waistband of his pants, Alexander turned out a gold nugget bearing Principal Julian's seal and dropped it into the tall Scot's palm.

After a cursory inspection, Tavish returned it to Alexander and said, "Well, you can't interview the councilor looking like a farm boy. My boy, Ioan, will take you to a resting room where you can clean the grime from yerself."

"Thank you." Alexander nodded, smiling at last when the dagger wielding Ioan came down from kill mode and sheathed his weapon.

A trek along a lengthy corridor, where faded tapestries lined the granite walls, ended at another hefty oak door.

Pushing it open, Ioan muttered, "When you are ready, follow this corridor to the end. The guard at the gate will direct you from there."

Alexander stepped inside the room, and the door slammed behind him. Pulling at his tattered shirt as he walked into a bathing area, he turned on the faucets, letting the steel tub fill while he stripped off his pants. Glad to be stepping into the water, he sank below the surface and lay on the bottom, thinking. The time for his meeting with Councilor Serge was set and he gathered his wits – he needed to be ready for anything. Five minutes passed, and when he surged back up, water sloshed out onto the tiled floor. It took seconds to step out, scrub a towel over his hard white skin and pull on the fresh clothes which had mystically appeared on a dresser. The rough serge fabric of the more-roomy charcoal gray pants barely registered and the white cotton shirt smelled of bleach – the ensemble was more rustic than stylish – but it was clean and therefore a huge improvement. He tidied his wet hair with clawed fingers, and his ice-blue eyes narrowed.

This is it. He left the privacy of the room and headed towards the iron gate Ioan spoke of. Following the directions of the gatekeeper, he descended a wide stone staircase into the lower levels of the fortress. At the end of a carpeted hallway, he found Councilor Serge's accommodation, and knocked on the door.

"Come in," a dry throat croaked.

Alexander entered and stared at the familiar wizened figure. The cold air tasted stagnant when he filled his lungs to speak. "Councilor Serge, how are you?"

Serge grinned, showing yellow teeth which, momentarily, made his jaundiced complexion look healthier. "Juror Alexander? I'm surprised to see *you*." Interest stirred in the depths of the councilor's reptile-cold eyes. "Perhaps it is fate."

"*Your* fate is in Principals Julian and Tavish's hands," Alexander said, suddenly feeling, when Serge's avid gaze crawled over his skin, as if he was held in the coils of a boa constrictor.

"Of course. And Doctor Connor? How is *he*? Has he delivered the answers to all our prayers?"

"That is no longer your concern."

Serge nodded. "Very wise. Better to say nothing when there is nothing to say." Serge sliced a glance over Alexander's tight expression. "Perhaps, I should tell *you* how it is?"

Alexander inhaled sharply.

Serge plowed on regardless. "It's two years on, no one is any the wiser about how the hybrid birth occurred, and Doctor Connor is playing you all for fools."

"It is *you* who played us for fools." Alexander forced a laugh. "How many humans did you claim Doctor Connor was hiding? Forty, wasn't it?"

They both knew Serge had lied, but the human concealed by Connor was pregnant with his child. In that moment Serge lost not only the battle, he lost the war.

"But I was right about one thing. A human-vampire hybrid is possible, and a hybrid herd would be the answer to vampire prayers. Replace the humans on the farm with hybrids – an immortal blood supply – and we still live forever. That's why Doctor Connor can't be trusted. He *loves* a human, and sired a hybrid." Serge spat the words. "He pretends to be better than the rest of us, but he is a traitor."

"Tread carefully, Councilor."

"You *know* he will never deliver, don't you? I can see it in your face." Serge's throat gurgled and he swallowed excess saliva. "Supervisor Matthew has never liked Doctor Connor. Now is the time to strike." Serge waited, the loose fabric of his empty coat sleeve rippling as he shook with ill-concealed fervor.

Alexander said, "You have *me* down as a traitor, too. I think you know better."

"I have you down as a vampire with a backbone. One who, if we have a champion for our cause, could take Doctor Connor down, and has the guts to do the right thing."

"A champion?" The moment the words left his mouth, Alexander felt the trap close.

Serge resisted the smirk tugging at his wrinkled cheeks. "The decision is in your hands." He spread his one hand in entreaty. "I've had word from one who is interested in the child. Sentinel Lars is keen to discover the answers Connor keeps hidden. You have nothing to lose. Lars' ship will be moored for one week at Inverness."

Alexander felt less of a traitor by just listening. *After all, I have not agreed to anything. I'll let him talk and deliver news of his plot back to Principal Julian.*

"Follow the south bank of Beauty Firth, I'm sure you cannot miss the ship." Serge licked dry lips. "It is his own creation, a small Viking ship."

Alexander was intrigued despite himself. "He has galleon slaves?"

"I'm sorry to disappoint you, but no. His oarsmen are vampires. It makes sense if you think about it. They never tire and can maintain top speed indefinitely. It will be a simple matter to pick the sentinel's brain about his plan. You have to pass the port on your way home." Serge's skin crackled as his wide-eyed innocence crossed the line into hideous. "And if you don't agree, then you can take the news back and warn Principal Julian. You'll be a hero."

When Alexander did not move, Serge murmured persuasively, "What have you got to lose?"

◇◇◇

Barely twenty-four hours after meeting with Councilor Serge, Alexander passed silently along the dark London streets. Inside the square mile known as the City, the soulless stare of oil-black windows settled the discomfort of guilt on his shoulders.

He had the feeling of watching a boulder hurtling down a hillside, unsure where it would come to rest and of how many casualties it would leave in its wake.

It's too late now.

Sentinel Lars had turned out to be a blindingly good-looking blond warrior of Danish descent. His smile was compelling, and even before he spoke Alexander was in awe. Sinews bulged above wide gold armlets molded to the sentinel's forearms and he wore a gold breastplate forged into a wall of hard abdominal muscles. Alexander felt certain it reflected what lie beneath.

Lars stood rock steady on the rolling deck of the ship, his briskly swaying cape betraying the true force of the choppy waters in the estuary.

Alexander's white-knuckled grip on the handrail left his handprint in the crumbling wooden fibers as he tried to imitate his companion's solid gait. He listened to Lars' plan and, at first, his chest felt tight with fear.

The Danish warrior's lips twitched in spiteful amusement.

Alexander drew himself up, hiding behind bravado as his voice rang out, "Sentinel Lars. I'm a juror of the London Hive. What you are suggesting would see me sentenced to death."

"Nej... no." Lars' bright blue eyes crinkled at the corners as he smiled. "We are securing the future of the vampire race. Who would condemn you for that?"

"Why do you not just command it?" asked Alexander. "I would back you in court. You outrank Principal Julian. Why not call a hearing and compel Doctor Connor to hand over S- the hybrid child?" Saying her name felt like he was betraying an innocent.

"You think that would go well?" Lars ran his fingertips over a marble smooth jaw. "I have heard about this Doctor Connor. He will not comply, and it will come down to combat, I fear. Your principal, he would feel obliged to fight for his hive, and I do not want to see good vampires die." The bright blue regard cooled to diamond ice. "Do you?"

The threat was clear, Alexander faced the death sentence whichever course he took.

The meeting ended quickly. Alexander was not party to the details and the coward in him rejoiced at that. He had only one task to perform – keep Doctor Connor busy.

The tendons in Alexander's shoulder creaked beneath the Dane's strong grip, and Lars' parting comment sealed his fate. "It is better you do not know the rest, it will make it easier for you to act the innocent, Alexander. You play your part, hold your nerve, and you will be rewarded."

Alexander tossed ideas around while traveling south from Inverness. Before he felt ready, the tall buildings of London loomed on the horizon like an avalanche of coal. Suppressing the feeling of foreboding, he veered west. *I can't do this alone and keep my own hands clean.*

The tall flood lamps around the perimeter of the human farm created a glowing halo of light. Alexander's gut tightened with every driving step which took him closer.

The chain-linked fence appeared as a gunmetal-gray barrier, and Alexander bit back the urge to shout out. *Act natural.* For him, natural meant 'easy going and optimistic'. The knotted muscle pulling a wire tight across his shoulders was a new experience. The warden appeared as if he stepped out from behind an invisible cloak, and Alexander forced a smile.

"Juror Alexander," the guard said and he unlocked the man-sized gate in the twelve feet high fence.

"Warden." Alexander nodded in greeting. "Is Supervisor Matthew in the siphoning sheds?"

"Shed number three, sir."

Two more security gates and another pair of guards later, Alexander loped purposefully across the vast lawn of the compound. A sweet aroma of blood clung to the siphoning sheds' walls. He could have zeroed in on them with his eyes closed.

The concrete ramp at the main entrance to shed number three had damp tire tracks running up the sloping surface attesting to the constant stream of human traffic. Trolleys either ferried humans who resisted their destiny and refused to walk, or transported metal crates filled with bulging I.V. bags – the blood ready to be decanted into vials and loaded up for the delivery run to the vampire hospital blood dispensary. Nothing got in the way of the harvest.

Pushing through three sets of doors, ignoring those leading to the storage areas and examination suites, Alexander entered the cavernous space of the siphoning hall. He did not often go inside and seeing the rows of bodies lying on metal examination tables, strapped in place as they gave blood, was something he would never get used to. Before the pandemic changed the face of society, humans who disagreed with the slaughter of animals for food had the luxury of becoming a vegetarian. For vampires there was no such choice. *That's one thing I have in common with Doctor Connor.*

He once overheard Connor saying he could pick out Rebekah by the aroma of her blood, by the iron-laden smell of it when it washed across his palette. *I wonder what that is like?* That Sentinel Lars had a conscience about the siphoning process was impossible for Alexander to imagine. And the tension across his shoulders tightened another notch.

Supervisor Matthew's angular bone structure was easy to spot, even behind the soft plastic mask worn by every vampire inside the hall.

Matthew frowned as Alexander attracted his attention with a raised hand.

Alexander stepped back out into the corridor.

Before a count of ten elapsed, the supervisor shoved his way through the door, pulling off his mask.

"Juror, is there a problem?" Uncertain of his next move, he dangled the mask from his fingertips and his eyes darted to the peg where his coat hung.

"I want to talk to you." Alexander turned, led the way along the hallway, and slipped inside one of the examination wards. He held the door open and closed it after Matthew entered.

The supervisor flapped his free hand. "Erm, forgive me, but you don't quite look yourself."

This time, when he moved, Alexander felt the sandpaper quality of the borrowed pants he wore and grinned wryly. "It is a long story. But the bottom line is, Doctor Connor knows how the hybrid child was conceived, and he'll need a nudge to make him divulge the information."

"Nudge? And how are you going to do that, exactly?"

"The details are not your concern." *I don't know them either.*

"Then what *is* my concern?" Reluctant exhilaration backlit Matthew's gaze.

"All I'm asking is that Doctor Connor is kept occupied at the right moment. You find a way to get him here, and make sure he cannot leave, for at least two hours."

"Why?" The supervisor's jaw jutted stubbornly. "What am I putting my neck on the line for?"

Shrugging, Alexander turned to walk away. "I can find someone else."

"Wait." Matthew flinched when Alexander whipped back around and closed the space between them to mere inches. Matthew swallowed noisily.

Alexander glared down, white lines of tension bracketing his mouth, and said in a disconcertingly casual tone, "Doctor Connor needs an incentive to run the hybrid breeding program. He has dragged his feet long enough. I thought you felt the same."

"Of course, I do." Matthew's gaze skittered around Alexander's face, unable to meet his eyes.

"It is simply a matter of applying pressure. I will leave it to you to decide the degree of humiliation he endures. I have no interest in your personal vendetta. I just need him out of the way for a while."

"I have an-"

"I don't need to know how you plan to do it," Alexander cut in. "Just make sure you get Doctor Connor out here at the right time. And do whatever you have to." Easing back and lightening the mood, he added, "If you'd rather not be involved, I understand. After all, Doctor Connor is very intimidating."

They emerged from the privacy of the side ward, the same ward where Doctor Connor performed physical examinations on patients. Often, they were spot checks to catch Matthew out. Matthew resented the implication that he was failing. He laughed grimly. "You can count on me, Alexander."

Alexander bristled at the familiarity. Turning his face away, he looked at the row of storage trolleys lined up outside the blood technician department, each one overflowing with I.V. bags full of blood. Alexander said, "And Matthew, try not to lose a human life in your plan. You... we don't want to bring Principal Julian's disapproval down on our heads."

Matthew's jaw snapping shut barely registered with Alexander, who nodded and swept from the siphoning shed, grateful to be filling his lungs with ice-cold night air.

Alexander covered the ten miles east into London in five minutes, losing his battle to suppress the distaste swilling in his stomach. *Matthew is gullible and spineless.* He ignored the worm of thought that said, *and so are you.*

The boulder was rolling faster now, but, at least he was watching from the top of the hill as it thundered away.

He slowed to a human jogging pace long before he reached the vampire council building. Walking up the flight of stairs from the sidewalk, deliberately setting a foot down on each tread, he stopped at the top and laid his palms on the solid oak barrier. It was too late to rewind the last twenty-four hours. As a vampire, he usually embraced the feeling of invincibility. But now, fear ate at his consciousness, and he felt as though the foundations were shifting beneath his feet.

He twisted the brass handles, pushed open both doors and entered. He focused on the pleasant aroma of the polished wooden paneling lining the corridors, and on the well-worn parquet flooring beneath his feet, and began to feel more at home. He stopped outside Principal Julian's chamber and rapped on the door.

"Come!" called a familiar voice.

Alexander took in a vampire breath, charging his lungs to speak and, knowing that Marius and Julian were waiting to hear his news, he prepared to deliver the performance of a lifetime.

He opened the door and entered.

Here goes.

Chapter 3

Connor descended the aged stone stairwell into the bowels of the hospital. A frown cut deeper into his face as he turned the corner and stopped at the door to his laboratory. He punched his eight digit PIN into a keypad mounted on the wall and, when a loud buzz sounded, passed through an airlock door into his personal dressing space.

At the opposite wall of the small square room, he pulled on a thick metal handle and rocked a cylinder-shaped stainless-steel drawer forward. He placed a plastic-wrapped parcel containing two dozen vials of monkey blood inside and rolled it shut again.

He stripped off wet clothes – soaked by the icy downpour of a blustery autumn day – dropped them into a laundry chute, and went through another doorway into a wet room. The rubber edging around the steel door hissed as the chamber was sealed.

His mind churned with thoughts of what his next experiment might turn up as he took his place in the center of the tiled chamber. He raised his chin and extended his arms while jets of steam blasted his naked form until his cold skin felt like granite warmed by scorching sun and clouds of vapor plumed into the atmosphere. His hair dripped onto his shoulders, the condensed water joining the rivulets pouring down over the hard muscles of his body and into the drain at his feet. As the air cleared, he waited for the hiss of the exit door lock releasing.

Inside the inner changing area, Connor scrubbed himself dry with paper towels, pulled open the packet containing sterile green surgical scrubs, and quickly dressed. He took a deep breath. He was in his comfort zone. The clock was ticking for Seren and Rebekah, and if being with them was where his cold heart wanted to be, his calculating analytical brain told him he'd find the answer here. *Solve this puzzle, and I can make them safe. Truly safe.*

The laboratory was hermetically sealed, but Connor did not need oxygen. He had no-one to talk to, so he stopped breathing.

Rolling the steel drawer open from the other side, he collected the package. The blood was still warm.

The visit to London Zoo, which was now populated entirely with species of apes and monkeys, had gone smoothly: Putting on a hazardous-material suit, locating the tagged specimens Connor wanted, and shooting a tranquilizer dart into the shoulder or rump of each one had taken him minutes. Drawing blood and placing the groggy simians into straw lined recovery boxes took but another few. He had performed the ritual hundreds of times. It was second nature.

Despite using the protective suit, he took no chances. He happily endured the laborious decontamination process because bringing bacteria or viral contaminants into his lab was unthinkable. No one but him was cleared to enter his domain.

Inserting a bovine-grade needle into his forearm, Connor drew two syringe barrels full of the cornstarch syrup-thick brown paste of his own blood. The vein collapsed, carving a trough under his skin along the path of the brachial artery. His fingers felt stiff.

Lying the syringe down, he reversed the process, injecting a vial of simian blood in to fill the vacuum and pumping his fist while massaging the vein. It was faster than drinking the sample and waiting for it to hitch a ride along his arterial system to rehydrate the tissue. His hand felt warm and his fingers nimble again when he picked up the rust-brown colored samples containing his vampire DNA and placed them in a Perspex box.

He pulled on a white linen coat and scanned the room while he tidied the collar. The laboratory had expanded to three times the size it had been before Seren's birth. The hum of five centrifuges whisking around in perpetual motion filled the air; all at different stages of the process of separating the red cells from the plasma in the blood samples of species ranging from gorilla through to spider monkey.

There had been a few promising results, where he felt the solution was almost within his grasp. But sadly, defeat came hot on their heels.

Connor's eyes were flint hard as he erupted into purposeful movement. Crossing to the bench, he flicked the switch on one of the hurtling centrifuges and listened to the whining noise decaying to a taunting whisper.

The rhesus monkey results were disappointing. Connor's hope was, that having been used before to unlock secrets of human immunity, the rhesus' blood cells would be compatible, but he was back to the drawing board.

White marble counter tops ran the full length of the laboratory on both sides. A peninsular spur, like the third prong in a fork, divided the room. The refrigerator units on the left side held human blood samples. The vampire samples sitting in the Perspex box were all his own. Every vampire had the same blood group. The congealed hardened nuclei of vampire blood cells absorbed the blood group of the human blood they drank. In other words, it varied according to diet, and he could easily replicate that process for himself.

Coming at the hybrid breeding challenge along the lines of organ donor compatibility, Connor aimed to discover *which* human blood group had the most resistance to the crystalized cells in vampire DNA. And in addition, if the odds of rejection were improved by a vampire donor switching to a diet of the same blood group as the human female his sperm was destined to impregnate. Human females were a precious commodity, and if surrogacy *was* to be trialed, Connor wanted to mitigate the risks.

Seren, when she developed the vampire sleep centers inside the womb, had almost ended Rebekah's life in the final stages of pregnancy. So Connor was determined to find a way of putting a mainline into the placenta and using sedation to control fetal aggression. If his hand was forced, he wanted to feel like he had some control. With Rebekah and Seren, he had suffered the horror of being completely unprepared.

But today, his focus would be on blood substitutes. He walked around to the right side of the laboratory. Opening the door of the walk-in refrigeration unit, he ran a finger along the edge of the shelves. They felt warm to him, despite the white-tinting of frost. He had the twelve digit batch numbers stored in his mind. Another vampire talent he took for granted; the limitless capacity of the filing system inside his head.

He took out the trays of test tubes containing the perfluorocarbons – PFCs – in a saline solution which he hoped could replace the ape-blood plasma. The artificial particles in the PFCs were one fortieth the size of blood cells. Connor had used them during the Second World War in the treatment of crush injuries. They could travel along collapsed capillaries which could no longer carry blood.

Centrifugal force had separated out the red and white cells from the plasma in the simian blood, isolating the properties for which the vampire brainstem refused to open. Connor planned to combine the ape blood cells with the finer PFC particles. He was convinced that, in the right ratios, the smaller simulated blood cells would unlock the gateway of the vampire brain, and let the simian blood through too. *Surely, one of the nineteen species of monkeys and apes will be able to complete the process of hydration.*

Using a syringe to siphon off the clear plasma from each test tube of simian blood, Connor replaced it with the saline PFC solution and loaded the glass vials into the slots inside agitators. He had just flipped the switch, activating the mechanical stirring process, when he swore softly.

The vibration of the klaxon siren's scream pulsing through the night air rattled his eardrums before the sound arrived. *Red alert.* A human was dying on the farm.

In an efficient flow of movement, Connor returned samples into cold storage, removed and hung his white coat. Like Superman rushing into action, he left the lab while still shrugging out of his scrubs. He tossed them into the linen chute, and pulled on outdoor clothes with barely a broken stride. Leaving was always faster.

Connor skimmed up the steps from the basement, emerging into the featureless environment of a white-washed corridor.

The wailing sound of the alarm finally arrived.

He barged through the heavy glass doors of the main exit, running out into driving rain which barely registered. Taking the fastest route, he hurtled through the London streets, heading west.

The shrieking noise would be unrelenting until he answered the call, and so, he forged a direct path through woodlands, leaving a trail of sawdust in his wake.

The floodlit compound came into view, and he honed in on the bulky shape of Anthony. They were both drenched, but, thankfully, the rain eased off to drizzle.

"Do we know what's happened?" Connor barked as he sluiced rainwater from his face.

Anthony shook his head. "I just got here."

Connor's chin jerked sharply. "Who's guarding the eco-shelter?"

"Don't worry, Rebekah and Seren are in the panic room."

The metal fabric of the tall fence jangled as the gate opened, and Connor nodded to the warden as the three vampires set off across the empty space between the perimeter fences. "What have we got?" Connor directed his comment to the stiff faced escort running along beside him.

"A human bleeding out. That's all I know, sir."

With a grim expression, Connor raced onwards in silence. Reaching the solid gunmetal gray wall of a siphoning shed, he called out, "Supervisor Matthew."

The supervisor appeared thirty yards away, framed in the main entrance of the next shed in the row, beckoning urgently. "He ripped his catheter tube out. He has torn the vein," he said as the pair approached.

Connor snorted his disapproval and went inside. At Matthew's direction, he made his way to the emergency suite. Shooting a glance in through the window of the observation room, he was pleased to see a vampire intern tightening a dressing and elevating the arm.

"Take him through to theater. Anthony and I will scrub in." Connor gave Matthew a baleful I'll-deal-with-you-later look.

The stinging smell of antiseptic focused Connor's mind as he pushed his jelly-soft synthetic mask over his nose and mouth. He scrubbed his hands under running boiling water, and then pushed them into latex gloves.

"Ready?" Connor backed up the muffled word with a keen glance at Anthony.

Anthony nodded – they both knew what Connor really meant was, 'are you in control?'. Anthony had recently fed and he packed his sinuses with gauze because free flowing human blood could fill his brain with a red cloud of hunger. His steady stare provided the answer.

He's ready. Backing into the room, Connor took his place beside the man's injured arm. He examined the two-inch tear along the anterior vein which led up into the bicep from the inner elbow, and met Anthony's fierce frown. *The pain must have been excruciating, how did he do this unnoticed?*

Connor quickly performed the intricate surgery using a needle which human eyes usually viewed through a magnifying glass. Assessing the patient's gray pallor, Connor acted fast. Swabbing away the blood, he pressed a fingertip to the wound, located the ulnar nerve, and injected a nerve block. The brachial nerve would be better, deadening the entire arm, but Connor decided the procedure would not be long enough for it to matter.

Happy that the patient would feel very little pain, Connor made an incision and exposed the severed vein. After using tweezers to grip the fibrous tissue and pull the ragged ends together, he used clamps to prevent the sheaths retreating up into the wound once more. Anthony held them steady while Connor put in a row of minute sutures.

Swabbing the blood, irrigating the area with sterile saline, and closing the gash took Connor moments. Stepping back, he gave a satisfied sigh.

"Porter," he barked.

A vampire scuttled in, gripped the metal frame of the trolley and wheeled the man out of theater into the recovery room. Connor and Anthony moved aside, holding their blood smeared hands in the air. They shared a glance which said they'd done all they could, and both left by the opposite door.

The silence in the scrub room pulsed with anger as Connor viciously scoured his hands. Pulling open his locker, he shoved his arms into the sleeves of the black shirt he yanked out. Doing up the buttons as he walked, with Anthony following on behind, Connor went in search of Matthew.

The supervisor raised his hands in surrender as Connor bore down upon him. "Before you say anything, you are right, it was our mistake."

"He didn't just pull it out, he butchered his arm. Principal Julian will hear of this," Connor said with deathly calm.

Matthew muttered, "Of course. I take the blame, as the one in charge."

A weight settled in Connor's chest as the supervisor agreed meekly. *What game is he playing?*

"Doctor Connor, while I'm not convinced you are committed to the hybrid breeding program, until I see otherwise, I will follow the council's orders to the letter. I'll do everything you say to improve the care of our inmates." Matthew looked resigned. "Let's at least, try to get along."

"The job of *supervisor* means something. Just step up and do your damn job. Maybe then, we will *get along*, as you put it."

Matthew held out a hand, and Connor smothered his annoyance and shook it.

"I wonder," asked Matthew, "can Surgical Assistant Anthony spare the time to visit the new medical block? I need advice on which vitamin and mineral shots to give the breeding females who pass the health checks. We should work together on this."

"Very well. But, I shall report this incident."

"I understand."

"Anthony, you go with Supervisor Matthew. I'll check on the patient. After I've spoken to Principal Julian, I'll be at the eco-shelter."

As Anthony and Matthew disappeared, a door down the hallway swung open, crashing noisily into the wall. An urgent voice called out, "Doctor Connor!"

Connor moved before he could think. He knew it was his patient.

"There is a subcutaneous bleed. The bruising is spreading fast."

The swinging door shut behind the retreating figure, and Connor followed the arcing motion and barged into the room.

The white coat of the vampire intern was a blur in Connor's peripheral vision as he crossed the polished floor, stopped beside the drugged man on the trolley, and inspected the operation site.

"There's no bleed," he said.

Connor sensed a presence at his shoulder. He straightened abruptly, felt a needle drive up into his carotid artery, and pressure as liquid was shunted quickly into his neck.

Twisting round and stepping back, Connor's legs folded beneath him and he hit the floor, hard. He lay, unable to move, looking up into the gloating expression on a young vampire face. It came as no surprise.

The last time Connor saw this face, the vampire had been hyperventilating behind the plastic film of an operating mask as bloodlust scrambled his thought process. On that occasion, Connor had pinned him to the wall before lifting and forcibly ejecting him from the room. A vampire who could not insert a siphoning cannula into a human farm inmate without losing control would never work in an operating theater.

Without hesitation, Connor had kicked the vampire off the surgical training program. Few interns made the grade, and he had not given the failing intern a second's thought.

The youngster's face vanished and Connor stared at the polystyrene ceiling tiles and tried to shift his legs, but couldn't. His anger boiled. *Muscle relaxant.* The intern was smiling when he reappeared in the line of sight, and in that moment, Connor knew it was an ambush. *Matthew? And who else?*

Clawed fingers dug into his slack muscles when the vampire hoisted Connor up from the floor. His head cracked on the wall as he was hefted onto a gurney and landed with a thump onto his back. The arm twisted beneath him creaked – there was no pain, but Connor worried about his tendons snapping. The vampire covered him over with a thick linen sheet. From the time it took to get his dead weight lying straight on the gurney, Connor knew his attacker worked alone. *But, he didn't plan this without help.* Putting Matthew in the frame was not a huge leap.

Connor felt the tubular steel frame of the gurney judder. It threatened to buckle under his weight as it started to move. The world viewed through the closely-woven fabric was pale gray with dark shadows passing overhead as the trolley wheels rumbled along a passageway. A minute elapsed, the gurney came to a halt, and pitch-black closed in around him. After a muffled thud faded, Connor detected the kind of stillness that scared him. He wasn't scared for himself, but for Rebekah, for Seren. *I've been taken out. They are making their move. But* who *are they?*

The cover over his face stiffened with the cold, sweet smelling stagnant air crawled into his throat and lungs, and Connor calculated he was in a disused blood-storage refrigeration room. *It could be weeks before anyone comes by here.* He suddenly wished he had stopped off to hunt before going to the lab and given himself a fighting chance. As it was, dehydration was closer than he dared to think about.

Chapter 4

Twenty-five miles away, Rebekah, Seren, Leizle and all the other humans galvanized into action when they heard the shrieking sound of the siren coming from the human farm. The procedure was hard-wired into their consciousness. An emergency on the farm exposed them to danger. As the hive surgical team, Connor and Anthony would have to attend, leaving Seth and Greg to guard the woodlands closest to London until Julian arrived.

The pair of Marines may be combat trained, but they were only human, and Rebekah tried not to think about what would happen in a confrontation with vampires. *It is less guarding, and more decoying and sacrificing.* No matter what the guys did, they were vulnerable.

Slamming shut the books they were reading, the three girls leapt up from their floor cushions. Rebekah grabbed Seren's hand and, following Leizle, raced along the passageway. Rebekah would never leave the younger girl to follow on behind.

From the library cavern to safety was a five minute, chest burning, sprint.

Darting through the arched doorway of the dining cavern, they wove a hectic path across the room, barely avoiding crashing into wooden tables, and scampered into the kitchen. Rebekah caught sight of Oscar disappearing inside the panic room carrying his usual box of supplies.

Greg stood guard, one hand gripping the handle of the steel-lined door.

Smiling tightly as the three girls passed by, Greg said, "Lock the door from the inside. You know the drill. We'll use the coded knock. Don't open it for anyone."

"Sure thing," Rebekah murmured.

The door shut behind them with a dampened thump. The grating sound when Greg dragged the wooden shutter into place remained a terrifying noise to Rebekah.

Feelings of safety and incarceration were hard to reconcile. *Shit, all this time, and I'm still scared.* But, Connor would say that was a good thing.

"Here," Oscar said calmly, holding out a bottle of water and the two pills sitting in his palm.

She swallowed down the beta-blockers with a noisy gulp.

"I know, it don't get any easier, lass." With a reassuring squeeze of Rebekah's shoulder, Oscar retreated and lowered himself down beside Evie to settle in for the night.

Rebekah sank cross-legged onto the soft floor, leaned back against the padded wall and got comfortable. With Leizle sitting on one side, and Seren on the other, she prepared to face the endless hours ahead.

Rebekah gripped Seren's relaxed hand and smiled. It reminded her of how Connor treated her like a mannequin made of spun glass. *He* was always scared of bruising her fingers if he forgot his own strength, or rather, how fragile she was. And now, it seemed, her daughter felt the same. Rebekah draped an arm around Seren's slight shoulders, suddenly aware that her daughter no longer fitted snugly into her side.

In the dim battery-powered torchlight, Rebekah looked down at Seren's serene features. "How tall *are* you, now? You've must have grown an inch, this week alone."

"Papa said one and a half."

Of course, Connor could measure Seren's height with one glance. "Well, it must be then."

Rebekah fell silent. *Maybe he's right. She grows fast because she has to survive.* The thought made her sluggish heartbeat quicken, and her stomach turned over, drawing an anxious glance from Seren.

"It's okay, Mama, I'll look after you," Seren said soberly.

Rebekah took a deep, controlled breath and said, "But, I'll look after you first, deal? You're the important one here. You stay out of sight, no matter what."

Seren's young face filled with fake innocence.

Rebekah stared at her hard. "I mean it young lady. Greg and Seth are running the perimeter until Papa and Anthony can get back. Anything happens here, you hide, got it?"

"Got it," Seren replied.

Rebekah's heartbeat subsided from slightly-agitated to can't-be-bothered-to-move slow. The downside of the modified beta blockers they used to suppress the human heart rate was it made getting out of the starting blocks more of an effort too.

This was their fourth night in a row of sleeping inside the panic room, and every one that passed felt like a nail in the coffin of hope. *If Connor succeeds in his research then we get to stay… with Leizle, Oscar.* Of course, having Connor was the most important thing, and if two weeks passed without hope, she would gladly face the unknown at his side. *But, let's pray we don't have to.*

Rebekah drew comfort from the sound of Oscar's steady, heavy breathing. Squinting into the gloom, she made out his large barrel of a figure laid out on a bedroll, with Evie tucked into his side, his arm holding her close. He could have been asleep, until she saw his dark eyes glisten in the dim light when he looked over and winked at her.

She smiled.

From where they sat on the floor, the view of the door was obscured by an igloo-type construction of boxes and crates. The smaller, cozier space hid them from sight and blocked out the draft from where the ventilation pipe cut through the padded ceiling in the corner.

Hours ticked by, and Rebekah's eyelids felt heavy, each blink becoming longer until it was easier just to leave them closed.

A lava flow of colors seeped through her brain, bringing with them tingling warmth that resolved into the fuzzy-edged images of a dream. Connor, wearing a white coat, looking like he had on the day they met, walked towards her. But when he gripped her arm the pressure of his fingers did not stop. White-hot darts of pain bit into her oxygen starved muscle, and the bone in her arm began to creak. Her eyes shot open and she woke with a yelp.

Seren's cold hand closed over Rebekah's mouth. "Shhh."

Rebekah's dream state evaporated and tension oozed in through the cracks. *What's wrong?* A sudden flush of sweat broke out on Rebekah's skin as she darted a glance at Seren. She read the cold warning in her daughter's eyes and wished, for the hundredth time, that she shared Connor's psychic connection.

Inhaling deeply through her nose, Rebekah nodded, focusing on easing the panic tightening her chest.

Seren slowly withdrew her hand, released the grip which had shaken Rebekah awake, and her arm throbbed. *The pain wasn't part of the dream.* Absently rubbing the site, she winced at soreness which could be a bruise tomorrow.

Straining to detect what Seren had picked up on, Rebekah could hear only silence, but she trusted Seren's senses better than her own.

Vampire? Rebekah mouthed silently.

Seren nodded, held up five fingers and shrugged.

Rebekah's smiled tightly. *Shit.*

The groan of crumpling steel jerked all five inside the panic room to their feet. Maintaining silence, even though every fiber inside her wanted to cry out, Rebekah darted a glance at Oscar. Pointedly taking in Evie at his side, she gestured him back. Oscar's chin went up as his hand found Evie's and he nodded reluctantly. Tugging Seren behind her, Rebekah passed her over to Leizle and shot a look over her shoulder that said 'hide'.

Rubbing her damp palms down over her thighs, Rebekah's hand jarred on her talisman; a kidney-shaped pebble which she kept in the pocket of her combat trousers. Connor had grimly nicknamed it the 'vampire slayer'. *It did no such thing, of course.* In fact, it had enraged her attacker and almost ended her life. But, at least she had the satisfaction of seeing the shocked expression on the vampire's face when she whacked the stone against the end-stop of a dagger and scored a groove into his marble-hard stomach.

Rebekah only survived because Connor came to the rescue, but, she had put up a fight. She hadn't thought it possible for Connor's face to get any whiter than the quartz shade she was used to. *Boy, was I wrong.* His angry disbelief had been incandescent. The white-hot kind. *But, my survival instinct is good, he can't deny that.*

Smiling wryly, she pulled the stone from her pocket and set it on a shelf beside the stacked bags of dried pulses and lentils. Opening a packet of dried chickpeas, she poured some into both of the deep utility-pockets on her thighs. Taking a steady breath, she pressed their Velcro flaps down and picked up the stone again. Keeping it in her fist, she turned to face the door and waited. *Here we go again.*

The creaking metal of the lock gave way with an explosive crack. The door sprung open, bouncing noiselessly against the padded wall, and a cluster of man-sized shadows flooded into the room. In that moment, Oscar fell further back, and Rebekah stepped forward around the wall of boxes.

She stared straight ahead, allowing four faces, their translucent-white complexions glowing in the dim light, to blur out of focus. The vampires froze as if their motors had failed. Rebekah, praying that Seren would stay out of sight, froze too.

The sound of a heavy footfall trickled dread down her spine as another assailant sauntered into the room. The vampires parted. A tall blond figure with ice-blue eyes stopped in front of Rebekah and smiled. "Where is the hybrid child?"

Rebekah did not pretend to misunderstand. "She's with her father. You won't find her. Not now, not ever."

As the vampire's brows arched in surprise, Rebekah drove all her strength into a swinging blow, aiming the 'vampire slayer' stone at his face. He easily caught her wrist and squeezed. The stone fell from her limp fingers with a clatter and annoyance twisted Rebekah's features. But, she did not expect to win; distraction was all she had to work with.

Gripping the front of Rebekah's shirt, the commander drew her slowly towards him. The sluggish pulse thumping inside her head faltered and Rebekah pushed up onto tiptoes, a tell-tale rasp grating in her throat as she choked.

"Mmm. You must be the mother." Leaning in close, his icy breath stung her cheek as he said, "How many bones will I have to break before you tell me the truth?"

Rebekah braced her free hand on the metal plate covering his torso and squeezed her eyes shut as ink blots clustered behind her lids. Unconsciousness would be a relief, but the vampire knew that. Sliding her back down his chest until her legs supported her weight again, he said conversationally, "I could start with a finger."

Suiting actions to words, he gripped her wrist tighter, the cartilage in the joint creaking as he moved her hand up in front of her face. Rebekah swallowed the groan of pain, her ears straining for any noise from behind as she willed them all to stay still.

"The thumb will hurt the most, but we'll get to that. The smallest finger first. Shall I snap, or crush the bone? What do you think?"

His pincer grip closed around her little finger.

Rebekah gritted her teeth as his gaze bored into hers. All she saw there was curiosity.

The numbing cold of his touch had just begun to bite into her flesh when his nostrils flared. He abruptly looked up, focusing in the mid-distance somewhere over Rebekah's head, and the muscle in his jaw twitched.

Feeling his attention slipping away, Rebekah panicked. "My daughter is safe, I don't care what you do," she muttered, and spat in his face.

His blank gaze slid back to study her. He tightened the pressure on her finger until she yelped in pain. Bruising blossomed as capillaries ruptured, the cartilage straining to hold the bones together.

Shooting a probing glance over her head, he said softly, "I can hear you, child. Smell you. Come out and I won't hurt your Mama anymore, or the others."

Through the tears, Rebekah saw his smile widen and his blue eyes glitter. She slumped in his hold, knowing she had lost. The blood pounding in her ears blissfully numbed her senses, but she felt Seren's presence behind her.

A keen expression carved lines into his diamond-ice complexion as he murmured, "There you are."

Pushing Rebekah aside into the hold of a guardsman, the commander stepped forward and took Seren's chin in his hand.

"Fascinating." His fingers probed beneath her mutinous jaw until they found the slow pulse in her neck. "Barely beating at all." Looking into her pale tight face, he coaxed, "Come quietly, child, and your three friends can live. That is fair, no?"

"And Mama? Let her go, too."

"Nej- No. I will need her. She will remind you to be good." The vampire's hand whipped out a fist, aimed into Rebekah's stomach, and with lightning reflexes Seren grabbed his wrist with both hands and stopped it dead. "See? You can protect her. If you both comply, no one gets hurt."

Lifting her chin and staring at the vampire with the candor of youth, Seren asked, "Who are you anyway? You're not from England. What crest is that on the brass plate on your chest?"

"Enough talking. Come." The commander jerked his head at the four guardsmen and placed a restraining hand on Seren's shoulder. They filed out of the doorway, the first pair holding Rebekah firmly between them.

"You're very blonde," said Seren sweetly. "You look like a warrior dressed for battle. Are you a king?"

"No questions," he said shortly.

"How did you know where to find us? Who told you?"

"Enough. Stop talking or perhaps I will change my mind about your friends, no?"

Seren looked into his cold face and decided he meant it.

Two vampire guards raced onwards through the tunnels. The remaining pair walked only as fast as Rebekah's shaky legs could move until, on a grunt of impatience, the commander barked, "Carry her, we don't have all night."

Rebekah was hoisted up and slung over a vampire's solid shoulder. Terrified of falling, she scrabbled to grip the folds of his leather tunic, her hip bones grinding painfully into stone-hard flesh. Seconds later, they emerged into the cold autumn night. Seren already stood beside the intimidating commander, waiting meekly. When Rebekah's feet touched the ground, she automatically sought out Seren's eyes, gratefully absorbing the gleam of certainty lighting her young face. *Connor will know she's in danger, she'll be showing him everything she sees. He will come.*

Two black horses loosely tethered in the pasture ambled forward, and Rebekah's feeling of still having some control plummeted when a sack cloth was pulled roughly down over her head. Cold callous hands gripped under her arms and hauled her up into a saddle. She collided with the solid bulk of a vampire already mounted up behind her. Her mouth filled with the hessian fibers, and she choked on the dust inside the sack when she gasped at the pain biting into her shoulder blades. The horse, whinnying nervously, bolted at breakneck speed as though trying to outrun the demon on his back. The hard metal of the breastplate jarring into her spine with each bounding stride confirmed her fear that she shared a horse with the vampire commander.

Rebekah heard her daughter's complaining cry. "I'll feel sick if I can't see."

Her heart sank. Seren's only visions now, would be of the inside of a sack. Rebekah wriggled in her seat, her thighs aching as they gripped the saddle, and she carefully burrowed her hands into her pockets. Filling her palms with the dried chickpeas, she eased them back out and, opening one hand, released the cream-colored pellets in a trailing shower onto the ground.

Holding her breath until the pressure in her chest throbbed like a bruise, she did the same again. A shout from a vampire running behind pierced the air, and the horse reared as the reins were pulled tight. Skidding hooves tore a trough into the earth and the spooked gelding's forelegs came back down, hitting the ground with a jolt. The horse shied sideways, yanking at the reins firmly anchored in the commander's unresponsive grip, and his arm around Rebekah's chest was all that saved her from being catapulted over the animal's head.

Still breathless from the blind fairground ride, she felt herself being hauled down from the saddle, and the sackcloth was whipped off her head. The heaving side of the horse pressed into her back, and she stared up into incredulous anger on a tight vampire face.

"You are leaving a trail?" His voice rose with disbelief.

Rebekah flinched when he grabbed her hand and, dragging her arm through his grip, pushed her sleeve up. With a frown, he inspected her skin. "You've never been siphoned," he said thoughtfully. "And this Doctor Connor has failed to tame you. I wonder what it takes to break the human spirit. What would it take to break your spirit?"

Jerking her chin up, Rebekah said grimly, "No one can break me. Not him, and not you. He protected my daughter, and that's all I cared about. Can you do the same? Stop her being used as a guinea pig?" Rebekah prayed Seren would understand. "I don't care who protects her, but I will die before I see her hurt. You will have to kill me first."

She slapped his face hard, hurting her palm, and she knew he had let her do it.

"So much fire. I guess I should expect nothing less from a woman who suffered through the birth of a hybrid child." Rebekah stared him down as he stroked a finger over her cheek. "You will have to tell me the story sometime. I wonder if you would survive another."

Rebekah suppressed the need to swallow and held her tongue.

Without looking away, the commander said to the other horseman, "Let's get going. The trail will die here." He smiled as he felt Rebekah's heart jolt despite herself. "Oh no, min skat, not you. Your Doctor Connor will be driven wild, no? The trail-" He gestured the poof of a magician's trick. "Just disappears."

Leaning closer, he delved into her pockets, his hands stroking roughly over her thighs as he turned out the remainder of the peas. Studying the glazed expression on her face, he laughed. Moments later, she was back in the saddle, and the wind chill of rushing cold night air made her eyes water and her throat burn even through the sackcloth. At least that was what she told herself.

Even though every muscle screamed with tension, Rebekah fought to stay stiff, hostility oozing from every line in her body. Keeping her head still became almost impossible as the breakneck speed of their mount slowed, and her chin dropped forward onto her chest.

The horse's pace eased to a slow rocking motion. The arm around Rebekah's waist pulled her back against her captor's chest. She fought him, flailing her elbows half-heartedly until he chuckled over her head. His touch was gentle as he tugged on the sackcloth hood and removed it.

The thick woodlands they ambled through were a landscape of oil-black and charcoal to Rebekah's eyes, although Connor had told her that vampire night vision transformed night into day.

"Sleep, min skat. We have a long way to go."

"Stop calling me that, my name is Miss Wylde, to you."

"Wylde? It suits you, but nej. You are the spoils of war, treasure, my treasure. It is what I call you," he said firmly.

Rebekah snorted but when the burn in her neck muscles became unbearable she found resting her head back against him was easy. His thick claret cape enfolded her body in soft warmth, and she fell asleep.

Her eyes snapped open and drowsiness dropped away with a jolt of panic when the jerking stride of the horse picking its way down a steep slope flung her body left and right. In the pearl gray light of dawn, she looked out over the sea, and it stole her breath away. The scenery was stunning, despite the glowering sky. The waves decorating the dark teal sea with frothy strings of lace raced into the shore and shattered upon the rocks.

The gelding's hooves skidded with terrifying regularity on the rock-strewn descent, but the horse seemed to know it well. The commander's hand splayed over her waist held Rebekah locked in tight to his steady frame and, despite her heart being firmly lodged in her throat, she felt safe.

The feeling of betrayal churned inside, and she muttered, "I should have fought harder. Better to have died."

"Tut tut. And leave your child alone? No, your doctor will know you could not do that."

Clamping her mouth shut, Rebekah gave him nothing else to play his games with. Looking down, she saw a ship. She had not seen a ship in almost twenty years and it was hard not to ask questions.

"Are we in Devon?"

"Not so far down as that."

"Dorset, then."

"No more questions," he said firmly.

The chalk face of the cliffs were a clue that it was the south coast of England, but that was all Rebekah could guess at.

"Can you tell me your name, at least?"

The surf pounded in time with her heart beat as she waited. *Will he unbend?* There were all kinds of ammunition. Any weakness would give her hope.

"Lars."

The word, whispered in her ear, made her shiver, and his harsh laugh ended the conversation.

The last minutes of the descent tightened the tangled knot of nerves inside her belly – they were leaving England. Making a break for it had barely crossed her mind when, as if reading her thoughts, Lars said, "Don't, min skat."

When the horse reached the pebbled beach, Lars dismounted and dragged Rebekah down with him. Carrying her, he waded into the surf, out to a rowing boat bobbing in shallow waters, and deposited her none too gently into it.

Already sitting in the stern of the boat, Seren waited quietly with her hood still in place.

Rebekah took her hand. "You okay, sweetheart?"

"Yes, Mama."

Rebekah called out to the vampire seated in the bow, steadily rowing the boat. "Can I take her hood off?"

"No."

She was tempted to pull it off, anyway, but the vampire's stern look pinned her to her seat.

Breaking the tension, Rebekah twisted around for a final glance behind. Scouring the flint-gray sky where it met the green-fringed line of the cliff-tops, she looked for a shadow which she could pretend was Connor, hard on their heels. *Where is he?*

The beach retreated at an alarming rate as the vampire's powerful oar strokes drove the boat forward, creating a stiff breeze that whipped her hair across her eyes. Dragging the strands back and squinting, Rebekah searched the pebble-duned coastline for the other vampires, but found that they were alone.

"Where did they go? The other vampires have disappeared."

"They're too heavy to share a rowing boat," Seren replied. "They are probably walking."

"Walking?" Rebekah took in a sharp breath and frowned. "Where-?"

Staring over the side into the water, clusters of shifting shadows in the murky depths captured Rebekah's fanciful imagination. *Walking? Really?*

Further out, the water became choppy and the rowing boat rocked violently. Rebekah abandoned her questions. She hung on tight, but was still thrown from the hard, wooden seat when the boat swung around and collided broadside with the wooden hull of the ship. The bottom rungs of a rope ladder fell into the bottom of the boat with a thud, and the vampire stood up.

"Climb," he said.

"I'm taking her hood off," Rebekah declared. Glaring into the vampire's blank white features, she did exactly that.

Seren climbed the ladder first, hopping nimbly over the wooden rail at the top.

Rebekah's climb was more labored. As the deck came into view, she almost took the hand Lars held out, but snatched her own back when she realized. Her cheeks burned as she ignored the smile twitching at his mouth. She clambered over the side and dusted her hands down on her thighs.

Once Rebekah and Seren stood side-by-side onboard the ship, Lars' levity melted. His features hardened, his eyes reflecting the bleakness of the sea.

Only the stinging force of the wind whipping across the bay disguised the color draining from Rebekah's face. *So, he has us. What now?*

"Come," Lars said and, swinging away, he crossed to a low doorway and pulled aside a thick canvas curtain.

Checking his stride only to make sure they were obeying the order, he ducked his head and descended below deck. Following on behind, Rebekah caught sight of his broad figure striding along a gangway and disappearing into a cabin.

His wet clothes left a dark trail on the wood floor and Rebekah raised an eyebrow at Seren. "Too heavy for boats?" she hissed. "*He walked?*"

Seren smiled.

Hurrying to keep up, at the door of the cabin, Rebekah fixed her gaze on her feet and concentrated on stepping over the high wooden threshold. She recoiled when Lars' brown leather boots came into view and he blocked the way. His cold fingers encircled her wrist without warning, but were quickly replaced by the chill of a metal handcuff. The other manacle clattered as Lars closed it around a metal pipe which ran like a handrail around the cabin.

Focusing an arctic stare on Seren, Lars said quietly, "You will be good, nej? I have some wire and a toughened steel cage, and I can post a guard inside the room, if you prefer?"

"I will be good."

He looked long and hard before, nodding sharply, he left.

Standing still, not quite believing they were at last alone, Rebekah held her breath and strained her ears, looking at Seren for confirmation.

Seren nodded. "He has gone, Mama."

"We have to keep looking for chances to escape. Send Papa what images you can and help him find us." Rebekah frowned. "Do you know where he is?"

"Mama, Papa is in a dark place. He cannot see." Seren's young face was tense.

"Don't worry, Seren, there'll be a simple reason. Papa won't let us come to harm." Her confidence was not as bone-deep as she wanted it to be. *A dark place sounds bad, whichever way you cut it. But he won't stop until he finds us, and Lars will regret the day he set foot in England.*

Dragging the metal cuff along the pipe, Rebekah sat down on the bunk, sighed heavily, and patted the mattress beside her.

"You know, Papa and I, we have been through worse than this." Hugging her daughter close Rebekah said, "He *will* come. And when he does, he will kick this arrogant commander's ass. Make no mistake."

Seren smiled, and Rebekah's heart lightened. *We just have to stay alive.*

Chapter 5

It was barely an hour before, after shutting the small group inside the panic room, that Greg slotted the wooden panel back into place and rubbed dirt into the edges. *Okay, good to go.* Pulling a black knitted cap on to cover his snow white hair, he set off to catch up with Seth. Both men sprinted through the tunnels, taking turns on point as they made their way out into the open, each one covering the other, their metal spiked maces at the ready.

They crossed the meadow at a crouched run, heading for the cover of the woods as fast as their pumping legs could carry them. In the damp, gloomy environment the ear-piercing wail of the human farm siren made staying in sight of each other critical, but they were combat hardened and watching each other's back was second nature.

Greg would be happier when the high-pitched noise drilling its way into his brain stopped.

They moved through the trees as if a tightrope was drawn between the two men, each forward step landing in unison. Every few seconds, Greg looked over at Seth's tight lipped, mud smeared features, which mirrored his own. *No reaction is good.*

Without warning, the shrieking noise stopped so abruptly Greg thought he had gone deaf. He froze in mid-step and raised a fist, signaling to Seth to do the same. They held their positions like awkwardly posed statues, both aware it was a knife edge moment. The wait for senses to adjust was the stuff of life or death. Neither man would move until they could hear again, had taken stock, and made sure the din had not allowed a threat to come close.

Many soldiers died in combat because they took their eye off the ball. When something which demanded all their focus suddenly disappeared, resisting the urge to relax was crucial. Both Marines had been here before.

As Greg took a deep, careful breath, the hairs on his nape prickled, and he knew something was wrong. He frowned because the cause of the unease evaded him.

Seth drew closer. His eyes glittered as he mimed their combat sign for a mounted opponent – one black-gloved hand patted the closed fist of the other – and he extended his fingers to indicate two as he cupped a hand to his ear.

And there it was, the sound that didn't belong, the beat of horses' hooves. Greg was angry. *What am I? A bloody rookie?*

"Raise the alarm," Greg muttered, jerking a thumb towards the peak of the hill.

Seth nodded sharply and broke into a powerful run that propelled him up the slope.

Reeling around, Greg took off towards the meadow below. For a bulky man, his step was surprisingly agile. Humans sounded like stampeding buffalo to vampire ears, but, right now, all he cared about was speed.

As the woods thinned, Greg reached out, grabbed hold of a tree trunk, and stopped dead. With every muscle braced, he scanned the rambling pasture below. It looked quiet, but panning left, through his night vision goggles he caught glimpses of dark and pale gray shapes moving through the trees beyond. He shifted his shoulders as his shirt stuck to the cold sweat soaking his skin. *Fuck.* Thumping the tree trunk, he swallowed a groan. Pushing the goggles up onto his forehead, he took a quick compass reading and burst out into the moonlight.

By the time he crossed the rough grass and entered the woodland opposite, even with the night goggles back in place, the trail was cold. "Damn it all to hell." His frustration ricocheted from the trees, taunting him. Now, he had a million questions. *Vampires can move too fast to show up on night goggles, but the horses were real. Had they left empty handed? Or-* "Shit, shit, shit."

As Greg double timed it back across the meadow, his eyes lifted to watch the yellow-tinted halo above the tree tops. A flickering glow lit up the night sky. Fireflies of ash danced higher, drifting on the breeze and disappearing into the stratosphere. *Good, Seth has lit the beacon. Julian should come, even if Connor is still tied up.*

Reaching the foot of the escarpment, he approached the camouflaged entrance of the eco-shelter, checking for anything out of place. Staring into the black hole carved into the hillside, an appetite for ice-cold revenge gripped him and he hoped to find a straggler, something to ease the pain of defeat – he wanted to beat the shit out of something.

Tightness cramped his neck as he yanked the black knitted skull cap lower over his damp hair. He wiped the sweat from his face with his thick gloves, took a deep breath and moved forward, dreading what he may find. Switching to his favored weapon, he drew his blacksmith's mallet from his utility belt. Sidestepping along, hugging one wall, he entered the eco-shelter.

It was quiet. Using the mallet head, he eased back the blackout curtain and let it graze across his chest as he slipped past. Still hugging the wall, ducking below each burning torch along the way, he covered another thirty yards before he heard crying. He continued on at a slow steady pace. He would not let a rush of emotion make him stupid.

Instinctively, he peered into each tunnel mouth he came to. His heart grew heavier as he recognized the crying as Leizle. He steeled himself to face the worst when, finally, reaching the arched doorway of the dining cavern, he walked in.

Evie and Leizle were seated at a wooden table with their arms around each other. Oscar stopped pacing like a caged bear, took one look at Greg's grim face, and nodded abruptly.

"They are gone," Oscar's face crumpled and then stiffened again. "I let them get taken."

Evie said quietly, "Don't blame yourself Oscar, please." She appealed to Greg. "Would you have done any better? If five, six. Lord knows how many vampires walked in here right now, could you stop them?"

But Greg, knowing what Oscar would be thinking, shook his head and injected understanding into the flint black intensity of his gaze. "Yes, you could have died trying. But what good would that have done?"

"It would stop me feeling like a spineless bastard."

Greg laughed darkly. "You'd not be feeling anything at all. The best thing you can do is get every word you heard straight in your head. We need all the help we can get." Crossing the room, he laid a heavy hand on Oscar's shoulder. "How did they find the panic room?"

Oscar shook his head. "They must have known. They didn't search. Nothing is disturbed except the wooden shutter over the door." Oscar's voice dropped to a dry whisper, "They knew exactly where to find them."

Greg knew the answer, but he asked anyway. "They took them both?"

Oscar nodded and lowered himself down onto a wooden bench. "What happens now?"

Greg squared his shoulders. "We wait for Connor. Take what shit he throws at us, and then we get out there and bloody find them."

"We just wait?" Leizle stood up. "Where *is* Connor? Where is Seth? There must be something we can do." Gripping the edge of the table, her white face flooded with sudden color as she shouted, "Don't just stand there, do something."

As though her desperate anger took on a tangible form, a breeze gusted around the room, snatching at her clothes and plastering them to her body. Her red hair whipped across her face.

"It looks like the waiting is over. He's here." Greg turned to face the door, weathering the force of the tornado which would be nothing compared to the storm which would hit when Connor appeared.

But it was Julian who rushed into the room, and, for a moment, everyone in the cavern was struck dumb.

Leizle recovered first. Stepping up onto a bench and then onto the table top, without thinking, she launched herself at him.

Julian absorbed the impact, catching her as though she was the feather-light weight of a fragile bird. He stroked a reassuring hand down over her back, choking on his obvious relief. He tried not to notice the faces which were missing, but he knew the beacon burning on the hill could only mean disaster.

He sought out Greg. "What the hell happened?"

Lowering Leizle gently to the floor, he looked down into green eyes the same shade as his own, running his thumb over her damp cheeks. He felt guilty because he was glad she was okay.

Guilt gave way to anger as he scanned the area. Turning to Greg again, he said, "And where the hell is Connor?"

Seth joined them in the cavern and leant against the wall while Greg rattled out a summary of what happened out in the meadow. In a hard tone, Greg summed up. "A group of vampires entered the eco-town. They knew where Rebekah and Seren were hidden, and they took them. They set off southwest on horseback about fifteen minutes ago, and we've not seen Connor."

A groan of despair from Oscar drew Julian's attention. Oscar's broad shoulders slumped in self-recrimination.

Greg cut in, "Oscar knows there's nothing he could've done, but you know the score." His voice faded as he added, "He's looked out for Rebekah since she was a child, and now-"

Julian grinned wryly. "Don't beat yourself up, Oscar. Let's concentrate on getting them safely home. We need to track down Connor, now. And where's Anthony?"

Greg shrugged.

"I've not seen either of them. A messenger from the farm confirmed the emergency surgery had gone well. I thought they'd be back here." Julian's fingers drifted down to squeeze Leizle's waist as he released her. "Greg and Seth, load up for a search party. I'll find Connor and Anthony and meet you back here. Oscar, write down everything you can remember." Addressing the group, but looking at Leizle, with a tight smile Julian said, "I'll be back soon, and we won't stop looking until we find them."

Julian took a direct route across country from London, arriving at the perimeter fence of the human farm in a record time for him. He had no intention of waiting for the guard. He leapt eight feet from the ground, grabbed hold of the wire mesh fence and crushed the metal into ingots inside his palms. Before the wire strands broke, he swung his legs up, and vaulted over the top. He mistimed the release, leaving it too late, and the razor wire sliced through his jacket and shirt. It dug grooves into his hardened flesh, but he didn't care.

He landed on the soft grass and loped towards the next barrier.

As he mentally ticked off places to search, frown lines cut into his smooth complexion.

He had already tried the hospital and drawn a blank. Charles had not seen Connor since the last blood delivery to the dispensary, when Connor had collected his daily allowance of human blood. He said he was going to the laboratory. Julian tried there next and found it empty. Although he could not get inside, the outer door was a good old-fashioned mortise key into a keyhole affair. If it was locked, then Connor was not in there.

Isaac had not booked Connor in to a cadaver drawer for grave-sleep, and Julian was running out of options. *And Rebekah and Seren are running out time. Where the hell is Anthony?* The idea that Connor was in trouble seemed less likely with Anthony missing too. *Perhaps they're already in pursuit? Let's hope so.*

As Julian rushed up to the next barrier. A vampire warden reached the gate at the same time, disapproval locking his features tight as he said, "Halt, and identify yourself."

Julian glared though the glinting metal and growled. "If you were doing your job, you'd have discovered who I was twenty yards back, at the outer fence. Open up."

Blasted by Julian's white-faced fury, the vampire's throat worked as he struggled for words. With dull acceptance, he muttered, "Yes, sir... Principal Julian." After opening the gate, the vampire stepped back as far as possible, almost tugging his forelock while he waved Julian through.

"Make yourself useful," Julian barked. "Find out what time Doctor Connor and Surgical Assistant Anthony left the farm."

The vampire blurted, "They are still here."

"What the hell?" The idea of an early pursuit died. Ignoring protocol, the need to get answers fast eating at him, Julian grabbed the vampire by the neck. "So, where are they?"

"In the new medical block, sir."

"Thank you," Julian muttered, releasing the guard who staggered at his sudden freedom. Reeling around, Julian rushed across the rough ground and on to the gate in fence number three.

The farm warden waiting at the inner boundary shot a wary glance at this new disconcertingly physical Principal Julian. Opening the gate in silence long before he needed to, he stood stiffly to attention and waited.

Julian shrugged out of his tattered jacket as he walked, tossed it to the warden and rolled up his shirt sleeves. "Get rid of it, please." Dismissing the vampire with rudeness that drew a raised eyebrow, Julian turned and walked quickly away.

Passing through the desolate vista which reflected the grim reality of being an inmate on the farm, he raced onward to the new medical block. Even in his distracted state, he registered that the newer facility represented an oasis in an arid and brutal desert of human existence.

In the main compound rows of wooden dormitories were raised up on platforms to protect against rising damp. The constant stream of human traffic to and from the siphoning sheds had long ago worn away the grass. The frequent downpours which plagued England in autumn made the ground perpetually muddy.

The human exercise yards that lay beyond the siphoning sheds were deserted. The pristine rubber-coated black surface glistened with the oily sheen of dewdrops. It was bare and uninviting. Frustration at Supervisor Matthew's continuing failure to make sure humans took exercise drew a grunt from Julian, his anger fueled by the futility he felt at Connor being missing.

I spend too much time in court and not enough time kicking Matthew's butt. That changes, right now. The human body was receiving less care than the human spirit, and *that* was precious little. He knew from experience that the vampire mentality of viewing humans as 'cattle' was hard to crack. *But I'll bust him down to a crop reaper if he doesn't up his game.* Getting the message across that humans needed recreation would be a mountain to climb. *But, that is what it will take for them to live longer.*

Survival options of the species were hurtling towards desperation point – they both live, or both die. What was needed was an epiphany where the human and vampire interests became symbiotic. *So, we need a damned miracle then.*

Reaching his destination, Julian shoved the thoughts from his mind. They were problems for another day.

He jabbed at a keypad mounted beside the tall iron-barred gate, entering his personal identity number, and with a click the lock released – passing through the gate into the new breeding compound was like stepping into another world. *This is better.* But his appreciation felt like one pair of hands clapping a virtuoso performance where there should be crowds cheering. But then, this was only for the 'chosen few', he reminded himself.

Here, instead of concentration camp steel-mesh fencing and razor wire, they had opted for a brick wall. Inside the enclosure, traditional picture-postcard-perfect red-brick built houses sat on their own plots behind white picket fences. The integrated drainage system meant there were burgeoning flower beds and lush lawns instead of puddles of mud.

A wide pathway led to the medical block. The sandstone paving slabs, which were golden yellow in both sunshine and in rain, reminded Julian of the yellow brick road in the Wizard of Oz. *Follow the yellow brick road...* Julian hummed the jaunty tune. *Ironic.* Of course, unlike the Emerald City, while the answer to vampire hopes may well lie beyond those doors, humans press-ganged into the hybrid breeding program would certainly not see it that way. *The wizard being merely a man would be a happy ending for them.*

Julian's announcement in court was a ploy, for now at least, and he found the prospect of the breeding program becoming a reality abhorrent. Connor was right about one thing, inducing hypothermia in human females as part of the fertilization process was not an option, and, as yet, there was no alternative. *If only Connor had taken Rebekah and Seren and left while he had the chance.*

He mounted the steps to the medical center and pushed open the door. The plush surroundings were an extension of the surreal dream. His eyes were drawn to the sage-colored carpet. Cozy down-lighting cast an amber glow over a waiting area populated with couches upholstered in brown distressed-look leather. The pretense was shattered when Julian caught sight of a thin young girl. The plump cushions of a couch seemed to swallow her up. Lank hair hung over her face in a curtain of strings and the knuckles of her hands glowed red with chapped skin. The vampire standing guard behind her tore holes in the illusion of comfort.

Turning away, Julian took the stairs three at a time, arriving at the landing where plush gave way to hospital pristine white. He walked along the corridor, opening each door and closing it again. The fifth door reaped rewards.

"Anthony." Julian recognized the broad back and glossy brown hair immediately.

The shocked expression on Anthony's face when he turned around puzzled Julian, until he caught sight of himself in a mirror.

His eighteenth century buttoned down reserve and immaculate appearance had taken a beating. The reflection staring back at him wore a torn and rust streaked shirt. Silver scrapes ran along the length of his forearm, like pink veins through quartz, and the tangled blond hair and manic glitter in his green eyes would certainly raise an eyebrow.

Julian couldn't care less.

Supervisor Matthew went to take a step forward, but then thought better of it. "Principal Julian, is there a problem?"

Julian ran his hands through his hair in a token attempt to restore order, and hooded the urgency in his gaze as he said carefully, "Where would I find Doctor Connor?"

Anthony frowned. "He said he would report back to the hospital. I'm just running through the shots they'll need to give to females that pass the health checks-" Julian noticed the frozen wink-wink expression, as they both knew that was never the plan.

"Doctor Connor has not reported back?" Matthew asked. "Perhaps he does not consider it important the council be kept informed. He can be a law unto himself, or so it seems."

Turning to Matthew, Julian cut in smoothly, "I need a word with Assistant Anthony, alone." When the door closed behind the supervisor, Julian said quietly, "Rebekah and Seren are gone, they have been taken-" He held up a hand to silence Anthony's questions. "Right now, we need to find Connor. He's damn well disappeared."

Anthony's jaw snapped shut.

"No, not disappeared. There is something going on here. The warden told me Connor has not left," Julian said slowly. "He's here somewhere, and we have to find him, now."

"I'll begin here. Search every room," said Anthony, reaching for the door handle.

"Wait. We need an excuse. The less Supervisor Matthew knows the better. Tell him Charles found contaminated blood in the dispensary. Two vampires are in anaphylaxis, and we need Connor to treat them. That should give him something to worry about," said Julian with a tight smile.

"You got it." Anthony left quickly and disappeared up the stairwell, and the noise of doors opening and slamming overhead marked his progress.

Finding Matthew lurking uncomfortably close to the doorway when he walked out into the corridor, Julian said, "Supervisor, assemble the porters in the foyer."

"Certainly."

The hint of a smile on Matthew's face irritated Julian. "Do it now."

Watching the supervisor scuttle away, he took a deep breath. *When this is over, transferring that smug bastard out of here is top of my damn list.* He allowed himself a second's peace before returning to the ground floor. He stood to attention as the last of the porters answered the summons, before walking along the row of twenty-six vampires. Staring into each attentive face, he said, "We have an emergency at the hospital and we need to find Doctor Connor. He is here somewhere-" Julian stopped walking as Anthony arrived beside him and shook his head. "I'm looking for a court clerk. Putting it bluntly, find Doctor Connor and you get a promotion."

"Search the whole compound?" a young vampire asked.

"Perhaps I should coordinate the search?" Matthew interrupted, frowning with shallow concern.

Julian ignored the supervisor and nodded at the keen youngster. "The whole compound. Leave no stone unturned." Jabbing a finger at each porter as he moved along the line again, he barked out search zones, finishing with the command, "Now, go."

Anthony and Julian followed on their heels, taking off to search the first siphoning shed.

The first shed was deserted. Anthony took the main hall, feeling ridiculous as he peered underneath the vacant siphoning beds. The locker areas at the rear of the shed were locked, but the screech of metal filled the air as he poked a hole in each door and pulled until the catches snapped.

Julian checked the examination rooms, pulling the supplies in the walk-in storage units from the shelves and onto the floor until he could see the steel walls behind. He would leave nothing to chance.

They met up back at the main entrance and set off together for the next shed.

Inside the main hall, eighty humans lay strapped to the metal siphoning tables. Extending from the catheter implanted in the arm of each donor, a transparent tube filled with blood snaked from the brachial artery down into an I.V. bag.

Anthony stopped in his tracks, casting an apologetic glance at Julian. His breathing on pause, he slammed a plastic mask over his face, nodded tersely, and diverted to the relative safety of the storage area.

Julian took care fitting his own mask. Pressing the soft plastic firmly around his muzzle filtered the alluring thick odor which was like syrup lining his palette. The ache to wash it down with a draft of fresh warm blood could be almost unbearable. *Thanks, Anthony.* But to be fair, Anthony knew his limits. Without Connor to coach him, he did not trust himself around so many bleeding humans.

Whipping along between two rows of occupied tables, Julian aimed for a closed door in the wall opposite. *The recovery room is fair game. They can't hide Connor out here in plain sight.* He stepped inside and scanned the area. The room was populated by drowsy patients. They had given their quota, received vitamin and iron shots, and would stay in the recovery room until they felt able to walk. Vampire interns paced the perimeter, keeping an eye on their charges.

Julian studied each of the circulating vampires, paranoia setting in. *Any one of them could be involved.*

The odor of blood pervaded the air. Minimizing his exposure, Julian moved quickly up and down each row of reclined bodies. The patients who fought the system exuded a cloud of ether. Julian checked the face of each human, again feeling stupid, but a comatose Connor lying on a table could be plausible.

When he drew a blank, a disabling cocktail of frustration and desperation hit. The smell of blood permeating his mask dragged a blade of hunger from his throat down into his chest. *I can't do this.* Just as he turned to leave, his prayers were answered.

Julian heard a shout and burst into movement. Retracing his steps, he beat Anthony out of the main door of the siphoning shed, skimmed down the polished stone ramp and hit the muddy grass at a run. He followed the fading sound waves of the shout across the compound and darted into the doorway of siphoning shed number six.

He almost collided with a vampire who stepped swiftly aside. Scudding to a halt as he overshot his mark, he swept back around, his hard perfect features cramped as he said. "Well? Where is he?"

Apprehension lurked in the vampire's eyes.

Julian's animation drained away. He asked again, "Where is Doctor Connor?"

"In the disused refrigeration facility, at the back of the shed," the young porter said.

As Anthony darted forward to lead the way, the vampire added heavily, "I think it's too late."

"Get some I.V. bags of blood down here, stat," Anthony shouted over his shoulder as he ran.

Anthony and Julian burst through the thick metal door which took them into a disused corridor. There were four open doors ranging down one side. Their shoes scraped over the rough quartz floor while they shuffled with indecision, until a vampire put one foot into the hall and beckoned from the doorway at the end.

Julian took the lead, waving the vampire aside as he darted into the darkened room. The stagnant atmosphere poured into his lungs like flood waters, making talking difficult. His keen eyesight easily picked out Connor's frozen features staring at the ceiling, his body still half-covered in a linen sheet.

Gripping the foot of the autopsy trolley, Julian dragged it into the center of the room, yanked the cover from Connor's torso, and tossed it aside. Doing the first thing that came to him, he slapped Connor's cheeks hard and shouted his name.

With a snort, Anthony barged Julian aside and wheeled an empty drip stand forward. He pressed his thumb into the back of Connor's hand, tore open his shirt and pressed firmly on his sternum, and then did the same on his cheek bones.

"What the hell are you doing?" croaked Julian.

"Calculating dehydration." Anthony turned his head abruptly and blasted the vampire still standing at the door. "Don't just stand there, get that blood in here, right now!"

Turning back to his patient, Anthony placed his thumbs on Connor's eyelids, pushed them back, and smiled.

"What?" asked Julian, elbowing Anthony when he didn't immediately answer. "What?"

"He's still in there," Anthony said quietly. "See the pupil dilation?"

Julian leaned in close. "What? Fixed and dilated? That's not good."

As Julian spoke, Connor's pupils contracted abruptly to pinpricks. His ice-gray eyes glinted with flint-like anger, before the pupils swelled to oil-black pools again.

Anthony laughed darkly. "It's the only thing he has control over, and I'd say he is good and mad.

A clatter at the door signaled the arrival of a vampire pushing a crate filled with I.V. bags. Their oily plastic skins glistened in the light spilling in from the corridor. Anthony scooped one up, hung the bag from the drip stand, and ran the line into Connor's carotid artery using a large bore needle – it took all his strength to shove its sharp tip through his mentor's skin.

After taping the I.V. tube in place, he glanced down into the crate.

"Shit," he said, and turning to bark out another demand, he stopped short.

A young vampire porter slapped a bovine grade syringe and a vial of adrenalin into Anthony's hands and he smiled.

"Smart boy, he's the one you want, Julian," he muttered, as holding the glass tube upside down, he pierced the cork stopper with the long needle, withdrew the plunger, and filled the syringe.

Tossing the empty vial to the vampire, he turned back to his patient. Locating the space between the second and third rib on the left side of Connor's chest, Anthony stabbed the needle into the heart and shunted the adrenalin into it.

Connor barely twitched.

"What's that for? Our hearts aren't beating," said Julian.

"Muscle relaxant speeds up the dehydration process. Adrenalin thins the congealed blood in his main arteries, hopefully, making it easier for the fresh blood from the I.V. to get around his body."

"Hopefully?"

Anthony inspected Connor's rigid face, where the tight skin clung to his bones. "Connor, I'll push the blood through fast, and get another pint in." He paused, making sure Connor's gray eyes were focused on his face, and then said in a low voice, "It's going to be close. We might have caught it before the fifteen percent dehydration point, but-"

Connor's pupils contracted like the shutters of a camera lens, which was the only signal he could give to show he understood.

Julian dropped back to look out of the doorway and beckoned to Supervisor Matthew. "Go to the council buildings and hand yourself in to Captain Gerrard's custody. You have some questions to answer."

The supervisor assessed Julian's impassive features and nodded.

As Matthew disappeared, Anthony joined Julian on the threshold, and his sober expression said it all. "I'll do what I can. Intravenous infusion gives him a better chance than ingestion, but still, it's in the lap of the Gods."

Julian grinned and said quietly, "In the lap of the Gods. Now, there's an irony Connor would appreciate."

"And I haven't even broken the news that he's going to have a crater in his neck to add to all his other battle scars. Talking of which-" Anthony raised a sardonic brow. "You really climbed over the fence?"

"Hell, yes," laughed Julian.

"Way to go," said Anthony, bumping his shoulder into Julian's.

Staring down the empty corridor, Julian said, "Keep me updated. I'll use the time to grill Matthew. Let's see if we can get to the bottom of this shit storm."

Chapter 6

In the council anteroom, the three jurors sat in throne-like chairs ranged along one side of a rectangular black walnut table. The polished surface captured their still images like reflections in a millpond. Closed hearings were rare, but in this instance, with Connor's life hanging in the balance, Julian was not in the mood to play to the gallery. His jaw muscle twitched as he listened for the ninth time to Supervisor Matthew's pathetic explanation. The excuses made him look like a fool, but Matthew made no effort to shift blame as he usually did.

Julian's smile was brittle. "So, that's your version?"

Alexander leaned forward, resting his elbows on the table and tapping his lip. He could not trust himself to speak. *I never expected Matthew to take Connor out, risk locked-in syndrome.* Alexander could not imagine the depth of hatred needed to condemn an enemy to suffer a hardened granite body with conscious thought intact for eternity.

"It is my fault. I misjudged his character. I took pity on the youngling," Matthew said. "I knew Doctor Connor kicked him off the surgical intern program, but working night shifts planting crops out in the fields seemed harsh. I took him on as a porter."

"And you have no idea how he gained access to the examination suite? Could he have known the access code from before, overheard or seen it used when he was an intern?" said Alexander.

Julian shot the young juror a disapproving look. "Juror Alexander, I'm sure Supervisor Matthew can fill in the gaps for himself."

Matthew looked apologetic. "As I said, I can't be sure. All I know is that I sent him to sound the siren and summon help when the male pulled his siphoning cannula from the vein. Where he went afterwards, I have no clue."

Alexander opened his mouth, then snapped it shut again when Julian raised a hand. "We will speak again, Supervisor Matthew, you can be sure of it, but for now-" Julian looked at his jurors for agreement. "That will be all."

Alexander masked his relief as he watched Matthew leave the room. *He has not slipped up, yet.*

"Well?" Marius said.

"I don't trust him. Perhaps this porter acted alone, but honestly? He's young-" Julian shrugged.

"And he holds a grudge? At least that's how I understand it," Alexander said, helpfully.

Julian drummed his fingertips on the lacquered finish of the table, his diamond-hard nails creating a cloud of scratches in the varnish.

Marius and Alexander waited, still as stiffened corpses, without blinking, while Julian deliberated.

"Okay." Julian slammed an open hand down on the table top. "Let's have him in."

Marius rose from his seat, his black floor-length robe barely moving as he crossed to the door and opened it. "Bring in the prisoner." As he returned and settled back into his chair, four guardsmen entered escorting the young porter.

The vampire's scattered to the four corners of the room, becoming a set of purple clad statues with their eyes locked onto their charge.

The young porter still wore the green surgical scrubs that proved his guilt. He stood in front of the jurors' table and his chin dropped to a defeated angle.

"What have you to say?" barked Julian.

"I called Doctor Connor into the side ward, injected him with muscle relaxant, and wheeled him into the old storage department." The events, laid out so starkly were all the more incomprehensible.

"But why?" asked Marius.

"I am a porter. Doctor Connor ended my chances of being anything more. I thought he would recover, that it would wear off," said the youngling, the note in his voice rising. "I just wanted to get back at him, make him feel like an imbecile. That's all."

"So, in your scenario Doctor Connor wakes up and what?" Julian's harsh laugh made the porter jump. "He sees the joke? Slaps you on the back and forgives you? What did you think would happen?"

The vampire's chin dropped further. "I didn't think, not really."

"It looks like *you're* the imbecile," Julian said quietly. "Let's come back to the dosage."

"I thought it would wear off. Doctor Connor uses it in vampire amputations-"

"Doctor Connor also uses it to prepare condemned vampires for internment in the storage facility. You were an intern, even if only for a short while. You know something about the dosage of medication. Try again," said Julian, staring coldly into the vampire's face.

The porter shook his head slowly. "I made a mistake."

"You made a mistake?" Julian stood up, and the vampire had the sense to look nervous. The heavy black fabric of his principal's cloak flared as Julian whipped around the table. His face appeared three inches from his victim. "You made a mistake?"

The porter flinched.

"Doctor Connor is in a coma because you made a mistake? You better start praying he makes a full recovery. That possibility, and your confession, are all that stand between you and a crushed skull. Who else is involved?"

In demonstration, Julian closed a clawed grip over the vampire's cheekbones, digging into the hard bones at his temples until they creaked. "I don't even need to send you to the death chamber, I could do it now, right here."

The vampire's clenched fists were his only reaction as Julian glared at him.

"He *was* a failure as an intern, Julian," said Marius.

The tension in Alexander's shoulders eased a notch. He had been biting his tongue, concerned that he had already raised suspicion defending the supervisor. *If Marius says it, I am safe.*

"We have to wait to hear from Connor before we can move to sentencing," said Marius.

"Oh, I think not," said Julian, "that is the beauty of a closed hearing. I decide."

"True," said Marius quietly, "Then I will be the voice of your conscience, Julian. Stay your hand until Connor's fate is certain."

The silence in the room was profound.

Julian slowly relaxed and stepped back. His grasp left craters behind in the vampire's petrified face.

"Very well. But, if Doctor Connor does not survive, neither do you." Julian swept away, his jerking stride tugging at his cape. "You better start praying. You will stay in the council building cells until we know."

At the signal of Julian's waved hand, the four guards collected the vampire and left the room.

Running fingers through his blond hair and straightening his white cravat, Julian murmured, "If Connor cannot help Seren and Rebekah, then it is down to us. We have to decide if we are declaring war or sending out spies, but doing nothing is not an option."

"Shouldn't we wait?" Alexander said.

Julian's grin was hard. "They have a twelve hour lead on us already. I need to go to the hospital and see if Connor is making progress. If he is not, then we must decide." Julian looked at Alexander. "Are you sure Serge gave nothing away? He did not mention a hive, or other visitors?"

"He rambled about the loss of his arm, and how Doctor Connor was pulling the wool over our eyes, for the most part." Alexander frowned, giving his answers serious thought. "Nothing comes to mind. I wonder if he is not suffering early dementia, after all, his human brain is seventy years old. I'm not sure he has all his faculties. He seemed irrational at times."

"Fair enough." Julian stood up and moved to the door. "I shall return with an update on Connor."

Alexander rose to his feet and went to the window to look out over the choppy waters of the River Thames. *Ironic. Beneath that boiling turbulence are calm still waters.* The opposite of how he felt. His peaceful face showed nothing of the knots in his stomach nor of the sensation that he had swallowed a bag of sand.

Supervisor Matthew had not cracked and, with the focus still on Connor, Alexander was hanging onto his control.

Before Julian returned from the search, Alexander had grabbed a moment alone with Matthew, as foolish as that was. The supervisor's face was tight with resentment when Alexander had blasted him for taking things too far.

"I said keep Doctor Connor there for two hours. Not this." His hand flapped as words failed him.

"I'm not the only one who has gone too far." Matthew's tone was cutting. "The hybrid child has been abducted? I think your crime outstrips mine."

"The porter. How did you get him to do it?" Alexander needed to know.

"I promised him an internship. He wants back on the surgical team and, in return, he will take the blame and play the innocent fool." Matthew frowned. "And he will succeed, unless Connor wakes up." The supervisor's voice faded in contemplation. "That vampire is made of steel. He should have been beyond saving."

"It is done now," Alexander said darkly. "I shall fight your corner, but if your intern cracks, you are on your own. Keep your head down and your mouth shut." Alexander's eyes were blue ice-chips. "Juror Marius and Principal Julian must see it was only a matter of time before the high council took charge. We merely jumped ship at the right moment. Our rewards will come."

Alexander did not believe the words, even as he said them. If he had one wish, he would use it to turn back the clock. Not because he believed in Connor, but because, right now, he feared the prospect of keeping company with the one other notorious vampire inmate in Storage Facility Eight. Julian had sentenced The Butcher to two hundred years. As decreed, he remained a shrunken granite effigy with a fully functioning brain, who could do nothing other than stare at the ceiling and consider his crimes.

I don't want to end up there.

Well perhaps you should have thought of that before, said the little worm inside his head.

Chapter 7

During the hours he lay abandoned in the storage room, covered in the linen sheet, Connor's mind was bombarded with pictures. He saw four tall vampires as though they were standing before him. Each wore a studded leather vest and a sword belt. The taller vampire, with the bearing of one in command, wore a gold-colored breastplate with a crest engraved in the center. The images shimmered with the intensity of Seren's emotions, and the last thing he saw, before the world he looked in on plunged into darkness, was Rebekah's defiant face.

Rebekah and Seren are in danger.

Unable to move or refresh the stale air locked inside his chest, every passing moment became a nerve racking eternity for Connor. He needed to get a grip. Anxiety would accelerate the rate at which his thirsty tissue devoured what precious moisture remained in his muscle fibers.

Connor pushed himself deep into the meditative state of revival sleep, preserving nervous energy and slowing his rate of dehydration. He hung onto the fact that Anthony would miss him and come looking. *And if Greg and Seth survived the attack and raised the alarm, then Julian will come looking for me too.* Hope crept through his temporal lobe, and, as he became impatient for his rescue, he shut it down. *They'll find me, but I won't be worth finding, if I waste energy.*

He locked down all thought process and slept.

It was Anthony pushing his eyelids open that dragged him back to the surface, bringing with it a rush of questions. *How long have I been here? Does anyone know Rebekah and Seren are in danger? Damn it, Anthony, DO SOMETHING.*

Frustration burned through every fiber, but Connor surrendered to waiting. Trying to yell when all you had was sight and hearing was a non-starter.

Connor silently congratulated Anthony along every step in the road.

The syringe needle shunting adrenaline into his heart caused uncomfortable pressure, and he was acutely aware of the whooshing sound as the blood infusions rushed into his carotid artery, filtered through his sinus cavity, and trickled down his throat. It pooled in his stomach and lungs, and then hitched a ride along his adrenalin flushed arteries until it reached his extremities.

His muscles tingled with warmth as the blood broke down the muscle relaxant in the fibers and the slow process of dilution began. *Is it too slow?*

As Connor stared at the ceiling, Anthony's face floated into his line of sight. Connor wanted to smile, but his flesh felt like heat melded plastic fused to his bones.

He pulled Anthony's face into sharp focus and listened carefully.

"I'll push the blood through fast, and get another pint in. It's going to be close. We might have caught it before the fifteen percent dehydration point, but-"

But? I could be in big trouble? No shit.

Connor heard Julian ordering Matthew to the council buildings. *Damn it, Julian, forget the 'who' and the 'why', just get to the eco-shelter and save them.*

When Anthony was left alone in the room, he stood at Connor's bedside like a motionless ghoul. He only moved to apply pressure to Connor's sternum, checking on his progress, and to change the rate of his I.V. drip.

I must have a word with him about bedside manners when this is done. A little conversation, some idea of what's going on, would make this go much easier.

Finally, Anthony inspected the pressure points on Connor's hands, feet, sternum, and his cheekbones, and decided they were ready to travel.

Anthony called for help to move Connor's dead weight on to a stretcher and dismissed the two porters when the task was done.

He pulled leather straps over Connor's body, yanking them tight and threading the ends into buckles welded to the metal frame. Once the belts were secure, he patted Connor on the chest, and said, "Let's get you to the hospital."

The cold night air buffeted Connor's still face and plastered his clothes to his body as Anthony dragged him along the forest floor. The straps across Connor's torso, hips and thighs creaked as they fought to hold him still. His spine jarred every time the foot of the metal bed grated over a rock. The steel stretcher moved at a speed that blurred the tree trunks on either side into a tunnel of brown silk.

The ride would be smoother with Julian's help, but I imagine he's rounding up suspects. Not that they matter much right now. Anthony could not trust anyone else to help. No one must know where he was taking Connor, so towing 'the patient' through the undergrowth was what they were left with.

The hard knocks and juddering halts did not cause pain, so Connor gave himself over to his own healing process. He drifted in and out of consciousness as his body worked hard at unknotting capillaries which had collapsed and become sealed. Trusting himself in Anthony's hands, Connor let his world fade to black.

When Anthony pulled on the I.V. line, stripping it steadily from Connor's carotid artery, the dragging sensation in his neck brought with it razor-sharp awareness.

In the sudden glare of clarity, Connor stared at the polystyrene ceiling tiles and wondered which room in the surgical wing Anthony had brought him to. In trying to see, he found he could turn his head a little.

"Welcome back." Anthony's hand settled on his shoulder. "I've pushed another pint of human blood through. It's time to find out how much movement we've got. Let's start with the toes."

"We?" Connor's stiff smile resembled a ventriloquist dummy.

Anthony laughed. "Okay, a smile, even a scary one, is good."

Connor croaked, "Seren. Rebekah."

"You know?" It took Anthony only a second to catch on. "Ah, Seren showed you. Okay, well Julian will be here soon. We'll put all the pieces together. In the meantime let's get you back on your feet. Now, as I said, toes."

Five minutes later, having worked his way up his body, Connor sat on the edge of the bed circling his ankles and massaging his thighs with his hands. He took a deep breath and said quietly, "We've got a problem."

Anthony unfolded his arms, wiped the 'proud parent' look off his face and said, "Problem?"

Connor awkwardly shrugged his open shirt from his shoulders and pulled it off. Twisting his right arm slowly, he revealed a patch of gray tissue, extending from his bicep and up over his shoulder, on the same side as the intern had shoved in the dose of muscle relaxant. A tight grin pulled his lips back as he said, "We missed a bit."

Anthony's cold fingers manipulated the flesh, feeling crystals crunching under the skin. "Hell. We were too late."

Dehydrated vampire tissue interrupted the blood network. A starved limb hardened to gravel, becoming a dead weight to drag around, or to amputate.

Flexing his muscles, Connor found he could not raise his arm above the shoulder. Audible crackling filled the air when he clenched both hands into fists. The muscle and sinews bulged in his left forearm, as they should, but he had little strength in his right hand.

He muttered, "I need to get to the lab before I lose the arm."

Standing up was easy, and within three strides Connor knew he had full function in most of his body. Anthony opened the treatment room door and followed a barefoot, half-dressed Connor out into the hallway. As he lagged behind the steadily increasing pace, he felt relief that there was nothing wrong with Connor's ability to walk.

Ignoring the surprised looks of the vampires he passed in the corridors, Connor finally headed down into the basement and stopped outside his laboratory door. Twisting to delve his left hand into his right pocket, he pulled out the key and unlocked the outer door.

It went against the grain, but they bypassed the decontamination procedures. Connor punched in the code to access the inner chamber and strode into the laboratory.

Anthony stopped on the threshold and gazed at the whiteboards where strings of numbers and equations extended way beyond his area of expertise. Standing motionless, content to observe Connor in his element, Anthony folded his arms. Connor would say if he needed anything.

Connor disappeared into a walk-in refrigeration unit, re-emerged carrying a tray of glass vials filled with clear fluid, and laid the tray on a marble counter. Working one handed, he pulled open a drawer, took out a pack of sterile syringes and tore it open with his teeth. He lifted his weak right hand slowly and closed his fingers around a glass vial, cursing when it slipped from his grasp.

It rolled across the counter, and a hand appeared as if from nowhere, catching the glass vial as it fell. Laughing quietly, Anthony straightened, and then raised an eyebrow. "Want some help? What are we doing?"

Connor grimaced at his own frustration, jerked his chin at the tray of vials and placed the syringe into Anthony's hand.

"Perfluorocarbon particles in saline suspension. They can carry oxygen to crushed human tissue that blood-cells can't reach, so I'm gonna play a hunch that they'll get fluid into vampire tissue, unglue the sealed capillaries, and let blood in. It's worth a shot."

"Okay. Let's do it."

Hoisting himself up to sit on the countertop, Connor rested his extended right forearm along his thigh and said, "Start with the brachial artery, feel along under the skin and inject a dose into each vein you can find."

The sound of a needle forcing its way through splinters of glass was one Connor had never heard before, and it felt just as nauseating, as the grains of crystallized blood were pushed aside.

Connor flexed his right fist and, feeling the tendon sheaths moving a little easier, he sighed. "It's working."

Anthony's brown hair flopped over his eyes; his thick biceps strained the fabric of his shirt as he pressed home the plunger on another full syringe. Frowning as he withdrew, he muttered, "It's working? Thank the Lord for that. Have you any idea how thick skinned you are?"

Connor chuckled as he ran his fingertips over the back of his neck, tracing the line of crescent shaped scars he had sustained in a brutal bout of unarmed combat. His flesh bore other battle scars – a glistening snail trail of hardened glue wandered across one hip and another ran down the triceps of his right arm. Anthony had done a good job patching Connor up after his fight to the death in the arena against Sebastian.

"I wouldn't want you to lose your touch."

"I broke a few bones in my day, as a boxer, but none since I was turned," Anthony muttered, shaking his head.

"Let's hope this is the last time you'll need to play nursemaid." Connor's expression sobered as he thought ahead. The golden breastplate of the commander declared him to be a warrior. *I won't get Rebekah and Seren back without a fight.*

Anthony set the needle down and pushed hair out of his eyes. "I doubt it will be the last time," he said absently as he pressed his fingers firmly along the veins in Connor's gray flesh, and looked for changes. "The color's fading to white. How does it feel?"

Connor compared his grip strength. "Improving, I think we are done." He hopped down from the counter, opened the door on a glass cabinet and pulled out a pair of granite pestles. Gripping one in each hand, he ground them both slowly to dust.

Grunting, he looked up and said, "Thank you, Anthony."

Anthony's eyes were serious even though he grinned. "We make a good team. You're the brains of the outfit, and I'm the brawn."

Connor smiled in return, his attitude becoming brisk as he slapped his friend on the shoulder. Sweeping past, he threw his words back into the room and disappeared through the door. "Let's find Julian. I've got my family to bring back."

◇◇◇

Once reunited, the three vampires moved through the woodlands, zeroing in on the eco-shelter at speed. Although they shared a common purpose, each was lost in his own thoughts.

Connor forged ahead of the arrow-head formation. Dread that he had failed the woman he loved and lost his daughter snapped at his heels like an anger driven demon.

Julian and Anthony labored under their own brands of guilt.

Anthony could not believe he allowed Connor's disappearance to go undetected for so long, and Julian regretted not following the compass setting Greg told him the vampires had taken when they left, and at least tried to track them. *Better yet, why didn't I make Connor listen, and take Rebekah and Seren to safety long before this? Hindsight is a wonderful thing.*

He hung onto Connor's coattails, shooting Anthony an apologetic glance when they crunched shoulders. Anthony ricocheted off a tree trunk, grinding a crater into the bark with a jab of his elbow as he launched himself back into the chase.

Their unrelenting speed across the wet meadow kicked up spray which soaked their clothes and plastered their hair to their foreheads.

At the eco-shelter entrance, Connor gouged lumps out of the grass as he dug his heels in and stopped dead. Scraping saturated hair back, he dropped to one knee and examined scuff marks left in the packed earth just inside the reception cavern. He ran his hands over each imprint and then surged to his feet.

"Five vampires, and you said Greg saw two horses," he said starkly. Striding into the dark cavern where a range of expedition equipment hung on metal spikes driven into the walls, he paused. Raising his chin, Connor tasted the air and listened. "They're all in one place, in the kitchen cavern, I'd guess," he said. "Why the hell aren't they in the panic room?" The shadows swallowed him whole as he rushed forward into the access tunnel.

Without hesitation, Julian followed.

Anthony faltered. He hung back, deliberately dragging his hard nails over the walls until a chicken-egg sized stone fell into his palm.

What is that noise? The grating sound ceased abruptly as Julian looked back over his shoulder.

Anthony had not been inside the human settlement for years, not since Rebekah had lost consciousness and Julian had dragged him down here to diagnose her illness. As their eyes met, Julian knew they shared the same thought. Her illness, which turned out to be pregnancy and the birth of a vampire fetus called Seren, had turned all their lives upside down. Anthony was an accomplished vampire surgeon, and he had come a long way in resisting humans, but- *As long as no one bleeds, he should be okay.*

Anthony's expression was grim as he sped up and regained his place on Connor's shoulder.

Connor, Julian and Anthony crossed the threshold of the dining cavern, and five human hearts jolted inside their owner's chests. Greg and Seth were closest to the door, standing with a white knuckled grip on the clubbing weapons they held diagonally across their bodies.

There was a moment of stunned silence, although, for the vampires the silence was crammed with human heart chambers clattering, plump blood cells swishing along arteries, and adrenalin soaked aromas. Their mouths watered, and Julian darted a look at Anthony.

Anthony's jaw worked and the grinding of his teeth became an added sound to the symphony.

"Are you okay?" Julian asked quietly.

Anthony opened his mouth, and Julian caught a glimpse of the pebble lodged in the back of Anthony's throat. It blocked his airway and dampened his hunger. He stopped breathing altogether as he gave a thumbs-up sign, but hung back and leaned against the wedge-shaped rocks which formed the arched doorway.

"All the better for a quick getaway, hmm?" Julian murmured and then advanced to stand beside Connor.

Greg lowered his weapon. His eyes glinted as he said, "When do we leave?"

"Why aren't you on patrol? And why are the others not hiding?" asked Connor bluntly.

"Have you ever heard the expression 'the rooster has flown the coop'?" Greg's face flushed red and his chest heaved. "We screwed up. Out there-" He jerked his head, indicating the nearby woodlands. "We're sitting ducks. We can't outrun a vampire for Christ sakes." Greg's expression hardened. "Me and Seth could've fire-bombed the suckers, caused a diversion at least, if we'd been in here. We screwed up," he said tightly.

"And you couldn't have called for help. Not from in here," said Julian.

Greg snorted. "The beacon? As I said, slamming the stable door after the horse has bolted. Big deal."

Connor nodded, walked over to a wooden table and sat down on the solid surface. Ignoring the fibers creaking beneath his dense vampire tissue, he planted his feet on the bench seat. Resting his elbows on his knees and gripping his hands together as though praying, he said, "Tell me exactly what happened, and then, Greg, we will go out there and bring them back."

Greg's utility belt clattered on the wooden table-top as he took a seat opposite Connor. "When the farm siren sounded, Seth and I went out on patrol." Greg's lip curled as he spoke. "Oscar, Evie, Leizle, Rebekah, and Seren were locked inside the panic room. I rubbed dirt into the gap around the wooden shutter. I guess a vampire could tell, but it looked just like the rest of the panels on the wall to me."

"Julian, get the others in here, I want to hear what they have to say," said Connor, without taking his eyes off the Marine. "Go on, Greg."

"There's not much to tell." Shooting a glance at Seth, he said, "The siren stopped. We were up near the hilltop and we heard horses. By the time we got to the meadow they were already moving out through the trees, heading southwest."

Julian, still listening to Greg, entered the kitchen, but then, his smooth features creased into a smile when he saw Leizle. "Hey, Red," he said casually. He took a deep breath, infusing his lungs with the delightful cocktail of aromas which were all Leizle. At the sudden ache in his chest, he crossed swiftly to her side.

He threaded his fingers into Leizle's glossy chestnut hair, tilting her chin and savoring her warm sigh on his cool skin, his thirst for her blood thundering through him. Molding his hand to her nape and settling his thumb on the pulse throbbing beneath her delicate jaw line, he drowned in the pool of desire that settled in his gut. The sharp blade of a knife cut him open as he kissed her, tasting the heat of her mouth as his lips brushed over hers. Suffering gladly, he held back the urge to bite.

"You won't be wanting me and Evie getting in your way, Mr. Julian," Oscar muttered. With an indulgent smile, he walked out of the kitchen pulling Evie along at his side.

Coming back down to earth, Julian moved back to look into Leizle's flushed face. "Red. I am so glad you didn't let me lie to myself."

She smiled gently. "You never had a chance, womanly wiles and all that."

Julian knew better. When they first met, Leizle had been eighteen and had never been kissed. She lived in a world where most of the men in the eco-community were old enough to be her father. Julian had tried to resist, but every time he caught her scent, and saw a new expression cross her face, he found it harder to stay away. He had, at last, got past the guilt of stealing her heart. Without her, Julian felt cold. Death he could cope with, but an existence without the heat of her body making his feel alive, not anymore.

He absorbed the teasing bravado that did not quite hide the worry lurking behind her gaze, and said, "We will find them." His hand drifted down her arm until he carefully entwined his fingers with hers. "Let's go and see Connor."

"You found him? Thank God," she muttered, tugging on Julian's immovable arm like a child trying to move a statue.

Her annoyed frown made him laugh as he let her drag him from the kitchen.

"Did you hear the vampires searching?" Connor asked.

Oscar shook his head. "Seren heard them first. We stayed quiet. We'd taken beta blockers, used suppressant spray. We were quiet."

"They knew then? Where you were?"

"It seemed that way. I'm sorry, Lad. I should have faced them, made Rebekah and Seren hide."

Connor shook his head. "You didn't stand a chance."

They wouldn't have stood a chance against *one* vampire, thought Julian, keeping a neutral expression on his face.

"And, there were five of them," Connor added.

"Perfect number for a covert operation," Seth muttered.

"Precisely," Connor agreed. "They weren't attacking, they were extracting."

Julian voiced what Oscar opened his mouth to say. "How do you know there were five?"

"Seren. She showed me." Connor suddenly looked up at the ceiling, frustration piling onto his shoulders. "I should have been here. Let the human on the farm die. I should have come home like I planned."

He slammed his hand down on the table and a chunk of wood hit the floor. He closed his fingers over the splintered edge and ground it to sawdust, making the hole bigger. "The leader had a brass or gold breastplate with a crest. The vampires wore battle dress, studded vests. I'd know them if I saw them again."

"Did you see anything else?" asked Julian calmly.

Connor sneered. "Nothing useful. Not the direction in which they went. I think they blindfolded Seren. A lucky break for them. But every now and again I get a flash of a small room with wooden walls, overlapping planks." His jaw muscle jerked as he brushed the sawdust from his fingers onto his thigh. "Rebekah, handcuffed to a pipe, and the beds in the room are narrow bunks."

"Handcuffed-" choked Oscar, his despair written clearly on his face.

"Don't blame yourself," Connor said. "Think about it. They knew who they came for, and you, Evie and Leizle were not part of the plan. If you had stood in the way, they would have killed you."

"You said flashes. Seren sends you only flashes," Julian cut in.

"Our connection has never been tested. I think the further away she is, the weaker the images."

"You know, traveling southwest from here, unless they doubled back up north, takes them to the West Country. Why would they go into a dead end, unless they had a ship?" Julian mused.

"No one has vessels anymore, except the super tanker vampires."

At Greg's puzzled look Connor added, "Super tanker nomads. They are vampires who have no hive. Pirates, kind of. They barter for blood. Use container ships to ferry food crops across the ocean. In return for their services, they get paid in rations from the blood dispensary." Connor shook his head. "This abduction is not their style, Julian."

"No. But, it's the style of a sentinel, and they can commission a ship. A sentinel who has heard of the hybrid birth and thinks he can gain from it."

Greg huffed impatiently. "And what the hell is a sentinel?"

Julian smiled, knowing that, for a tactician like Greg, getting to grips with vampire hierarchy was like fighting ghosts, blindfolded. "Sentinels are the next step up from principals. They are overseers and handle disputes between hives." Turning back to Connor, Julian said, "This gold breastplate, did she see the crest clearly, or his face?"

Connor frowned as he sifted through the images Seren had shown to him. "Blonde hair, blonder than yours, Julian. The crest had a lion, or a dragon, on a shield, and a medieval knight's helmet in profile on the top edge."

Connor looked at Julian and waited.

"Sounds Danish, Scandinavian. Sentinel Lars," said Julian.

"How would this Sentinel Lars have the Intel to pull this off?" asked Greg.

Connor said flatly, "We have a traitor in our hive. Supervisor Matthew?"

"He may be part of it, sure, but no, he hasn't the guts to put this together."

"Have you any idea who?"

"No, not yet."

"Shit," breathed Connor.

Three seconds passed before Connor launched himself from his perch. Planting his feet firmly, he rose to his full height and said, "That will wait. Let's work on the theory that we are going to… Denmark?" He looked to Julian for confirmation. "Okay, Denmark, to find this Lars character."

Greg lowered a boot and twisted to face Connor. "You can count me in."

Seth drew Connor's gaze with a curt nod that said, 'me too'.

"Anthony will have to stay behind and cover for me at the hospital. It looks like we have ourselves a squad of four. Julian, go and smooth the path in London, and keep it need to know only. I'll get things ready here."

◇◇◇

Both council jurors looked around at the sound of the door opening and watched Julian enter the antechamber.

Alexander turned away from where he was studying the scenery outside the window. Pushing away from the wall, he became absorbed in dusting down his jacket, removing minuscule flakes of paint from the dark fabric. A human eye would not have seen them, but to Alexander, the white flakes were a like a snow fall of dandruff.

Marius still sat in his juror's chair at the polished conference table, and, were it not for the red tint to his lips and the less-white sheen to his face, Julian would have suspected Marius had not moved at all during the hours he had been gone.

Tapping a fingernail on the table top where two vials of human blood lay side by side, Marius said, "I picked yours up while I was there."

He has been to the blood dispensary, then. "Did Charles ask about Doctor Connor?"

"Of course. He seemed like a rudderless ship, not knowing if he should wait before allocating the next blood delivery from the farm."

101

Julian's eyebrow lifted. "You reassured him that starving the vampires in the hive was not a good way to go, I hope?"

Marius nodded sagely. "He is happy to know Anthony will take charge during Connor's... incapacitation."

"Good." Julian smiled. "Emergency averted, then."

Alexander stopped fidgeting with his jacket cuffs, barely waiting for the two to finish speaking before smoothly filling the gap. "What *is* the news on Doctor Connor?"

Julian crossed to the jurors' table, absently running his fingers over the glass tubes. "Connor's awake."

"Well, that is good news," said Marius. "Does he remember anything? Is the porter in the frame?"

Julian's reply was short. "These are all questions that will have to wait. Rebekah and Seren have been abducted."

"What?" said Alexander, his eyes widening in disbelief.

Marius' stare shone like black beads. "Abducted? And what is the plan?"

Julian's grin was brittle. *Marius always cuts through the crap.* "*If* the plan is to succeed, the details must not leave this room. We have a traitor in the hive."

"That makes sense," said Marius. Rising to his feet, he stopped behind the tall back of his chair, a hand closing over a decoratively carved scroll. "Supervisor Matthew will break if I push him."

"Not yet, Marius. We have to rescue Seren and Rebekah first."

"Which brings us back to my question, what is the plan?" Marius' brow rose as he idly carved a new groove into the hard wood scroll with his fingernail.

"As far as Matthew, and the rest of the hive are concerned, Doctor Connor is still in a coma. That will cover his absence for a few weeks, a least. Anthony will step up while he is gone."

"And your absence from the council?" asked Marius. "I assume you are going, too?"

Julian chuckled. "There's no fooling you." He looked at the ceiling, his eyes searching the ornate plaster cornices for inspiration. Thinking aloud, he murmured, "The hive will have to know the hybrid child has been taken. The rumors will already be out there. They already know that Councilor Serge is a sworn enemy of Doctor Connor." Julian scanned Marius and Alexander's faces. "It would not be unusual for me to travel to Scotland to interrogate Serge."

"I wonder if he *does* know something," Marius said thoughtfully. "After all, as you say, he hates Connor. What better way of getting back at him?"

Alexander frowned. "I think Councilor Serge would have gloated if he thought Doctor Connor was about to suffer. He would not have been able to help himself."

"You may well be right." Julian shifted his shoulders and drew up to his full height. "Report in council that Connor is still in a coma, and I have gone to Scotland to gather information on the abduction."

"And in truth, do you have any idea where to start?" Alexander asked. "Who is holding them?"

Marius' glanced sharply at Alexander's intent features. "I imagine Principal Julian would rather keep those thoughts to himself." Studying Julian, he said, "I'm sure you know what you are doing but, perhaps, if sentinels arrive here to make arrests, the less we know the better?"

"Thank you, Marius," Julian said. "I had better get going." He almost made it to the door, but then turned suddenly. "Marius, have the porter released from the cells. Let Matthew think we bought his pathetic line about making an innocent mistake and only wanting to embarrass Connor."

Marius nodded. "Perhaps Supervisor Matthew will relax his guard, and slip up?"

"Precisely," said Julian, and then, he vanished from the room.

He had one more stop to make before the rendezvous with Connor, Greg, and Seth. Instead of heading left towards the front doors, he turned right and walked the hundred yards of hallway which took him to the guard room.

Inside the sparsely furnished space, uniforms hung on open rails. A wall of carved panels framed an innocuous looking door, behind which, was another smaller room, with one wall made of steel. High velocity guns and tungsten bullets were kept under guard in the hardened-steel walk-in safe. Two key operators were needed to open the combination lock on the door. Julian held one key, and Captain Gerrard the other.

And that is how it will stay. Julian absently traced the outline of the key, concealed in an inner pocket that only he knew about, and pressed his lips together. *Perhaps Marius? But no.* His instincts told him to trust no one.

Julian trusted Captain Gerrard, with good reason. He had stood by when Connor had executed a guardsman, discharging a bullet into his ear and listening to it bounce around inside the indestructible vampire skull until he had no brain to speak of.

Captain Gerrard had instructed his men to stand down, and stood shoulder to shoulder with Julian in defending Connor's actions. *I can trust him, but not Matthew. And who else?*

Julian walked in to the captain's office. As he expected, Gerrard was already standing to attention, having heard the outer door.

He was not surprised to see Julian. "Is Doctor Connor okay?" he asked briskly.

Weighing up his options, Julian stared at the captain's sober expression. Detecting genuine concern in the composed features, he opted for honesty. "He is well on the road to recovery, but it was no accident."

Gerrard's lips tightened. "I heard he was injected with something. Seems like a cowardly thing to do."

"We have a porter who has confessed, but Doctor Connor and I agree he was a pawn in a larger game. He will be set free as bait, and that's where you come in."

"Anything I can do to help, consider it done."

"Keep your eyes open and your ear to the ground. I have to leave the hive for a while. I need someone I can trust to try and get to the bottom of all this. You must keep this between you and me. No-one else needs to know." Julian paced the floor in front of the captain's desk.

"Any particular targets?" said Gerrard.

"Supervisor Matthew is my hunch," Julian said. "But even *he* could not have worked alone. So, take a hard look at anyone he comes into contact with."

"Certainly, Principal. And who do I report to?" Gerrard's voice was brisk.

A cloud lifted as Julian knew he'd chosen wisely. "Just me, Doctor Connor, or Surgical Assistant Anthony. No one else."

"Very well."

"Thank you, Gerrard. I know Connor will be happy to know you are on the case."

"Give the doctor my best. He's a tough nut to crack. I wouldn't want to be in the slippery bastard's shoes when we find out who did this."

Julian raised a hand in farewell and, satisfied he had done all he could, set off to keep the rendezvous with Connor in the woods outside the eco-shelter.

Chapter 8

At the same time Julian disappeared from the dining cavern, to focus on his task of facing the jurors, Greg's attention centered on Connor. "Get things ready here? What are you thinking?"

Studying Oscar, Evie, and Leizle, Connor took in the three grades of concern written on their faces. Oscar's jovial features wore a look of defiance he had never seen before. Evie's eyes glistened with unshed tears, and Leizle's youthful features wore an expression of determined optimism.

He said quietly, "They can't stay here, Greg. Not while we are gone."

Seren's birth had thrown the eco-shelter into the limelight. Uncle Harry's skills as a bio-chemist, and the modified drugs he had synthesized to suppress the human heart rate and reduce pheromone levels were useless now.

"The exclusion zone is unenforceable with Julian and I out of the picture."

Oscar tuned in to the conversation. "You're right, lad. We'd be safe with Seth's people, though."

Seth pushed away from his usual leaning spot against the cavern wall, thumping Greg on the shoulder as he stopped beside him. "You're beginning to wonder what you'd all do without us 'tree dwellers', huh?"

"Yeah," Greg drawled, "bumping into you out in the field was the best thing I could've done. I remember your sparkling wit from the Marine Corps. What would I do without it?"

The two eco-groups were separated by twenty-five miles and rough terrain, unaware of each other's existence, until Greg went out on a long-range foraging mission and a chance meeting reunited him with Seth. Now, like cogs in the wheels of a survival machine, the groups rotated away and seemed destined to come back together again.

"To be honest, you are more like one group, now." Before the Marines started a pissing contest, Connor said, "Harry, Thomas and

Seth's men keep the arsenal stocked and safely stored, and you guys are the front line. Let's leave it at that."

Both Greg and Seth grunted in a 'let it go' fashion.

"Seth?" Connor studied the wiry marine's content features and smiled. "It will be good to see Adam. How long has it been?"

Mention of his son made Seth's grin wider. "It will, yes."

"Are the shelters still sound? I haven't visited in a while." Connor frowned.

"The ones you renovated are good."

Seth's community chose to live in Anderson-type shelters, half submerged into the woodland floor. The tree dweller label came from the solid platforms they had erected high up in the thick forked branches of ancient oak trees.

"I gotta say, if you and Julian ever want to set up as Robin Hood and Little John, we'd take you in," said Seth. "I know we were just lucky to avoid the round-up to the farm, but hell, we have the edge now."

The tree dwellers remained undiscovered, and the longer it stayed that way the better. Their back-to-nature approach to survival, while more brutal, had proven to be less risky. Without knowing it, they had avoided setting up camp in the backyard of any vampire hives.

Uncle Harry and many of the eco-shelter humans had chosen to stay and make the Anderson shelters home when Connor was forced to defend Rebekah and his unborn child.

An opportunity to see old friends caused a ripple of excitement in the cavern.

Oscar took a deep breath, and Connor knew what was coming.

"No, Oscar, the best thing you can do for Rebekah and Seren is to stay safe until they return. So, while we are away, you will join Adam, and you'll do as you are told, no arguments."

Seth hoisted his kitbag up onto his shoulder. "If we set off now, we can intercept Adam on the recon trail through the big oaks clearing. We have ten miles to cover, but-" He looked at Connor. "If you go on ahead and tell Adam we are coming, he will wait. He can take Evie, Leizle, and Oscar back with him to the wood-dwelling. Julian can ride shotgun and give us the heads up if vampires are on the move."

Connor's lips twitched as he caught the glint of amusement in Anthony's eye. *Seth may be a man of few words, but there's no arguing with his logic.*

"Makes sense," said Greg.

"Looks like we've got our orders," said Connor. "I'll head out, check the woods are clear, and wait for Julian. Greg, Seth, get everyone kitted out and ready to move. Wait in the reception cavern as soon as you are done here."

Anthony pushed away from the wall and from where his shoulder had compressed the stones a shower of gravel hit the floor tiles. His huge bulk hunched and he looked sheepish – with the pebble still lodged in his gullet, he could not speak.

"Anthony, go to the blood dispensary and talk Charles into allocating a generous amount of human blood vials to the patient."

Oscar frowned. "What patient?"

Anthony choked on a laugh, thumping his chest hard, as he straightened his coat.

Smiling, Connor said, "Me. I'm in a coma, in case you haven't heard."

Anthony coughed the stone up into his palm, his brown eyes alert as he quipped, "Lord knows why, but Charles will do anything for you. I'm sure he'll be very generous. I'll be back with supplies before you leave."

"Thank you, Anthony. Let's get moving."

As both vampires swept to the doorway, Connor threw over his shoulder, "Get kitted-up as quick as you can, and we'll see you up top."

The group immediately dispersed, each scurrying away to their own small caverns to change into traveling clothes.

In less than twenty minutes, the humans were assembled quietly in the reception cavern, standing well back from the pool of moonlight which spilled in. Greg and Seth dropped their sixty pound backpacks to the ground, and inspected the trail bikes parked up in an excavated alcove.

"We could start out on these, if Connor has checked out the woods," said Greg.

Seth stopped chewing on a cigarette-sized splinter of wood. "We could. They make us sitting ducks, though."

"Leizle will go with Julian, no bike required there. If Evie lets Connor carry her, then us three men can abandon the motorcycles when we get bogged down in the undergrowth."

A dust storm of grit whisked around their feet. The alcove plunged into darkness as Connor, from mere inches away, said, "If you do that, I'll have to bury the bikes to cover your tracks and they'll not be fit to ride again."

Both men jumped, and the jolt of adrenalin rushing through Greg and Seth made Connor's mouth water.

Seth chuckled as Greg spat, "Fuck, Connor, give me a heart attack, why don't you?"

Despite his mountain of hard muscle, Greg recoiled when Connor's hand flashed in front of his face and a cold finger pressed into his neck.

Baring his teeth in fake ferocity, Connor grinned. "Oh, I think you'll live. Got a good strong pulse there, for now."

"Funny," said Greg, lashing out at Connor's hand, but finding it had already gone.

Still smirking, Connor moved back out of reach. "Well, the woods are clear. Ride the bikes if you want to. If you guys are packed up for the journey, I'll send Oscar over."

Seth nodded. "Where's Julian?"

Connor said, "He and Leizle have already set off. I think he wants time alone with her. He doesn't know when he'll see her again."

It was a sobering thought, and Seth and Greg exchanged silent looks.

Connor's gaze dimmed to ash-gray and cold determination etched hard lines into his face. "The sooner we deliver Evie and Oscar, the sooner we get to track down that bastard Lars. Load up."

Diving out of sight for a moment, Connor returned with two packages. "Have you got room for these in your kitbag?" He held out the transparent zip-lock bags; the ruby glow of blood glimmered inside glass vials. "They're shatterproof – plastic-coated glass – so you don't have to be too gentle."

As the men repacked their kitbags, Oscar checked the gas tanks, and chose the three bikes with the most fuel. Greg and Seth shouldered their packs and mounted up. Within seconds, each of the three men kick-started his engine. Winding open the throttle and dropping the clutch, in quick succession, they darted out into the meadow cloaked by the dark gray of dusk.

Connor listened to the sound of the bike engines fading, the change in note telling him when they entered the woods. He felt confident they would make steady progress. All three men were well practiced in dodging tree trunks, even when viewed through night-vision goggles. *They'll be fine.*

Connor turned and looked around for Evie.

He could see her face clearly even though she hung back in the shadowed entrance of the access tunnel. Her rushed breathing grated over his eardrums. The synapses in her brain firing in a lightning storm of panic were easy for Connor to detect. He took a step closer, faltering at the cloud of adrenalin-infused human perspiration. *Okay, maybe getting up close and personal with a vampire is something to freak out about.* Of course, being older, unlike Rebekah, Evie remembered the days when vampires did not exist. *She never knew they did, at least.*

Spreading his hands, as though Evie was a thoroughbred about to bolt, he said, "Julian and Leizle will be traveling fast. We need to get going." He summoned his best 'reassuring doctor' expression. With a raised eyebrow, he drifted to within striking distance and, in a smooth seamless action, he swept her up into his arms, not allowing the embarrassment stinging her cheeks to deflect him.

Standing still for a moment, he said gently, "It's okay, Evie."

Connor could feel her heart racing despite the beta-blockers she had taken. Ignoring the sweet fumes of blood assaulting his senses, he set off at an easy run, holding Evie steady. The shuddering of her body vibrated through his. Evie's head bowed beneath his chin as she focused on the fingers she had clasped in her lap, and the thirst for the rushing tide of red and white cells pumping beneath her skin clawed its way into Connor's chest.

Even keeping his embrace gentle, Connor felt bone fibers creaking and the cartilage in her joints groaning as he moved. *Early osteoporosis.* Connor calculated that Evie was in her late sixties and, respecting that, he capped his speed. Julian would make the trip in half the time, but it wasn't a competition.

The whining sound of the trail bike engines echoed through the woods, the note stuttering with each gear change as they were pushed to their limits. Connor quickly caught up with the three hunched forms of bikes and riders, and he slowed to match their pace. Two miles further in to the woods, the engine notes abruptly rose to screaming banshee levels. The bike wheels spun, splattering mud and tearing up the sodden ground. *End of the road.*

After setting Evie down at a safe distance, out of range of the barrage of debris the bikes were pelting into the undergrowth, Connor reached up and tore a sturdy limb from a tree, essentially cleaving it in half. Dropping the thick log onto the ground and bedding it in with a firm thump of his boot, he waved a hand to indicate her newly formed perch. "Sit there a moment. The men need my help."

Waiting until she was settled, Connor reeled back to where the bikes remained bogged down in the mud. "You get going, guys, the clock's ticking."

Shouldering his pack, Seth took a compass bearing.

Connor pulled a trowel from a pouch in Greg's backpack and said, "I'll deal with these. Go now."

Seth, Greg and Oscar set off through the trees at a brisk run.

Using the trowel, Connor easily excavated a deep hole in the packed dirt and mulch. Gripping the skeletal frames of two bikes – one in each hand – he lifted them from their mud-filled trenches. Tires skimmed the undergrowth as he swung each bike forward and let their sliding weight carry them to the bottom of the pit. He pushed the final bike down into it and metal creaked when he used his foot to bend a handlebar which refused to lie flat. Moisture hissed as the hot exhaust pipes sunk into the water pooling in the bottom of the crater. Connor covered them over, throwing mulch and leaves, and anything else his hands brushed across, over the burial site. He surveyed the results and, with a sharp nod, turned away.

Taking a quick detour to a nearby brook, he used gravel from the stream bed to scrub his hands clean, and then he returned to Evie.

Her half smile reassured him.

"You're getting used to traveling by vampire, hmm? It's not so bad," said Connor. Indulgent amusement lit his eyes as he scooped her up. "It will just be a few more minutes, and then we can rest a while, Evie."

True to his word, ten minutes later the trees thinned, and then parted, revealing an enclosed area of rough heathland. An owl's call echoed through the woods in answer to Connor's own, and he grunted with satisfaction.

Adam walked into the 'big oak tree' clearing. The impressive girth of the tree trunks could easily shield four men, and the overgrown meadow they surrounded was once a Druid ceremonial site. A moss-covered stone altar marked the center of an oval space, and the ring of deep holes in the ground surrounding it marked the placement of standing stones which had long since crumbled or been felled and stolen.

"Hello, Adam," said Connor, as he set Evie on her feet.

The serious youth, ever the gentleman, untied his leather cape and, folding it, he set it on the ground for Evie to sit on. "Hello, Doctor Connor." He swallowed nervously.

Connor studied Adam's matured features. *It must be two years now since I saved him.* An adder snake had bitten the youth. Connor had terrified the members of Seth's away team when he swooped in and bit into the stricken boy's leg. The team of four men froze, but, instead of the blood-sucking horror and carnage they feared, Connor sucked out enough blood to extract the venom, and no more. Although, he had enjoyed the snack.

Connor inhaled, filling his nose with Adam's familiar scent. *It took all my strength to stop.* The two did not meet often, and welcoming vampires as friends still unsettled the tree-dwellers. *Perhaps, 'allies' is closer to the truth* – friendship was a bridge to cross further down the road, or so Connor hoped.

Adam poked at the ground with his wooden staff, keeping it between him and his vampire companion. The muscular young man wielded the weapon with skill.

It was harmless to Connor. *But, it makes him feel more comfortable.* "Your father and Greg will be here soon. They are hiking through the woods with Oscar."

The solemn young man nodded.

"Adam, can you stay with Evie while I go on ahead and talk to Rebekah's Uncle Harry?" He wanted to break the news of the abduction in person. "Julian should be along soon." Connor frowned for a moment. *He should have arrived first. Maybe he and Leizle are saying goodbye.* "You remember Julian?"

"Yes, I remember him." Adam rubbed a hand over his cropped brown hair. "Blond hair, tall." He grinned. "Vampire. Hard to miss."

Connor chuckled. "Well, if you need proof of identity, he wears a gold ring with his principal seal on it. Right hand, middle finger. And he'll have a red-haired girl with him."

"Leizle," said Adam.

"That's right. Good." Connor smiled. "Tell Julian I'll be back soon."

A short flight through the woods later, Connor found Harry, as expected, inside a large purpose-built Anderson shelter, attending to his makeshift still. Connor scanned the slate counter tops where Harry had lined up Calor Gas adapted Bunsen burners, and a well-stocked supply of glass beakers, test tubes, and jars containing liquids and pills.

"Harry," Connor said.

The old man leapt out of his skin, the glass beaker in his hand rattling as he lowered it sharply onto the bench.

As always, unable to control his irrational fear that meeting Connor's gray gaze might turn him to stone, Harry focused on a spot in the center of Connor's chest and said, "Doctor Connor. Are Rebekah and the baby okay?"

"The *baby* is two years old." Connor shook his head. Harry would never get a handle on his niece loving a vampire. *Perhaps, if he hadn't pushed her into marriage with a bastard who almost raped her, I could feel sorry for him.*

"Of course," said Harry quietly. "Two years."

The rest, news of the adolescent Seren who grew at an alarming rate, Connor decided could wait until Harry found the guts to visit. "They aren't doing so well."

Harry met Connor's eye for the very first time since they had met. His mouth formed shapes, but the words refused to come.

Connor's rigid expression softened as he said, "I'm sorry, Harry, they have been taken. Kidnapped. Julian and I are setting off to find them."

"No." Harry reached out, grabbed the edge of the counter, and sank down on to a stool. His skin turned gray as he took a deep rattling breath. With tear-glazed eyes, he stared up at Connor.

The battery-powered bulkhead light above Connor's bowed head scattered sapphires through his hair. Shadows pooled in the hollows of his cheeks. With chips of ice glittering in his blackened eye sockets, he embodied a fierce avenger. His voice was hard as he said, "We will find them. And the vampire who took them will die."

"Just you and Principal Julian are going after them? What about the other one. The boxer?"

"Anthony? No," said Connor, "he'll stay behind. Greg and Seth are coming with us. But if it gets too dangerous, they'll set up camp and wait it out." *That part they don't know yet, but I won't have their deaths on my hands. That is non-negotiable.*

A sudden sense of purpose glinting in his eyes, Harry rose from his stool and opened a drawer. Running his finger over batch labels, he extracted two jars of pills, and two small plastic bottles of liquid, dispensed by trigger pumps. "Here," he said, holding them out for Connor to take. "The latest compound of beta-blockers, works faster than the ones we had before, although, Greg and Seth will feel weak if they stay on them too long. And pheromone suppressant pumps. It neutralizes odor. They spray it onto their hands and rub it onto exposed skin. It's quick and easy to use."

Connor raised an eyebrow. He had never heard Harry talk so much. "Thanks, Harry. I better get back, I just wanted to tell you in person." As, carrying the jars and bottles, he ducked his head to leave the shelter, Harry called out, "Connor."

With one foot over the threshold, Connor turned his head and smiled stiffly. "Just Connor?" he said, "Not 'doctor'? This is a night of firsts."

Harry took a deep breath. "You bring them back. Do whatever it takes and bring them back. Promise me."

"I will, Harry, you can count on it."

Chapter 9

The wind howled and the hull of the ship shuddered.

Rebekah peered out through the salt-streaked glass of a small porthole in the cabin, out over the ragged surface of boiling water. She hoped it would keep the sea sickness at bay. *Sea sickness.* At least, she guessed that was why her stomach was churning. The human world had ended when she was six years old, so, on the list of all the things she had never experienced, sailing on the sea was one.

For her, growing-up hinged upon survival skills and staying under the vampire radar. If you asked her to dig a fox hole and survive a night in the field, or how to sharpen a knife on a whetstone and butcher a pig, no problem. Ask her what music she liked or her favorite film, and, apart from nursery rhymes and cartoons, she had no clue.

"I don't much like boats," Rebekah decided.

Seren was standing beside her. "But, the sea is beautiful." Her tone swelled with awe.

Rebekah smiled as the sun's rays draped a gauze of glitter over the teal-blue, ever-moving surface. "I wonder how they can still row the ship in the sunshine?" Rebekah asked curiously as the steady creaking of wood, groaning of straining ropes, and splashing of oars continued on at an unrelenting metronomic pace.

"They are probably wearing tanned leather from head to boots, and helmets to shield their faces," said Seren. "Papa says he can go out in sunshine in his greatcoat and leather gloves, if he's careful. He says, vampire skin gets soft if covered too often, and then, in a fight, another vampire can slice you open like a kipper."

"Seren!" Rebekah did not like to hear such a graphic phrase from her daughter's lips.

Seren smiled. "Papa says survival is not a bed of roses. He says sometimes it comes down to the small things, so he doesn't cover up unless he has too." Seren looked thoughtful as she scanned the wooden walls. Crossing to the doorframe and digging her hard-clawed finger in between the fibers of wood, she uncovered the head of a nail and pulled it out. "If they are soft, then maybe we can hurt them?"

Rebekah turned, unsettled by Seren's youthful intensity as the girl inspected the four-inch spike of her improvised weapon.

Disguising her fear, Rebekah said, "Just you against them? Your strength will be no match, and they have numbers on their side." *The commander, alone, could crush you with one hand.*

Seren grasped the nail, and, with a stabbing motion, she buried half its length into the wall. Using the heel of her hand, she thumped it home. "I'm stronger than they realize, I think. That's where our advantage lies. They believe I'm young, but Papa says my human bone marrow gives me greater strength than most. He taught me where to hit a vampire and cause the most damage."

"I'm sure your papa also told you that an ounce of planning is worth a pound of muscle." At her daughter's mutinous expression, Rebekah added, "I'm not saying we'll go down without a fight. I'm just saying we must choose our moment."

"We will watch and wait, Mama," said Seren, but she did not meet her mother's eye.

Rebekah stepped back from the porthole and walked over to Seren, the noise of the handcuff scraping along the corroded metal of the warm pipe setting her teeth on edge.

The ship pitched, and Rebekah staggered, losing her balance. Her breath hissing between clenched teeth when Seren's hand darted out to steady her, bruising her arm.

"Sorry, Mama."

Rebekah waved it away, her concerns were for her daughter. "Please, Seren. Just give Papa a chance to save us. Our biggest weapon is not your strength." Rebekah laid her palm on Seren's cool white cheek, the contrast making her hand look wash-day red raw. "Our biggest weapon is that you can show Papa where we are, see where he is, and help him find us."

Seren stared hard at Rebekah with understanding beyond her years, and she frowned. "Mama, *I* might be strong, but you are not," she said, taking Rebekah's hand and pushing up her sleeve. She studied the faint imprint of her palm and fingers, where crushed capillaries bled under Rebekah's skin. "Papa would want me to keep you safe until he gets here."

"It's nothing, sweetheart." Laying a comforting arm around her daughter's shoulders, Rebekah noticed Seren's height was getting closer to her own five feet and six inches. Lightening the mood, she said, "We'll keep this Viking vampire on his toes, you and I. We'll run circles around him. He has no idea how sorry he will be that he picked a fight with your papa."

As though the words summoned the Viking, the door whipped open, and Lars walked into the room. "Ah, such a touching scene, no?"

Rebekah dropped her arm away from around Seren, wriggling her fingers to drop her sleeve back into place. She hoped he would not smell the bruising. "What do you want?" she said flatly.

Lars laughed. "I come in peace."

"You're taking us home, then?"

Lars' eyes glittered in the gloom and his smile stiffened.

"I thought not," said Rebekah sweetly.

Seren slumped, shrinking an inch or two in height. A sullen cast darkened her features as she scuffed the rubber sole of her shoe across the wooden planks with an irritating squeak.

Way to go Seren. She had never looked more childlike and defenseless.

"Come," Lars said, "I am inviting you to dinner."

Rebekah thought about refusing, but she was hungry. Letting herself starve would not help their cause. Instead, she grinned, lifted her arm, and clanged the handcuff against the pipe. "I'm sorry, I'm a little tied up right now."

"Ah, min skat, good to see you still have spirit," said Lars.

Inhaling with irritation, she almost choked when he appeared in front of her. She smothered the recoil when his finger lifted her chin, but the rapt expression on his face as he inhaled told her he knew she was scared.

The handcuff tightened around her wrist briefly before it hit the floor with a dull clang. "Problem solved, nej?" Lars said quietly, stepping back and brushing the metal filings from his fingertips.

Rebekah blindly felt for Seren's hand, and, presented with Lars' broad back, they followed him out of the cabin.

Lars' burgundy cape flared behind him, each powerful stride driving him further away. Rebekah glanced at Seren's focused profile. Her chin jutted as she studied every move their captor made before he accelerated out of sight.

"Be careful, Seren. A little reluctant cooperation will work better for us, trust me. It will keep him off balance until Papa gets here."

Seren's rock-steady gait gave Rebekah something to hang onto as they walked along the deserted gangway of the rolling ship.

Around the next corner, a pool of light spilled out into the gloomy corridor through the open doorway of a cabin up ahead. All the other doors remained closed. Having come this far, they had no choice but to carry on walking. Inside the bare cabin, they caught sight of cream-colored walls and a large table laid for fine dining – the tablecloth was so white it appeared to glow, and the silverware and crystal winked in the lamplight.

Standing eerily still beside it, Lars waited.

Rebekah stepped over the high threshold first and surveyed the dining room. She ignored Lars' outstretched hand, as she said, "I suppose I should be grateful I'm not the main course."

"Enough," Lars said, impatience printed on his face. "Sit down, please."

The table setting was for four diners. Rebekah chose the seat that allowed her to gaze out over the horizon, where the sinking sun lay bleeding as the dark sky crushed it slowly into the gravel-gray water.

Seren sat beside her.

After freeing his heavy cape from the gold buckle fastening on each shoulder of his burnished breastplate, Lars took his place opposite Rebekah.

Hating the idea that Lars would know she was rattled, Rebekah glanced pointedly at the fourth chair. "Is someone joining us?"

"After you have eaten. He has no patience for the pretense of manners."

Foreboding trickled through Rebekah. *He? Why does that sound sinister?* But, asking more questions tasted of defeat, so she resigned herself to waiting. She glanced up sharply and jumped when a blond-haired vampire entered the room, but relaxed when she saw he carried a tray bearing silver-domed platters. Lars' half smile of amusement at her skittishness irritated her.

The newcomer wore a leather vest with gold studs which marked him as a warrior, not a servant, and judging by the grim look on his face, he resented the role.

"Serve, Erik, please," Lars prompted.

Erik set the plates down in front of Rebekah and Seren, lifting the domed covers to reveal delicately seasoned cod fillets and vegetables. He placed a third plate in the empty setting space, and a glass of thick red liquid in front of Lars.

"Leave the plate covered, Erik," Lars said, and the vampire melted quickly away.

"Please, eat," he said, watching Seren closely.

Dropping her gaze and exuding the air of a shy young girl, Seren took a mouthful of the fish.

"Fascinating," said the commander as Seren steadily devoured half her meal. "Do you eat every day?" he asked.

"I do not have to, no."

"We're tired, can't the questions wait? After all, we are not going anywhere," said Rebekah with a hard stare.

Lars lifted his glass and the long draft he took stained his lips red.

Rebekah averted her gaze as a dull flush flooded his high cheekbones.

"Come, min skat," he said. "Your mate must drink blood?"

Rebekah jumped as, without warning, he reached out and plucked at the neckline of her shirt.

"Unless?" he said.

"None of your damn business," Rebekah spat, clutching her collar.

"Very well." He inclined his head. "And you, youngling. Your name?"

"Seren."

Lars' shark-like smile filled the silence.

Rebekah kept her breathing even, fighting the urge to hold it, knowing it would make her heart race and draw further attention from Lars.

A sudden pool of shadow moving across the wooden deck broke the tension and jerked Seren's head around. A silent figure blocked the doorway.

"Heinrik, good of you to join us," said Lars, his smile disappearing.

"Sentinel." Heinrik approached the table and sat down opposite Seren. He lifted the cover on the untouched meal of raw liver and beefsteak, sitting in a pool of thin blood. "So, she ate the cooked food," he said as he inspected Seren's face.

Her own food turned over in Rebekah's stomach as she glared at Lars. "Who is this?"

"This is Doctor Heinrik. He will document Seren's development. Take blood, and… samples, and so forth," said Lars. He shrugged.

"Over my dead body," muttered Seren.

Lars laughed. "That is what we are here to find out. Where does the dead body and the living one converge?" Lars' hand shot across the table and his fingers closed around Seren's wrist. Pressing his thumb to her veins, he closed his eyes. "Fascinating," he said again. "Heinrik, she has a pulse. Only twelve beats per minute. No, wait – it has stopped now." His eyes snapped open as he gazed into Seren's glazed expression.

She must be slipping into revival-sleep, I'm sure of it. Connor had explained revival sleep was a form of relaxation that reduced stress, and right now, Seren was surely under stress. Rebekah didn't want Lars drawing any conclusions. Every piece of information he uncovered put more power into his hands, and even Rebekah was in the dark when it came to how Seren ticked.

"You're scaring her," Rebekah insisted. She gripped the stone flesh of his bicep, above the gold armlets which encased his forearm from wrist to elbow. "Let her go."

Seren's complexion became waxy and gray beneath Lars' inspection.

Releasing his grip reluctantly, he murmured, "Child, we have much to learn, and I wish to do this the easy way. So tell me, do you know yet how often you need to breathe? How long your body can go without oxygen?"

Seren shook her head, her words slurred as she answered, "I do not know."

Lars darted a sharp glance at Heinrik, his tone steeped in reverence as he said, "It looks like we are in for an incredible journey of discovery, nej?"

"Indeed." The doctor nodded slowly. His pupils glittered like jet beads.

The hairs on the back of Rebekah's neck prickled, and her chair clattered over as she shot to her feet and glared at Lars. "The questions *will* wait. Seren is *my* child and you will respect my wishes."

Lars stood up, his own chair scraping slowly back, and towered above her, the uncompromising gleam in his glacial-blue eyes freezing her heart. He drifted around the table and stopped at Rebekah's side.

Her gaze tracked his face, her chin lifted in defiance. She hoped she exuded the iron will which frustrated Connor, at times.

"You have your way, for now. But once we dock, and you have your quarters in my home, my wishes will be obeyed. You understand?"

"No," she said firmly.

Lars laughed. "How did this vampire of yours not break you? Train you? He must be weak."

"He is everything you are not."

Rebekah's hand whipped through the air and slapped his face. Her anger evaporated when he caught her fingers and bent them back until they creaked. Pain shot down her arm as he said, "Careful, min skat, do not mistake my tolerance for kindness. Take Seren back to your cabin. We are at sea, so I will not chain you, but there will be a guard outside your door. Now go."

He released her, returned to his place and sank gracefully back into his chair. His long pale fingers curled around the stem of his glass as he swirled the blood, inhaling the aroma like a connoisseur, before swallowing it down.

Not taking her eyes from his face, Rebekah reached out and shook Seren's shoulder gently. "Come on, sweetheart. You need to rest."

Like an automaton, Seren rose to her feet and allowed Rebekah to lead her from the room. With both her hands on Seren's shoulders, it took all Rebekah's strength to guide her child around corners and into the final run towards their cabin.

Back inside, Seren shook off the lethargy and, for a moment, she was confused to find they were no longer in the dining room. "I'm sorry, Mama," she said, dropping down to sit on the bunk.

"What happened in there, Seren?"

"I was scared. I tried the relaxation exercise Papa taught me. Imagining rooms inside my head, I chose the calming one, and I found him in there. Papa. He is no longer in darkness. He has not left London, yet, but he is with Uncle Julian, Greg and Seth." Seren's voice dropped to a whisper. "They are coming to get us, Mama. They will come."

"I know they will." Rebekah sat beside Seren and held her close. "I know they will."

Rebekah believed it. She just hoped it would be soon. *I think this relaxation she talks about is revival sleep. But hell, I'm not a vampire. Where is Connor when I need him?*

Chapter 10

Julian had already said it – getting off the island of Great Britain undetected would be almost impossible. Greg and Seth sat, hunkered down at the base of an oak tree devouring the contraband delivered by Anthony. The pre-packaged meals destined for the human farm consisted of jerked beef, cheese, nuts and seeds, washed down with milk. Neither Marine knew when they would get the chance to eat again.

Connor strode back and forth, the speed of his pacing clearing the autumn leaves from the ground around him more efficiently than a leaf-blower could have managed.

Julian waited with his arms folded across his chest, biting back the urge to throw a rock at Connor and put a stop to his perpetual motion. Instead, he fixed his eyes on a knot on a tree trunk and observed his friend's profile, each time he passed by.

Connor stopped. "Our options are limited. It's more than twenty-four hours since Rebekah and Seren were taken." Frowning fiercely, he said, "We have to think outside the box."

As principal, Julian could muster up a seagoing vessel. Working shipyards in Southampton and Bristol each had a fleet of ships in dry dock. Nothing hugely impressive, but even vampires were not smug enough to burn *all* their bridges. Just as Noah needed the Ark, if ever they needed to transport their herd of humans across the English Channel, they had stored the ships they could need.

"We don't know who we can trust, so getting our hands on a vessel, but keeping it a secret, now *that* requires a miracle," said Julian.

Both vampires could walk across the seabed, but the last time Julian had made the crossing, around a decade ago, he discovered that the ravine-like walls of the deep trench marking the shipping channel were unstable. Even if it were just he and Connor, and they tried the crossing on foot, if their dense body weight triggered an avalanche in the bedrock, the sea could become a watery grave.

"We need to board a vessel no one will miss if it disappears," said Connor, "So, how do we do that with two humans, and without being noticed?"

Bristol, on the west coast of England, was the main transportation port of the goods vampires considered essential. Some vampires hung onto human comforts, and, whether it was a penchant for Italian made shoes, or a weakness for vintage clothing which reminded them of the year they were turned, Bristol was the bartering capital of the British hives.

Connor scowled as he ran through all the options he could think of.

He had visited Bristol. The vampires there did not bustle, but they did create a constant stream of bodies walking up and down the gangways to the floating pontoons giving access to permanently moored barges. They were shoppers; their attention would be focused on the Aladdin's cave of treasures. *Maybe we could slip by unnoticed.* Vampires come in all shapes and sizes, and Seth and Greg, with the help of beta blockers, would pass a cursory inspection. *But, casting off on a boat that has not moved for years? Stupid idea.*

"Come on, Julian, think of something."

Julian's raised eyebrows said 'really?'. "If you're thinking of Bristol, it's over two hundred miles across country, and we don't have that kind of time to waste."

"No," Connor said slowly, "but the East London Docks are on the doorstep, and worth a look."

Getting moving felt better than standing doing nothing, and within an hour the group of four were crawling across rock strewn ground which ended in an escarpment of loose gravel.

Their vantage point overlooked the soot-black skyline of London. The River Thames meandered below, glistening in the moonlight like a discarded ribbon of silver-blue silk. The yellow painted girders of the dockyard's fixed loading cranes stabbed into the sky, their bony fingers pointing towards the heavens, and the black outlines of tugs and tender vessels berthed in rows shimmered with the oily sheen of cockroach shells.

"Perhaps we can steal a boat?" suggested Greg.

Julian frowned. "We won't get our hands on anything larger than the tenders which carry small loads from ship to shore. We can't get you across the channel in one of those."

Moving back into a crouch, Connor surveyed the deserted quaysides and silent machinery. His harsh sigh rippled unrest through the four men as he took out a map and laid it out on the ground. He traced his finger along the blue line of the Thames.

"This is just an outpost from where we ferry food up the river, moving perishable supplies out of the cold storage sheds and then on to the human farm." Withdrawing his hand, Connor stabbed his fingers roughly through his hair. "The sentinel's ship is still at sea, but my connection with Seren is breaking down. We have to get moving, Julian."

Seren's pictures were like the revolving beam shining from a lighthouse. The flashes illuminated a room for only fractions of a second, and the tall blond vampire commander featured in too many of those glimpses for Connor's liking. The protective instinct of the alpha male vibrated through his hard muscles and he wanted to hit something. "We have to make a decision, now."

"I'll go to Bristol. Perhaps, alone, I can steal a merchant's boat?" said Julian.

"We won't find anything seaworthy there, either, but there is a way to get across to Europe." Connor folded the map, pocketed his compass, and stood up.

Julian's brows rose. "Meaning?"

"We need to head down the estuary past the Thames barrier." A brittle smile tightened Connor's features as he asked, "Which vessel comes and goes every few weeks, sits out in the estuary, and no one would ever wish to get close to it?"

"The super tanker nomads? You've got to be kidding," said Julian.

"The vessel is the size of a small town," said Connor, "and perfect for hiding humans."

Julian's green eyes narrowed. "*And* is home to a vampire crew so close knit that they move as one entity. How the hell are *we* gonna slip past them, let alone *humans*?"

"Right now, I have no clue, but have you got a better idea?"

Connor studied the shifting expressions on Julian's face as he looked for solutions.

"Hell, Connor," he muttered, getting to his feet and brushing the dirt from the back of his coat.

"Precisely." Connor lifted a hefty khaki-colored backpack up onto his shoulders and sliced a penetrating look towards Greg and Seth. "If you're up for the challenge, guys, it's a twelve-mile hike, so let's get going."

Julian and Connor carried the bulk of the equipment. They looked mildly ridiculous doing it dressed in their vampire day clothes, but it was necessary. If they had to bluff and talk to any other vampires along the way, wearing combats would raise serious eyebrows.

It took under an hour and a half to complete the cross country run. Greg and Seth flatly refused to travel under vampire power, but they were able to run faster when Julian and Connor dumped their own packs at their destination and doubled back to relieve the men of their loads. The vampires eased the tension of what lay ahead by indulging in good natured taunts, urging the human pair to dig deep and get a move on.

Regrouping on high ground, Greg and Seth sank to their haunches to catch their breath while Connor and Julian commando-crawled forward and looked down the sheer face of a cliff. They watched in silent awe as the swarm of vampires set about unloading cargo from a fleet of 50 ton trucks into steel containers – each one the size of a three-floor tower-block lying on its side.

Their speed and efficiency defied belief.

The super tanker's cranes were bolted to the deck. On the shore, four vampires jumped nimbly up onto the roof of a transport container sitting on the concrete causeway. Each crew member effortlessly dragged a chain as thick as a body builder's thigh over to a different corner. Squeezing open the spring-loaded G-clamps on the end, they anchored them into holes drilled into the angled metal framework.

The chains groaned and rattled when the crane arm rose, taking up the slack. A scraping noise of metal scuffing the concrete grated through the air, and then an eerie silence swelled when the container swayed and became airborne.

As the ground fell away, two vampires dropped twenty feet, landing back on the quay side with easy grace. The moment they touched the ground, they were moving again, repeating the process with a new pair of crew mates.

The two vampires left behind stood on the container roof and rode across to the tanker ship, their hands hanging loosely at their sides and their eyes staring straight ahead. Gales beat their clothes against their bodies and snakes of hair whipped about their composed faces, yet both figures exuded easy relaxation.

Four vampires waited on board at the rectangular landing site marked out on the deck. The steel container loomed overhead, casting them in deep shadow as they reached up and rotated the colossal weight with skilled hands. As the crane lowered it swiftly onto the deck, the air beneath the container whooshed into their rigid faces, plastering their black garb to their bodies.

Laid out on his belly in the coarse grass next to Julian, with his eyes still glued to the action, Connor said, "We need to get down there before they finish loading."

A ten-strong crew crawled over the dockside in purposeful coordinated movement, like an organism that divided and sub-divided in a display of perpetual motion. The pack of vampires backed trucks up into the loading bays, drove forklifts at speed through spaces that were constantly changing, and hosed out empty transport containers, preparing them for loading onto the ship.

"How they don't collide with each other, I don't know," muttered Julian.

"They are like magnets that repel each other. They know the position of every member of their group," murmured Connor.

"Surreal, isn't it?" Julian glanced at Connor and added, "We're wasting time. There is no sneaking past this lot."

"No, you're right," said Connor firmly. "I'll act as decoy, and you smuggle Seth and Greg on board inside a container."

"And what are you going to say? 'Hi, guys, I was just passing by, any chance I can get free passage across the channel?'" scoffed Julian.

"You're right." Connor said again.

"Thank God," sighed Julian.

"They'll want something in return. I could be defecting from the London hive. It will be easier to convince them of that if I have a pet." Connor's calculating tone did not bode well, but Julian knew there was little point arguing.

"Well, it won't be the first hare-brained scheme you've pulled off." Julian's smile did not reach his eyes. "All you've got to do now is convince Greg or Seth to let you bite them. Good luck with that."

Connor turned an innocent gaze on Julian. "Have you never heard the phrase 'close your eyes and think of England'? Rebekah and Seren's lives are on the line, I think you'll be surprised at how far Greg and Seth are prepared to go."

Both vampires reversed their commando crawl back to where the men were kneeling, hiding behind thick shrubbery. Connor wasted no time. He rose to his feet, explained the plan, and asked the question, "Which one of you is up for being a sacrificial lamb?" He left the two Marines alone for a minute, saying, "Come find me when you decide. I know it's a lot to ask. I can go it alone, but it would make the story more plausible."

Connor disappeared into the sparse undergrowth winding his way between a cluster of trees.

Waiting out of sight of the others, Connor heard ponderous human footsteps approaching. He knew who was standing there by the pH balance of his skin and the sweaty aroma radiating from hair still damp from the exertion of his run. *Greg.*

With his back still turned, Connor said, "Are you sure? You can go now if you want, and I'll not think any less of you."

Greg shook his head and swallowed.

When he took in a breath to answer, a thump on his chest rammed him back against a tree. Searing pain burned through the flesh in his neck like a shower of hot needles. Instinctively, he tried to raise his hand and shove Connor away, but his fingers tingled and his arm felt like a lead weight as his blood pressure plummeted. As he opened his mouth to cry out, the pain stopped.

Greg knew he was volunteering to have bite marks imprinted in his flesh, and to run the gauntlet of walking into the den of a group of vampires whose reactions even Connor could not predict. Greg staggered back, his hand reaching for the reassuring support of a tree trunk. "Is it over?" he croaked.

Connor stood twenty feet away, his fierce white features dappled by shadow where the leafy canopy obscured the moonlight. "I thought it best. Give you no time to think."

Greg needed to hear the worst. "I'm not a vampire now?"

"No, that ritual is far more excruciating. You have to be drained to the point of death, and drink from a vampire in return." Connor laughed gently. "You are still you."

As Connor wiped blood from his mouth with the back of his hand, Greg gingerly felt along the series of teeth marks in the skin at the base of his throat. Feeling foolish, he said, "Thanks."

Connor's gray eyes glinted as he stated flatly, "I'm in danger, too. I have no idea if they'll buy it. They may decide to kill us both on the spot, but they'll lose a few men if they do." Connor approached until he was close enough to lay a hand on Greg's shoulder. "Think about the most exhausting experience you ever had when in the Marines, and channel that. You are a pet, you are drained, you are weak, and just walking is the hardest thing you have ever done."

Greg's shoulders slumped beneath Connor's grasp and his features slackened to exhaustion.

"Good," said Connor. "The blood I took will help. It has lowered your blood pressure and the wounds smell of my venom, marking you as my property." Slapping Greg on the back and almost knocking him off his feet, Connor said, "Take a beta blocker, a slower heart rate will convince them you are struggling to survive. Let's go and round up Seth and Julian. And Greg?"

Greg's face wore the expression of a man who had walked to the gallows and lived. He straightened the collar of his combat jacket and winced. The bruised sensation in his neck proved he had not just had a nightmare.

Connor smiled indulgently. "It was a tough call. Thank *you*."

◇◇◇

The loading was well underway when Connor walked up to the gate in the wire fence surrounding the docking area. Pushing his fingers through the linked chain fabric, he shook it so hard that the hinges of the gate began to crumble.

Three black-robed figures instantly appeared, the shadows at their feet oozing over the concrete like a spill of oil.

Connor shot a glance along the perimeter, satisfied that his noisy arrival had drowned out the rattle of Julian and Seth climbing over the fence about sixty-yards away.

Without breaking their stride, the three vampires swarmed over the top of the fence and surrounded Connor in a synchronized movement. He groaned when they shoved him face first up against the wire mesh, and the tallest of the nomads gripped Connor's skull. With irresistible force, he increased the pressure until Connor's brow and cheekbone bent the metal strands.

Their complete silence was eerie. Through the limited view of the eye not crushed closed by the wire mask, Connor saw the vampires exchanging looks and glancing off into the middle distance.

Someone is coming. As the thought filtered into Connor's mind, from the other side of the fence, a voice whispered into his ear – the compelling tone penetrating the sound of creaking steel.

"What do you want?"

When Connor tried to turn his head, the fence shuddered as a vicious shove on his spine slammed his hard abdomen into the clattering links of metal. The vampire holding him captive rammed a knee into Connor's back. Again, there was silence, until Connor got it. *It's my turn to talk.* "I want to speak to the captain."

"You *are* talking to the captain."

The take-me-to-your-leader scenario was not working out like Connor had hoped. "Are you taking on crew?" said Connor, as clearly as the distorted mesh of wire would allow.

The vertebrae in his neck popped as Connor was yanked backwards. His teeth snapped shut when the movement stopped dead and, from three feet away, he got his first view of the captain.

The captain looked Connor up and down and then stared into his eyes. The shadows eased back from his face as he lifted his chin and said, "Start talking."

Man of few words, huh? "I'm on the run."

The arrogant moon-bleached features showed surprise. "Running from what?"

Here goes nothing. "From the London hive." Connor sneered as he said, "Fifteen years of being spoon fed cold human blood, shit. I'm sick of patching up vampire idiots that get caught out in the sun on cloudy days." His voice became wistful as he sighed. "Humans made war on each other, and I enjoyed killing them for fun." The smile he allowed to spread over his face dripped with malice. "Just when they came back from the battlefields, thinking they had tasted victory, I'd snatch it away." Connor's gray eyes gleamed as he sought the captain's agreement. "Human blood tastes thicker, richer, when they are pumped with adrenalin, don't you find?"

Connor was prepared to continue on until interrupted, and, thankfully, the interruption came in the form of a rumble of laughter.

"Climb the fence and we'll talk," said the captain, his jet-beaded eyes glittering.

Said the spider to the fly. Connor stood still long enough to make the captain angry.

"Crush his skull and let's get going," he barked.

As large calloused hands closed over the back of his head, Connor growled, "Wait-"

The captain's leather coat flapped around his thighs like oiled silk as he turned back. He grinned. "I don't need you. Muscle like yours is ten-a-penny. You're just another mouth to feed."

"I have someone with me," Connor said flatly, forcing each reluctant word through a clenched jaw as his neck strained against the rotating force the cradle of large hands still applied. The reticence was real. Tactical suicide went against every grain in his body. *If I climb that fence Greg will be stranded here alone. It's all or nothing.*

The two flanking vampires turned and scanned the undergrowth of the embankment.

"You won't find him," grated Connor.

Tilting his head, the captain stepped forward to within inches, his eyes boring into Connor's brain. "*We* don't have to find him. But, it seems, you can't leave him."

Connor gave up another enticing tidbit. "He's my property, and you do need me."

The captain's gaze sharpened. "A human?" His slick gaze reassessed Connor.

At a gesture from the captain, the clawed grip framing Connor's head slipped away.

Easing the stiffness from his neck, Connor said, "You have humans onboard." It was a stab in the dark.

The captain's eyes narrowed.

So, the rumors are true. A vampire closed in behind him once more, and Connor cut in, "And I'll bet you lose them to sickness, injury. Overdraining? I'll also bet they are getting harder to replace. Not so many strays out there, now." Contemplating the blank impassive features of the commander, Connor played his ace. "I'm a doctor. You need me."

"I see."

Connor said bluntly, "I want in." He jerked his chin at the looming outcrop of the super tanker skulking in the harbor. "And my pet comes too, but he remains my property."

"I make the rules onboard ship."

Stillness seeped into Connor's body as he said, "Fair enough." And as triumph lurked in the captain's grin, Connor added, "I think I'll pass."

Breaking through the cloud cover, moonlight captured the reluctant admiration in the captain's expression, softening the harsh effect of the four scars slicing down the left side of his face. The silver threads glistened as he spoke. "The human is your property, and no one touches him. Come, we are leaving."

Clearly, the force of nature in command of the tanker was accustomed to having his own way. By the sudden shuffling of vampire feet behind him, Connor sensed he had been awarded a huge concession.

Connor nodded curtly. Moving fast, he crossed the street, jogged twenty yards along the perimeter fence and then left the sidewalk. Bracing his boots on the steep bank of silt and mud, he dug Greg out of the shallow grave where most of his body had been buried beneath the dirt.

As he pulled the Marine to his feet, Connor muttered, "They are watching, lean on my shoulder. You're weak, remember?"

"Did Julian get in?" Greg mouthed carefully.

Connor nodded, and, as part of the act, gripping Greg by the back of his collar and underneath one arm, Connor helped him stagger convincingly back to the compound.

The vampires unlocked the gate, and once Connor and Greg were inside they were led to the loading bay. To keep pace with their escorts, Connor took Greg's weight and whisked him along, dragging the soles of his boots over the concrete.

Keeping a close eye on the broad shoulders of the vampires flitting along in front, Connor inspected the grime-encrusted coats. The group moved with the effortless coordination of a flock of birds. Connor grinned. *Maybe vultures fit better. 'Super tanker nomads' might as well be written in the dirt on their backs.*

They lived by their own rules, existing outside the laws of vampire society. They were answerable to only one, the tall powerful figure of the captain, who had, for now, disappeared.

On the quayside, Connor quickly worked out the vampires were herding him and Greg towards an open container. *It makes sense as transportation. We really have no choice.* Connor sensed Greg's moment of realization when the Marine's body stiffened in his grasp. "We need to get onboard that ship, Greg, so just go along," Connor whispered.

Releasing the Marine and letting him walk unaided, Connor followed him into the empty transporter container. Before they could turn around, the sheet-metal doors slammed shut with a doom-laden thud.

Darkness descended and the stench of rotting vegetation made Greg cough. "Can't your lot smell?" he spluttered.

"I thought you'd be more worried that we could die here if the captain has hoodwinked us, but you go with the smell?" scoffed Connor. "Of course we can smell, much better than you." Wasting the humor of a leering sneer that Greg's human sight would never see in the pitch-black, Connor added, "But, we can also hold our breath for, well, forever."

"I hope you know what you're doing, getting us banged up in here," Greg said.

"If I was the captain, I would do the same. It gets us onboard, and he knows where we are. That's all," Connor replied.

"Fair enough, but-" A noise overhead cut Greg short.

Chains dragging over the roof sounded like tigers with steel claws trying to get in, and then the wet metal panel beneath them shifted abruptly in a gentle arcing motion. Neither wanted to sit down on the greasy floor, and Greg swore as he groped around for an anchor point on the wall. Connor stood solid as a rock, listening to the scrabbling sounds with wry amusement. Finally, taking pity on Greg, he strode over and offered his arm. "Hang on to me, the crossing will be bumpy."

Greg grunted, reluctantly gripping Connor's sleeve with both hands.

"When we're on board, keep your head down and say as little as possible." Connor cast a skeptical look over Greg's huge muscular frame. "We are going for two hundred and fifty pounds of invisible."

"Where are Seth and Julian?"

"They boarded the same way as us, except the vampires did not know it," said Connor. *That was the plan anyway. Let's hope they aren't waving us off when we leave.*

"Hey, did you notice, these guys look like the walking dead? The zombie kind, I mean," said Greg under his breath.

Connor's lips twitched. "Is that a compliment?"

Greg had hit the nail on the head. The vampires' bluish, waxy-toned skin had clearly not seen even a cloud-filtered ray of daylight in decades. Connor wondered at their strangely tribal existence. They were eerily silent, and rumor had it they were inbred. The story went that, when they were turned, each vampire had fed from the other and a telepathic connection ran like an electric current between them. Connor was inclined to believe it.

The container touched down, shuddering to a halt with an ear-piercing screech.

In the seconds left before the doors opened, Connor said urgently, "Just stay close. I'll insist you stay where I can keep an eye on you, but if they take you, I've got your scent and I'll track you down. Just keep your head down and cooperate."

Greg had time to nod, before the darkness lifted to pale gray and two black silhouettes blotted out the view of the starlit sky.

Connor walked out onto the deck and took stock of his surroundings. "Nice place you've got here," he murmured as he made a note of the coiled mounds of thick chains, the ax cradled in a wall mounted bracket, and massive reels of steel cable.

"Come, the captain is waiting," said the shorter of the two vampires. Their skin may look like it belonged on a corpse which had floated in the estuary for a week, but the muscles bulging beneath their coats warned Connor not to underestimate them.

With one nomad leading the way and the other bringing up the rear, Connor and Greg walked through the maze of secured container units until they reached the outer deck. The distant whine of the tanker engines made the ground thrum beneath their hurrying steps, and Connor acknowledged that the only way left for them now, was forward. *The plan will play out in our favor, or fail. But I'll die before I concede defeat.* The vampire guide moved aside at the bottom of a flight of metal stairs, allowing Greg and Connor to ascend to the top.

There were three flights, welded to a wall of steel on one side and ending on a square platform exposed to the sea on three sides, except for the metal door in the panel to Connor's left. Frothy white horses cantered over the rough gray water, rearing and scattering into the white lace of wind-blown spray. The gusts tore at the smooth skin of Connor's face, and Greg hunched his shoulders and groaned at the icy-chill.

Connor shoved the door open, shielding Greg from the gale-force blast as he helped him bodily over the high threshold and into the square room beyond. The door slammed behind them, muting the pitch of the screaming squall.

Predictably, they were on the bridge. Presented with the broad back of the captain, Connor gestured to Greg to stay quiet and moved forward, taking up a position between them. *He knows we're here. Making me wait is part of the game.*

As Connor waited for the captain's attention to turn to them, he looked around.

Unusually, for the bridge of a vessel, visibility had been sacrificed in the interest of shelter. The vantage point had more metal panels than glazed panes. The thick glass glistened with a skim of UV protective coating, and Connor recognized it as a vampire construction.

He wondered how many features, from bow to stern, a human crew would find familiar. If Connor was any judge, the tanker had been *redesigned* rather than re-fitted.

None of the creature comforts humans needed remained. A wide console winked with an array of lights, and the captain appeared intent on flicking several toggle switches on or off. Three black square buttons lit up at his touch and then he sank into stillness.

Here we go.

Greg flinched when the black cloaked figure whipped around, becoming the ominous blur of a tornado.

Facing Connor, the nomad commander said, "Welcome aboard. My name is Captain Blake." He waited, raising an eyebrow.

"Doctor Anthony," Connor replied.

Blake's attention slid across to Greg's wary face, partially obscured behind Connor's left shoulder. "And this would be your pet?"

Connor did not bother to nod. He prepared for Blake to make his move. *He'll strike early, a show of force.*

Greg did not see it coming – he gasped as the freezing cold of the window pane bit through the clothes on his back and set his teeth chattering. Blake's face appeared mere inches away, his strong grip turning Greg's head and exposing his neck.

Nanoseconds later, Connor shouldered Blake aside, staking his claim, and giving the captain time to get only a quick glance at Greg's bite wounds. *He'll expect to find some bites older than others.* Shoving his body in-between Blake and Greg, baring his teeth, Connor met the black glare of the captain, and said, "Hands off."

Blake inclined his head and, in the lightning fast switch in direction Connor was beginning to expect, he said, "Once we are underway the crew will gather below decks and feed. And you will meet your shipmates." It was not an invitation.

"I'll come alone." Connor jerked his chin towards where Greg convincingly sagged in a heap of tired muscle, resting heavily against the wall. "He needs to sleep, and, as you say, I do not yet know who I'm dealing with."

It was a calculated insult in the battle for the upper-hand. Blake had checked Greg for evidence of having been fed upon, and Connor made it clear he was offended.

"He looks dead on his feet," said Blake, smiling ironically. "I'll extend *my* hospitality to you for tonight. I'm sure you must be hungry."

"Once he's settled, you can show me the ropes. And, I'll need to see my patients." *And search for Seth and Julian.* Connor would rest easier knowing he and Greg were not alone.

The captain bristled, his coat pulling tight across his shoulders. His blue-tinted features were carved in ice. "You'll meet half of your patients tonight, the rest will wait until we're at sea. As you say," Blake stared at Greg. "Our keeping of pets is only a rumor, but, it would seem we are all in the same boat, and risking the death penalty."

Connor gritted his teeth.

A challenge glinted in the depths of the captain's keen glance, and Connor wondered how bad it was going to get. *I'll take whatever he throws at me, and fight if I have to.* Walking away in one piece was all that mattered. How much devastation Connor left in his wake was down to Blake.

"I tell you what." Blake scooped up a brown paper parcel and tossed it at Connor. "Take a food pack to feed your human, and hide him wherever you wish, as long as it is below deck. Sliding about inside a container in high seas is a short cut to broken bones. Fair enough?"

Connor inclined his head. "Fair enough. And what time will the crew assemble for the rap-sleep gathering?"

Blake craned his neck to read the clock on his console. "An hour will see us in the North Sea. So, call it oh-two-hundred. Follow the sound of the bilge pumps."

Connor arched a brow, and the captain added grimly, "The room is purpose built. It makes it easier to sluice out the space afterward." Blake shrugged. "Accidents happen."

As Connor and Greg retraced their steps to the stern of the ship, looking for a door which led down into the bowels of the vessel, Greg asked heavily, "You're going to a what-gathering?"

In a toss-up between telling the truth or fiction, Connor decided Greg should know what dangerous company he was keeping. "Rap-sleep gathering." Without looking at Greg, Connor slowed to a casual human pace. Cutting it down to bullet points, he said, "A vampire brain has three compartments, and each one needs human blood to rehydrate it. During sleep, we can only open one door at a time. Our personalities change, depending upon which one we choose to unlock." Darting a look at Greg, Connor finished, "A rap-sleep gathering is like a drunken brawl. We feed, we fight, and sometimes, vampires or humans, die."

"You're going to be outnumbered," said Greg.

"I didn't know you cared," said Connor. "And here was I expecting you to be horrified."

"I've killed men in combat. Sometimes, survival instinct is all you've got to work with."

Connor nodded soberly. "Talking of which, if I'm leaving you on your own you'll need a weapon."

Greg laughed. "Got a nuclear bomb handy? Anything less is like water off a duck's back."

First checking that the deck was deserted, Connor pulled opened a rust-stained door in the wall of riveted gunmetal-gray paneling which ran the length of the inner deck. Peering inside, he said, "Wait in here. I'll be back in a minute."

Moments later, arriving back at the site of the transport container inside which he and Greg had hitched a ride, Connor took the ax down from its bracket on the wall. Ranging his gaze along the deck, he spotted a large metal storage chest – rust boiled through its white painted surface like weeping sores. Stopping in front of it, he crumbled the padlock which secured the lid and flipped it open.

"Ah," he sighed, in a eureka moment. Reaching inside, he knew he'd found the nearest thing he could get to Greg's nuclear-bomb.

Returning to the closed metal door where Greg was hiding, Connor whipped it open. Delighting in the alarm that skittered along his friend's spine, Connor wielded the ax, wearing the manic smile of the psychopath he was parodying.

"Funny," muttered Greg.

Laughing softly, Connor flipped the weapon round, and held out the handle.

Greg yanked the ax out of Connor's hand. His lip curled at the sound of the blade grating over vampire flesh. "Like I said, water off a duck's back. Might as well try cutting granite with a butter knife. I won't even get a swing in. Bloody bloodsuckers move so fast." Slicing a sharp glance at Connor, he added, "No offense."

"Quit whining and move it, Marine," Connor said lightly, dodging through an inner door and moving along a gangplank at a pace which Greg could only match at a forced run.

Following Blake's instructions, they headed below deck. In the cavernous storage hold, hugging the wall, they passed row after row of head-height wooden crates. Writing stenciled on the planks declared the contents as food: dried, tinned, and vacuum packed. Weaving in between the rows, they found other crates containing textiles and clothing, and, finally, at the back of the storage space, huge metal and plastic containers marked as laundry.

Connor leapt up on top of one and pulled open a hatchway in the sloping section. Holding it still, he ordered, "Hop in."

Greg recoiled at the rancid stench of stale sweat. "You have to be kidding."

"Think of it as camouflage. Safest place in the house. Just get in."

Greg hoisted himself up, swung his legs over the top, and, holding his breath like a deep-sea diver, he dropped down inside. Connor almost laughed, watching as Greg struggled to find his balance. He grabbed at handfuls of fabric, pushing the garments aside until he found a firm footing and was able to stand, waist high in a sea of crumpled clothes.

Connor grinned down at him. "It's going to be pitch-black when I close this lid. I'll use the owl call signal when I come back for you. In the meantime-" Connor reached inside the flap of his greatcoat and pulled out a flare gun. "Here, I found something pretty close to that nuclear-bomb."

Planting the ax handle in the dune of fabric, where it stood to attention like a tree sculpted by Salvador Dali, Greg reached up and took the gun in one hand and the four spare cartridges in the other. Compressing his lips, he said, "That's more like it."

"They have to find you first. You're not a threat and they won't be concerned with keeping quiet if they come looking. You should hear something. If they open this hatch, you aim for the face. You can't penetrate their skin, but eye sockets, nose, and ear canals are open conduits into the skull. With luck, you'll fry something."

Greg nodded and said, with more reverence this time, "Impressive."

"Glad you approve. I'll tell Julian to listen out, and he'll come running if I'm erm… detained."

Aware of the ticking clock, and not wanting Blake to come looking for him, Connor made a lightning fast detour, emerging back up onto the loading deck. He scouted along the row of containers, his attention focused on the upper edge, where the vertical sides of each container met the roof, until he found one with a crease folded into the metal.

Leaping from the deck, he hung by one hand from the gulley running around the top, and ran his free hand over the paint until he found Julian's mark scratched into the steel. Folding back the serrated cut in the panel, Connor eased his body, feet first, through the tight space. Silence greeted him for a nanosecond, followed by the reassurance of Seth's careful breathing.

"Julian-"

His friend materialized silently and punched Connor on the shoulder.

"Nice job," said Connor, jerking a chin towards the neatly scored cut in the metal.

Julian grinned. "Teamwork. My fingernails, and Seth's hunting knife."

Connor frowned. "I'm in with the crew, but Greg's out there on his own." Connor quickly filled Julian in on Greg's location on the ship.

"What does 'in' mean, precisely?"

Connor's gray eyes glinted like ice. "I have to attend a rap-sleep gathering with the crew."

"Just be careful. They could use the chaos of rap-sleep to kill you."

"I need to keep Blake guessing. He's enjoying sparring with me. Once we dock in the next port, we are out of here."

Connor turned to go, primed to launch himself towards the petal shaped fold of metal overhead.

"Hey, Connor, be careful."

He met Julian's penetrating stare. "I'm not going to fall at the first hurdle. Rebekah and Seren are waiting for me." Seconds later, he swung back through the gap, the metal creaking as he took the time to fold it back into place. After using dirty water from the gulley to add a layer of grime and wipe away his own tracks, he dropped down onto the deck and made his way back inside to the tanker's living quarters.

Chapter 11

The thrumming beat of the bilge pumps vibrating through the hull gave the tanker the illusion of life. Every passageway looked the same, and at each intersection Connor stopped to listen, before setting off in pursuit of the ship's beating heart.

He was not surprised when he rounded a corner and Captain Blake's resting figure blocked the gangway, his grim features bathed in the red glow of the bulkhead lamps. The black eyes glinting in blood-red sockets could have belonged to the Devil himself. Then the nomad smiled, and made the Devil look like a pussycat.

"So, you found us, Doctor. I didn't want to start without you," said Blake. "Come."

Connor fell in behind.

The leather tails of the captain's oil black coat flared, giving him the illusion of flight.

Up ahead, a Perspex dome emitted a strobing red light, and Blake zeroed in on the door beneath it.

Gripping the spoked wheel in the center of the steel door, an effortless spin from Blake retracted the locking mechanism, and the rubber seals sighed. The four-inch thick hatch creaked as he pushed it open and invited Connor to enter first.

Stepping over the threshold, Connor found a chamber alive with rich colors and textures. After the bare metal of the storage rooms and the riveted panels of the gangways, it felt as though he had stumbled into a setting of the Arabian Nights.

With a raised brow, Connor glanced at Blake, watching him climb through the door and shoulder it shut. The scars carved into the captain's face proved he was no stranger to conflict. Connor wondered if – like Shahryar of the Arabian Nights fable – Blake could be capable of killing a human girl each day for a thousand days, as his impassive face suggested.

Closer inspection of his surroundings revealed the rot beneath the opulent facade. Like the rocks on a sci-fi movie set which turn out to be made of polystyrene, nothing was as it seemed. The

Persian rugs and richly colored cushions scattered on the floor in the center of the room were threadbare and stained. Dull-brown patches smelled of copper to Connor's vampire senses. *Blood, then.* The curved tapestry-upholstered benches forming a large circle around the rancid cushions looked more menacing than cozy. *It's a holding pen. A human cannot leave without a vampire allowing it.*

Connor mirrored the captain's voracious smile, creating an air of pretended enthusiasm. As though he really cared, he said, "So, how many humans are we feeding from tonight?"

Blake's hooded gaze reflected approval as he slapped Connor on the back. "Wait and see, Doctor. I'm sure you'll find something to your taste."

The corners of the room were in deep shadow, and it was only when Connor heard the rustle of fabric that he realized the vampires were already assembled.

The flick of a switch illuminated a weak yellow bulb buried in the ceiling. It cast a funnel of light that focused on the tumbled pile of cushions, like a spotlight on a stage. Captain Blake entered the arena through the only break in the circle and took his seat. As though a silent dinner gong had been struck, movement erupted around the room as the ghoulish-looking tanker nomads filed into the enclosure and sat down.

Connor took the last remaining space in the circle, nearest the 'exit', feeling in control of some things anyway. With Greg safely stashed and Julian in the loop, he could focus all his attention on keeping Blake off balance. *It sounded easy when I told Julian.* Now, surrounded by the fifteen-strong group of vampires, he was not so sure.

The seconds ticked by, and Connor began to wonder, what now?

Slowly, the silence dissolved as the vampires began to talk, the low conversational tones grating over rusty vocal cords. Connor listened in; gathering the words spoken, by even the occupants of the farthest seats in the circle, presented no difficulty to his acute sense of hearing. It was a matter of singling out a vampire's face and tuning into the pitch of his voice. *Simple, and yet.*

The nomads' eyes skittered over Connor's face with disconcerting frequency, and it dawned on him that the talking was for his benefit. He realized other exchanges were going on inside their heads, and became more interested in reading the faces of those not speaking. *If only I could read their thoughts.*

He wondered again, how do they do that? His connection with Seren was like a revolving lighthouse beacon sweeping through his mind, illuminating in moments of crystal clarity, but then fading again.

In over one-hundred-years as a vampire he had never 'turned' a human, but Seren was *part* of his blood. *Is that what fused the connection?* Though his bond to Rebekah was incredibly strong, he could not read her mind. *More's the pity. I might have saved her from some of the scrapes she got herself into, but, I'm certainly in tune with her biorhythm.*

Captain Blake made a noise, a deep inhalation of breath which killed the conversation and grabbed every vampire's attention.

On the far side of the room, a metal panel screeched as it grated along a track. The odor of human sweat and hormones thickened the air – the 'food' had arrived.

One girl walked ahead of the other humans. Cutting across the middle of the circle, she sank gracefully down to sit at the feet of the captain.

So, is she his private property?

Despite himself, Connor was intrigued. She was far removed from his Rebekah in appearance, but the defiant tilt to her chin and the lively spark he caught before she veiled her gaze was the same. Her olive complexion was darker than an English rose in summer could ever achieve, the Mediterranean pigmentation giving her skin the scent of warmed oil. *Spanish descent, perhaps?*

As her head turned, the silken black mass of her hair, shot through with dark golden strands, came alive. Her eyes were the deepest brown Connor had ever seen.

He watched her closely, ignoring the progress of the other humans shuffling past. *Something sets her apart, other than Blake's favoritism.* Then it hit him.

She was holding a telepathic conversation with Blake.

When the captain's narrowed gaze raked over Connor's intent face, with a half-smile, Connor inclined his head, expressing respectful admiration.

The charged atmosphere arced between the two vampires. The others became absorbed in the conflict, their hunger in abeyance, their speculative glances shared silent communication behind the impassive facades.

The captain's features broke into a brittle grin. Extending a hand, he indicated the huddle of humans sitting on the scatter cushions within the circle.

Blake's earlier words haunted Connor. *I'm sure you'll find something to your taste.* Connor had noticed them only as interruptions to his view of the intriguing Spanish girl. Forced into surveying the room, it dawned on him that some of the seats in the circle were already empty, and he had not seen that happen either.

Just when Connor was wondering how things worked, a vampire lurched forward, grabbed a human boy by the hair, and yanked him to his feet. His other hand gripped the boy's upper arm and, using those two anchor points, the nomad dragged the youth out of the circle and into the shadows beyond.

Connor did not need the wafting odor of fresh blood to fill in the details of the scene. The humans could barely see in the gloom. *They just see vampires dragging their meals away like lions retreating to their den.* Vampire vision proved to be a mixed blessing. Connor studied the boy's terrified features, which slackened to stupor when his body hung limply in the vampire's hold, his blood draining from his face.

The unfed stragglers in the circle reclined in their seats and waited. Sensing Blake's growing impatience, Connor resigned himself to the inevitable. *I have to feed.*

And the captain decided that too. Catching the eye of a slight girl with a stringy curtain of greasy blonde hair hanging down over her dull expression, Blake jerked his head in Connor's direction. Her folded posture took up the space of a bag of bones, and, rising awkwardly to her feet, she almost toppled over.

Her legs appeared disconnected from her brain as she unsteadily picked her way through the obstacle course of cowering bodies, trying not to step on her fellow sufferers. With the stuttering grace of a day-old foal, she stopped in front of Connor. He arranged an inviting smile upon his face, feeling Captain Blake's eyes boring into his features.

When Connor went to get up, Blake's whisper oozed across the space. "No, stay."

Connor darted a glance towards the captain. The fresco of his Spanish girl smiling as Blake stroked her hair aside revolted Connor. Her warm bronzed skin took on a jaundiced hue in such close contrast to the blue-tinted paste of the captain's. His corpse-white tongue slid along her jawline and dipped into her mouth. Connor buried his repulsion, knowing he was being tested.

Settling back into his seat, he turned his attention to the thin girl, looking past the swaying strands of lank hair. Her eyes were closed as though she was sleepwalking. *Or dreaming of better days?* His narrowed gaze traveled over her adolescent frame and he knew there were no better days for her to dream of.

The floor vibrated as Blake tapped his boot, telling Connor his time was up.

Reaching out, Connor took hold of her arm. Her skin was clammy and nowhere near as warm as Rebekah's, but still the fluttering pulse in her wrist when his grip slipped downward shot a surge of excitement through him. Saliva flooded his mouth. The smoky odor of her unwashed body made his lip curl, and a disconcerting blend of hunger and disgust tore a path through his tight gut.

She offered no resistance when he drew her fragile bird-like weight down onto his lap. The protruding bones of her pelvis grating over the hard muscles of his thighs drew a gasp of pain from her faded rose-tinted lips.

She leaned against his chest as though it had taken every ounce of her energy to arrive there. Connor dipped his chin and turned his face to hers. She dropped her head back, exposing the steady pulse in her neck. It was thick and slow. It smelled like nectar with all the sweetness removed, but it was compelling just the same. Licking his tongue over her carotid pulse, Connor darted a glance around the room. As he expected, many sets of eyes were watching, and he bristled with irritation at the salacious anticipation contorting the captain's face.

Blake's lips drew back to expose teeth that were artificially sharpened for fast feeding. His gaze glittered like beads of jet.

Connor took a deep guttural breath and surrendered. The girl's torso rippled as he sank his teeth in, closing his jaw in a relentless sucking motion. For a moment, he paused as her blood rushed into his mouth, filled his throat, and trickled down inside his chest like a flow of burning lava. Satisfaction tightened every muscle in his body and he pressed her closer, and it was all he could do not to tighten his embrace and break the bones which were already creaking beneath his touch.

The mewling sound in her throat stripped away his veneer of civilization, and his own throat rumbled in response. Barely hanging onto the thread of humanity, suppressing the urge to feed until her heart ceased beating and her blood thickened to syrup, he stopped before the girl died in his arms.

As he stroked his tongue over the tear in her neck, congealing the seeping wound with the coagulating balm of his venom, the red clouds draped across his vision thickened, and a tingling sensation burrowed into the base of his skull. The inmates of his thirsty brain centers clamored at the cell doors, and his desire to let them out clenched a strangle hold around his throat.

The girl slipped from his slack arms, and Connor was only vaguely aware of humans being helped from the room by the ones who still had enough strength left to support the weight of their friends.

The psychopath of grave-sleep rattled loudest inside his head, but Connor was still the master of his fate. He knew the drunkard, the fighter with no conscience, was the cellmate he would need to liberate tonight.

Connor swung around snarling as Blake landed a hard blow on his shoulder. "Come, Doctor. When we party, we like to play."

The nomads were disappearing through a doorway, stripping the grime-encrusted coats from their shoulders as they walked. By the time Connor joined them, they had drifted into another circle. The solid wall of vampire flesh stood shoulder to shoulder.

Blake took his position in the center. Rotating on his heel, he dragged his gaze across the tense faces of each crew member as he said, "Play hard, but try and stay in one piece, hmm?" His eyes found Connor's blood-glazed expression. "You enjoyed your meal, Doctor?"

Connor nodded cautiously.

"And now, you pay."

"Pay?" Connor fought against the tide of rage burning the back of his neck. "I'll treat your humans. They are malnourished and sick. My debt is paid."

"But where is the danger? The edge that makes rap-sleep enjoyable?" Blake appeared inches in front of Connor. "If you are going to fight, and you are, you need a good reason to win, wouldn't you say?"

Deathly calm settled in Connor's chest. "Go on."

"Your pet."

"Non-negotiable," spat Connor.

Blake shook his head, laughing gently. He gripped Connor's shoulder squeezing near the base of his throat. "If you win, you can keep him, and he is safe, always."

"And if I lose?"

Blake tilted his head and said casually, "He dies."

Connor weighed up the chances of warning Julian and getting them all out of there, fast.

Blake watched, calculation written on his face. "Ah, you're thinking that he is hidden."

Connor smothered his reactions, giving nothing away.

"He is, of course. But unless he can leave the ship and swim in the freezing waters of the North Sea, then he will be found." Blake shrugged.

And a search will uncover more than just Greg. "I will fight." Connor studied the row of guarded faces. "How is the winner decided?"

"Surrender or die. The winner does not stop unless the loser surrenders."

"I will fight. Do I choose my opponent?"

"You will fight *me*," Blake said, frowning when Connor barked with laughter.

"No. Choose a champion. I will not fight you."

"Scared?"

"*You* should be scared." Connor forced his words through clenched teeth. "*When* I beat you, there's no way you will bear the humiliation and turn the other cheek. This is not the movies." Connor grimaced, indicating the wall of vampire flesh. "And with you gone, they will not let me live. So, choose someone else."

Blake's anger hummed through the air.

Connor's casual stance disguised primed muscles as the captain's affront crashed through his men with the force of a tsunami. Like a pack of hounds, each vampire became alert and ready for battle, held in check only by their commander's will. *I'll take as many as I can with me. Julian will hear something, I won't be going quietly.*

The simmering annoyance abruptly drained away when Blake bellowed with laughter. "Very well." He approached a nomad of huge proportions and placed a hand on his arm, drawing attention to the vampire's thick biceps. "You will fight Viktor. Now."

Connor shrugged out of his coat and handed it over to a bemused vampire. "Take good care of it. I want it back."

There were no rules. Immediately, Connor allowed the human blood in his system to rush up his carotid artery, past his brainstem, and flood into the gray matter of his brain. Sinking into rap-sleep, the rampaging aggression of the belligerent drunk kicked in, and he swung around, roaring as he charged at Viktor. Ducking low and gripping his foe around the waist, Connor drove the vampire back, hammering him into the wall. He dug his shoulder in hard, exhilaration singing through him when Viktor's ribs cracked. The metal panel behind their grappling bodies crumpled.

Keeping his body rammed into Viktor, Connor launched a powerful right hook and made juddering contact with the tall nomad's square jaw.

Viktor shoved at Connor's crushing weight. The hard girdle of his muscles twisting, the towering nomad slammed a descending elbow down between Connor's shoulder blades. Connor instinctively dropped to one knee, and the blow scraped down along his spine. As he hit the floor, Connor drove an upper cut into the vampire's abdomen and felt the muscle wall tear.

A roar echoed from the walls as Viktor reared up. Clenching his hands together, resembling three-hundred-pounds of incensed gorilla, he swung a double-fisted hammer blow down towards Connor's crouched figure.

Twisting away, Connor gritted his teeth as the clubbed fists crunched onto his shoulder and skidded down his arm. Springing to his feet and backing away, Connor spread his arms and gestured to Viktor to come and get him. At six-foot three-inches tall, Connor rarely, before today, had to look so far up into another vampire's face. *But the bigger they come, the harder they fall.*

Viktor charged like a raging bull, his face contorted as if in a silent battle cry. In the moment before impact, Connor whipped around, drove his leg up in an arc, and crunched his boot into the side of Viktor's head.

Viktor's jaw dislocated and he hit the metal floor face first.

Moving fast, Connor dropped down onto the nomad's broad back and planted one knee on each solid shoulder. He gripped Viktor's head and, digging his fingers into the vampire's scalp, jerked his chin up from the floor.

The tendons in Viktor's neck creaked as Connor growled, "Surrender."

Viktor bucked beneath Connor's weight. In an explosive blow, Connor slammed the nomad's face into the floor and broke his nose. "Surrender."

Still the vampire fought, rocking wildly until Connor's knee slipped from its anchor point.

Bracing his hands beneath his massive chest, Viktor surged up from the floor, forcing Connor into retreat.

Backing casually away, Connor muttered, "To the death, then?"

With the thick blood of his human meal trickling from his shattered nose, Viktor rushed forward. Diving low, he caught Connor in a vice-like bear hug, pinning his arms to his sides.

Connor's ribs groaned as the bear-hug tightened with the power of a boa constrictor.

Saliva dripped from Viktor's mouth as he grinned.

Feeling the fibers in his ribcage shriek, Connor snapped his head forward, butted Viktor in the face and cracked his cheekbones. Blood splattered Connor's face, and a startled Viktor relaxed his hold. Twisting around, and reaching back, Connor dug the clawed fingers of both hands into the straining tendons of Viktor's neck. Jerking back into action, the nomad's iron grip crushed Connor around the chest again, the knot of his clenched fists grinding into Connor's sternum. In the seconds before his ribcage could implode, Connor jabbed his fingers deeper into Viktor's thick neck and swung both his legs out in front – the sudden lurching shift of weight knocking the heavier vampire off balance. When Viktor staggered, Connor drove the pendulum back down. He planted both feet back on the deck, yanked hard on Viktor's head, and flipped the nomad over his shoulder.

The thump of Viktor landing on his back rumbled like thunder through the chamber, and Connor pressed his boot down on Viktor's throat.

"Surrender," Connor growled. He shot a fleeting glance at Blake.

Viktor stared at the ceiling, gurgling quietly as congealed blood pooled in the crater where his face used to be.

Blake nodded, and Connor stamped down and broke Viktor's neck.

Without turning his head, Connor detected the confusion rattling through the circle of watching vampires, as though a link in their chain had snapped. In stunned silence, they clamored to find a way of closing the gap. Their frozen disbelief stretched into a minute and Connor began to wonder if he had cut off the head of the snake. *Will they all keel over like a line of dominoes?*

Just as Connor hoped it would be that simple, as though a reboot switch flicked on, the eyes of each nomad rekindled with emotion and they appeared to teeter on the brink of the aggression of rap-sleep.

He could smell the electrical storm of activity inside their brains. He prepared himself for the worst. An orchestrated attack of the collective seemed inevitable. *They really are like one organism... maybe that strength is also their weakness.*

Then Blake said calmly, "Come, doctor. We will leave them to it."

Viktor's head rocked back when Connor slowly lifted his boot as though retracting from a landmine he thought might detonate.

There was a surreal moment of thinking, 'do I pick it up and hand it to his crew mate, like a football after a match is over?', but, looking around, he saw Blake already disappearing through the doorway. Deciding that getting out fast was the wise choice, Connor collected his greatcoat from the slack grip of a stone-still, preoccupied nomad – who still looked like a mannequin in a freak show – and shrugged into it as he walked. He followed the captain back into the feeding room.

Before Blake closed the door, Connor heard fighting break out in a symphony of snarls and the thumping of colliding bodies.

Captain Blake took his place at the focal point in the arcing circle, a wave of his hand inviting Connor to join him.

"That was impressive. Though I would have beaten you, of course."

"Of course," said Connor. "Just as long as we understand each other. I don't enjoy looking over my shoulder. I had that in the London Hive."

"As I see it, one out, one in." Blake's lack of concern rankled. "Viktor is out, you are in." He extended his hand. "Welcome aboard."

Chapter 12

Malachi walked slowly forward, feeling every grain of sand beneath his bare feet as though he was reading Braille. The gilt-lined walls of the excavated square tunnels, polished to a mirror finish, gave Malachi a clear image of his regal appearance – enhanced by a solid gold headdress fashioned into a cobra which coiled around his forehead, and rose up, with the snake's hood flared in an attitude of attack.

Malachi smiled. *Egyptians have long been enchanted by snakes and serpents. It would seem they find cold-blooded creatures hypnotic.* His presence here in the ancient tomb was proof of that.

The reflection of the thin tanned hide stretched over the angular bones of his skull was, as always, a source of sadness. He still felt like a young man of nineteen human years. He had not *aged* as a vampire. His internal organs, his mind, and his skeleton all retained the vigor of youth, but, before he could learn the lessons of survival, close encounters with the scorching Egyptian sun had dried his skin to parchment.

To hide from the sun, he had resorted to burying himself in desert sands. The glass-like splinters had pitted and torn at the fabric of his flesh. *They don't call it sandblasting without good reason.* Malachi smiled in self derision. And his twin, Numu, had fared no better.

He looked closer to his two thousand vampire years than he would like. It was only when he met others of his kind had he realized that if you were fortunate and learned the lessons early, you could stay forever unchanged.

He had felt anger, at first, but the impotence of that had finally made him laugh – or perhaps 'howl at the moon' was more accurate. *I can't change it.* Moving forward was the only option left to him – or end it, and that he would never entertain.

In his undead span, he had witnessed many things – atrocities and breath-taking acts of heroism – and, just when Malachi thought mankind could no longer surprise him, he discovered the existence of the Earth Walkers. Each time he returned to reconnect with them, their generations may have expanded, but essentially, they remained a beacon of incorruptibility.

Drawn to their strength and their faith, in the end, he considered their community his home, and he stayed.

He continued on in what was, for him, a painfully slow procession to the feeding chamber. Human eyes had to be able to *see* him and to drape his 'demonic appearance' in an air of acceptance. *Deity.* Not a mantel he chose, but labels provide the comfort of boundaries. The dryness of the chuckle in his throat reminded him that the 'gifting ceremony' was overdue.

Hundreds of years before *this* day, the Earth Walkers' high priest, Amenomopet, who now lay buried in an opulent chamber within a subterranean temple, had prepared the ground for the tribe's survival when he had foreseen the rise of vampires. Amenomopet had not merely preached about the 'end of the world', no, he had been far more specific. He predicted that 'blood' would outstrip 'gold' in value. He urged humans to be vigilant and guard against the 'eaters'.

Hearing the prophesies, Malachi had sought out Amenomopet. On the peak of a stepped pyramid at Saqqara, the two had sat and exchanged views on philosophy and survival. Malachi, after experiencing sixteen hundred years of Egyptian culture, had taken to traveling the world. While he knew not what form it would take, he, too, sensed an ill wind. *I knew mankind could not insult Mother Earth without suffering her wrath, and I was right.*

When, in faraway parts of the globe, the prophesy came true, Malachi arrived in the Valley of the Kings, seeking out Amenomopet to warn him that the pandemic killing hundreds of thousands of humans across North America marked the rise of the 'eaters'. Malachi hoped to persuade Amenomopet to take his community of priests and priestesses, and establish a settlement in the deserts, where they would not be found.

But, without him realizing it, three hundred years had passed since his last visit. The manifestation of his ghoulish figure terrified Amenomopet's descendants, but, Malachi, jaded and needing to find some worth to his existence, longed to help them.

When the elders of the tribe looked upon a face where the eyes glistened like fish scales and taut skin stretched over the protrusions of his skull, they could not hear Malachi's words. All they heard was the thundering of their panic-stricken hearts.

Only one among them showed more curiosity in the skeletal figure. Imhotep, a direct descendant of Amenomopet, had heard tales of Malachi. The tall warrior held the rank of Lord Protector, and his healing powers were gifts handed down through his blood line – he shared the name 'Imhotep' with a mortal ancestor, once hailed as a God of medicine, magic, and raising the dead. It was merely folklore, but Malachi felt the powerful aura the warrior wore like a cloak, and detected that others feared him. But he was only one voice on the tribe's council; others reacted with fear and closed minds.

Malachi admitted defeat, and returned to the desert where he built underground accommodation similar to the network of tombs near Thebes, before sitting back and waiting until the Earth Walkers needed his help.

In Egypt, as, in time, it would in all the other parts of the world, when the hammer of disease finally dropped, vampires rose to the top.

The vampire hive in Egypt reared up like a serpent, making its nest at the mouth of the Nile, where the logistics of feeding captive humans was simpler.

Human Egyptians were at the mercy of Mother Nature to enable crops to grow.

Vampires had no such difficulties. The vast delta region of the great river was soon protected by a vampire built sea wall. Digging trenches in the seabed was a cinch when you did not have to breathe, and dense vampire flesh withstood the water pressure of a deep ocean trench with ease.

In a matter of weeks, vampires laid claim to the rich farmland of the region, punctuating their sea wall with dams and sluice gates to regulate the irrigation of the fertile soil – the region no longer depended on the annual flooding of the plains.

The day came when a vampire attacked the Earth Walker tribe and the combat skills of the warriors could not even dent his skin.

Even though Malachi thought his location was unknown, Imhotep arrived at his door, as if drawn by the pull of a magnet. "The elders cannot understand a being who moves without a beating heart." The tall warrior dropped to his knees. The silk curtain of his black hair fell forward as he bowed low. "It is time the elders awoke. An enemy is coming."

Malachi knew that, too, but because he scouted the area. How this man – because his heartbeat and the warm nectar shuffling along his veins told Malachi that Imhotep *was* a man – could know of the impending doom, presented an intriguing puzzle.

Without question, Malachi followed his new-found comrade. Traveling at a slow pace for a vampire, he tracked the powerful run of Imhotep, and wondered at a physiology which allowed the warrior to run the dozens of miles without pause.

Malachi arrived at the Earth Walkers' settlement just as a sandstorm transformed the air into unbreathable silt. Imhotep sought refuge inside a mudbrick habitat – one which acted as a gatehouse and shade from the sun. Malachi did not need to tell Imhotep that the sandstorm was driven by a source other than the wind; a vampire was heading in at speed.

The human screams inside the settlement began when the vampire made his move – with the speed of a bolt from a crossbow, he felled his first victim. Malachi tracked the slipstream of the vampire's path, and caught up with him as he threw a corpse aside like an empty container. Malachi killed the vampire, first putting out his eyes with his thumbs and then increasing the pressure until the vampire's skull crumbled. His enemies often underestimated Malachi. They failed to see the young man beneath the desiccated shell.

Malachi accepted the Earth Walkers' gratitude and was elevated to the role of Lord Protector. Imhotep readily handed over the coronet of his office and became the oil on the wheels of communication – the ancient vampire gained the trust of the tribe.

The banks of the Nile were the lifeblood of Egypt, but human settlements were founded in the desert where the floods did not reach. Vampires would be searching, and some would have their own interests in mind, and not that of the hive. Killing humans in this time of shortage was not 'community spirited', but old habits die hard.

When Malachi told them other 'eaters' would come, they believed him, and he led them further into the desert to their new home.

The tribe came to accept, embrace even, Malachi's presence, and the 'gifting ceremony' became part of their culture. *I need to be fed.* It was a fact of life, or rather, of his death. *And now, it is time.*

Living here in a facsimile of his pharaoh's tomb, built by the human tribe he protected, he could suppress his bitterness as he took some satisfaction in watching the Earth Walkers grow old. Though they were magnificent specimens of humanity and, even to Malachi, the ageing process seemed to happen exceptionally slowly – and in Imhotep's case, hardly at all.

Imhotep's vitality earned him the honor of being the Seer of the tribe, and he sat at Malachi's right hand in tribal gatherings.

But this is the gifting ceremony, only the few need to glimpse the monster in their midst.

Emerging from the passageway, Malachi crossed the polished stone floor, mounted the steps up onto a quartz dais, and sat erect on his throne forged in gold.

The chamber walls were inlaid with gold leaf and painted with the pictorial narrative of Egyptian fable. Over the centuries, the depiction of curiously erect awkwardly-posed Egyptian figures, with their faces presented in profile, had changed little.

The two warriors standing like human statues on either side of the doorway remained immobile until Malachi waved a dismissive hand. "Go, now," he said quietly.

Side stepping into the mouth of the tunnel, each one bowed low over their praying hands and walked backwards until they were out of his presence.

Left alone for a moment, this was the time Malachi enjoyed the most. It was like coming home. The flickering candles danced over the statues of ancient Gods – some boasting the strange animal heads of birds, jackal, or beasts – and the glint of gold saturated the room.

Malachi felt weary. He knew them all from his childhood scriptures: Horus, Anubis, Khnum. *But were they Gods, or Demons?*

Malachi's death occurred in a space similar to this one. He had been in a burial chamber with the pharaoh he served when the ballast of sand had shifted, and the dislodged stone slab which hurtled along the channel cut into the tomb wall had sealed him and his brother Numu inside. *We expected to die.* But the vampire living in the tomb decided their deaths would be only the beginning.

He recalled the silent, knowing smile on the face of his maker. It still haunted him. *He left without a word, and we did not even know we were vampires at first.*

Malachi had been alone for a hundred years now, but he had protected his brother for many hundreds of years before that. Numu had a weakness of the mind, and vampirism created a psychotic killer. *I protected him as long as I could. It was inevitable he would go too far.* Malachi carried regrets about the humans who died at Numu's hand, but he also felt pride in the one he had chosen to save. A young doctor in London who proved to be strong, his fighting spirit drawing Malachi in. *If the doctor and Numu's death weren't so closely linked, would I have stayed and made him my eternal apprentice? Perhaps.*

The rising whisper of bare feet brushing over the sloping tunnel floor ignited a glow of excitement inside Malachi. His wistful thoughts dissolved, he smoothed the white fabric of his costume over his thin legs, rested his forearms along the solid gold arms of the throne, and prepared for the ceremony to begin.

The air this far underground was hot and stagnant, although Malachi only registered that fact when the procession of priests filed into the room, sweat beading on their brows. Six attendants followed them into the chamber and ranged themselves at intervals around the walls; the muscles in their reed-like arms strained as they moved huge gilt-edged silk palm leaf fans, stirring a gentle current in the warm air.

The white linen skirts the four priests wore as modesty flaps, which brushed their thighs, accentuated their narrow hips. The caramel-colored skin of their bare chests glistened with the residue of the aromatic lotion which preserved the succulence of the flesh Malachi envied so much.

Each member of the Earth Walker tribe of warriors were *also* priests, and Osiris, their Wenuty priest, was the keeper of the sundial chamber – he was the hour-watcher. He made certain the temple rituals were performed on time during each day and night throughout the year.

Osiris entered the chamber last and took center stage.

The serene expression on his youthful face suggested gentleness completely at odds with the finely-honed musculature of his body. The edifice of his abdomen tensed as he moved, and his biceps rippled beneath gold serpents which wound around each of his sinewed arms. Even the strongest of men would reconsider challenging Osiris in combat.

Malachi knew where Osiris was in the room, even when he moved out of sight.

Osiris' bare feet moved soundlessly as he drifted across the polished floor until he reached a marble shelf embedded within an alcove. He lifted a jewel-encrusted hour glass, slowly rotated the sand-filled bowl to the top, replaced the time piece on the shelf, and bowed reverently to the scorpion statuette forged in gold which shared the polished marble shrine.

"I call on the deity of blood, the deity of death, the keeper of hearts," said Osiris solemnly. "Take our blood in your hand, take our lives in your palm, and bring us peace."

Osiris' words echoed from the walls, and as they faded, a priestess walked with balletic grace into the chamber. She was a vision of white silk, simply adorned by a single strand of rubies suspended from a gold necklace; they ran down over her bodice like a river of blood-red droplets.

In her wake, a tall man matched her steps. As the pair reached the foot of the dais, the girl paused, and the man took his place at her side. A priest stepped forward, placing a bowl fashioned from beaten gold into her hands, before melting into the background once more.

Malachi extended his hand, beckoning with a hypnotic rhythm. "Come, Aapep."

The man ascended the glacier-smooth steps and knelt at Malachi's feet, his arms slack at his side and his head bowed. The girl knelt beside him, holding the gold bowl out in front of her.

Leaning forward in his throne, Malachi closed a bony grip around Aapep's wrist and drew his arm forward. With his other hand, he found the pulse beating hard in the crook of the man's elbow, and, with a stabbing motion, the blade of Malachi's thumbnail sliced into the vein.

Aapep hissed involuntarily. His blood splattered into the bowl, gushing at an alarming rate.

Malachi's preternatural sight captured the entrancing display of diamond and ruby blood cells swirling within the plasma cocktail, and his eyes darkened to the silvered glow of mercury. The red-berry scent filled his sinuses. His lips compressed to hold back venom-tainted saliva. Settling back in his throne, pressing his bony spine into the hard metal, Malachi savored the hunger tearing through his body.

The priests and the handmaiden began to chant. "Eternal sleep came to us through vanity, the second time through falsehood, the third time through greed, the fourth time through conflict. We offer this blood, beloved master, so you shall live, and vanity, falsehood, greed and conflict cannot harm thee."

As the last words died away, Malachi leaned forward and ran his tongue over the deep cut in Aapep's arm. His venom stemmed the flow, the last drops of blood becoming a row of red dewdrops over the wound.

The chanting voices rang out again as Malachi accepted the bowl and, in a long draft, he swallowed down Aapep's offering.

Setting the empty vessel on his knee, he waited, as motionless as a statue carved in white marble. His peaceful expression belied the battle raging inside. Each heart beating in each human chest was a siren call he resisted. Locking his muscles down and summoning years of experience, he suffered to let them live.

He could hear the sand trickling through into the bottom of the hour glass, and tuned into the calm aura of Osiris. *The young warrior fills them with peace,* thought Malachi with a smile.

As the last grains slipped through the glass, Osiris spoke.

But Malachi did not hear the words. Suddenly every muscle in his body jolted and his attention was sucked into a black hole of awareness. Thoughts that were not his own punched a hole through the red curtain in his brain and he saw a woman. *No, almost a woman, it's a girl.* Her face was snow-white, her hair glistened with the sheen of darkest obsidian, and her eyes were an arctic ice gray.

It was a female, and yet one name swelled to fill his mind. *Connor.*

As the girl's face tightened with defiant fear, he saw through her eyes, and his gut churned. He looked in on a room where vampires, wearing leather tunics decorated with metal studs, circled around her. The scenery whipped by in a blur of colors and then snapped back into sharp focus. *It is Connor.* He could see him now. He stared into a shattered face with flesh the translucent blue-veined texture of a jellyfish. Malachi's last view was of the vampire's decapitated head rolling over a greasy metal floor.

The exhilaration of the fight he witnessed made Malachi's fingers twitch. They curled into fists as he unraveled the threads of his visions. *This girl and Connor, they have a psychic connection. He has turned a mate?* Riding the zip-wire of the connection back across to the girl's mind, he realized her heart was beating. *Not a mate then. Impossible.*

The gold bowl slipped from his senseless fingers and bounced on the hard floor. The strident note rang out around the room, vibrating through the air like the hum of a tuning fork. Malachi snapped back to awareness as the priestess stooped to gather the bowl, her red rubies falling forward like a river of blood cascading from her throat.

Osiris appeared at Malachi's side, the spent hour glass still in his hand.

"Master?" he said. Concern creased the young Egyptian's brow, and Malachi knew that Osiris had seen the vision too.

"Who is she?"

Malachi reached out and laid a hand on the head of the tall man still kneeling before him. "Your blood is your savior, and I bring you peace, Aapep," said Malachi, uttering the words which brought the ceremony to a close. He stared straight ahead as the four priests, the priestess, and the tall man retreated slowly.

Osiris did not move until they were alone. "Master, you had a vision." He knelt in front of Malachi.

"Yes."

"What did it mean? Who is the girl?"

"I do not know."

Malachi studied Osiris' keen expression. His Egyptian bloodline showed clearly in his dark coloring and eyes that were almost black. Malachi could not remember how old the young man was, but, in any case, being an Earth Walker changed the meaning of passing years.

Meditation, stillness of mind and body, had long ago become part of the daily ritual, reducing their metabolism and making food supplies stretch further. *And lengthening the lifespan of those in the tribe.* The scented lotion blended with the sap of plants harvested on the banks of the Nile shielded their skin from the sun. Malachi wondered at the properties of the cocktail of plant extracts which they drank daily as part of their detox diet. He knew other tribes thought they had found an elixir of youth. *But the truth is more visceral, and can be traced back to Imhotep. To die before the age of one hundred and twenty years was rare for an Earth Walker.*

The Earth Walker warriors hunted in the cool evenings, when the Egyptian sand dunes resembled piles of coal-dust in the gloom. They took the easy ten-mile run to the lush green acres of the flood plain through which the Nile meandered.

The warriors brought their prey back alive, hogtied and draped over their shoulders, and then killed the animals in a purification ceremony. Linen sacks carried by other Earth Walkers contained the succulent alfalfa shoots and plant tubers they dug out from the soft black earth of the delta. They caught fish and transported their catch back in baskets woven from tall reeds.

They had survival down to a fine art.

Malachi played his part. The Nile vampires stored food to feed their human herd on the hive farm, in warehouses, but never guarded. After all, who would steal it? Malachi would, and did. He contributed sacks of rice, grain, and dried beans to the Earth Walker diet.

Malachi gazed around the walls of the ceremonial chamber and wondered, when these frescos of Egyptian legends faded, what would replace them? *Blood and death?* Osiris, the image of his father, had become a warrior who could have stepped from the vibrant gilt-edged vista painted on the walls. Excitement stirred in the pit of Malachi's stomach.

"I do not know the girl. But the vampire, Connor, I am his maker." Malachi said quietly, "Something is happening to him. Just as I could share his visions and show him my own, this girl can do that too."

"So, she must be a dream giver? She can project images?"

Malachi nodded. "But I'm not sure how. She is not a vampire, but her connection to Connor is strong."

"What should we do, Master?"

Malachi smiled. Osiris always spoke as though he and Malachi were one. *After all, I was there at his birth.* They had shared many adventures. If Malachi was the perfect companion when vampires attacked, Osiris repaid the act by providing Malachi with blood. *Yes, together we are as one.*

"It is ninety years since I have been to England and seen Connor. Perhaps it is time I found out how much my protégé has learned." *Something to breathe new life into my existence. What is he doing, I wonder?*

Malachi retraced his steps along the polished stone corridors. His face showed nothing of his intrigue as he dissected the visions and looked for their meaning. His journey ended in a chamber holding his own tomb. Like that of Tutankhamen, his sarcophagus was a parody of a Russian doll. The huge stone shell, intricately sculpted with his likeness and decorated in the soft twenty-four carat gold-leaf as befitting a pharaoh's resting place, held another within. Inside the second coffin, once the lid was slid away, the illusion of tradition shattered. Malachi rested inside a toughened steel box with a hasp and lock on each side.

As the Wenuty priest, and Malachi's familiar, Osiris was in tune with Malachi's sleep patterns. When the murderous rage of grave sleep rattled inside the vampire's head, Osiris locked Malachi's body inside the three layers of confinement. As the final touch, the young Egyptian rolled a large boulder across the entrance, blocking the doorway.

In grave sleep, Malachi would clamp his muscles down and let the raging fire of voracious thirst burn through him. *If vampire dementia strikes, and my mind goes the way of my brother, then Osiris will dislodge the coping stone protruding from the ceiling and, like an hour glass, this chamber will fill with sand.*

Even that would not contain Malachi, but it would give the Earth Walkers a chance to make their escape.

Osiris' solid shoulders filled the doorway as his jet-black gaze tracked his mentor's movements – his muscles braced and at the ready.

Malachi removed his ceremonial costume and pulled on the drab gray garb of vampire camouflage. He scraped fine, spun-silver strands of hair back from his face, and his thin brows drew together in a frown as another vision flashed into his head. He muttered, "Connor's pale companions are tanker nomads. What on earth is he doing? Leaving England then, and headed to Europe, but why?"

When the old vampire rushed towards the doorway, Osiris swung back and cleared his path, and, within seconds, took his place at Malachi's shoulder.

The pair whipped along the tunnels.

As if he could read Malachi's mind, Osiris asked, "When do we leave?"

"Now. I think we should leave now. Let us find your father."

The ironic consequence of vampires coming out of hiding was that attacks on the community were a thing of the past. Ferals – vampires who had allowed starvation to drive them into dementia – were a minor threat. They were hive outcasts and unpredictable, but they were solitary creatures. *My leaving for a while is not such a cause for concern, now.* Malachi wondered what he would have done if he had had to choose between Connor and Imhotep.

The delicate scent of beeswax ointment grew stronger when Malachi and Osiris entered a chamber with a wide arcing ceiling. Earth Walker ancestors were duplicated around the domed space – battles won and lost were etched into the grim vista of illustrated conflict – and sitting on his throne at the epi-center of it all, was Imhotep.

His black eyes snapped open. "Greetings, Lord Protector, you seem agitated."

"Greetings, Great One."

Imhotep shifted in his seat, studied both his subjects avidly, and then relaxed. "Your news is not of immediate danger, or a threat to the tribe. What troubles you?"

"Straight to the point, as always, Imhotep," Malachi said.

"Time is not something to waste, my friend, we both understand that."

Malachi nodded, taking three steps to enter the circle of light the dancing candle flames threw across the gilt adorned floor.

"I have seen-" Malachi's aged skin crumpled as he searched for the words. "I don't know what I'm seeing, but an undead of my making needs me. That I do know."

Imhotep nodded slowly, his brows climbing in questioning surprise. "I have known you a very long time, and this is a first."

Malachi shook his head as though shooing away a swarm of flies. "That is why I must go."

Osiris coughed from where he stood with his arms folded across his chest and impatience written on his face.

Darting a glance at his son, Imhotep muttered, "How would he have fared, Malachi, in the enforced confinement of the pyramid, waiting for the sword of Damocles to drop."

"Thankfully, he has not had to fight for his survival, as we have, old friend, not yet."

"He has time to learn."

"Great One-" Osiris' shuffled his feet, lost for words, his leather sandals scuffing over the gleaming floor.

Imhotep held up his hand, silencing the youngster and seemingly sucking all the energy from Osiris' body.

Looking at Malachi, Imhotep mused, "Which of us two will have the longer lifespan? I'll always be thankful you saved Osiris, thus I give his life to you, but, old friend, the years have been unkind to your physical being." Imhotep straightened shoulders that expanded his chest into a wall of muscle. "I may yet outlive you." His amusement reverberated from the chamber walls.

Malachi's tight skin creaked as he joined in the laughter. "Indeed, who can say which of us will prevail. Your gift is unique – unknown. Akin to a gift from the Gods; I hope we shall have untold decades to debate." His expression stilled as though distracted by a distant sound.

Imhotep laid a hand on Malachi's thin shoulder. "Go. I can see the visions are clouding your sight. This protégé of yours is buried deep inside you to have a pull so strong. Osiris will be honored to serve you. You are his father, also. I gave him form, but you breathed life into him. Go."

"Thank you for your blessing, father," Osiris said quietly, his face still and serene.

Imhotep's dark eyes gleamed as he nodded slowly. "Blessings be upon you, Osiris, although we both know you command healing powers far superior to even mine. Go, and be well."

Leaning back into his gold encrusted throne, the tension left Imhotep's body and his hooded gaze exuded relaxation.

Imhotep, despite the knots of metal and crystal shards digging into his back and thighs, achieved a state of meditation within seconds. His slack hands released their grip on the throne and rolled slowly over – pale pockmarks which dappled Imhotep's forearms glowed in the dim light.

The sites in various stages of healing revealed where his lifeblood was literally tapped into and shared by his warriors. Like the witch-doctor of early Briton tribes who ate a measured dose of Deadly Nightshade, and then the tribesmen drank his urine and experienced shared hallucinations – Earth Walkers shared Imhotep's life-giving blood. It was why the Earth Walkers enjoyed long lifespans. *Blessed be the Gods.* Malachi wondered if maybe, he too was enhanced by Imhotep's offering – he drank from the warrior tribe, completing the cycle. *My visions of Connor are certainly sharper than in the past.*

As though leaving a sleeping child, Malachi and Osiris backed silently from the chamber.

"How old is he?" asked Osiris, as he flanked Malachi, skimming away along the slick stone corridor.

Malachi glanced at the young priest, and it pulled back into focus the unknown hazards which they faced. It was no small thing that Imhotep gave his son into Malachi's care.

"Your father? Years mean nothing when the body can regenerate. His journey to the suspended state was merely different to yours." Malachi's smile revealed yellow pegs embedded in pale gray gums. "You know 'time' means nothing. As the Wenuty priest, you know how it stretches and folds in the mind."

Malachi suddenly jerked into a spasm which threw him sideways. In an instant, Osiris steadied him, his hand cushioning the old vampire's collision with the polished quartz wall.

"Another vision?" Osiris asked.

"Yes. It is as well our journey begins now."

"I shall gather what we need and meet you on the surface." Osiris was already disappearing as he spoke.

Malachi barely acknowledged the young priest's departure as he focused on traveling the tunnels, ascending the final ramp, and emerging into the cold desert night.

The temperature outside had plummeted, and the glow of the moon transformed the sand into a stormy sea of glittering crystals.

Osiris arrived barely ten minutes after the restless Malachi.

Dropping down onto his haunches, Osiris sorted through the camel hide sack he carried, and pulled out an earthenware jar. He rose to his feet, and, ignoring Malachi's scowl, he smothered every inch of Malachi's exposed skin with the thick black mud of the Nile delta.

Malachi complied, knowing the desert sunrise came quickly. Both travelers pulled on capes made from a patchwork of boar skins. The tanned hides shimmered with the linseed oil used to fill in the puncture holes made by the needle and blocked out every ray of sun.

Replacing the jar of mud, Osiris hitched a sack containing a parcel of dried crackers and leather water canteens up onto his back, and said, "Master, we are ready."

Osiris rode camels, horses, elephants, and, when the occasion called for it, vampires.

"Finding a way to get you across the Mediterranean will take time we don't have. We'll head east and cross into Asia at the Sinai Peninsula. We should make it to the west border of Turkey by morning, if we set off now."

With Osiris' strong grip anchored to his shoulders, Malachi accelerated into a run. In seconds, he reached cruising speed, his feet barely skimming the undulating sand. Osiris rode the buffeting wind like a para-glider rides the thermal currents in the sky.

Chapter 13

The walls of the cabin drifted in and out of focus as Rebekah fought sleep. Shifting position on the thin mattress of the bunk and sitting up straighter, she tried to clear her head. *How many miles have we sailed? How many hours?* Her frustration faded to resignation as she lost the battle to stay alert. Each time she pulled her eyelids open, she wondered how much time she had lost. Her stomach complained. Hunger, sickness and fear swirled inside it. A dull pain rode another spasm, and Rebekah couldn't make out which sensation had the upper hand.

The porthole of their prison looked out over a sea of undulating oil-black satin. The commander had agreed to light the lantern hanging from the beam overhead, so Rebekah could, at least, see some of her sparse surroundings. The lantern swung violently when the wind picked up and tore the black satin of the sea into ragged strips. Rebekah decided seeing did not help.

The crashing impact of the waves shuddering through the ship's timbers was so much worse than anything Rebekah had previously experienced. The vessel reared and the floor shifted beneath her feet. Her stomach lodged in her throat, and, when the weightless free-falling sensation hit rock bottom, Rebekah groaned. *I definitely don't like boats.*

Seren, as a mark of solidarity, sat beside her on the narrow bunk, allowing Rebekah to grip her firm white fingers. Lars had been true to his word. Rebekah had not been handcuffed when they arrived back in the cabin, but walking across the rolling floor was beyond her, so making a run for it was the last thing on her mind.

She gave up on scolding herself for being spineless. She could almost hear Connor's voice saying, "Swimming in the North Sea is suicide. Bide your time, Rebekah, stay safe and I will find you." The seasickness eased when she closed her eyes and drifted into a world where his intense white face and the melted mercury of his avid gaze made her feel safe. Warm relaxation settled in her bones and Connor beckoned to her as he receded into black shadow.

But she jerked awake with a yelp, as though the bed springs delivered an electric shock, when the ship pitched violently. A falling sensation tumbled through her insides, and the comfort of Connor was ripped away.

"It's okay, Mama," Seren said quietly. "The wind's dropping. I think the rough weather is passing."

Shuffling her waking thoughts back into order, Rebekah sighed. "Hey, I think I'm winning the biggest baby competition."

Seren laughed. "I guess vampires don't get seasick."

Another reason to become one. But Rebekah kept that thought to herself. Seren accepted that she was the perfect blend of her human mama and vampire papa. But for Rebekah, the joy of seeing her daughter grow into a beautiful young woman was tainted by envy. Both Connor and Seren, if Connor was right, would live on for centuries without her. *I'll persuade him to turn me, or die trying.*

Rebekah laughed at her own joke, and Seren cast a concerned look her way.

"Don't worry, sweetheart, I'm not becoming hysterical. We have enough to worry about, without that." The smile melted from Rebekah's face as she said quietly, "Is there any news on Papa and the others?"

Seren shook her head. "Papa and Greg are together, but Papa can't see Julian and Seth."

As her voice tailed off, Rebekah said, "Is Papa in trouble? You can tell me."

In an awed voice, Seren said, "I think Papa had to fight. The room kept moving, and he hit another vampire." She bit her lip.

"But, he's okay?" Rebekah asked, the careless tone spoiled by the white knuckled grip she had on her own knee.

"He's waiting for something, I think."

"A little like us, then. Waiting to see what happens next." The helplessness of that drained her.

As the sea calmed to a gentle rocking motion, Rebekah admitted defeat. She pulled the animal hide blanket up over her shoulders and rested against the hard wall. Even the wooden panel pressing against the back of her rocking head could not disturb her. She fell asleep.

A cold hand on her cheek woke her. Every muscle jumped as she heard Seren say, "Mama, someone is coming."

Opening her eyes, she stared at the varnished wood of the cabin ceiling, and realized she was lying down. She frowned. "How long did I sleep?" Fighting her way from underneath the heavy goatskin blanket, she freed her legs and sat up. A misty funnel of light cut a path across the room, ending in a pale gray patch on the floor. "Is it dawn?"

"Almost, yes. You slept about three hours." Seren repeated, "Someone is coming."

Rebekah focused on the cabin door, struggling to see in the dreary glow of dawn. The lantern chain creaked as it swung. Irritation knotted her insides as her human ears could hear nothing else. She looked at Seren for help.

"There are three of them."

Cold sweat trickled down Rebekah's spine. Breathing made her chest hurt. "Three?" Laughing harshly, she said, "Any chance you can tell what they are thinking?"

"I know one is the commander, does that help?"

Distracted for a moment, Rebekah said, "How?"

Seren grinned. "When he touched my arm, he left his scent. And his stride is, well, determined."

"Ah, the power of deduction." It was like discovering the 'trade secret' behind a magic trick. *Not psychic powers then.* Before the humor dancing in Rebekah's eyes found expression, the door whipped open, and she jumped.

"You scared me," she blurted. "Don't you people ever knock?"

Lars stopped just inside the room, and, as Seren had correctly said, two guards stood beside him, one at each broad shoulder. "We are at our journey's end," he said slowly, dangling a set of handcuffs from his fingertips. "I don't want you to get any ideas about jumping ship, so-" Lars extended his hand and waited.

Rebekah walked over and took the metal bracelets. As her fingertips skimmed his palm, she wondered which was colder, his skin or the metal. Staring defiantly into his face, she closed one cuff over her wrist and then turned away. Ignoring his gaze burning into her shoulder blades, she retraced her steps, sat down on the bunk, and snapped the other cuff closed around the pipe. "Satisfied?" she said quietly.

"Godt," he said, and the door closed behind them.

"At least we're getting off this ship. We'll have a better chance of escape on dry land," Rebekah said calmly. "I must try being nicer to him. Perhaps he'll drop his guard if he thinks we have accepted our fate." She looked at Seren. "Don't believe everything I say, okay?"

"Sure."

While they waited, Rebekah eased the pull of the handcuff chain by holding onto the warm pipe. The muscles across her shoulders burned.

Seren stood motionless, looking out of the porthole, her head tilted as she listened to the sounds vibrating through the deck overhead. The splashing of oars stopped, and the ship glided through waters which glittered with a sprinkling of diamonds in the pearl-tinted dawn.

The hull groaned noisily, and Rebekah guessed they had weighed anchor.

Without warning, a vampire guard appeared, swathed in a leather cloak which rippled like silk. Rebekah quashed the swell of disappointment that the tall blond figure of Lars was not with him. She wanted to know where they were going, but the closed face of the guard peering from beneath his hood killed all hopes of picking his brains. *Being charming to the help will get me nowhere.*

Released from the handcuffs, Rebekah and Seren were escorted up on deck. The ship appeared to be deserted when they emerged into the early dawn, climbed down a rope ladder and into a small rowing boat. The vampire made short work of setting off for the shore.

A deep belt of sand bridged the gap between the gently lapping waters and a flat landscape of endless green pastures. In the distance, the pre-dawn light picked out a halo of pale green on the horizon which Rebekah took to be a line of trees. It might as well be Mars as far as Rebekah was concerned. After all, she had lived beneath the ground in Kent since she was six years old. Her experiences were limited to foraging in the deserted city streets of London. Uncle Harry's library had little by way of books covering world geography.

She sighed heavily. *What were you expecting? A sign saying welcome to dot-dot-dot, only x-number of miles from the coast of England. Idiot!*

As the rowboat swept in an arc, changing direction, Rebekah gasped and her face drained of color. She froze, looking the closest to a vampire that she ever could and still feel her heart thumping in her ears.

"Mama, breathe," whispered Seren.

The vampire in the boat hissed, his nostrils flaring as Rebekah's accelerating heart-rate threatened to break her ribs, and, without warning, he slipped over the side of the boat and disappeared beneath the water. The boat lurched left and right, almost throwing her from her seat.

Rebekah dragged her gaze from the sight of the castle perched on the water's edge, where a skirt of sharp tumbled-rocks held back the unrelenting assault of the sea. Tall, vertical slits of dozens of black soulless windows interrupted the expanse of biscuit-colored walls, the peak of each arched frame as sharp as an arrow-head. The dull slate gray roofs of the sloping turrets added to the bleak impression, and the battlements crowned the walls with blunt fang-like points which threatened to devour the dark clouds drifting overhead.

Everything about the castle looked ferocious, and filled her with dread. *Connor will never find a way inside that.*

"Mama," Seren called.

Rebekah turned her attention back and scanned the length of the boat, confused. "Where'd he go?"

"I think your panic attack made him hungry."

Knowing their guard had abandoned the boat rather than risk hurting her made Rebekah feel better. The importance of her life, her keeping it anyway, had obviously been drummed into the guards by their commander.

It took another half second for Rebekah to shift quickly onto the empty plank seat opposite and grab an oar. "Quick," she hissed. "Seren, row."

Seren moved to sit beside her, picked up the other oar, and they began to row.

"Easy does it," croaked Rebekah, her words stuck in her throat as sweat broke out over her skin.

As the castle began to retreat into the distance, a ray of hope stabbed through the black cloud clinging to Rebekah's heart. *Easy does it, easy does it.* The words accompanied each stroke of the oars, focusing her mind.

"Mama," said Seren, resignation heavy in her tone.

"Keep rowing," said Rebekah, even though she too could see the wave racing along the surface of the water – the eddying current going against the tide and carving a trough which defied the laws of nature.

Because it's not a force of nature. Tears blurred Rebekah's vision and she swiped at them with one hand, transfixed as the spearhead of turbulent white foam gained on them.

She knew it was coming and still she screamed when a white hand appeared on the stern of the boat. The vessel stopped as though it hit a brick wall, and her body jerked backwards.

The water had darkened his blond hair to burned toffee, but, as he surged out of the surf and climbed effortlessly aboard, Rebekah knew it was him. In case she was in doubt, the sea water pouring down his face flowed over the gold breastplate and dripped from the leather strap hanging from his belt. *Lars.*

Her cramped features hid a grim smile. Her nerves clattered.

The dark clouds overhead bruised the sky and cast shadows across his still features. Reading the mood of a bronze statue would have been easier. At least an artist might give their creation some emotion.

Rebekah steeled herself for his anger, clenching her hands into fists.

"Give efter, min skat," he said, his jaw muscle twitching as he shook his head. "Ja?"

Rebekah frowned. *Not angry then. Just irritated.*

Putting out his hand and bracing his feet to steady the boat, Lars pulled Rebekah to her feet. "Give up, my dear, yes?"

In a fluid movement which grazed his breastplate over her body, Lars switched places, and Rebekah took her seat back in the stern beside Seren. He took charge of the oars and rowed with forceful strokes back to shore, covering the distance in minutes. Stepping out into the surf, he dragged the boat a dozen yards up the white sand. Holding out his hand, he said, "Komme."

This time, Rebekah needed no translation. Her shoulders sagged and she did what he wanted. Taking his hand, she climbed out and stood on the beach, stubbornly silent. The wind snatched at her shirt and tossed her hair into a tangled mass. She welcomed the biting cold and the numbness it laid over her skin.

Without taking his grim gaze from her face, Lars whistled, and, at his signal, a vampire led two horses down onto the sand. Mounting the black stallion, Lars leaned over, both his hands reaching for Rebekah. To step away had barely crossed her mind when her feet left the ground and she found herself seated, as before, with his metal armor pressing into her back.

Seren co-operated, climbing up onto the other horse.

Rebekah kept her body rigid, but even in the midst of her hardened emotions she was mesmerized when the galloping stride of their mount transformed the lush grass of the meadow into a glacier of cool green.

They raced towards the castle, passing beneath a high stone arch before taking the final approach up to the imposing gates. The horses rode two abreast along the causeway over a chasm, where the vertical drop either side ended in a trench lined with flint-like shards of rock.

Rebekah realized that filling the moat with water would not deter vampires. *Perhaps, the glass-like pieces are designed to make noise, but they'll be lethal to humans, if they fall.* The chances of

Connor, Julian, Greg and Seth entering the fortress unheard and unseen seemed to become smaller with every feature she noticed.

The horses slowed to a skittering halt. Colossal wooden doors, embedded with black studs, blocked their progress.

Lars called out, "Sentinel Lars, kommer." The commander's presence was like a physical force which moved the gates swiftly aside.

And Rebekah felt it too. He held her close to his chest and his exhilaration hummed through her body like a charge of static.

The horses' hooves clattered over a courtyard of cobblestones, and the saddle beneath her rocked alarmingly until the animal came to a stop. Rebekah slipped gratefully from Lars' grasp, her knees feeling unsteady for a moment, even though she was on firm ground.

"Are you going to obey?" Lars asked lightly. He dismounted and released his horse, but appeared more interested in watching it amble towards the stables. Finally looking back at Rebekah's closed features, Lars added quietly, "Pity."

Turning away, Rebekah expected the interior landscape to be austere and forbidding, but a flash of deep green caught her eye and her jaw dropped open. Beyond a set of carved marble pillars lay an immaculate lawn bordered by trimmed hedges. Even in the half-light of approaching dawn, adorned in a dramatic display of autumn color, the gardens were breath taking.

"Beautiful, nej?"

Irritated at being caught gawping, Rebekah snapped her mouth shut and took Seren's hand. "Where are we going?"

Lars laughed dryly and with a jerk of his fist, he summoned four vampires dressed in the now familiar metal studded leather vests. They were no more than half a second from cover if the sun broke through the determined bank of cloud, so they no longer wore their flowing leather cloaks and hoods. With their faces uncovered, Rebekah recognized the blank stare of the vampire who had abandoned them in the boat, and she wondered if vampires bore grudges.

Dwelling on that unnerving thought, Rebekah gripped Seren's hand tighter and followed the guardsmen into the castle keep. At the defiant lift of Rebekah's chin, Lars' laughter filled the air.

They descended a spiral stairwell into near darkness, and the air grew more stagnant with every tread. Running her fingers over the roughly hewn walls, Rebekah waited for her eyes to adjust, but soon realized the blend of soot and ghost gray was as good as it would get. She felt the weight of incarceration slotting into place. *Now we are* inside *the castle, what dangers will Connor have to face?*

Their footsteps echoed on a stone floor and the temperature plummeted as they walked the length of a dark corridor. Their escort stopped outside a black door reinforced with metal crossbars. The lead vampire used an iron key in the lock, pushed the door open, and stepped back.

Crossing the threshold, Rebekah felt relieved to see the flicker of candles. *At least we have light.* From the sweeping curve of the opposite wall, she realized the prison cell was in one of the castle's turrets. She crossed to look out of the rectangular aperture cut into the bricks, set with vertical iron bars, but no glass. The crisp breeze lifting her hair chilled the sweat on her skin as she gazed out over the water, barely noticing the vista of sapphire and diamond studded silk. The candles guttered at a sudden gust coming in off the sea, and she shivered, rubbing her arms. Inspecting the makeshift animal hide window-cover hitched back over a rusted hook buried in the wall, Rebekah flipped the hem with a disparaging finger. Without looking round, she said, "We'll freeze to death in here."

A stilted vampire voice replied, "There are a stack of heated rocks in the hearth, and warm clothes and blankets."

"Very thoughtful," said Rebekah.

The clanking sound of metal dragging across the floor cramped her stomach. "He wouldn't," she blurted, turning around quickly.

But, he would. A large toughened steel ring protruded from a flagstone in the middle of the floor, and a vampire knelt beside it separating out two thick lengths of chain. Ignoring her protest, he opened the metal cuffs welded to the end of each one. The closed door made escape impossible. *Not to mention a matter of vampire versus human.* Rebekah took refuge in silent contempt as a guard fitted the shackle around her ankle and secured it with a padlock.

After repeating the process with Seren, the vampires left the room.

Rebekah took stock of their new home. The row of candles ranged along the length of a deep stone shelf and the lumps of masonry missing from the wall above it suggested there had once been a shrine which included a plaque or statue. *Did praying help them, I wonder? I doubt it.*

The wooden table in the room was bolted to the floor, likewise the bed frame. A pair of stout carved wood armchairs faced the fireplace, and they looked comfortable, at least, with deep cushions tied onto the seats and backrests.

As the vampire had said, heat radiated from the hearth, but not from a fire. Curious, picking up the chain to prevent it dragging on her ankle, Rebekah went to investigate.

"The granite stones must have been warmed in the sun," said Seren, placing her hand on a hot stone.

Rebekah pointed out some carbon-streaked blocks. "And those were warmed in a fire and moved here afterwards. They're like storage heaters. Clever."

Lighting another four candles, using the ones already burning, chased away most of the shadows to the corners. Rebekah had never been afraid of the dark, but inspecting their prison for weak spots such as loose mortar, or a piece of sharp stone which could be used as a tool, would be easier if she could see.

An hour later, Rebekah sat on a padded wooden chair feeling hot and exhausted. She clutched a sliver of flint-like stone and a long metal nail which Seren had managed to prize out of the solid wooden door.

"Perhaps we can work the door hinges loose," Rebekah said, and she began to wish she had not sat down. It suddenly became impossible to decide which was harder to bear, the hunger or tiredness. She reached out and dragged a parcel of folded fabric across the table. Opening it, she inspected the contents. "Bread *and* cheese," she muttered. "Count of Monte Cristo, eat your heart out." She picked up the chunk of cheese and bit into it.

Seren dropped down into the chair opposite and said heavily, "Sentinel Lars is coming."

"Really?" Rebekah quickly put the cheese back, got to her feet, and tucked the stone and nail under the cushion of her chair. 'Be nice', she told herself.

A key ground in the rusted lock and the door opened.

Rebekah stayed standing, turned to face the door, and made the most of her five-feet and six-inches in height. Pushing back her sweat-soaked blonde hair, she wiped all expression from her face.

Lars entered the room, paused inside the doorway, and stared at her with calm arrogance.

A sick feeling welled in her stomach. *Why is he here?*

He stepped aside and a surreal parade unfolded. Two vampires, each carrying a bucket of steaming hot water, strode into the dungeon. They marched across the floor to where a hanging tapestry covered the wall.

Rebekah's attention was torn between Lars and his henchmen. Shifting position, she kept them all in her sights.

The first vampire held back the heavy curtain. The other entered the crudely hewn alcove behind and set the buckets down on a gnarled bench of aged gray wood.

Rebekah's dirt encrusted skin cried out for the refreshment of the water, but she merely stared at Lars, raising a sardonic brow as the vampires retraced their steps. "Is that all?"

"Not at all," he replied, taking a further step into the dingy room.

Doctor Heinrik appeared at the sentinel's side, holding a menacing looking black leather case.

"What does he want?" whispered Rebekah.

Seren sidled over and reached for her mother's hand. "What do they want, Mama?"

"Whatever it is, they can think again." Lifting her chin, Rebekah glared at Lars.

"Doctor Heinrik is here to make a preliminary examination of the girl. He will record her vital signs and take blood." Lars' eyes moved to Seren. "We just want to understand how you tick."

Seren glanced at the doctor, his pointed features intent, and said, "I don't want to."

There was no mistaking the zealous gleam in the doctor's eye. Rebekah knew they had no choice, but she tried anyway. "You heard her. Please leave, Sentinel Lars."

He laughed. "Enough, min skat. The easy way, you stay, and the child cooperates. The hard way, you go, and my guardsmen return to help the doctor. I know which I would choose, nej?"

Rebekah looked at Seren, begging her to understand. "I don't think we have a choice, sweetheart. I'm sorry. They won't hurt you, there is too much at stake. We just have to stay safe." *And Connor will come.*

The tightness in her chest eased as her daughter's dark eyes stirred with comprehension. Rebekah looked at Lars. "I stay."

He nodded abruptly. "Godt."

Seren sat quietly in a chair. Rebekah stood at her side, and they both watched every move the doctor made. He opened his case on the table and began his tests. He took Seren's blood pressure and recorded her temperature, as well as taking swabs from inside her mouth. Taking blood was a comedy of errors, but at least the doctor had thought things through.

He began with the finest thirty-two-gauge needle, and, when it buckled as he tried to insert it, he moved up through the graduations of thickness. Applying force which made Rebekah cringe, Doctor Heinrik finally managed to find one that penetrated Seren's skin.

The examination progressed in an eerie silence Rebekah found chilling. *He'd be better off working as a mortuary attendant.* The doctor's inspection came to an end, and she pretended to ignore the sentinel as he walked away, following the meandering length of her chain from the shackle around her ankle to the anchor point in the floor, seeming to peer at each metal link.

With the width of the room between them, Lars turned and adopted a casual stance.

Apprehension pricking at the hairs on her nape, Rebekah gripped Seren's hand, offering comfort and taking strength from her daughter's calm features.

As the doctor packed away the five vials he had filled with Seren's blood into foam lined slots inside his bag, Rebekah said with a smile, "It's over, sweetheart."

Doctor Heinrik snapped his case shut and stepped back, nodding at the sentinel.

Lars swooped in and yanked Seren to her feet. His hand darted out to save her when she stumbled. "She is strong, for a human, but not so much for a vampire, I think," said Lars thoughtfully as he released her and joined the doctor.

As the door closed behind them, the pieces slotted into place. "Ah, he was testing your strength, to see if you can escape from your chains."

Seren smiled. "I know."

"So, you faked it? Clever girl," said Rebekah. The embrace she folded around Seren fell away as the door opened again.

"Dinner will be in one hour." Lars inclined his head. "You will join me."

When the door closed, a stunned Rebekah stared at Seren.

"I hope the doctor is not there," muttered Seren. "When he touched me, his fingers were vibrating as if he was nervous. No, not nervous, exhilarated. Mama, he and Lars, I think they mean to separate us."

"Don't worry, sweetheart," Rebekah said firmly. "I won't let that happen. We just need to keep them guessing, distracted, until Papa gets here, hmm?"

"Perhaps we can ask for steak for dinner? Rare, of course." Seren smiled, her lip drawing back into an instinctive sneer which reminded Rebekah of her father.

Rebekah looked apologetic. "I'm sorry, I'm still trying to work it all out. Do you need to feed?"

"Not yet, but steak knives are sharp." Seren pulled the nail out from under Rebekah's seat cushion. "And a better tool than this, Mama."

Rebekah believed in covering all the bases. Right now, it might seem there was nothing to be achieved by wielding a stone, a nail, *or* a knife. However, if previous encounters with vampires had taught her one thing, it was that sometimes, the simplest thing can make the difference between life and death.

"Of course. Steak, it is." When Rebekah shrugged, her shirt clung to her skin, the fabric still damp with sweat. She quickly decided that if they were going to eat dinner with the sentinel, she would cope better if she felt clean. "Let's wash-up before they come back for us."

Slipping behind the tapestry curtain and into the concealed alcove, she washed her face, neck, and hands in the bucket of warm water. Scrubbing at the mud and residue of salt left her face tingling, but not in a good way.

Seren found the process simpler. Dirt wiped away with little effort from her harder skin, brightening her complexion to its usual striking milk-white color.

Rebekah still looked like a scarecrow, but, as she and Seren meekly followed their vampire escort along the passageway and up the spiraling stone staircase, she felt better equipped for a sparring match.

They crossed the threshold into the cavernous space of the great hall. Dozens of tapestries lined the walls and dampened the echo of their reluctant footsteps. Weak sunlight picked out the edges of the thick fabric hanging over the tall, arched, stained glass windows at one end of the building. The main source of light came from a circle of what seemed like a hundred church candles set into an enormous wooden hoop suspended dozens of feet overhead, like a chandelier.

On both sides of the central chamber, pairs of stone pillars ran the entire length, supporting an intricately carved wooden ceiling. Each towering arc of wood formed part of a succession of sweeping domes. Rebekah wondered if they were created by vampire hands.

She gazed down the center of the room, her eyes following the path laid down by the wide gold carpet. At the furthest end of the hall, Rebekah could only see three chairs at a table, and she shot a comforting glance at Seren. *So, we won't have to suffer the doctor's company, that's good.*

Looking no less threatening from a distance, Lar's rose from his seat and waited.

With a deep breath, Rebekah strode forward to meet the challenge. *Best get this over with.*

The furniture, rendered small by the cavernous surroundings, became more imposing as Seren and Rebekah drew closer.

The banquet table itself was over thirty feet long and eight feet deep, and dwarfed the three place settings laid out on its surface. The aged scored wood was clearly steeped in history. The gouged knife holes and dark grease stains formed part of the fabric of the grain.

"How old is this table?" Rebekah blurted.

Lars smiled. "Sixteenth century English, I believe." He ran a finger along a deep groove in the wood. "Legend has it that this mark was made by the Tudor King, Henry the Eighth, when he cut off the hand of a serving wench who spilled wine on his doublet." He pulled out the solid oak chair as though it was made of balsa wood and beckoned to Rebekah to sit.

Lars took his seat again, at the head of the table.

"Sentinel, Seren has asked for rare steak for dinner." Rebekah looked at him, masking the tension as she wondered if *she* could get away with stealing a sharp knife. *Would he cut my hand off, too?*

"Of course," said Lars.

Alarm leapt inside her at his words, even though it was irrational. His agreeability unnerved her.

He added thoughtfully, "Doctor Heinrik said her iron levels are low for a human, and that she will need to drink blood just as pure vampires do. I imagine rare steak fits the bill."

"It seems you have it all worked out," said Rebekah.

"Perhaps. Do I need you at *all*, I wonder?" Lars smiled invitingly. "Maybe the girl alone will provide the answers?"

"You can watch her grow, and document it, but you take her away from me over my dead body."

"I wonder what your body would feel like, dead? This Connor has not cared enough to change you, protect you. Why?"

Rebekah cast around for a convincing lie. "Because, if Seren becomes ill, only my blood will save her. My *human* blood. She will go into anaphylactic shock with any other."

Lars' eyes narrowed, surprise lurking in their depths.

Rebekah had no idea if he bought the story. *But heck, what else have I got?* "Until she's full grown, and we know more about her immune system, Connor will not turn me. Seren *needs* me. *You* need me."

Lars sat back and considered Rebekah with predatory amusement. The veneer of gentile civility could not hide the exhilaration of the chase as he said, "Touché, min skat. For now."

The spike of dopamine tingling through her muscles urged her to run, and ignoring her survival instinct took every ounce of willpower. She pressed back down into her seat, and Seren's presence across the table steadied her nerve, helping to uncoil the tension.

A knowing sneer rippled across Lars' hunger-sharpened features. "Let's eat." The hefty wooden arms of his chair creaked beneath the pressure of his clawed grip, and Rebekah knew she was playing with fire.

As if in confirmation, Lars muttered, "You will make things, interesting."

The smell of food brought a sense of relief. The atmosphere in the room lightened at the distraction, and Rebekah could breathe again.

The stiff lines of Lars' body relaxed, and his sardonic grin appeared genuine as he said, "Dinner is served."

A platter of rare sirloin steak swimming in pink blood was placed in front of Seren. Rebekah was presented with a steak too, but cooked until medium-rare.

At her raised eyebrow, Lars said, "If your blood might be needed, you had better eat. We must make sure *your* iron levels stay healthy too."

"Of course," said Rebekah. She was happy to eat in silence, consuming her food quickly, but trying not to arouse suspicion.

"You are in a hurry?" asked Lars, sarcasm bowing lips stained dark red by the venison blood he drank.

Rebekah's look of blank innocence disguised the mental kick she gave herself. Acting natural was hard when she had no idea what natural was anymore. "It's been a long, tiring day." *And you scare the hell out of me.*

Although it was only late afternoon, Lars did not argue. "I'm sure you are tired, but you will stay."

The notion of 'a good night's sleep' had long since come to mean nothing to humans and vampires alike, and Sentinel Lars was certainly in no mood to hurry. If Rebekah's nerves were not already shredded, she would have been bored. Lars sank into periods of deep contemplation, sitting unmoving for endless minutes at a time.

Rebekah glanced through veiled lashes, and the sight of his impassive face knotted her stomach. *If only I knew what he's thinking.* Slumping her shoulders and trying to look weary, Rebekah reached for her glass, knocking it over, and the spilled water flooded her plate. Leaping up to avoid the rushing tide headed for her lap, she scattered her food, silverware, and the plate across the table.

Lars rose to his feet, and, dropping the linen napkin from his lap onto his chair, he materialized at Rebekah's side. He shunted her chair sideways, his cool hand resting on her shoulder to make sure she did not fall. The water poured onto the floor, followed by her plate, which shattered.

Rebekah muttered, "I'm sorry." Trying to make amends, she dabbed at the puddle with her napkin, and knocked over the glass of blood. Lars' white fingers closed around hers, pulling her up short.

Pain flared in the joints of her hand and tears glistened in her eyes. "I'm sorry. I'm just tired."

"No harm done, min skat." He cast a glance over the devastation littered across the table, and Rebekah held her breath. "So, have you eaten enough?"

She nodded. "I just need to sleep."

"Very well."

The rush of adrenalin drained away leaving her skin cold and clammy and the tiredness became real. Lars' eyes glinted, greed flashing in their cool blue depths. Adjusting his hold on her hand, his thumb moved to cover her pulse. His voice roughened as he said, "Go back to your room."

Rebekah tugged away from his cold hard grip, and muttered, "Thank you."

Walking away with Seren at her side, Rebekah shot a glance back over her shoulder.

A vampire guard was busy gathering the broken crockery and collecting the spilled food. Rebekah might have been amused, but the intensity of Lars' calculating stare sent shudders down her spine.

By the time a vampire had escorted them back to their dungeon, the sun was low in the sky. Dusk fell quickly in autumn, and by four o'clock, the candlelight would cower in the face of the growing shadows.

Remaining still while the vampire snapped the shackle closed around her ankle, Rebekah looked out of the small window, tuning out the depressing effect of the bars. Now she was here on dry land, she could appreciate Seren's observation. *The sea is beautiful.* The tide was in, and the water glittered with scraps of silver foil as the wind rippled over its surface.

Rebekah was in turmoil, but she hid it well. "I hoped the chains would be forgotten," she said playfully to Seren, when they were alone once more.

"Ah, vampires never forget. You should know that, Mama." A worried frown tugged the black wings of Seren's brows together. Lowering her hand, she dropped a steak knife down from inside her sleeve into her palm, and inspected it closely.

"You did it. Clever girl. Do you think he suspects?"

"No mama, he was looking at you."

Attracting Lars' interest is dangerous, even Seren knows that. Rebekah said, "It was not exactly a smooth operation, but if Lars is intrigued, maybe he'll make mistakes." She shrugged. "Perhaps, it's a good thing."

Seren's glance said 'it is never a good thing'.

Rebekah thought so too. *But it's too late now.* Tearing a strip of fabric from the sheet on the bed, Rebekah sank to the floor and wound the linen around the metal cuff where it had already begun to chaff her skin. Without looking up, she said briskly, "We need a plan of escape. Something to make it easier for Papa."

"At least the chains are long," said Seren.

Getting back up to her feet, Rebekah said, "I agree with that. Thank goodness."

There was nowhere within their dungeon cell they could not reach, and right now, with plotting on their minds, that was a blessing.

Seren went to the window. "Perhaps I can loosen the bars," she said hopefully, running her nails over the lumps of mortar on the window ledge. Using her vampire strength, Seren set about using the steak knife to dig at the base of an iron rod.

"Good idea." *If she can escape, she can find Connor and guide him to the castle.*

Rebekah settled to her own task. Sitting down again, she made a start on sharpening the end of the nail on a stone. *If I can sharpen the end to a point, and if, as Seren says, their covered skin is softer, I may get in a lucky strike.* Half an hour later, Rebekah ran her thumb over the sharp point and grunted. "Greg makes it look easy."

Still scraping at the mortar, Seren said, "He has bigger muscles than you, Mama. I can try in a while. I have more strength than you, too."

"Gee," laughed Rebekah. *I'm pretty useless really.*

A gleeful yelp escaped Seren as she finally uncovered the end of one bar, having showered the floor with obliterated cement. Gripping it tightly, she dragged the iron rod towards her, pulling hard until the upper fixing also crumbled.

Rebekah leapt up and rushed over to take a look. "Well done."

Seren eased her head into the wider space between the bars, pushing through as far as she could. She scanned left and right. The hundred-foot high wall of the gray stone fortifications swept away until it collided with the graceful curve of the next turret. The long narrow windows Seren could see glinted with the orange glow of candlelight, reminding her of pictures she had seen of a castle in a fairytale.

Just below the window, green moss stained the footings of the walls to a height of ten feet or more. Waves lapping at the foundations had polished the stone to a pumice-gray glacial finish. Even to Seren's preternatural vision, there appeared to be very few handholds for climbing.

"Can I see?" asked Rebekah quietly.

The rusted bars still in place grazed over Rebekah's cheeks as she pushed her head through the gap. Salty spray stung her eyes as she strained to see. "I wouldn't be able to climb down the walls. But maybe we can use the sheets and the tapestries. They'd make strong ropes. We'll get onto that tomorrow."

The task loomed as a mountain they needed to climb. Rebekah pulled back from the window, brushing flakes of rust from her reddened cheeks. Feeling drained, she said, "Let's just sit and rest a while."

Seren opened her mouth to say she didn't need rest, and Rebekah interrupted, "I know, but humor me. Come and give your Mama a hug."

The iron bar bowed a little as Seren slid it back into place. She filled the holes at the base with a jigsaw of mortar pieces. Satisfied with her handiwork, she stepped back.

Rebekah's chain rattled as she climbed up onto the bed.

"You know, it won't be a surprise to Sentinel Lars that I'm stronger than a human. What will it matter if I remove our chains?" Defiance tightened Seren's features.

"We don't know how long we are going to be here. The less they know about where your human half ends and your vampire half begins, the better. You understand that, right?"

Seren relaxed and hopped up onto the bed. "You're right."

Rebekah smiled as she shoved a feather pillow down behind her shoulder blades and settled back against the wall.

Sitting side by side on the bed, with their feet hanging over the edge of the narrow mattress, Rebekah nudged Seren's toes with her own. "You've grown again. Not too big yet for a hug, though," she said, as she put her arm around Seren's shoulders.

In the time they sat in quiet contemplation, whispering their thoughts now and again, dusk donned the heavy cloak of night. Buried underneath a pile of blankets and cradling a warm stone on the bed beside her, Rebekah listened to the wind picking up. The flames of the candles guttered alarmingly and the dancing shadows thickened each time one lost the battle to stay alight.

Rebekah was so absorbed in dreading the moment when complete darkness descended that she didn't notice Seren's chin drop until she slumped heavily against Rebekah's side.

"Hey," said Rebekah quietly.

Seren toppled sideways, her cheek resting in Rebekah's lap. She was asleep. Rebekah smiled as she brushed a swathe of jet-black hair back from Seren's face and stroked her cheek. "Sleep, sweetheart."

Exhausted too, Rebekah wished she could sleep in the same way Seren did. For Seren, human sleep fell like a blackout curtain. It happened infrequently, so Rebekah did not know how long it would last, and, worse still, there would be no waking her. *But she is safe for now, surely they will leave us in peace 'til morning.*

The whistling wind eddied around the stone chamber and the waves crashed against the solid walls in a muffled assault. The bombardment of the storm created a strangely hypnotic rhythm that relaxed Rebekah until her eyelids drooped, and she, too, fell asleep.

As all her senses came under attack, Rebekah was not sure exactly what woke her. A flash of lightning bleached the room with stark white light, and the growl of thunder battled with the screaming gale, but the sensation that jerked her into action was the sloshing of ice cold water over her feet and ankles. The candle flames were all dead, but the glare from the lightning confirmed Rebekah's fears. With every wave which crashed onto the castle wall, a cascading spray of sea water poured in through the window.

Each rush of water added inches to the lake already flooding the cell.

"Seren! Seren!" Rebekah shook Seren's shoulders hard but she did not stir. "Damn it, why didn't I let you get rid of the bloody chains."

The soaked linen binding around Rebekah's ankle cuff clung like cold fingers and fear tightened her muscles. Shifting her legs beneath the heavy wet folds of the blankets felt like wading through mud.

"SEREN!" Rebekah unashamedly shouted into her comatose daughter's ear, patting her face briskly. The cold firm texture of Seren's cheeks should not have sent panic crawling through Rebekah's heart, but it did. "Don't be stupid," she breathed, "she's half vampire, she can't be dead. Can she? Shit."

Slamming the shutters down on paranoia, Rebekah kicked away the smothering weight of the blankets and lowered her tethered ankle into the ice-cold water until her foot touched the floor. Lying Seren down close to the edge of the bed, Rebekah stood up, relieved when the water reached only to her knees. Both her feet slipped on the glacier-like cold stone, and a bone-deep shiver shuddered up her spine.

Casting a frantic glance around the darkened space, she focused on a funnel of moonlight glistening on the rippling oil-black lake. Desperation cramped her throat. *How high will the water get?* Another blinding flash of light imprinted an image of the room on her retina, and the row of white wax candles lined up along the stone altar shelf became a beacon of hope.

Inhaling sharply when the cold water lapped up over her knees, Rebekah waded across the room as fast as the dragging chain would allow. She pulled a wooden chair into place beneath the shoulder high shelf, reached up, and pushed the candles aside. Gritting her teeth, she concentrated on shuffling her feet to make the awkward turn. A deluge of water thundering in through the window struck her full in the chest. The blow, like the slam of a baseball bat, left her gasping for breath. Coughing until she thought she would choke, Rebekah rubbed her stinging sternum, easing the pain as she waded back across to the bed.

"Baby, Seren, Honey." Rebekah dropped to her knees in the bitter cold water and rocked Seren's shoulders again. "Please, wake up," she whispered. Seren's body was a strange combination of hard, but slack. Rebekah laid her forehead on Seren's firm shoulder and counted to ten inside her head. "Okay, here goes nothing."

Another rush of water crashed through the window as Rebekah struggled back to her feet, battling against her sodden clothes, which seemed more water than fabric, dragging down over her skin as she moved.

Summoning strength she never knew she had, she pulled Seren to the edge of the bed. Taking a deep breath like a weight lifter, she prepared to bear the deceptive weight of a slight girl with densely-packed vampire tissue. Every muscle in her stomach screamed as she lifted her daughter, grunting loudly, "Arrgh."

Each labored stride through the water stirred a current that scattered pins and needles into the places where she still had feeling left. Clutching Seren close to her chest, leading with her free foot and then dragging the other one into line, she counted down the steps to the other wall. She stopped, sensing she was close, but needing another flash of lightning, or shaft of moonlight to confirm it.

Her teeth chattered loudly, and, before her prayers were answered, her knees took up the rhythm. The wall bleached to ice-gray, and thunder joined in her mental applause. "Yes. Thank God." Hitching Seren higher in her arms, Rebekah stepped up onto the seat of the chair. Trying not to graze her stomach on the jagged edges of the stone shelf, she lifted and pushed, and rolled Seren's body onto the flat platform.

Before her energy died, she braced her hands on the pitted stone surface, and dragged herself up until she perched on the edge of the shelf. Nudging Seren back into the crumbling crater in the rear wall of the alcove, from where the shrine had been removed, Rebekah made enough room for herself, and sat at one end of the platform.

Grabbing hold of Seren's chain first, and then her own, she hauled the excess up onto the altar shelf beside her, folding her legs up so it was not pulling on a dangling foot. Rebekah curled into a ball and rested her chin on her bent knees. She placed her hand on Seren's shoulder and descended into a mindless trance of exhaustion.

Perhaps, I'll fall off if I sleep. Will I wake-up, or drown? Staring downward, she found the glimmering light winking on the oily surface of the flood hypnotic. The blood staining the binding around her ankle appeared black in the moonlight, and the hands she clenched around her knees were white, *too* white.

Her shivering stopped. *That's a bad thing.* When she touched Seren's cheek, it no longer felt cold to Rebekah. *That's definitely a bad thing.*

Dropping her head back against the wall, she barely registered the cold fingers of frost drifting over her neck. When she closed her eyes, her face felt stiff. The black clouds of unconsciousness filtered into her brain.

She smiled as her head filled with soot-colored cotton wool, and she heard a splashing sound which drove a tidal wave of sloshing water across the room. Cold hands closed over her shoulders, and the voice of death said urgently, "Min skat, wake-up." The weight of her chain fell away, and her ribcage creaked in an iron embrace that swept her up and through the air.

Chapter 14

On the deck of the super-tanker, Connor stared out into the gray haze of the gathering storm. Squinting and shading his eyes from the icy needles of driving rain, he picked out the coastline of Europe. *Captain Blake said the next port is still three hours away. Will that take us past Hamburg and onto the Danish coast?* Connor hoped so. The closer to Sentinel Lars' fortress they landed, the faster he could track him down and take back what was his.

The boiling flint-gray surface of the North Sea swelled and troughed, spray reaching for the clouds overhead and trying to devour them. It was four in the afternoon, but night had ridden roughshod over the sky and cast a veil of darkness.

Perfect weather for a vampire, thought Connor.

The banshee wail of the gusting air was welcome after the thick silence of the nomads. Connor's senses were strained to breaking point. Talking was so small a part of communication onboard that his eyes ached in their sockets.

Wrapping his greatcoat tighter around his chest against the wind trying to rip it from his shoulders, Connor walked along the deck. Impervious to the blizzard, his solid frame forced the squalls of rushing air to yield to his presence.

He easily opened the metal door that took him below deck, and it slammed hard behind him, setting a vibration humming through the bulkhead. As the sound faded, Connor sensed he was being watched and waited the nanosecond it took to find out by whom.

At his shoulder, Captain Blake appeared.

Turning his head, with convincing nonchalance, Connor asked, "To which port are we headed?"

"I haven't taken the decision yet."

Connor laughed. "I get it. Knowledge is power. I'm a doctor. I understand that better than most."

Blake nodded. "Perhaps." The hearty thump on Connor's back tested his patience. "We are two of a kind."

Connor thought about Rebekah and Seren, and of the Spanish girl who was clearly Blake's pet.

"More than you know, I think."

Blake's eyes glittered with interest. "Oh?"

"Knowledge is power," grinned Connor, bracing as Blake once more slapped his back, hard.

Connor did not bruise, but his ego was tired of taking the battering. He made himself a promise to deck the captain before they parted company for good. *Until then-*

Beneath their feet, the vessel shifted violently as the tanker fell from the crest of a wave and hit the floor of a trough like a car slamming into the bottom of a ravine. Connor's boots slipped, and he shot out a hand. His fingers dug holes in the riveted panel of the wall, using them as anchor points to hold him still.

As the ship steadied and the hull creaked, Blake said, "That's why I'm here. I have some seasick humans in the hold. Can you do something?"

So, he's finally asking for a favor. Not a sign of trust, but something he needs at least. "Sure. Medication is out, that must be taken before you set sail."

Blake's eyes narrowed in speculation.

"Do you have ginger? Peppermint?" Connor knew the answers before he asked. *Power, my friend.*

"Hardly," drawled Blake.

Connor grinned and punched the captain on the shoulder, enjoying the small taste of retribution. "No, course not. Dry crackers and acupuncture it is then." He could also show them how to use the pressure points inside their wrists, if needles freaked them out, but Blake did not need to know the details. *I wonder if the Spanish girl will be there?*

With little to occupy his time during the hours at sea, Connor's curiosity about her was building with every passing hour. *Yes, she's telepathic. Maybe she drank blood from Blake, but she's not a vampire. So, what is she?* He tried to ignore the voice which whispered 'hybrid'. *Impossible.*

"How many humans are sick?" Connor asked. As an afterthought he added, "And is there any difference between the humans who were fed upon at the party and those who were not?"

Blake said bluntly, "I have no idea."

Enjoying needling Blake, arching an eyebrow that implied, 'Well, what are we waiting for', Connor said briskly, "Let's get going."

The captain accelerated away, covering the length of the storage area in a moment. At the back wall, he stopped and pulled on a concealed handle, opening a metal door which had escaped Connor's notice in his earlier explorations.

It led to a part of the tanker Connor had not seen before. Following Blake over the threshold, he obeyed the captain's sharp command to close the door behind them. The swish of Blake's leather coat brushing against the metal walls whispered through Connor's head, breaking the profound silence, and his mind slid smoothly onto full-alert. *If there are humans down here, they are very quiet, too quiet. It could be an ambush.*

Buttoning up his greatcoat to cover his throat and add another layer of thick fabric over his chest, Connor dropped back until he had Blake in his sights, from head to toe. He watched keenly as the tall figure in front arrived at another door and effortlessly rotated an airlock wheel. The door sighed as Blake pulled it open and the stench of human filth escaped in a toxic cloud that rippled a sneer over Connor's face.

Without looking back, Blake disappeared inside, barking over his shoulder, "Seal the hatch."

As the marinade of scents permeated Connor's sinuses and drifted down his throat, hunger rose to meet it like bile burning in his gullet.

"Distracting, isn't it?" said Blake. "Now you understand why the sealed bulkhead hatch."

Connor grinned, and his suspicion down-graded from red-alert to amber, his mood complimenting the yellow-tinted lights illuminating this 'human sector' of the ship. It also gave his vampire features an almost human-like warmth.

Connor suspected that was deliberate. *There is more to Captain Blake than a farm produce merchant.* Curiosity got the better of him.

"What did you do before the pandemic? How did you blend in?"

Blake laughed. "I was a penitentiary governor. High security. I saw a lot of hard men broken and crying like babies. And I saw a lot of hard men too tough to break. *They* killed more men inside prison than those that had earned them their sentences. And they enjoyed it, too, until I decided it was time for them to taste their own medicine."

"Death Row, with a twist?"

"Precisely." Blake turned to look at Connor. Despite the scars carved into his jawline, he too, when bathed in golden light, looked almost kind when he smiled. "These humans are sheep rather than lions. They will eventually die by vampire hand. I certainly don't want them getting stir crazy and killing each other, so a little kindness goes a long way."

Connor wrinkled his nose. "It smells like a cattle farm. Where's the kindness in that?"

"They feel safe. You will be the first vampire to cross into their enclosure in a decade." At Connor's curious expression, Blake said, "A human has the role of a warden, of sorts, and holds the keys. She eases their path, chooses the ones strong enough to be fed from, and makes sure all of the herd get the food they need."

It was on the tip of his tongue to ask if the warden was the Spanish girl, but instead he said, "And you have had a warden from the start?"

"Enough questions." Blake's features hardened. "You have a job to do."

Connor said easily, "How long do they live?"

"You're onboard to make sure they live longer. That's all you need to know." Blake turned away and started walking.

From the captain's reaction, Connor guessed that the human warden was his Spanish pet, and that he regretted letting it slip. The satisfaction of knowing more about Blake than he should, and that he may soon get a closer look at the girl, put a spring in Connor's step.

Minutes later, Connor faced a red door. Another airlock. As Blake rotated the wheel with a flick of his wrist, he said, "This will be your consulting room. I'll have the seasick humans sent through to you."

The room was painted in warm cream and muted-amber, and the bulkhead lights made it look almost cheerful in contrast to the dark shadows which filled the vampire inhabited sectors. "I guess the colors are for their benefit?" asked Connor.

Blake's answer was a slammed door. The bolts shot home in the hatchway behind him, and Connor stared at the other door, trying to imagine the living conditions of the humans somewhere beyond it.

He scanned the room, taking in the examination couch, a privacy screen three panels wide, on wheels, and the pile of cotton examination gowns, each one sealed inside a plastic bag. In this setting, the mundane familiarity of the items seemed absurd.

Opening the door on the chilled storage unit, he ran an expert eye over the contents, and found it stocked with every form of medication he could ever need, and quite a few he would never need. *Not unless smallpox makes a resurgence*, he thought wryly.

"What I do *not* have, are acupuncture needles," murmured Connor.

He opened drawers and found a stock of syringe needles of all gauges. Tearing open the outer packages of the ones marked as the finest gauge, he turned them out into a sterilized kidney-shaped specimen bowl.

Over at the stainless-steel basin, he scrubbed his hands with sterile handwash. He picked out a needle and used his fingertips to bend over the blunt end and fashion it into a solid ball. Idly surveying the room, he worked his way through the first six packs, until his eyes alighted on the examination screen. Metal hoops secured the panels of linen to the steel frame via metal rimmed eyelets.

"If they get undressed, I'll just have to close my eyes," he muttered as, abandoning his task, he crossed the room.

Starting at the bottom edge, Connor ran his hand along the fabric, pausing to press each ring between his finger and thumb until the metal crumbled. The space he made in the hoop allowed it to fall into his palm and then, with a twist of his wrist, he tossed each one across the room to land in the basin with the unerring accuracy of a circus performer.

Connor repeated the process along the top edges until he was left with three large sheets of material lying in crumpled heaps on the floor, three empty tubular steel square frames, and a sink full of sea sickness pressure-point bracelets. *Or they will be, once I scrunch the ends into balls.*

A knock on the internal door announced the arrival of his first patient.

Connor approached the airlock door, not painted danger red this time, but a welcoming pale green.

He whipped the wheel around, opened the enlarged oval hatch and stood back. Instinct told him that this was as far as he should go. The human aromas rushing into the room smelled sweeter than the stale ones trapped in the other corridor, and so much more enticing. He swallowed down his venom-tinted saliva and arranged a half-smile of welcome on his face.

A thin young man staggered over the threshold, guided by the human hand of another. Connor's brain jumped to full attention when the Spanish girl appeared beside the pale distressed youth. Her face remained hidden behind a curtain of glossy black hair as she concentrated on escorting him across the room and helping him up onto the examination couch.

Connor disguised his interest, focusing on the patient but aware of the girl standing back and leaning against the wall. The gray, clammy complexion of the youngster and the groans he could not keep inside were easy to diagnose. Collecting a broken curtain ring from the sink, Connor rolled the sharp ends into balls and slipped it around the man's wrist. His cold fingers bent the bracelet and adjusted the fit until it pressed into the pressure points of the joint.

Stepping back and nodding, Connor said quietly, "It will take an hour or so to take effect, but you should feel better soon." Switching his attention to the girl, he added, "Give him some dry crackers when you get him back."

Under Connor's watchful gaze, the patient shuffled out, staggering when the ship swayed beneath them. He hoped they would all be as easy as that one. *The Spanish girl didn't stagger. Her footing was rock solid.*

The procedure became pedestrian as one after another of the seasick humans were escorted in and then out again. Connor felt like a boy on a first date. Whenever the room was empty he rehearsed opening lines to draw the girl into conversation.

He sensed that when the last patient was taken away, he would have missed his opportunity, and he wouldn't know it until she failed to return to knock upon the door again. "Dry crackers," he said again, adding carefully, "you are not seasick?"

Her eyes met his for the first time, suspicion in their velvet-brown depths. "No."

"I'll need to check on them again. But this-" Connor waved a hand and shrugged. "Eighteen patients. It would be easier if I came to you."

The girl's face shut down. Her hair swung forward, masking her closed expression as she held out a hand to help the woman perched on the edge of the couch. With the new bracelet in place, the woman, already looking less green, eased one foot down onto the cold linoleum floor.

"Come, Una," the girl said.

"And *your* name?" Connor persisted.

"It is not your business."

"I know what you are." He had been treating the humans, but gathering his evidence on Blake's pet.

The girl smiled with muted confidence. "You think you know?"

"I *do* know. Your heart beats slowly, and you can stop it at will."

She shot him a sharp glance.

"You forgot, and stopped breathing in here a couple of times. You are both vampire and human."

"Stay away from me."

"I won't hurt you. I just want to know how."

The girl lifted her chin and laughed. The sound, like a shower of crystals on glass, died abruptly as she said, "He will hurt *you*."

"Look...?"

"Hera," she said.

"Hera." Connor's face was serious. "I'll be at that door in one hour. You take me down to check on my patients, and if, on the way, you want to tell me your story, I want to hear it."

Without speaking, Hera helped the frail woman from the bed, and, holding her arm gently, she walked her from the room. The green door closed behind them with a thump.

Connor ran a hand down over his face and swore. "Shit." He did not feel like he had made a mistake, but Hera had given him no clues.

Leaving by the red door, he retraced his steps along the corridors. Like a rat traveling along a maze of identical drainpipes, he knew exactly where he was within the colossal shell of the vessel. As the second airlock door came into view he exuded a relaxation he did not feel.

The door opened before he reached for the wheel, and Blake's broad frame blocked his path. He stared at Connor, currents stirring in the dark pools of his eyes, and then broke into laughter. As it died, he said cryptically, "Of course. How many were sick?"

Connor filled in the blanks. *He forgot that I can't hear his thoughts. He has to speak aloud.* "Eighteen. I'll check on them again in an hour." It was not a question and Connor's straight look defied the captain to argue. Connor concentrated on picturing the faces of each and every patient, not once thinking about Hera. He was taking no chances.

Walking forward, Connor forced Blake to yield, and he stepped through the door into the storage hold.

"I'll send my first officer to accompany you." Blake hesitated as he turned away. "We will be docking in two hours."

"Where do you want me?" Connor asked dutifully.

"All hands' on deck for the unloading and loading. We assemble at the stern."

Connor watched Blake's tall figure recede in a blur of fast moving shadow, and then did some fast moving of his own.

He raided the refrigeration unit where parcels of food were lined up along the shelves. The outsized canvas duffle bags were empty, so the lunchtime delivery to the humans had not yet happened. *They won't miss one, and Greg must be getting low on glucose tablets.* The checklist of tasks he'd set himself galvanized him into action. The upcoming appointment with Hera rattled bones in the closet of his good sense. *But, being cautious has never been my strong point.*

Connor made his way back to the containment area. The laundry hamper in which Greg resided was thirty feet away. Connor checked that the storage room remained empty, and then, clutching the food parcel in one hand, he negotiated the maze of huge crates.

He flew soundlessly down the length of the cavernous space.

It was easy to attract Greg's attention with a whispered owl call. Connor jumped down inside the container, landing beside Greg. After he handed over the parcel of food, he compressed a pile of laundry into a makeshift seat. While Greg demolished the food, Connor alternated between talking and listening for intruders.

"Okay. The tanker docks in two hours. The storm is dying down, so there should not be too much delay."

Greg gave the thumbs up. Human speech carried to vampire ears better than a dog whistle to a canine's, so he would say as little as possible.

"I'll go now, and tell Seth and Julian to be ready. When Julian comes for you, leave the flare gun and cartridges behind. I'll collect them and put them back."

Greg shrugged and frowned.

"Why? Because you're abseiling over the side of the ship, and Julian will have four kitbags and two humans to worry about. You won't need it, and if it turns up in the wrong place it may spark a search." Connor grinned. "Excuse the pun."

Greg took a swig of water and, leaning closer, he stabbed a finger into Connor's chest.

"Me? How am I getting off?" All expression slipped from Connor's face as he mused aloud. "It depends on how close an eye Blake is keeping on me. He seems to be beyond distrust in any case. I'm not exactly in, but he's not got me under surveillance, so I'll wait and see. Julian will head inland three miles, due east of our landing spot, and wait. I'll find you."

Greg pulled his black leather gloves back on and tapped his watch.

Connor mimed an ironic salute and in an effortless gliding motion, he pushed open the hatch above their heads, and flowed, rather than vaulted, over the side. *Okay, give Julian and Seth the heads up, and get back to the examination room in half an hour.* Connor set off at a fast run.

Taking the long route, he dodged along the open deck between the rows of containers where the wind once more threatened to strip Connor of his coat. Sea water spray dripped from his hair, down his face and onto his lip, and his skin tasted of salt when he licked it away. The storm had abated, but he was in a wind tunnel.

Approaching the bottle-green metal box from the rear, Connor executed a free-running maneuver. Jumping up, he gripped the metal lip of the roof and launched his boots at Julian's serrated tear in the metal. A judder of stressed steel vibrated up through his arms as his solid mass forced the metal sheet back, and he forged his way inside the dark, damp space.

His feet touched the floor, and a thick arm folded around his neck and lifted him off his feet. A fist drove into his kidneys. Another assailant hit him over the head with a metal pan before Connor got really pissed off.

Gripping the arm which crushed his wind-pipe and prevented talking, Connor kicked out behind, his boot making satisfying contact with a knee. He shoved the vampire back into the wall behind and, with some fast footwork, doubled over and heaved the attacker over his shoulder.

Julian landed on his back, putting his hand up to shield his face as he sprung back to his feet, stopping abruptly when Connor hissed, "It's me."

"Damn it, Connor. We weren't expecting you 'til we dock."

A metal bar rolled across the floor as Seth collapsed into a crouched position against the opposite wall and muttered, "Bloody vampires."

Even in the near dark interior, Connor picked out the bruises on Seth's face at a glance. "What the hell happened to him? Were you attacked?" Being jumped by Julian made immediate sense.

Julian scowled, reading Connor's shocked conclusion. "You got attacked because you bowled in here like a demented bat without giving me the signal."

His lips twitched as Connor realized the weather had driven everything else from his mind. "I think you're hearing must be failing, old man," He said innocently, before returning to his earlier concern for Seth. "What's with the black and blue look?"

"Seth got thrown about a bit in the storm." Seth glared, and Julian added, "He's not a fan of using a vampire as an anchor, and the going got rough." Ignoring the snort from Seth's corner Julian forged on. "But he'd be a lot blacker and bluer if I *hadn't* held onto him."

"Guess weighing as much as a lump of concrete has its advantages," joked Connor. Remembering Hera, he changed the subject. "Julian, we're docking in about an hour and a half. Soon as the coast is clear, collect Greg, and get off the ship. I'll meet you three miles due east. Got it?"

"Got it." Julian did not waste time asking questions.

He'll know I have a plan. What he'd say if he knew about Hera, I don't know. It's best I don't ask. Clapping Julian on the back and saluting Seth, Connor sprang from the floor, gripped the torn edge of metal, and disappeared.

Connor and the escorting crewman arrived at the red-painted airlock door at the appointed hour. Staring into the glowering expression which had not changed since the vampire appeared beside him, Connor lifted a brow and said, "This is as far as you go, I believe."

The twitching muscle in the vampire's clenched jaw was a sure sign that the barb had hit home.

With a brisk nod, Connor opened the door and left the vampire standing outside.

The consulting room was empty, and a few tense minutes passed by with Connor standing at rest, imitating a statue. *Will she come?* His smooth complexion creased as he considered, for the first time, that perhaps his curiosity would endanger her. For himself, he would take that risk. *But will Blake lay* all *the blame at my door?*

Just as he decided he should leave Hera in peace, and turned to go, the green door opened and she stepped into the room.

He had no time to wonder why she kept the rendezvous. She shot a glance at his neutral expression, and said, "Come."

Connor jerked into action as her slender elfin form disappeared, and like a dark woodland sprite she whisked away along the corridors. He could easily have caught up, but he felt more comfortable merely keeping her in his sights. Doubt crowded his mind. *If she's a hybrid, why does it matter?* He provided his own answer. *Because Seren's life could depend on it.*

He focused once again, just in time to catch a glimpse of her fleeting heels as she disappeared through an open doorway. The knee-high thresholds to the hatchways were designed to prevent floodwater becoming a rushing river in a disaster. There was no graceful way of clambering through them, and yet, Hera managed it.

Connor followed and slipped seamlessly into the room. He found her waiting.

"Come. Sit."

"The patients?" said Connor, looking around at what was clearly her personal space.

"We can talk first," said Hera. The intensity in her dark eyes compelled Connor to do as she said. He took a seat on a tapestry covered ottoman.

She sank into a graceful cross-legged position on a cushion on the floor. Her loose-fitting combat trousers and khaki T-shirt enhanced her exotic air, adding a rich coffee cream tone to her soft skin. "What do you want to know?"

"How it happened? Were you born human?"

She nodded slowly, the obsidian silk of her hair shimmering with each movement. "I was the same as them. The rest of them."

"The other humans?"

"Yes. But, one night, the captain, he chose me as his-" Her features tightened as she struggled to say the word.

"And after, he chose you every time?" Blake's behavior had told Connor that much.

"Yes."

"So, how were you changed, without the transformation being completed?"

"I can tell you what I remember, that is all." She shrugged delicately. "It was during a storm, much as tonight." Her hands flowed through the air, imitating the waves of the ocean. "The ship shuddered and a screaming sound tore through my head. I found out later, in hugging the coastline and hiding from the weather, the ship hit the rocks." Hera's eyes fixed on a spot on the wall, her lips moving soundlessly.

"Are you okay?"

"Yes, finding words," she said quietly.

Connor wondered if talking was difficult for her. *Out of practice, maybe.*

Her next words came out in a rush. "The screaming I heard was a hole being torn in the hull. Five of us drowned that night. I did too. I died, or would have. I remember feeling ice cold, and then the tingling fire burning in my belly, and I was so thirsty my throat felt raw."

"So, he resuscitated you. And when it was failing, he made you drink his blood?"

"I think so, yes." She smiled. "He is not so bad. He shows me the things he keeps inside his head. His life before, he was a good man."

"Thank you, Hera." Connor had a lot to think about. Seren's conception had happened when Connor saved Rebekah from hypothermia. Hera had been cold, but perhaps her bone marrow cells, protected from the chill by the insulating properties of her bone fibers, retained warmth and continued to function. *It looks as though the chemical reactions caused by Blake's venom only reached her tissue and organs.* Connor took a breath to ask more questions, but Hera jerked to her feet.

"He comes," she said. "Say nothing."

Her heart jumped in her chest before she brought it under control and slowed the beats to a somnolent waltz. *She's not scared for herself.* Amusement at this slight, exotic creature protecting him made Connor smile.

Hera frowned and repeated urgently, "He comes."

Connor stood up as Blake glided into the room. His black eyes swept the scene in a tidal wave of speculative disapproval, coming to rest on Hera. His narrowed gaze searched her face, and the tension in Blake's expression faded a little.

"So, all was well?" He spoke to Connor without looking at him.

"Yes, the bracelets are working well," Connor replied briskly, praying it was true. Wondering what silent interrogation the captain was subjecting Hera to, Connor cut across Blake's concentration. Looking at Hera, he said, "I can tell the captain, too, now he is here."

Blake's black hair glinted with needlepoints of gray as he pushed it back from his forehead, and his cutting glance honed in on Connor.

I've got his attention. As though continuing an interrupted conversation, he said, "They need a regular dose of vitamin 'D'." Shooting an inclusive glance at Blake, Connor shuffled through his recollection of the patients he had examined and came up with a candidate. He said, "The man with the beard, and the scars on his arm...?" He looked to Hera for the answer, waiting for her response.

"Arnold," Hera provided.

"Yes, Arnold," Connor continued. "His rash is caused by lack of sunlight."

Blake snorted as he said ironically, "Sunbathing is not always possible."

Connor felt encouraged. At least the captain seemed distracted. "I suggest you remove the roof of one of your transport containers and let the humans get some sun whenever you can."

Blake nodded, his eyes returning to Hera as he smiled. "We have plenty of time to talk about these matters once we set sail again."

Connor watched Blake's implacable profile. *Has he bought it?* Masking his concerns for Hera, he glanced at his watch. "You're right. It must be time to gather up on deck."

Blake's black eyes were dead pools as he replied, "It is. Come."

Studiously ignoring Hera, Connor followed the captain from the room, imitating Blake's purposeful stride as they made their way through the bowels of the ship. The thick silence was not reassuring, and Connor resigned himself to watching his back.

Fifteen minutes later, Connor left the storage hold and prepared to become a drone in the hive of activity on deck. The tanker had docked and the signposts around the harbor were in Danish. The prospect of setting foot on dry land and moving closer to Rebekah and Seren was a heady cocktail of exhilaration. It took monumental control to stay and finish the charade, but he knew he had to give Julian, with his human handicaps in tow, the chance to make their escape.

Connor felt relieved when he lifted the lid on the laundry crate and found the flare-gun abandoned by Greg, as agreed. *If the nomads found him I would know by now.* Assuming everything had gone according to plan, Julian's party of three would already have abseiled down the side of the ship onto the quayside. *What could go wrong?*

Connor tucked the flare gun firmly into his belt at the small of his back. The metal weight was a tangible reminder that, right now, everything hung in the balance.

Negotiating the maze of twenty-feet-tall steel shipment containers, Connor zeroed in on the cluster of vampires at the stern of the ship. The group was already dispersing. Pairs of crew members scattered across the width of the deck, disappearing into different alleyways.

Having spied on the nomads in London, Connor recognized the scene. *The preparation for hoisting the containers onto the quayside is underway.* The vampires worked in pairs and as Connor stared into the hostile eyes of a muscular mousey-haired vampire who was clearly waiting for him, he had the distinct feeling he was literally stepping into Viktor's shoes. *Great.*

"Goran," the vampire muttered through creaking vocal chords.

Connor nodded, and, studying the strangely silent dance of those around him, he followed suit. Every move Goran made, he mirrored. They worked in concert, unclipping huge spring-loaded clamps at the base of each container. With an effortless squeeze of a vampire hand, each metal latch fell open, landing on the deck with a resounding crack, before the crew moved onto the next.

Once all the anchor points were released, they swung open each set of doors and pushed back into place any crates inside which had slipped during the storm. In some containers, the crates were empty, ready to be filled with whichever food crop the nomads collected. Some already contained bananas, kiwis, and other exotic fruits which the hives in Spain and Italy grew in abundance. Those the nomads would now barter in northern territories in return for blood rations. *It gives their humans a short respite.* The number of weeks the tanker spent at sea outstripped those in dock, Connor was certain.

Connor joined Goran inside a container, following his lead and sliding the steel boxes back into place, and pulling on the nylon-webbing straps until they were tight. Once the lower crates were secure, they both climbed to the higher levels and used a ratchet to tighten the toughened steel restraining cables. Job done, they jumped down, left the container, and closed the doors.

Another team of vampires moved seamlessly through stage two. The rumble of thick chains dragging across the steel deck sent a shuddering vibration through Connor. The vampires tossed hefty coils of the chain up onto the top of each container as though they were shifting bales of hay. The sure-footed crew members up on the roofs, dragged them into place, and the links screeched over the metal panels like claws grappling for purchase on the slick wet steel.

Continuing with his small part in the process, Connor struggled to concentrate on the mindless repetition. He and his comrade closed the doors on the twenty-seventh container unit, and Connor wondered how many more.

At that moment, Goran's head whipped around, his murky gaze narrowing as his body jerked onto point like a hunting dog. Silence hit the deck like a combat blackout, and nothing stirred except the oily fabric of their coats buffeted by the gusts of wind scurrying along between the boxes.

Up on the observation deck, Captain Blake's silhouette carved his shape out of the dark gray evening sky, and Goran's features tensed. *Receiving orders telepathically?*

When the activity started up again, Goran said, "Come. We check the first set of containers going out, and hitch a ride inside. The trucks are on their way." Goran rolled his eyes, his irritation showing on his face. He resented Connor as an outsider and a liability.

Connor grunted at the concession of speech. He took off after Goran, keeping up over the hundreds of yards of slippery steel, and dodging the rivets on the floor which anchored the handrail running along the outside of the deck. Beyond it, the rippling sheet of gunmetal-gray water undulated gently, fracturing into white foam when it hit the mammoth hull. The sound of the slapping water disturbed the eerie silence which was crawling into Connor's brain, and unease cramped his gut. *Something is not right.*

As the pair reached the forward row of metal units, Connor caught glimpses of bluish-gray faces staring down from their vantage points. Like frozen sentinels, they stood on the container roofs, ready to make the ride through the air from the ship to the quayside.

Goran jerked his chin towards a container already hooked up to the super tanker's crane, the chains pulled tight like a four-legged spider. Connor's scalp prickled as he felt a dozen pairs of eyes piercing his skin. *Vultures waiting for a kill. Is Goran a hyena or a lion?*

"Come," barked his companion. Goran pulled open the door and gave a hand signal to the nomad in the cab of the crane. Connor hadn't seen him before, because he would have remembered the grin which oozed across his face.

Still on guard, Connor was wondering what would happen next, when Goran beckoned, and disappeared into the black shadows inside the container. *Okay.* Connor took a step forward. The crane winch began to whine as it took up the last few inches of slack, and the four chains creaked as the links grated together.

Taking the plunge, Connor went through the doorway. He felt grim satisfaction when the door slammed shut behind him, but not before he felt the breeze of Goran's passing by. Connor was left alone in the dark. *I knew it.*

He braced when the floor shifted suddenly and swung beneath him in a lurching arc, and the nylon webbing holding the crates in place sighed when the load shunted from one side to the other. In pitch-black even vampires could not see, so, while his hard flesh crawled and his brain searched for the reason why, he closed his eyes.

In the nanosecond before Goran's shape blotted out the moonlight and the door closed, Connor saw something else. *But what?* The whining sound overhead continued, and the crates grated together. The rocking motion became a jerking swing. Connor's realization hit at the same moment as the air thrummed with a feral growl, and the odor of ionized breath filled his nostrils.

A snarl tightened Connor's own muzzle when disembodied words, grinding through a locked jaw, reverberated around the cluttered space.

"Viktor is out, and so are you, doctor."

The static charge of the mystery vampire's brain made the hairs of Connor's nape stand up, and his worst imaginings fell into place.

Shit, Blake. In grave sleep. The word 'doctor' melted into a rumbling, saliva-soaked spluttering breath.

Keeping his eyes closed, Connor started to run. With explosive forward propulsion, he ran up the mountain of crates, feeling Blake's clawed grip snatching at his coat. The psychopath had been unleashed inside Blake's head and the time for talking was past.

Connor hit the platform at the top of the crates and heard the screech of Blake's sharp fingernails puncturing the steel wall at Connor's feet. Turning around, his coat swinging in an arc, Connor reached behind and drew the flare gun from his belt. With unerring certainty, he fired it into Blake's snarling face.

The solid thump on the opposite wall sucked all movement from Connor's body. The explosion of red light saturated his vision even through closed eyelids.

A sizzling sound preceded the crackling pops of Blake's eyeballs disintegrating, and his throat gurgled. The smell of burning flesh pluming in an acrid cloud of ash turned Connor's stomach. He opened his eyes. In the dying light of the flare's embers, Blake's mouth glowed orange as his tongue cooked inside his mouth.

The captain was injured but not down. The container rocked in the high winds, and Connor knew it was not over.

Blake's enraged bellow galvanized Connor into action.

With a burst of acceleration, he unfastened a steel restraining cable from around a nearby crate. Gripping both ends in one fist, he darted to within Blake's reach.

The hunger of grave sleep focused Blake's brain on the movement, and even with a ruptured face, he bared teeth and dug his claws into Connor's shoulder.

In a lasso-swing, Connor dropped the toughened cable around Blake's neck. He yanked the noose tight and whipped the end around one of the cargo hooks set in the metal panel behind. Connor's coat tore as Blake's teeth burrowed into his shoulder. The sharpened edges gouged holes in Connor's hard muscle until he slammed the butt of the flare gun down on Blake's head. The enraged vampire bellowed, and Connor ducked away.

Stepping back, with the only light inside the container the ashen glow of Blake's contorted demented features, Connor sank down on his haunches. He watched the blurred tornado of Blake's movement as he struggled to reach Connor, the wire cutting deep into his neck. Feral instincts were all that functioned inside the captain's brain.

Connor rested back against the opposite wall, primed to move if the hook gave way and unleashed Blake to hurtle around the space like a projectile in a pinball machine. *He can't see, hear, or taste, but he may get lucky.*

He waited for the ride across to the quay side to be over. *And what then?*

Certainty struck him with the force of a hammer blow. *I can't go out through the front door.* The swaying movement steadied, and the container rotated more slowly, Connor pictured the vampire hands reaching up to guide his metal prison to the ground.

Pushing back up to his feet, he silently climbed to the top of the stacked crates and commando crawled on his stomach into the small space. The ceiling scraped over his shoulder blades. His knees buckled the steel lids as he shunted his heavy weight forward until he could rest his palm on the back wall.

His fingertips absorbed the vibrations rippling through the structure, and he could hear the creak of the chains overhead. Shutting out the spluttering growls of Blake from below, focusing on timing his escape, Connor waited.

The metal skin shuddered when the concrete of the quay grated beneath the settling mass, ending in a final thud as the crane dropped it into place. A cacophony of creaks and grinding moans vibrated beneath his spanned fingers, and Connor punched a hole in the back wall.

Instinct told him that the nomads, anticipating the circus performance of Blake's victory, would be crowded around the front doors. Forcing his arm through the hole and folding back the edges of the fractured steel, Connor drove his head and shoulders through the space. The unrelenting pressure of his rock hard frame stressed the metal until it tore to fit his form.

Connor heard the shrieking protest of the chains dragging over the roof and the thud as the two vampires who rode across on the top jumped down onto the ground. Connor grinned. *I guess they don't want to miss the show.* Easing his body through his escape hatch, he hung from the gutter of the container by one hand, the edge of the metal scoring a line in his granite white palm, taking a moment to quickly scan the compound.

He dropped silently to the ground, and, as a bellow echoed from inside the container, like a sprinter bursting out of the blocks, Connor took off across the concrete. The wire strands of the perimeter fence snapped like spun glass, the fragments exploding into the air as he rammed his way through.

Beyond the boundary of the docks, he darted erratically, dodging the tangled steel skeletons in a graveyard of rusted cranes and broken-down loading machinery. *Tossed over the fence by the nomads, I guess.* A spike of metal grazed across his thigh muscle, tearing his pants, when he dived headlong through a space between two mangled girders and rolled on the ground.

A compressed wave of rushing air plastered his clothes to his back as he regained his feet and hit his stride once more. *Shit, they're gaining, and how many?* Dipping down to the ground, Connor scooped up a handful of scrap metal nuggets, and, spinning on his heel, released a Claymore array of shrapnel. He scored four direct hits. With a series of thuds, chunks of metal embedded themselves in the mud-soft layers of their damp leather tunics and drove the vampires back on their heels.

Swinging back into his run, Connor spurted forward, his mind turning to concealment. *The window of escape is closing fast.* The train tunnel rush of air at his back whipped his hair over his eyes. He hit a glistening wet ribbon of asphalt and veered left, hugging the grass embankment which ran alongside the path.

Connor's survival instinct went into overdrive when he heard scrambling movements deep inside the steep slope of dirt. *Rabbits? Badgers? Who cares?*

His legs pumped hard as he left the asphalt and ran up the bank. Spotting the deep pothole of a disused animal burrow, Connor jumped and landed on both feet. His determination spiked when, as he hoped, the ground disappeared beneath him. Scrabbling to excavate more earth from around his body, scooping it upwards, he forced his way into the burrow until he slipped down into the animals' den. Reaching up over his head, he caved in the soil above until clumps of mud fell onto his face, filling his nostrils and pressing onto his eyeballs.

He kept his eyes open, and the thick veil of dirt gave him hope that his makeshift grave was deep enough to escape detection from above. How long he lay frozen, motionless, his body absorbing the vibrations of preternatural movement overhead, he did not know. The tread of the searching vampires came perilously close to his scalp at times, and Connor prepared to fight his way out if he had to.

The pasture of grass above him finally became as still as the grave in which he lay, and his rock-solid weight sank further beneath the surface. The network of burrows he had invaded crumbled around him, and the tight grip on his chest was strangely reassuring. His hiding place felt more secure, and he settled in for a long wait, knowing Blake's anger would take hours to burn out.

He locked his throat shut. Preserving a clean airway, he descended into the refreshing state of meditation. His last meal of human blood still oozing through the network of veins in his heart and chest shunted a leisurely path up his carotid artery into his brain. He allowed the tranquility of the chilled-out persona of revival sleep free rein.

Enforced solitary confinement gave him time to reflect. He ran through the events leading up to this moment and wondered how Julian, Greg, and Seth had fared. Red vapors of blood filtered gradually into his mind, thickening to a crimson mist, and then, an eddying vortex punched a hole through the surface. A vision of a castle emerged, the sea crashing into the foundations, spraying white mist up over the walls and turning the pale stone to flint-gray.

Connor's grinding teeth juddered through his skull as he battled to hang onto relaxation. Seren's voice drifted in to his head like a whispering breeze. "Papa, we are safe."

The words should have eased the lump in his throat, but the image of the foreboding fortress became a twisting kaleidoscope of color. Now, he was looking at Rebekah's face. Her blonde hair clumped into hanks and her brown eyes were huge saucers of anxiety. *Not fear, my Rebekah would not despair.* He realized that the window into this world was through Seren's eyes. The chain on Rebekah's ankle clanked as she moved, and the crimson clouds inside his head thickened to rage.

Seren's hand reached out in front of him, and she shifted a metal bar in the dungeon window, pulling it forward and lowering it out of place. He would need no such device, the bars would crumble when he got a hold on them. Seren, too, could bend them if she found the confidence to try.

What does this mean? They're planning to escape and cover their tracks? The cliff-like edifice of the castle walls and the jagged skirt of rocks at the base filled Connor with dread. The sudden uninvited image of Rebekah's body lying on the rocks like a broken doll, blood trickling from a battered face, caused his body to convulse and his fists crushed sods of earth into rocks of carbon.

Don't do anything rash, Squirt. I will come for you. Could Seren keep Rebekah from taking matters into her own hands? He hoped so. The wisps of cloud in the vortex shifted again, and a pair of pearl-tinted eyes filled his mind. The intruder gathering his thoughts had thin hair framing an aged, paper-white face. The shimmering image of the vampire evaporated before Connor could grasp the details. They were hauntingly familiar, but the name he needed to give them meaning evaded him.

Fighting back the impulse to throw caution to the winds, erupt from the earth and rescue his family, Connor relaxed once more. *Use this time wisely.* Allowing his brain to fully rehydrate would give him an edge, and he knew he needed that. Unheeding of the dirt pressed to his face like a shroud, he slept.

Chapter 15

As consciousness returned, Rebekah stirred but found that she could not move her limbs. *Am I dead?* She didn't feel dead. A cold rock sat inside her stomach, and her chattering teeth rattled the headache lurking inside her skull.

Finding the strength to explore with her hands, she discovered that it was a heavy padded comforter weighing her down. The soft mattress trying to swallow her body was dry. *So, the water, the flood... none of it was real.* She smiled while a dream she'd been having billowed into her mind once more – Connor, surging up from a lake of water, the sapphire strands in his black hair gleaming in sunshine and his silver gray eyes alight with triumph. The sun reflected in an ethereal glow from his carved features, and happiness reached out to grip her. Only in her imagination had she ever seen his face bathed in sunlight. *But, he'll come for us.*

The feeling of pressure, as if hands spanned her ribcage, dragged unwanted memories to the fore. Her recollections of another vampire who had surged from the surf, his wet hair glinting with dark copper and light refracting from the brass breastplate he wore, solidified in her mind. *Lars.*

Rebekah jolted fully awake and her eyes snapped open. *I'm in a strange bed.* Her heartbeat racing, she stared up at the heavy ruby-red swags of fabric draped around the square frame above. The imposing four poster bed, with intricately carved wooden posts at each corner, was reminiscent of a medieval fairytale, and her mouth fell open.

Her head jerked round as she looked for Seren, and the cramped feeling in her chest eased a little when she saw her – daintily reclined on an impressive chaise longue, Seren's black hair splayed over a velvet cushion. Sleeping Beauty, another fairytale, came to mind.

Throwing back the covers revealed a dress Rebekah had never seen before. *How did...?* A hot flush burned her cheeks and she shied away from the thought of *any* vampire hands undressing her, let alone the sentinel's. She swung her legs over the side of the bed, huffing as the cotton petticoats beneath the ridiculously long skirt wound around her calves.

"For goodness' sake, what does he think this is? The 16th century?" Looking down at the heavy brocade material, she traced her fingertips over the starched fabric of the bodice and began to wonder. "Maybe he *does* come from the 16th century." The uncomfortable idea that these clothes could mean anything to Lars, maybe hold a human attachment, made her break into a cold sweat. It trickled down between her breasts.

Grabbing at distraction to push the thought aside, she padded in bare feet across the floor and perched beside Seren. *At least, he kept us together.* Her hand rested on Seren's cool cheek. *How long has she been asleep?* Seren's breathing was so slow that Rebekah began to panic, but then her eyelashes fluttered, and rolling movements beneath her eyelids showed that the girl was dreaming. Rebekah wondered if she, too, was dreaming of Connor.

Rebekah surveyed her surroundings. *Where are we?* Her bare feet sank into the thick pile of a woolen rug, and the cavernous walk-in fireplace glowed brightly. Orange flames of a long-established blaze danced over the blackened wood and ash gray lumps of coal. Weak sunshine struggled through the tall arched window. *So, we have been here a few hours, at least.*

The crashing fury of the sea had subsided to the gentle murmur of a lullaby which drifted on the air. Crossing quickly to the window, her stomach turned over. The gleaming surface of the sea was dozens of yards below. This room, with its gently curving walls, was in another turret. *He's moved us further away from Connor. We have to get back to the dungeon somehow.*

Rebekah squinted into the sky. True, it was daylight, but, judging by the nip in the air and the purple and gray cloud cover, this part of the world was further north than Kent. Rebekah shivered, the exposed flesh of her collarbones and shoulders suddenly feeling cold. Casting her eye around the room, she dragged a thick shawl from the back of a wooden throne chair and pulled it around her shoulders.

"Mama?"

Rebekah turned quickly, a smile lighting her eyes. "Hey. Morning, sweetheart. Or afternoon, I can't say for sure."

With a frown, Seren rolled easily up, swung her legs around and sat still. "What happened? How did we get here?"

"Well. You fell asleep, and we nearly drowned. I nearly drowned," corrected Rebekah. "And, yes, I'm okay," she added at Seren's look of concern. "Apart from sleeping too long." *And feeling like my bones are made of ice.*

"Where are we, now?"

Rebekah sat beside Seren. Pushing a tress of raven black hair behind the girl's ear, she said, "I'm not really sure. The dungeon flooded. The storm, high tide, who knows." Rebekah shrugged. "Anyway, you were asleep, and I got us both up onto that altar shelf. I passed out, I think, and I woke up here."

Seren remained silent, plucking at the skirt of her own absurdly outdated gown. "Mama. I dreamed of Papa."

Rebekah smiled. "I did too."

"No. I mean I saw through his eyes. He's under the ground, buried under the ground."

Taking Seren's hand, Rebekah said quietly, "Perhaps he's sleeping too. You know, Papa has to sleep sometimes."

"I showed him the castle and the window in the dungeon. I can get you out to meet him, if we can get back there."

Rebekah said, "I know your father well enough to know he will be cursing under his breath at your plan. But, yes, as soon as you can tell where he is, when he is close, we'll have to get back to the dungeon, somehow."

Seren sat completely still, apart from her scratching fingertips which tore a hole in her dress.

"Honey?" Rebekah said gently.

"I saw someone else, a strong presence who is sucking information from Papa's mind. I'm scared, Mama."

"Do you know who it is?"

"No, but, he is very old, his skin's wrinkled."

Rebekah sighed. "It's not Sentinel Lars, at least." The worst thing she could imagine was that Lars could read minds too, and would discover Connor's whereabouts.

Noticing Seren's busy fingers worrying at the hole in her skirt, Rebekah gripped her chin and looked into her face. The changes were glaringly obvious even to her human sight. Capillaries resembling threads of silver lace were spreading throughout the quartz-like translucence of Seren's skin. "You're dehydrating, sweetheart. Do you feel okay?"

"A little stiff. I hadn't noticed. Sorry Mama."

Rebekah knew 'a little stiff' was an understatement. In preparation for raising a hybrid child, Connor made sure he told her everything they might expect. The stiffness translated into shrinking tendon sheaths gripping the sinews, which would feel like a hacksaw blade sawing through them.

"I think you need to hunt," said Rebekah thoughtfully. "The sentinel will understand that, and it will get us out of the castle. I'll ask him." She shot to her feet with sudden urgency written on her face.

"Mama?"

Rebekah said, "If you get the chance to escape, do it." As Seren protested, she added, "Don't worry, I know it's unlikely, but if we make a show of trying, perhaps he'll put us back in the dungeon. It's worth a gamble, hmm?"

Seren shot her a 'you know what Papa would say' look, and Rebekah ignored it.

Beating on the door with the flat of her hand, Rebekah shouted, "Hello?" Before she could call out again, the warm wood was whipped away and she almost toppled forward. Regaining her balance, she looked up into the neutral expression of the vampire called Erik. *He was not thrilled at waiting on the table onboard the ship. I guess it's a vain hope that babysitting is his dream job.*

"Erik?"

His eyes didn't narrow, but the dead brown pools thickened in discomfort.

Okay, trampling all over his toes, then. Starting again, she said, "I must speak to Sentinel Lars, please." The door slammed in her face, and Rebekah burst out laughing. "Charming."

She barely had time to wonder what to do next when a sudden breeze whisked around her bare ankles, and she stepped hastily back. She knew the rushing vortex of a fast approaching vampire when she felt it.

The door vanished. Rebekah didn't see it move. It was simply replaced by the tall imposing figure of Lars, his golden breastplate glowing in the fading afternoon light, and his cape still swaying wildly, slapping over sturdy, leather-covered thighs.

The fanned flames in the hearth leapt in greeting and shot his hair through with burning amber highlights. The power he exuded made Rebekah's mouth dry with nerves. Lars' moods were like a boiling cauldron, and she never knew which reaction would rise to the top. The sinews working in his forearms mesmerized her and the heat creeping up her neck flushed her cheeks. She knew, instinctively, he had carried her into this room.

Meeting her eyes, his icy stare melted as he seemed to guess her thoughts. His regard alight with the glint of crystal, he said on a feral smile, "Min skat? You have need of me, nej?"

Rebekah's flush drained away to a cold sweat. "Sentinel, Seren is hungry-"

His eyes stayed on Rebekah's face. "I will bring her food."

"No, she needs to hunt."

Understanding dawned, a purr stirred gravel in his throat and his attention snapped over to Seren. His eyes narrowed when he saw the girl's translucent complexion. His movement leaving the blur of a comet's tail, he strode the ten yards across the chamber, stopped in front of Seren, and lifted her chin. He stared into her dilated pupils, and at the ashen smudges around dehydrating eye sockets, and breathed, "So you do. Human sleep takes its toll, hmmm?" His head tilted as he absorbed Seren's scent, dragging it over his pallet. He found the muted pulse in her neck with his thumb, and his features slackened with fascination. "Incredible."

Worried that Seren could be taken from the room without her, Rebekah blurted, "I am coming too." *Let's face it, if he* wants *to separate us, what could we do?*

I want Mama with me," said Seren.

Caught in the midst of his enchantment, Lars murmured, "But, of course. We will leave at dusk."

Rebekah was not sure if it was the knotted excitement of possible escape which caused the pain in her chest, or Lars' arm clamped across her body as their horse galloped at a terrifying speed over rough ground. Despite the more sensible riding clothing Lars had given her to wear, the bitter wind numbed her flesh, and her windpipe felt as if icicles were being forced down her throat. *But I'll be damned if I'll let on I'm in pain.*

Seren ran on ahead, her driving stride eating up the distance without once stumbling in the long grass of the meadow. Rebekah gritted her teeth, grateful to see the olive-green smudge of the woodland up ahead separating out into individual trees. Her pain should soon be over.

Passing beneath the canopy of rustling leaves brought Rebekah immediate relief.

Lars reined in the horse, easing it smoothly back to a walk. His barked command to Seren, telling her to wait, echoed through the woodlands as the horse came to a restless halt.

Rebekah slipped thankfully down from the saddle. When her knees almost folded beneath her, she grabbed hold of Lars' boot, but snatched her hand back as if the leather delivered an electric shock.

Lars' laughter drifted through the trees.

When Rebekah squinted up at him, the exhilarated glitter in his gaze chilled her to the core.

The ground vibrated as Lars dismounted and landed heavily beside her. His stare shifted to Seren, and Rebekah hoped this hunting expedition was not a mistake.

Seren joined them and tucked her fingers into Rebekah's clenched hand. Smiling, she said, "It will be okay, Mama. I can hear a lot of wildlife in the woods. It'll be quick."

"Mount up, min skat," said Lars. "You can follow on behind. And in case you are wondering, Erik will be close by, to make sure you don't get lost."

"I won't get lost, but thank you," said Rebekah, stiff with annoyance. Ignoring the helping hand Lars offered, she gathered the reins, put her boot into the stirrup, and swung up into the saddle.

"Make sure you don't," Lars said quietly, before turning to Seren. "These woods are stocked with Roe deer, the same as those in England, so you should feel at home, nej?"

"What else can I smell?" said Seren, her voice vibrating with impatience.

Lars scented the air and frowned. "It seems we have an interloper, a lynx. It has probably escaped from the enclosed hunting ground fifty miles to the south."

"May I?" asked Seren.

Lars' lip curled and his tongue collected the visceral saliva glistening on his bared teeth. "If you think you can take him, I'd be interested to see it."

In a burst of movement, Seren and Lars took off through the woods together. Rebekah nudged the stallion into a canter, weaving expertly between the tall slender tree trunks, desperate to keep Seren within ear shot, at least. Knowing Erik was stalking her laid an uncomfortable tingle down Rebekah's spine, communicating fear to her jittery mount and making the ride tougher than it needed to be. *Get a grip, Rebekah. Erik is a babysitter, nothing more.*

The trail of sap weeping from broken branches and trampled undergrowth made tracking Seren easy, although Rebekah could hear nothing except the thudding of her horse's hooves and the beating of her own heart. She tried not to let the frustration of not knowing what was happening make her careless.

Will there be a way for Seren to fake a convincing escape attempt? Because, that is all it could be. A feint, aimed at getting them back to the safety of their dungeon. *Unless.* The glimmer of hope that, against all the odds, Seren's escape attempt might work, became hard to quash. *You never know.* Her stubborn optimism stalled when the woodlands ahead erupted with the sounds of slaughter. There was no other word for the splattering noise of wet blood.

A gurgling, whimpering cry tore through the silence, followed, a split second later, by a heavy thump and the noise of bone cracking.

Pushing down into the saddle and using her heels, Rebekah urged the horse into a canter. Gripping both reins in one hand, she crouched low and used the other to shield her face from the low-hanging foliage which grazed over her back.

Rebekah burst into the clearing in time to see Seren rise gracefully to her feet and wipe the back of her hand across her mouth. The black leather hunting jacket she wore glistened with the oily sheen of fresh blood, and manic excitement glittered in her eyes before she hooded her gaze.

The horse balked, rearing and wheeling round at the smell of blood. Rebekah twisted in the saddle to keep Seren in her sights. Smiling widely at her daughter's impassive expression, as though every mother had the same milestone to negotiate, Rebekah said, "Was it the lynx?"

Seren smiled, relief glinting in her wide dark eyes.

Lars' voice floated out of the shadows. "You would have been proud of her. She is magnificent. So much speed in one so slight."

Rebekah felt sick at the possessive note of pride in the sentinel's tone. *It is Connor who should've been here.* But to mention him now would give Lars power, reveal her weakness.

Lars arrived at Seren's side and set a hand on her shoulder. "You were right, little one, it was quick."

Rebekah buried the revulsion aching in her throat and with a smile, intended only for Seren, she said, "Do you want to go back now?"

Seren's wry grin caught Rebekah unawares. *She looks more like Connor every day.* Her daughter's long stride as she shrugged off

Lars' hand and jogged across the grass reminded Rebekah of him too.

The stallion shied at her approach, and Seren grimaced. "Ah, I guess I'm not a pretty sight right now."

There was nothing that could be done about the blood smeared over her face and hands, so Seren said lightly, "I guess I need a bath. Let's go back, Mama."

Tightening her reins, Rebekah controlled the horse's jerky retreat, although the stallion continued to huff nervously through velvet nostrils. She patted the animal's shoulder and clucked her tongue, turning his head to face the way they had come.

The journey back through the woods should have been more relaxed. Although, her mount seemed determined to outrun the smell of blood-soaked vampire, so the speed became more high-octane than Rebekah wanted.

Seren dropped back a few paces, allowing the horse the relief of a few more yards. She chuckled. "Wise animal. There's no convincing him he wouldn't be food in a heartbeat."

Rebekah couldn't see Lars, but she felt sure he would cruise along behind, orchestrating events. The horse was his, and would be certain to obey his command.

Tossing her words into the wind, Rebekah said, "You've fed, so we'll be okay for a day or so." The look Rebekah sent said 'we'll soon be at the castle and will have to find another way to get back to the dungeon'.

Seren nodded her understanding and accelerated ahead.

Rebekah watched with fascination. Back when Seren was a baby, Connor had tried to explain what their child would go through. She envied them both, wishing she was a vampire who could experience the fully-fed, lubricated feeling of unleashing propulsion through tendons that had the tensile strength of steel. Seren appeared oblivious of the icy windchill of traveling at such devastating speeds.

Beyond Seren's racing form, across the meadow, the fortress loomed as a fairytale castle, its walls bathed in the muted gold of a sunset, and the windows reflected a fiery orange glow that promised warmth for Rebekah's shivering flesh.

The tension of the hunting expedition made Rebekah's tight shoulders burn. *Is it so bad I'll be relieved to return to the peace and quiet of a locked room?* But, the lure of the castle was forgotten when, from the corner of her eye, Rebekah noticed Seren stop sharply and then shoot off on a new trajectory. Seren's chin jerked up, and Rebekah wondered what she had seen, and then, she saw it too. A hawk glided overhead.

The drifting mass of the bird in flight stalled as though it hit an invisible force-field. The taloned feet swung forward as it dived. Rebekah watched, but did not understand, not at first. Reining in the horse, she focused on the unfolding scene. She did not hear Lars until his low amused tone broke her concentration.

"A little sport, I think. It's like a cat, No? The movement pulls her in."

The hawk's swooping path accelerated, and so did Seren's.

Rebekah held her breath as Seren disappeared into the distance, the path she carved drawing her ever closer to the bird hurtling towards the ground like a feather-clad stone.

Rebekah darted a look at Lars, whose profile reflected the same intense purpose she saw in the hawk. The sinews in his arms pulled tight when he clenched his fists, anticipating the kill.

The hawk hurtled downwards, honing in on a rabbit scrambling in the grass. As his talons splayed and the dagger-sharp points formed a deadly clawed grip, Seren leapt into the air. Thirty feet above the meadow, their bodies collided. The honeycombed construct of the bird's ribcage crumbled in Seren's embrace. Crushing a wing and gripping the avian skull in her hand, she twisted until the fragile neck snapped with a sickeningly cheerful pop.

They dropped from the sky in a tangled mass, until Seren released the bird. She landed on her feet, letting the carcass thud into the long grass beside her.

Lars stared, the satisfied cast on his taut features shifting to disbelief when Seren stepped over the dead hawk and took off, making a break for the distant wood. The metal of his breastplate creaked with the eager feral breath he took, and then, with a bark of harsh laughter, he accelerated in pursuit.

Thinking as fast as a sluggish human brain could manage, Rebekah dug her heels into her mount until it bolted in the opposite direction, rushing away towards the distant castle.

Lars was already a hundred yards away, intent on catching up with Seren.

Not allowing herself time to do anything more than pray, Rebekah threw herself from the horse. She screamed in genuine terror as the ground rushed up towards her and, suddenly, there was too much time to think. She landed in thick moss-strangled grass, rolling into a ball when her shoulder hit the ground, just as Greg had taught her. She came to rest and groaned. The sharpest points of her skeleton burned in agony. Rolling over onto her back, she turned her head and squinted through the curtain of green fronds. She wondered if Lars had even noticed.

Rebekah fought to control her rasping breathing. It scratched at her dry throat and she tried not to cough. She hoped that having got this far, Seren would keep running... *and escape.*

The first thing she saw was his boots. When she looked up, the dim light could not disguise the annoyance in his frosty stare.

Holding out an imperious hand, Lars said, "Komme."

Ignoring the cramped knot in her stomach, Rebekah struggled and sat up without his help.

He dropped to one knee beside her and said, "Er du ondt?"

"Am I hurt?"

Lars nodded, his head tilting to one side as if he was listening to a tune which Rebekah couldn't hear, and she knew he was still tracking Seren.

Instantly moving, Rebekah braced her feet on the ground, tried to get up, and whimpered. "My ankle. I hurt my ankle."

In a fluid movement, Lars lifted her foot, removed her boot, and, cupping her heel, pressed carefully over the joint with firm fingertips.

Rebekah leaned sideways to see over his shoulder, happy that Seren had disappeared from human sight. She let out a gasp when Lars' bitter cold hands closed around her ankle. She silently prayed. *Please, God, let her get away.*

Lars closed his eyes, inhaled, and then his eyes snapped open. His glare was diamond-hard as he surged to his feet. "There is nothing wrong with your ankle." He flexed his fingers in irritation.

"But it hurts." Rebekah had forgotten vampires have many more senses to use.

"I think not. Human muscle tears. The tissue bleeds beneath the surface at the slightest injury. There is no sprain." He tilted his head. "You will have bruises, yes. But, that is all."

Pulling her boot back on, Rebekah let her hair fall forward to cover her red cheeks. She awkwardly tried to stand.

With a cold grin, Lars carefully held her arm until Rebekah regained her balance.

She braced herself to meet his disdain.

"You were lucky. But stupid, no?"

Before Rebekah could answer, his stiff smile faltered and his head shot around. Lars contemplated the empty meadow, and an adrenalin rush of genuine fear for Seren made Rebekah's bruises throb,

Laughter rattled in the sentinel's throat, and Rebekah staggered when the support of his hand vanished.

"She has made it to the woods already. She is quick." Lars stepped back, his thick ruby cape flaring as he spun on his heel. "Erik," he said lightly, "watch the mother."

Rebekah watched him take off across the pasture until he faded to a blur.

Erik stood a comfortable ten yards away, with his usual reluctance crimping his features.

Rebekah grimaced, rubbing a hand over her backside. *That will be the biggest bruise tomorrow.* She waved to attract Erik's attention. "I don't suppose you could catch the horse? I'll wait here. Scout's honor." Rebekah put up three fingers in the Boy Scout salute, and Erik stared blankly.

Nothing. I wonder if he's simple?

Like a coma victim waking up, Erik's face reanimated. He gave what could only be called 'a long-suffering sigh', and grew three inches in stature. In a low clear voice, he said, "Du vil bo?"

Assuming they were talking about the same thing, Rebekah nodded soberly. That appeared to be the right response because Erik turned and left.

She stood in the middle of the empty pasture, evening gathering around her like a shroud. The longer it took Lars to return, the more she dared to hope.

When a hunchbacked silhouette emerged from the rapidly falling shadows of dusk, Rebekah squinted, trying to make it fit the mold of a vampire alone. A rhythmic beating noise reached her, and the approaching mass separated into two figures. Lars' stride devoured the distance. His glowering features accentuated a stone set jaw. Seren was slung over his shoulder, and Rebekah realized the beating sound was her daughter thumping on his back, her fists playing his ribcage like a xylophone.

Rebekah could not help but smile. Seren had no hope of escape, but, like a mosquito tormenting a lion, she made sure he could not enjoy his triumph.

Lars did not falter, continuing on past Rebekah.

She called out, "Hey."

Swinging around, Lars barked, "Erik will bring you home on the horse. I think we have had enough adventure for one day, nej?" Turning away again, he broke into a jog, accelerated to a dark streak, and then, he was gone.

Staring after him, Rebekah barely heard Erik riding up beside her, and she jumped when he leaned over in the saddle and touched her shoulder. When she looked up, her tears blurred the oval of his white face. Rebekah accepted his help to mount the horse and leaned back into the disconcerting comfort of his solid body. The horse broke into a canter which stirred the sick feeling in her stomach like a fairground ride. *Lars won't separate us, surely?*

Darkness had dropped like a curtain by the time they passed beneath the spiked portcullis. The horse's hooves clattered on the cobblestones of the inner courtyard until Eric reined in their mount. The aged wooden doors swung shut with a groan and iron grated on iron as they were locked. Once back on her feet, Rebekah waited for Erik to turn left and lead the way towards the keep, but he didn't. *So, Lars is not returning us to the dungeon.*

Rebekah hung back, dreading the moment of walking through the enormous doorway and into the body of the castle. The huge oak doors slammed shut behind her, the dull thud reverberating like a death knell. Her skin prickled with the discomforting feeling of being swallowed by a monster. The cavernous great hall loomed like the empty stomach of the beast.

Without warning, a concealed stone panel in the wall glided open, and a smiling Doctor Heinrik appeared.

Rebekah jerked to attention. "Where is Seren?"

Heinrik's deliberate silence closed an icy grip on Rebekah's heart. Finally, his black-beaded stare narrowed. "Poor child is too agitated to obtain reliable blood pressure and biometric readings." His clipped tone drained the sympathy from his words. "Sentinel Lars tells me the girl is indisposed until tomorrow."

"Enough." The word echoed around the great hall, and Rebekah did not have to look around to know Lars had arrived. "I'll take you to your room."

Rebekah met his cool blue regard, and said, "We would understand if you return us to the dungeon. It will be dry by now, and-" Darting a pointed glance at Heinrik, she added, "Perhaps we would be safer under lock and key."

Lars took a step closer and tilted Rebekah's chin with firm fingers. "But then, I would not see the lengths you are willing to go to in protecting your child." His expression was speculative as he said, "I've seen your daughter in action, and you remain as undaunted by me as ever. Why would I miss the chance to see you break, hmm?"

"Just take me to her. Is she in our room?" Rebekah asked sweetly.

Lars laughed. "Komme."

Realizing the doctor was not joining them, Rebekah readily hurried along behind Lars' gliding gait. The exertion of running up the stairs caused her bruises to throb again, and she wondered how much of her skin would be purple by tomorrow. By the sudden jerk of Lars' chin, she realized he could smell the ruptured capillaries seeping blood into her skin. Her heart accelerated to rib-cracking proportions and she swallowed carefully, trying to calm her nerves. Measuring her stride, she dropped back.

Minutes later, the sentinel opened the door to their bedroom of last night, and Rebekah staggered when Seren flew across the room and threw her arms around her.

"Mama! You're safe."

Rebekah dropped a kiss onto the disarray of her daughter's hair and chuckled. "I am safe, Honey. And so are you."

The door closed, leaving them alone together, and they stood for endless minutes holding each other.

Moving back, Seren said, "Sentinel Lars. Do not trust him, Mama. I could read his mood, he is hiding behind smiles." Seren frowned, "He's a cruel man, I think. A warrior. He has many broken bones from when he was human. As a vampire, he thinks nothing can touch him."

"How can you know that?" Rebekah found the bleak look on her young daughter's face frightening.

Seren smiled, lightening the mood. "His broken bones are like a tuning fork with the frequency interrupted. The notes changed when I banged on his ribs."

"So, you cannot read *his* mind? It is just Papa?"

"No, I can't read his mind. But when he chased me down out there, I got scared. My chest got tight, so I ran away inside my head." Seren's voice dropped to a whisper. "I found a door and when I went through it, I felt calm. I saw him clearly. Lars' face was smiling, but I could feel greed."

Wishing Connor was here to explain, Rebekah followed her own suspicions. "Seren, I think maybe you were in revival sleep. Do you remember when we were at dinner on the ship? I'm certain now.

Remember, Papa told you there are three vampire sleep centers inside his head?"

Seren nodded solemnly.

"I think this is the first one. There are two other... doors inside your mind. The others are not so soothing." Rebekah smiled reassuringly.

"Papa said I would learn how to sleep my vampire brain centers. He said one will make me angry and throw things, and the other, he said I should be alone for. I'll want to eat anything I can touch, as long as it's living, of course." Seren quirked a smile so much more mature than her words.

Rebekah silently thanked Connor for finding the right things to say.

"Do tell me Seren, when you're feeling new things. I'm your Mama, I want to help. The throwing things and being angry comes next, I think. But, try not to throw things at me, hmm? I think I would come off worst." *It seems, puberty arrives early when you're a vampire.*

Rebekah watched her daughter's serious face and wondered when she last saw an infectious smile there. Seren swept the swathe of her jet-black hair back over one shoulder and lifted her chin.

Rebekah saw the concern in her gray eyes and waited.

"What's it like? Pain? Papa said you bruise easy. What's it like?"

A child shouldn't have to worry about the parent. "You know, if I were as feeble as you imagine, you would not be here," Rebekah said gently. "I fought hard to bring you into this world, and we're not going to let anyone tear our family apart. That's all we need to concentrate on, for now. Okay?"

Seren closed the space, slipped her arms around Rebekah and squeezed, gently. "Okay," she whispered.

Chapter 16

The earth surrounding Connor's still form shifted as grains of dirt filtered into the spaces made by the passing of earthworms. He heard the clicking and crunching of insect mandibles devouring leaves and grubs, and the sounds lulled his refreshed mind into concentrated focus. It was an uncomfortable truth, but feeding on the super tanker humans had saved him from vampire coma. *Blake did me a favor, if I had to fake using Greg as my food onboard, I'd be facing a dehydrated brain, about now.*

During the hours after the search for him had been called off, he burrowed deeper into the soil and, in a rare opportunity, slept each of his brain centers in turn. He relished the process even when the hunger burning in his gut carved a path up through his chest. In grave sleep the psychopath rattled around inside his head, filling his mouth with saliva that pooled in the back of his throat. Resisting the warm blood of any creature became almost impossible.

A mole, its claws excavating a path which collided with Connor's shoulder, scraped its way onto his chest, its pink nose snuffling over the vampire's collarbone. The urge to plow his hand through the dirt, grab hold of the svelte body, and bite into its flesh tested Connor's one hundred years of control; his cramped muscles and the restraint of tightly wound sinews saved the mole's life.

Slamming the cell door shut inside his head and locking away the lunatic, finally gave way to heightened awareness where he felt the weight of every grain of dirt lying on his skin

The earth pressing into his face grated over his skin when he smiled. Being buried was not a new experience, but not one he would ever enjoy. His widening smile rode a wave of bloodthirsty satisfaction as Seren once more projected images onto the canvas inside his head. He saw, not only a clear picture of Sentinel Lars' face, but a detailed impression of his towering height, and the battle dress which covered muscles seemingly carved in stone.

His eagerness for Seren's images fired the synapses inside his fully hydrated brain, and the battle plan raced through his mind in a fast forward rehearsal of events to come. His fingertips twitched as his body joined in the illusion, performing the actions which would save Rebekah. A scene where the Danish sentinel's hand touched Rebekah ignited the banked fires of his anger into incandescent rage.

Connor sneered. Soil filled his mouth as he anticipated the exhilaration of his teeth tearing through the hard flesh of Sentinel Lars. His body jolted as he imagined Lars' cold blue eyes glazing with the frost-like effect of death. He visualized crushing his enemy's cranium to dust.

Suddenly, cataracts clouded Lars' eyes to a pearly fish-scale kaleidoscope of muted colors. His vigorous youthful expression wasted away, and a tanned parchment of shrunken skin clung to his skull. The facial muscles beneath Connor's grasp shifted, and the face transformed into one he had not seen in almost a hundred years. *Malachi.*

Connor's mind recoiled. The vision smiled and the rows of hideous yellowed teeth stabbed into white gums were just as he remembered them from the day Malachi tore his human life from him.

He had come to know the monster well, and in more ways than he would admit, it was Malachi who helped him become a vampire of fearsome strength; one who could control the craving of bloodlust which caused other vampires to crumble.

The sentinel, and now Malachi. Feeling that his fate bore down upon him and all he had to do was act it out, he drove up out of the earth. He erupted through the surface and regained his feet, scattering clumps of soil in a shower of black rain. Grateful to leave his makeshift grave behind, he dragged his fingertips down over his face, scooping the soil from his eye sockets and spitting out the emulsion of dirt which filled his mouth. He roughly filled in the crater left behind, moving the tumbled avalanche of rocks and lumps of mud with his boot.

Three miles east, I told Julian, Greg, and Seth. He set off at a fast run, the earth falling from his coat becoming a dirt storm in his wake.

When a fast-flowing stream crossed his path, he dropped his watch into his coat pocket, and tossed both the coat and his boots across to the opposite bank. He waded into the fast moving current and dropped to his knees. Ducking his head beneath the cascading surface, he rinsed the dirt from his face and sluiced water through his hair until the strands slipping through his fingers were slick.

He waded to the other side, with his shirt and pants plastered to his body, climbed out, sat on a log, and pulled on the boots. Retrieving his watch from the pocket, Connor held up the greatcoat by the collar. Sentimental attachment meant he would never risk ruining the garment in the stream, so he beat the worst of the mud from the fabric. Once the earth dried, what remained would work its way out from between the woven threads, especially when he put it through the wind tunnel of traveling at top vampire speed.

He shrugged into the coat, and by the time he covered the last mile to where Julian waited, his clothes were dry.

As if a beacon marked the spot, Connor stopped precisely three miles east of the dockside. He spotted Julian standing beneath the shaded canopy of a cluster of beech trees and both vampires smiled.

Tilting his head as he arrived at Julian's side, Connor tuned into the slow steady heartbeats of Greg and Seth, and said, "So, it all went according to plan?"

"They are hunkered down behind the trees, resting." Julian laughed at how simple Connor made 'the plan' sound. "Luckily for us, there was a distraction when the ship docked. You. It's the first time I've understood what 'looking daggers at someone' really means. From what I saw, the nomads' eyes could've bored holes in your back. I imagine your escape was not so simple."

Connor shrugged. "I got more than I bargained for, but mission accomplished." Turning to look out from beneath the cover of the tree canopy, he inspected the alien landscape. He watched the mist drifting over acres of dew-laden green grass. "It's very flat, Denmark."

"Well, yes. It *was* in the path of a glacier millions of years ago."

Julian's sarcasm went unnoticed as Connor squinted and scanned the horizon.

Joining him, Julian nudged his shoulder. "It will be dawn in two hours. We'll have to wait until afternoon before we leave the woods." Jerking his chin to indicate Greg and Seth, he said, "They need rest, in any case."

"Do you know where the castle is?" Connor asked.

"I went ten miles out to the east. I could see it from there," Julian said.

"Well, that's a fifteen-minute run. We leave Greg and Seth, and go now. We'll be back here with Rebekah and Seren within the two hours."

They both knew Connor was fantasizing, but Julian played out the game. "So, how are we going to get inside unseen? And *where* are they in the castle? Unless you're planning on plowing through every wall between you and them, and taking out every vampire guard along the way, I think we need to do some reconnaissance first, don't you?"

Connor said, "Seren sent me images of their dungeon, *and* the chains on their ankles."

Julian laid a heavy hand on his friend's shoulder.

"I know what Sentinel Lars looks like, and how to defeat him. I just need to get close enough." Connor smiled bitterly. "Seren is her mother's daughter, they will be ready when we come."

"Let's go and pick Greg and Seth's brains. Four heads are better than two, even if two of them are human," Julian joked.

Connor's narrowed gaze did not shift from the hazy landscape.

Julian's grip tightened on his shoulder. "What?"

"I don't know. Something. I saw Malachi."

Julian's head jerked around. "Where? Here?"

"No, when I was in revival sleep." Connor's lips twitched. "Although, there was not much by way of relaxation."

Julian's tone was uneasy. "Perhaps Seren tapped into your own memories, and *she* put him there?"

Taking a deep breath, Connor turned back into the shade of the trees. "You're right. Let's go and plan an attack." Dismissing his reluctance to move, Connor walked away at Julian's side until his greatcoat twitched around his thighs in an eddying breeze.

It was a mere whisper, but Connor froze in his tracks. *I'd recognize that smell anywhere.* The dried parchment aroma which clung to his maker like a shroud was unmistakable. But, Connor could hear a faint heartbeat riding on the breeze, too" His smooth skin creased with confusion.

"Malachi," he muttered as he abandoned Julian and returned to his vigil.

A dark silhouette appeared on the horizon, hurtling forward at the speed of a runaway freight train, and, as the ashen-gray details of Malachi's face came into focus, so did the dramatic bronze-toned features of his companion.

Connor struggled to make sense of the odor of aromatic oil and the configuration of the two bodies, until the dark stranger swung his legs into view and hit the ground running, in a light-footed parody of a parachute landing. *So, surfing in Malachi's wake?* His attention locked onto the forceful young man's somnolent heartbeat. Despite the trauma of riding at vampire speed, Malachi's passenger was the epitome of composure – as the hurtling velocity faded, the black curtain of his hair fell back into place and his face exuded calm.

Osiris. Connor's unasked question was answered when he pulled the strange name from thin air. He knew by Malachi's arrogant smile that his mentor had put it there.

Julian joined Connor and watched their final approach. "Why is he here now? Be careful Connor, look beneath the surface. Why would Malachi turn up?"

"He's here for a reason." Connor took his eyes from the approaching crow-like outlines for a brief moment to look at Julian. "And his companion is interesting. We'll hear him out, at least."

Julian had known Malachi much longer than Connor and had more reason to distrust him. Malachi had made Julian's role as principal of the London hive difficult, at times. The final straw occurred in 1910 when Malachi shielded his brother, Numu. To cover up the brutal murders his twin had committed on the city streets, Malachi had lied to the council.

Malachi had protected his brother for thousands of years. Julian sometimes wondered if he should have sentenced Malachi to death, but then, the aged vampire had turned Connor and saved him from being Numu's final victim. Julian could never really know, and that irritated him, too.

The incoming vampires finally stopped six feet from their welcoming committee.

"Principal Julian. This is a pleasant turn of events." Malachi's oyster-tinted gaze widened ingenuously. "I'm happy Doctor Connor has someone on his side."

Julian cut straight to the point. "What do you know?"

Malachi tilted his head, putting a hand on Osiris' chest and blocking his path as the Egyptian took exception to Julian's tone and made to take a step closer. "It's okay, Osiris, the principal and I are old friends."

Julian reared slightly, inhaling Osiris' human scent and finding the same confusing information Connor had already registered.

Ignoring the focus on Osiris, Malachi said, "I know only what Connor knows, and about the girl."

Connor and Julian spoke at once. "The girl?"

Malachi bared yellow teeth, transferring his keen gaze to Connor. "You have a protégé? You turned a girl? I had not expected it-" The aged vampire snapped his attention back to Julian. "And I thought it was forbidden to reduce the food supply by even one human. But then, Connor is your friend," Malachi said slowly, his voice trailing off.

Connor's narrowed gaze remained trained on the bronzed skin of Osiris' face as he listened to his heartbeat, and inhaled the smell of incense. Without looking away, he said, "Who is your companion, Malachi? Not a vampire, but, exceptional."

Glancing pointedly at the lightening sky, Malachi said, "We have much to talk about. We should be comfortable."

The elder vampire's garb could withstand the weak hazy sunshine of a Danish winter's day, but to a roaming vampire's eyes he would be visible for many miles.

Connor moved aside. "You're right, of course. Join us."

Malachi stepped into the shaded canopy with Osiris glued to his side. Sweeping back the hood of his gray cape unveiled a sparse covering of silver-tinted strands of hair over a putty-colored scalp. Malachi laughed gently. Looking Connor's muscular frame up and down, he said wistfully, "It is good to see I taught you well. Come. I think we both have stories to tell." With a wave of his bony hand, he added, "You, too, have humans in attendance. A lot has changed in the ninety years since last we met."

Connor laughed gently. "You're right."

Malachi's dry skin crackled as he said seriously, "So, there is a girl, a woman, a castle, and a warrior?"

Connor was past surprise. "That about sums things up. All we have to do is work out how to get the girl and the woman out of the castle."

"And the warrior?" Malachi chuckled at Connor's venomous glare. "Ah, I see."

Julian's impatience erupted with deathly calm. "You see everything, it seems. Why are you here?"

Ignoring the principal, Malachi smiled, his mist-colored gaze glittering. "So, who are they?"

"Why do you not just visit my mind and find out?" asked Connor.

"There is a lot going on in there. I can see the pictures the girl is giving you, but I need more explanation."

The black sweep of Connor's hair ruffled in the sharp gust of air as Malachi pounced and clamped his bony fingers around Connor's skull. A kaleidoscope of pictures rushed through Malachi's head, and anger boiled inside Connor because he relived it all. Lars sharing a horse with Rebekah, and then, tenderly, to Connor's mind, dropping to his knees, removing Rebekah's boot and touching her skin. Connor's rage was palpable when he saw the Danish warrior carrying his child, slung over his shoulder like a sack of grain.

Malachi's eyes widened as he absorbed Connor's incandescent fury. "You are in love?" he said, "and she is your child? Incredible."

Malachi's awed tone drew Osiris to his side. "Master?"

Turning to look at the impassive Egyptian, Malachi said, "In time, Osiris, I shall explain."

Julian said sharply, "It is your turn, Malachi. Why do you have a human consort? You and Numu always traveled light."

Malachi blinked slowly as Julian's barb hit home. "Osiris, show them."

Osiris stepped forward and eased a finger beneath the adornment of a golden serpent coiled around his bicep. Slipping the armlet downwards to his elbow, he revealed a bamboo catheter embedded in his vein with a wax plug sealing the end.

The smell of blood drifted up Connor's nostrils and he said in amazement, "He is your food?"

Malachi nodded. "I told you, surviving in Egypt is harsh, but it is my home. A human would not set off into the desert without water, and I would not set out without blood. He comes from an ancient tribe of Earth Walkers. They are masters in the art of meditation, and have great spiritual control over their body chemistry."

Would that account for the unusually steady heart rate? Connor wondered. Osiris returned his regard with quiet certainty.

Julian asked softly, "Why did you set out at all?"

"Connor knows." Malachi studied Connor's stiff face. "You may not like it, but this warrior will not give up easily. You need us."

"Show me what you know, Malachi."

Malachi's eyes dominated his gray features, glistening like clear water pools as he shared Seren's pictures with Connor.

Jealousy tightened a band around Connor's chest when he saw the blond vampire eating meals with his family, and, even though he sensed the tension in their exchanges, Connor didn't like the cozy picture it made.

"We have to make our move as soon as the light fades," Connor ground out.

"And that is where I come in. Osiris and I will walk up to the front gates."

Julian laughed. "And you'll say what?"

"Osiris will be a distraction. But, I will tell Sentinel Lars I can feel Seren's telepathic powers, and use that to gain his trust. I will reveal that Seren is in contact with Connor."

Julian closed his fist around the slender branch of a tree and crumbled it to dust. "And what will that achieve? Apart from losing us the advantage?" His eyes settled on Malachi's neck, the threat clear.

As though Julian had not spoken, Malachi continued, "I'll tell Lars that if I can lay my hands on her, I can tell him everything Seren knows by reading her mind."

"And why would he believe you?" asked Julian. "Telepathy is uncommon, unless there is a blood link between maker and protégé."

"Why? Because he will want to. Because he will be thrown off balance by the possibility of Seren being in contact with her father. To be able to know when his enemy will descend? Of course, he will want to believe." Malachi let his words sink in. "It will distract him, Connor, and allow you and Julian to get close."

"You'll keep him occupied long enough for us to enter the castle? It could work." Connor looked at Julian, and his friend nodded.

"It could work. Osiris' presence will certainly cause confusion," Julian said, pushing his sawdust covered hand into his pocket, the white flag of a truce implicit in his half smile.

"Greg and Seth will stay here, in camp," Connor cut off the words he could not say. *In case things go wrong.*

"I shan't tell Lars of Rebekah's power," Malachi mused aloud, and Connor forgot everything else.

"What powers?" he asked sharply. "Can she read Seren's mind too? I don't feel her."

"Not powers." Malachi smiled. "Her power: an unbreakable spirit. Seren is here only because of that. Humans call it 'the will to live'. Or 'mind over matter'." His bony fingers rested on Connor's solid shoulder. "Few have a spirit as strong as hers. You may not like it, but she will do whatever it takes to keep Seren alive and in one piece."

Connor laughed nervously, recalling all the occasions when her intractable spirit had put her in danger. "I think you'll find I saved her more times than you can imagine."

"So you may think. But, did you ever wonder, how was it that she was still there to be saved?"

Chapter 17

Lars rested his hands on the parapet wall at the top of a castle turret. He looked out over the sea. The icy wind dragged his hair back to a blond helmet which gleamed in the dim afternoon light, flared his cape, and plastered the soft leather of his trousers to his body. A bitter expression was frozen on his face. He did not like complications.

Their bond is strong. I don't like it. He had not expected the hybrid child to have emotions that intrigued him. And the mother, she was a mere human, but her spine seemed forged in steel. *Does nothing cow her?*

What he really did not like was that he enjoyed having them around. He told Heinrik they could learn much more by observing first, before they cut into the girl. But now, letting the doctor lay a hand on either of his prisoners rankled.

He chuckled grimly. When he took her back to the room she shared with her child, he could smell the bruises blossoming inside her flesh. *Throwing herself from a horse and hoping Seren would escape. She'll be black and blue by morning.* He shook his head. *Such guts.*

The heavy oak trapdoor in the floor behind him eased open, and he felt the depressive cloud of Doctor Heinrik's presence. He sneered. If he had been asked to define it, he could not. *Is it the formaldehyde tainted odor which infests his clothes? Or the death rattle in his chest when excitement gets the better of him?*

The door fell back onto the wooden floorboards of the ramparts with a soft, controlled thump, and the shadow Heinrik cast reached out until the vampire himself appeared in Lars' peripheral vision.

Lars fought off the distractions inside his own head and reluctantly acknowledged the small weasel-like countenance of the doctor with a brief glance.

Smiling uncertainly, Heinrik asked, "Why are we keeping the woman, Rebekah?"

"We?"

"You-"

Clouds covered the dying sun like dirty rags, and Lars' silent disapproval thrummed in the gloom. He enjoyed hearing Heinrik's facial muscles twitch.

With quiet calm, Lars finally spoke. "Her mother's presence soothes Seren. We cannot take the child's bone marrow for transplants until she is fully grown." Lars embraced the building force of the gales as purple-tinged clouds came billowing in over the horizon. It suited his mood. "It amuses me to watch the woman try to protect her child."

How far will she go, I wonder? She claims this Doctor is a mere convenience. Picturing her defiant face, Lars felt curiosity flowing through him like a vein of gold in the bedrock of lack-luster granite. *Doctor Connor fell under her spell, and she led him like a bull by the nose. She will find not every vampire so weak. Perhaps, I shall teach her that lesson.*

As if he felt Lars' attention drifting elsewhere, Heinrik's wheedling tone rose like toxic vapor. "What are we waiting for, Sentinel? We have the child. The mother cannot stop us. I just take stem cell samples from her tissue." Casting a sly glance, he added, "I don't believe the child needs her mother's blood. I think she is playing you for a fool."

In a split second, Lar's shot out a hand and tightened his grip around Heinrich's throat until the words became a croak. "I think you should stick to your laboratory and blood samples, and leave the military campaign to me." A harsh laugh rumbled through Lars. "Your solution is to dispose of the mother, yes?"

The doctor's vertebrae creaked when he nodded.

Lars released his hold, and Heinrik swayed, but stood his ground.

As if talking to an imbecile, Lars said, "If they come for the child, and this cuckold is faced with his human woman in danger, do you not think that will distract him? Give *us* the edge?"

Reluctantly, Heinrik nodded.

"Precisely. She is entertainment at the moment, nothing more. But in battle, she becomes a weapon. Now get back to what you're here for. Go and prepare your laboratory to receive the samples.

Your opportunity to harvest stem cells is small. I expect the blood samples will be largely contaminated by vampire cells. Her bone marrow is all you've got, so use your time wisely."

Heinrik blinked slowly, his mud-colored gaze dull with defeat.

Satisfied, Lars gave his verdict. "At dinner tonight, I shall calculate how much the child has grown. Her adult height should exceed her mother's five-foot six-inches, but we can set that as a bench mark." Lars' thoughts wandered once more. Her father's influence was evident in Seren's cobalt highlighted hair and gray eyes that glittered with quartz fragments. He wondered, with his golden blond coloring and ice-blue eyes, what *his* hybrid child would look like. *Rebekah is blond too.* Although, warm red strands betrayed her Celtic origins. *Her eyes are brown.* Images of her determined jaw and the rose flush of her skin filled the spaces inside his head. Lars pulled himself up short.

Birgitta would have something to say, of course. He was anticipating the next meeting of the European hive principals with keen interest. The turf war, or rather, *access* war to the vampire safari parks had come to a head. The 'parks' were the only places where vampires could satisfy their feral nature and hunt prey strong enough to inflict wounds in vampire flesh. *The Stockholm hive will offer me Birgitta, and in return, I increase their hunting rights. It has been agreed.*

He had seen his prize. The tall blonde vampiress drifted in an illusion of delicate grace, but she too was a warrior. *She wins, also, having a sentinel as her protector.* Most females had perished in the early days after the pandemic drove vampires out into the open to form a society. Pound per pound of muscle, females were still the weaker sex. Human males were defenseless, but not so their vampire counterparts.

Will she stand by and see the human woman become part of my household? Lars lifted a fatalistic brow. *Once I have a child, then the mother can go to the farm.* He mentally shrugged. *And, if Birgitta will not accept my hybrid offspring, then I shall decide which I want to keep.*

A ripple of old-fashioned desire skittered through him, tightening his groin. He was still a man. Burying himself inside the human heat of Rebekah and feeling her soft flesh molding to his in the moment he made his vampire child shone as a beacon. Why should he resist?

The wind picked up and the noise of flapping fabric reminded Lar's he was not alone. Heinrik's presence irritated Lars. "Meet me here tomorrow at dusk. I shall tell you when you can take your samples."

"Very well," replied Heinrik.

Dismissing the frustrated doctor, Lars dragged his flaring cape from the grasp of the wind. Turning smartly, he strode to the open hatchway and descended the stone staircase. When he set foot on the flag-stone walkway high above the great hall, he stopped on the edge of the sheer drop to the tapestry covered floor below and yelled across the void. "Guard."

The sound of grating stone heralded the arrival of the guardsman emerging from a concealed doorway opposite. The secret tunnels connecting locations within the castle formed part of the defense system Lars had built into his domain. When he convened council hearings, presiding over the hive principals as they brought their grievances before him and waited for his verdict, he knew they had no idea of the manpower he commanded, hidden inside the walls.

Only once had violence broken out, and Principal Vincenze had not lived to launch the dagger he aimed at Lars' head. *Meant for my eye socket.* Knowing the Italian's penchant for revenge, Lars had been prepared. *Interestingly, I've not seen the London hive principal, Julian, for decades. He is either a fool, or he is in league with this Doctor Connor. Perhaps, I should summon him on some ruse and find out the truth.*

The guardsmen arrived beside Lars and waited. Seconds ticked by to a minute and he raised a hand to his lips but stopped short of the insolence of coughing to draw the sentinel's attention, and Lars realized he had been lost in thought once more.

"Dinner is in one hour. Bring the hybrid child and the mother to the great hall." As the vampire turned away, Lars said, "Has the delivery of human blood arrived from the farm?"

"Yes, Sentinel."

"Good. Dismissed."

Watching the guard walk away, Lars felt a little easier.

The castle's guardsmen had been on tight rations since before the capture of Rebekah and Seren, and having warm blood close to hand was a risk. They will also be weakened by not being fully fed. *I don't expect a counter-attack. Juror Alexander is a weak link, but he is wise enough to know he has signed his death warrant with Principal Julian if his involvement is discovered. And Serge?* Lars' lips twisted into a bitter smile. *As long as this Doctor Connor suffers, he'll be happy.*

He surveyed his domain, admiring the twenty-foot tall stained-glass window which cast a muted harlequin of colors over the floor below on moonlit nights – in daylight a drawn curtain obscured the beauty of it. *It is a pity, but good sense must prevail.* The thirty-foot long banquet table was dwarfed by the dimensions of the room. He had lived for centuries, just *how* many he himself had forgotten. Now, with vampires in ascendance, he finally owned the setting he craved.

He fell in love with castles as a symbol of status and strength when he had been the captain of the guard to King Christian IV during the 18th century. As a vampire, he was surprised by feeling something close to sadness when his time in Copenhagen Castle drew to an end. It had been home to every Danish king from 1417 onwards, and seeing it demolished in 1730 to make way for Christianborg Palace left Lars with a hunger to live in a castle of his own one day.

Palaces are impressive, but a castle is beyond compare. Now, I'm the king of the castle. To father a child would be the final glory. *Perhaps the secret of the hybrid birth is the mother.* Other human women failed to conceive. But running tests on Rebekah, putting her in Heinrik's hands, was distasteful to him. *Perhaps I should woo her? Pretend to, in any case. Smooth the path.*

Lars studied the hefty chain taking the strain of the intricately carved wooden hoop of a chandelier, filled with burning candles that danced shadows across the rafters and created an atmosphere of splendor. He sighed gently as the thermal currents set it swaying gently in a movement undetectable to human eyes. *Medieval grandeur is surely a lifestyle Rebekah would find bearable in return for her life?*

"Over dinner, we shall see," he murmured thoughtfully.

Pacing the floor of their room, Rebekah was wondering what would happen next when the vampire called Erik appeared in the doorway. "You will dine with Sentinel Lars in the great hall this evening," he said, in a deadpan voice.

"Seren and I would rather eat here, in our room."

Erik's raised eyebrow and a slow blink were the only indication he heard what she said. "I shall return in an hour," he said, and turned away.

Staring at the door he had closed silently behind him, Rebekah clenched her fists and spat a string of unintelligible words, her face screwed up as she vented her irritation.

Seren touched her arm. "Mama."

"I'm sorry. I just despise talking to a brick wall." Rebekah relaxed and gave a wry smile.

"Papa is close now. Maybe, dinner is a good thing. If we can get the sentinel to send us back to the dungeon, then there will be only one brick wall between us and escape."

Alright, it was an eight feet thick brick wall, but the scenario of Connor bursting through the masonry seemed entirely reasonable. Looking into Seren's polished-steel gray gaze, Rebekah said, "How close? How long?"

"He has seen the castle. He's planning an attack."

"Okay." Rebekah took Seren's cold hands in hers. "Let's charm Lars. And if that doesn't work, you have my permission to throw the biggest tantrum of your life." Rebekah smiled, realizing that she and Seren were almost the same height, and yet, her instinct to protect her child was as strong as ever. "I imagine Lars will happily throw us back in the dungeon if you pull out your best shrieking banshee impression." Rebekah grinned grew wider, calculation glinting in her eyes as she said, "But first, let's throw him off balance a bit."

She crossed to the door and hammered her fist on the wood. "Bring us water." Like a demented shrew, Rebekah shrieked, "What do I have to do to get a bath around here? Go tell the sentinel, I'm not eating dinner feeling like a vagrant."

Crossing the room and looking in the mirror, Rebekah saw only the dirt ingrained lines around her neck, and matted dull blond hair. The striking bone structure and the spark of intellect stirring a current in her deep brown gaze passed her by. Lifting her arm, Rebekah took a sniff and grimaced. "It's a wonder the sentinel would want to share a table with such a sloven. I thought vampires had a keen sense of smell?" Rebekah threw an inquiring glance over her shoulder.

Seren plumped herself down in the armchair, laughing as her own grubby skirts puffed up around her. "Perhaps, he figures the smellier we are the easier we are to track?"

A sharp knock on the door made them both freeze, and Rebekah's delicately arched brows rose. "Come in."

Like in a surreal pantomime, a parade of vampires wearing battledress entered the room bringing everything Rebekah needed to bathe across the threshold. The leading pair carried a large tin tub already half filled, their leather-studded vests becoming splattered with water until they lowered it in front of the fire. The three vampires following on behind held a full bucket in each hand, and poured the steaming hot liquid into the bath before turning and leaving the room.

Rebekah watched with her mouth hanging open until, from the open doorway, an amused voice said, "So, min skat. I can still surprise you?"

Rebekah's teeth snapped shut and her head jerked around.

Lars stood in the doorway looking mildly ridiculous because his chin brushed the top of the pile of fluffy white towels he held and the flowing satin of the two dresses draped over his arm made it look as if he was wearing a skirt.

She swallowed her amusement, planted her hands on her hips and glared.

Lars drifted across the room, set the towels on the top of a black oak dresser, and, with a flourish, laid the dresses out on the bed. Turning to Rebekah, he inclined his head and said quietly, "You are right, of course. A bath is not too much to ask, I shall have one drawn for you each day, min skat."

Rebekah's eyes glittered with hostility, but she bit back scathing words. *I'll not give him the satisfaction.*

Lars said carefully, "I think we shall get along better, if we are kinder to each other, hmm?"

Rebekah's bath became more urgent as sweat erupted on her skin and trickled down between her shoulder blades. Lars' hooded blue gaze did nothing to ease the sudden flush of alarm.

"Basic human rights are all I need from you, Sentinel, thank you." Rebekah's voice croaked in a dry throat as the irony of the words hit home. *It's been a long time since humans had any rights.*

Lars moved without warning, arriving in front of her and tucking a strand of damp hair behind her ear. Her heart leapt into her throat, making talking impossible. Lars took a deep breath and, clearly absorbing her agitation, he smiled.

"We shall talk over dinner. You can make your demands of me then. I want you to be happy." He stroked his thumb down over her cheek before withdrawing his hand.

Rebekah caught only the blurred image of his broad back when he retreated to the door, and it closed behind him. She frowned, irritated by the feeling that Lars kept changing the rules of the game. "So, now he's being nice, and I don't like it."

"Neither do I," said Seren from the depths of her armchair.

Rebekah shook off the uneasy feeling. After checking that the door was closed tight, she unlaced the bodice of her dress, shrugging it from her shoulders as she drifted her fingers through the water in the bath. The warmth made her bones ache with longing, and a few moments later, as she reclined back in the tub, she relaxed for the first time since they had arrived at the castle.

Closing her eyes, she murmured, "If he's being nice, perhaps he will let things slip at dinner that we can use. That *you* can use." Rebekah lifted her head and met Seren's glittering gray eyes. She didn't want to say the words aloud, but Seren's nod confirmed she understood what her mother meant. *You can help, Papa. Tell him what he's up against here, with Lars.* For the hundredth time, Rebekah wished Seren could read her thoughts too.

After washing her hair, Rebekah climbed out of the bath. Holding up the burgundy red dress, she grimaced at the scooped neckline.

With a grunt, knowing she had little choice, she pulled it over her head, shook out the skirt, and smoothed the fabric down over her body. Her cheeks burned when lacing up the bodice pushed her breasts higher. The dress was more revealing than she expected. *If that's possible.* Seren's forest green garment turned out to be a demur high-throated affair, and that eased the tightness in Rebekah's chest a little. If being nice became as tricky as she feared, at least it was only her virtue that appeared to be at risk. *Lars is not a fiend, at least.*

Somewhere in the castle a dinner gong sounded.

Locking eyes with Seren, Rebekah took a deep battle-ready breath, and nodded. "Here goes nothing. Remember, eyes and ears open, and if there is no other way, you know what to do?"

The door handle rattled and a key turned in the lock.

"Okay?" Rebekah insisted.

"Okay, Mama."

Rebekah caught Seren's fingers in hers as they faced their vampire escort. *Not Erik this time. Perhaps, Lars took pity on him.*

This unfamiliar vampire was of a similar daunting height and his closed expression resembled the one Erik usually wore. The leather of his vest strained over a wall of muscle when he beckoned, and it seemed like an implicit warning.

Moving past him into the hallway, Rebekah asked, "Where is Erik?"

The vampire ignored her question, closed the door, and turned away.

If Erik doesn't understand much English, maybe that's true of all of them. The stranger presented his broad back, and, even though she guessed that trying to 'befriend' any of them was a waste of time, Rebekah actually missed Erik.

Their footsteps echoed from the stone walls as they walked along behind the strolling vampire. A fleeting glimpse of his white face appeared every few seconds. Rebekah smiled. *I wonder what his punishment would be if he lost us.*

Emerging onto the high-level walkway was a head spinning moment for Rebekah. Even though the ledge was at least twelve feet wide, the sheer drop to the floor of the great hall on one side took her breath away. She glued her eyes to the center of the vampire's back and trailed her fingers along the wall.

At the top of the flight of stone stairs, she paused and took a steady breath. Her nape prickled as she descended each step, and she knew Lars was down there somewhere, staring up at her. When her foot touched down on the flagstone floor, Lars appeared and offered her an arm.

Even though she expected it, she still jumped, and the heat burning in her cheeks made concentrating hard. She could feel her heart thudding.

"The dress fits beautifully," said Lars, his voice so low it vibrated inside her head.

Rebekah's chin jerked up. "I am cold and uncomfortable."

Lars chuckled. "I shall remedy the situation with a shawl. But, after dinner, no?" His blue eyes blazed, and when the flush on Rebekah's skin deepened, his smile became fixed and tense.

Get a grip, girl. You'll be dinner if you don't control yourself. Dragging her hand from his arm, Rebekah strode over to the banquet table and lowered herself into an elaborately carved throne-like chair.

Lars pushed her seat closer to the table, his cold fingers tracing over the bare skin of her shoulder blade as he said, "You have some war wounds, I see."

Rebekah gritted her teeth and stayed still. "It's nothing," she said, although, since the bruises were on her back, she had no idea.

The sentinel took his place at the head of the table and smiled lightly. "It is just as well we make peace, I think. Black and blue is not a good color on you, min skat."

Rebekah replied carefully, "Even if we make peace. I do not trust your Doctor Heinrik."

Seren added, her voice trembling delicately, "He means to hurt me."

Lars, with Rebekah seated on his left and Seren on his right, gazed steadily down the length of the table. "He follows orders. Do not worry little one, you are safe. Let us eat." He raised a hand, and, like a conjurer's illusion, three vampires appeared from thin air.

Silently, Rebekah watched them set out the silverware. Crystal glasses winked in the candlelight. Silver domed covers were removed from platters, revealing an array of different foods, some of which Rebekah, with her limited life experience of foraging for crops, did not recognize.

Sitting there like a child who did not know which fork to use, she suddenly felt warm and claustrophobic, as if the departing vampires had sucked the oxygen from the room.

"Here, drink." Lars leaned over and held out a glass. The hand he rested on Rebekah's shoulder was cool and refreshing.

Rebekah took the glass and gratefully drank the water.

"I am a bad host, it seems." Taking her hand in his, Lars placed a thumb on her skin and, when he removed it, inspected the site keenly. "You are dehydrated, thirsty, so drink."

When Rebekah lowered her glass, he filled it again, adding, "And eat."

Lars reclined in his seat, swirling the claret in his glass. Although, the deep red stain that bled between his lips told her it was not wine at all. As she ate, her curiosity at discovering new flavors disappeared, and being nervous made each fork full taste more like sawdust. Three glasses of water eased their passage.

Seren ate daintily, and Lars appeared to find this fascinating.

Rebekah risked a glance through veiled lashes, and seeing Lars' relaxed attitude brought a glow of hope.

"Sentinel?"

"Lars, please," he murmured.

"Lars. Seren and I have been talking. We want to return to our dungeon quarters." Lars hitched straighter in his seat, and Rebekah rushed on. "It will be dry by now and you said it has never flooded before." The words came easier if she fixed her eye on an aged knot of wood on the table and let them tumble out. "Put us under guard if you want to. That keeps us safe from Doctor Heinrik, too. We'll join you for dinner, if that's what you want, but please-" Rebekah ran out of steam, clenching her hands in her lap as she waited.

The silence stretched, and just when her twisting fingers began to cramp, he said, "No."

"But-"

"No." The flat intonation remained the same, and that chilled Rebekah more.

"Okay," she whispered.

Rebekah locked eyes with Seren. Five minutes of suffocating silence settled like a thick blanket, although Lars appeared unconcerned.

Suddenly, Seren's chin dropped and the sound of tearing fabric filled the air as she wrenched at the high neckline of her dress. The veins on her forehead bulged and a gargling sound rattled in her throat. "Mama-" The strangled word grated over Rebekah's ears.

"What's wrong, honey?" Rebekah leapt to her feet, leaning over the table and reaching out to Seren. "Something's wrong. Do something," Rebekah screamed.

Seren's convulsing body slid from her seat to the floor, and her head snapped back. The tendons in her neck strained, pulling tight like knotted twine, and her ethereal white pallor faded to dull gray. Her shoes came off as her body jerked in frenzy and the gargle in her throat became a feral growl.

"Lars-" Rebekah tracked the blur of movement as he rose from his chair and dropped down on one knee beside Seren.

"I think she's in grave sleep. Help her, please. She's never done this before. Please."

Lars' large hands pinned Seren's arms to her sides while he studied her face.

"The dungeon. Please don't put her in a box. She'll be scared. The dungeon will hold her."

Lars looked up at Rebekah. "Stay here. I'll take care of her."

"No, please. I can wait outside. I need to be there when she wakes up. Let me come too."

Fear gripped Rebekah as Seren's convulsions erupted into violent spasms.

"Enough," barked Lars.

"Just do something." Rebekah choked back tears. All thought of play-acting had whisked out of the window – this was terrifyingly real.

Lars swiftly tore the top skirt from Seren's dress and bound her ankles and wrists. Glancing at Rebekah, he rose, lifting Seren in a deceptively caring embrace. He looked every inch the Viking king, the halo of his blond hair glowing as brightly as the gold of his breastplate, the sinews in his forearms threatening to burst the gilded cuffs he wore. Planting his feet wide, he held Seren to his chest and said, "You will stay." And with a flare of red velvet, he spun on his heel and disappeared into the mouth of a dark corridor.

Rebekah ran after him and collided with the broad chest of a vampire blocking her path. "Get out of my way." Her fists beat on the stone wall of vampire flesh until, when all hope of following was gone, he vanished.

Out of breath and fighting back real panic, Rebekah backed away and subsided into her seat at the banquet table. Her mind scrabbled for comfort. *Please, God, let her be faking it. If Seren gets back to the dungeon, then Connor will find her. He must be close.*

Rebekah looked up when the vampire guard reappeared and stood by the wall. He took on the qualities of a marble statue, and she allowed his image to drift out of focus while she reset the goals.

Okay, plan A had been Seren fakes grave-sleep, and they would both end up in the dungeon. *Even an adjoining one would have done.* Connor's rescue mission would have been much simpler. But now, they were left with plan B, and bile rose into Rebekah's throat at the thought of it.

She began pacing. The table length was a satisfying prowl of thirty feet, and striding back and forth soon made her light headed as her ribcage struggled to expand inside the tight bodice of the dress. She noticed the glasses of water, the dregs blood in the sentinel's, and suddenly wished she could numb the dread with real wine.

He will be back soon. Something had changed in Lars this evening. Keeping him occupied and distracting him with her charms suddenly seemed like swimming with a shark. When he had been curt and distant, charming him felt safe, somehow. But tonight, an undercurrent had shimmered in his icy blue eyes. *He is different.* And different felt bad.

Rebekah drained her water glass and decided that sitting and waiting would only shred her nerves. *He said 'kinder to each other'. What the hell did that mean?* Leaping up from her seat, she strode to the foot of the stone stairs where the guard stood. "Tell the sentinel I've retired to my room. If he has news of Seren's condition, please let me know immediately."

The blood rushing in her ears drowned out the soft brush of her satin slippers on the stone steps. Dragging her fingers over the rough wall kept the feeling of vertigo at bay as the hall disappeared into the distance below.

She scurried along to her room. When she stepped inside, relief squeezed the breath from her body and wouldn't let her catch another. She leaned against the door, pressing back into the wood until it hurt, and tears seeped out from beneath her closed lashes. She stood there until the tears dried, making her face feel stiff, and then gave herself a lecture. Wiping her nose with the back off her hand, she paced the room. *Connor is on his way. Get a grip. He'll find Seren in the dungeon, and then come for me.* Swinging around, she chased her thoughts back across the room. *Okay, plan B, charm and distract Lars. Easy.* She felt in control again, resolutely ignoring the whispering voice that ridiculed her.

The shifting air stirring dust devils in the corners of the room went unnoticed in her distracted state. But, she could not miss the sudden gusts snatching at her skirt. It felt like standing on a platform in the subway ahead of the rushing train.

Someone's coming. She clung to the idea that the door would open and reveal Connor. The sun had lost the battle for control of the lowering sky, and storm-gray shadows filled the room. When the door swung open, the silently graceful movement was somehow more terrifying than the dizzying speed she expected. Her hopes died. The breastplate meant she didn't need to see his face.

Once over the threshold, he did not move, apart from stretching out a hand and resting it on top of the oak chest beside him, just as though he was human.

"It's funny," Rebekah blurted. "Even though we all know what you are, still you pretend. Vampires, I mean." Her tone curdled with ridicule and she laughed. "You all breathe, blink, lean, sit. None of it is necessary, I know."

"You know, min skat?" Lars pursed his lips in a fleeting sad expression. "We have feelings. I am only trying to make things easier."

"Well, let me go to Seren, if you really want to make things easier."

"Of course."

Hope flared and she looked at him more closely. "Of course?"

Lars nodded slowly. "In three hours, or so. I think she will awake by then."

Rebekah's throat dried up.

Lars walked further into the room and closed the door. "In the meantime, tell me about the hybrid birth. How did it feel? Being touched by this Doctor Connor."

She flushed, and Lars smiled.

"I can see how he lost his good sense." Tilting his head, the blue ocean in his regard shimmered. "I wonder if the secret of the hybrid birth is not standing before me. The child is fascinating, but perhaps it is *you* that is different to other humans."

His words crawled over Rebekah's skin. Before she could speak, she was imprisoned in Lars' insistent embrace, the metal of his vest crushing her breasts. His hand spread over her back and held her still. His cool breath fanned her face. "Perhaps, I shall be your protector, and find out what this doctor found so hypnotic."

His kiss was gentle. His tongue tentative and soft.

In the stony stillness of his arms, Rebekah fought the impulse to hit out. *It will do no good.* Instead, she embodied a stillness of her own. Swallowing down her revulsion, she let him explore her soft mouth, feeling the cool draft of his breath when he laughed.

Raising his head, his eyes glittering with ice in the gloom, he said, "You could never be cold, min skat." His fingertip dipped between her breasts, lingering on her flushed damp skin. Her heart pounded in her ears and her underskirt clung to her clammy flesh. Of course, he knew she was scared.

His hand drifted up her throat, and he cupped her jaw gently. He opened his mouth to speak and suddenly his chin shot up, annoyance written on his face.

He's listening to something. Connor? Rebekah could barely breathe, but she needed to hold his attention. She stroked her palm up over his cheek, and his eyes jerked back to hers, registering surprise.

"I have nothing to lose." Rebekah chose her words carefully. "But I have suffered broken bones and bruising. I think it's harder than you imagine." Embarrassment at what she was about to say knotted her stomach. "Connor was strong, but he found a way to be gentle. Can you do the same?"

Placing his hand over hers, Lars smiled, but the chill in his eyes froze Rebekah's heart.

So, he's playing a game. It was a relief to know the sentinel was a cold-hearted reptile. It made wishing him dead less cruel.

"I have to go, min skat. I have visitors. But I shall return, and we can see how gentle I can be, hmm?" With that, he released her, stepped back, and the door rattled in its frame.

The room was empty, but she had not seen the door move. *Visitors?* Excitement leapt in her chest and Rebekah began pacing the room again.

Chapter 18

The castle's glowering silhouette dominated the skyline as Malachi and Osiris crossed the rambling pasture of dewy grass. Their gliding strides covered the ground at speed. They were the first wave of contact with Lars, and being in plain sight formed part of the plan to draw the eye of any lookouts the sentinel had posted.

It is all about the preparation. Malachi memorized the configuration of each window and each damaged stone in the towering edifice, knowing it would be useful information for Connor in planning his less high-profile assault on the fortification.

Osiris moved with a deliberate, cumbersome gait. A loose tunic masked his honed physique and concealed the gold serpent armlets molded to his biceps.

Being the master, Malachi showed no such reticence. He displayed the serpent ring which wound around three of his fingers, the head of the cobra resting upon the back of his hand as though it was about to slither up his arm. *The first impression will be crucial.*

Malachi touched the pendant hanging from a chain around his scrawny neck, a gold-encrusted cage protecting a glass vial. The brown paste inside it was the blood of his twin brother, Numu. Malachi had carried it for more than ninety years. It reminded him that vampires were not truly immortal and sharpened his focus when facing danger. *As we are now.*

The grime-encrusted clothes they still wore, stiff with the dried mud of their marathon journey from Egypt, provided convincing evidence which would back up their story.

Leaving the uneven ground of the meadow, Malachi and Osiris stepped into the middle of the wide paved road. Pausing in the shelter of the stone arch, they studied the causeway which led up to the twelve-foot tall wooden doors. Even though it was deserted, in his peripheral vision, Malachi noticed cloud-gray faces moving behind the oily surface of the glazed windows.

"They know we are here."

His comment was met by comfortable silence. Osiris' sluggish heartbeat told Malachi he remained relaxed, but his tensed muscles revealed he was alert.

"Lars is a Viking warrior. He will welcome the challenge of a vampire pet that confuses him. Are you ready?"

The curtain of Osiris' hair shimmered like black silk as he assessed the construction of the fortress. "It is crude, is it not?"

"Compared to the pyramids, I guess you are right." Malachi smiled. "You must forgive them. They are interested merely in function."

Tilting his head and unfolding his arms, Osiris murmured, "If we keep Sentinel Lars busy on the west side of the castle, Doctor Connor and Principal Julian should have no trouble finding a way through the crumbling mortar below sea level." Osiris wrapped his grimy cloak around his body, throwing a flap of fabric over his shoulder, and the sea wind plastered it to his chest.

When the solid doors swung open and two horsemen burst through them, Osiris' shoulders sagged, and he embodied the long-suffering servant of a vampire master.

Malachi trained his pearl-tinted gaze on the face of the leading rider. His wizened features took on a haughty cast, he lifted his chin and glared. Part one of the puzzle slotted satisfyingly into place. The vampires wore studded leather vests and supple leather sleeves clung to their arms. *The same garb as the child, Seren, showed us. We are in the right place.* Malachi held back a grin when Connor's visceral pleasure cascaded through his mind. It was as though his protégé stood at his side, and was not merely a psychic connection.

The mounted vampires circled the pair of travelers, drawing ever closer to them until the velvet coat of the horses' flanks dragged at their cloaks.

Malachi remained implacable, staying silent. Osiris stared at the ground, watching the polished hooves flashing in and out of his view.

"Who goes there?" Both vampires' eyes flicked time and again to Osiris, their blown pupils reflecting the conflict inside. Osiris represented a heroin fix to a man making do with the poor imitation of methadone. *There's nothing quite like a warm gushing pulse to set the saliva flowing.*

"I am here to speak with Sentinel Lars."

"And your name?"

"My name is not your concern. Just tell the sentinel I know about the hybrid child."

The vampire rider stiffened in surprise, and the unforgiving pressure of his thighs almost cracked an equine rib. The horse reared, pawing the air in agitation, and Malachi ticked off another box. *The child is still a secret.*

With a final penetrating glance, the leader of the pack jerked his head towards the fortress. The reaction was immediate. Their black capes flaring from the metal buckles on their shoulders, the vampires raced away and disappeared into the yawning chasm of the opened gates. The heavy thud of the doors slamming shut faded, and Malachi and Osiris waited in silence.

Minutes later, a tall vampire walked towards them. He wore a vest with a jeweled buckle on each shoulder. Rings adorning the middle finger of both hands twinkled with diamonds, and anchored the leather sleeves of his tunic in place.

"I am the captain of the guard. Sentinel Lars bids you welcome."

He stared resolutely into Malachi's ash-gray face. Lowering his chin in salute, he turned away and led them along the causeway, and into the dark shade of the granite wall which framed the open castle gates.

The gates swung shut behind them. Malachi directed his attention at the tall captain's back, exuding an air of importance despite his tattered attire. The horticultural splendor of the garden went unnoticed. He was more concerned with gathering the details of the castle's defenses and sharing the visions with Connor.

The progress of the party of three was marked by the echoing footfalls of Osiris alone. Being a human, clumsiness was expected, and he delivered his performance to perfection. He shed the grace and power of his Earth Walker descendants, becoming the cowed, drained pet of a belligerent vampire.

Entering the castle through an imposing sculpted doorway, wide enough to accommodate eight men abreast, it gave way to the expanse of the great hall. The captain of the guard left the tapestry runner of the central aisle, passed between two stone pillars, and stopped abruptly.

"Sentinel." The captain inclined his head. "The visitors, sir."

The captain stepped aside, and Malachi got his first sight of the impressive blond figure of Sentinel Lars. *In the flesh, at least.* Even without the enhancement of the childlike fear which colored Seren's projected impression, Malachi conceded the vampire's aura was daunting.

Lars stood beside a cavernous walk-in fireplace, within which sat a cooking pot resembling a giant's cauldron. In a trick of perception, he took on the dimensions of a small man. But, when he walked towards them, Malachi was forced to look up to meet his eye and realized Lars' height easily exceeded six feet.

The sentinel's attention slid from the thin, aged figure of Malachi to his stout young companion, and he lifted a brow. Inhaling slowly, Lars' hooded gaze reflected pleasure as he said, "You have a human pet."

Malachi smiled, deliberately revealing yellow stumps in bone-white gums. "I need to feed frequently." His self-deprecating sweep of a hand, exposing the stick-thin bones and stringy sinews in his arm, filled in the rest.

The mercurial currents moving behind Lars' eyes were easy for Malachi to read. *He is wondering what hold can a weak ineffectual, vampire have over a human of Osiris' obvious good breeding.*

Lars' assessment sharpened, and he shrugged, discarding idle speculation. "How did you learn of the hybrid child?"

A sardonic smile spread across Malachi's stiff features. To Malachi, the soft leather the vampire guardsmen wore still smelled of the animal flesh it had once covered. "I will talk, when you dismiss the death squad," he said.

Surprised, Lars laughed loudly. "Very well." A click of his fingers triggered a flurry of activity, and the eight-strong guard melted away.

"Eight? I am impressed that you consider us that big a threat," chuckled Malachi.

"I see there is more to you than meets the eye," replied Lars.

Even more than he can possibly know. In one hour, when dusk fell, Connor and Julian would make their move.

Lars returned to the empty fireplace, took a seat and indicated that Malachi should join him. Osiris took his place at his master's shoulder, standing behind his chair with a hand resting lightly on the elaborately carved contours of the wood.

"So, tell me, how did you hear of the hybrid child?"

Malachi was pleased they were past pretending. "I did not hear of her."

Lars' chin shot up. "Her?"

"I sensed her presence. Perhaps others will too, but I think not."

"Go on."

"She has a psychic connection, and she is reaching out to her father."

Lars' jaw muscle ticked as he absorbed the old vampire's words. "Her father?"

Malachi shook his head wryly. "It can be no surprise to you that the hybrid child has a connection to her father. His blood flows through her."

"He knows she is here, then." Lars piercing blue eyes searched Malachi's face. "Is he coming for her?"

Malachi laughed. "You should know the answer to that. He cannot come. He is in a coma in the London hive." Tilting his head with bird-like curiosity, he asked, "It was your doing, I assume?"

Lars smirked. "I cannot claim the credit, but it is good to hear."

Osiris fidgeted, unwrapping the thick fabric of his cloak and readjusting his stance until it fell away from his shoulder. The fragrant aroma of his skin plumed into the air, accentuated by the strong pulse stirring the blood in his veins.

Although his eyes stayed on Malachi, the flare of Lars' nostrils gave him away.

He smells the blood. Distracting, isn't it? mused Malachi, enjoying the disruption to the sentinel's concentration.

"And what brings *you* here? Curiosity? Self-interest?" Lars bared his teeth, reasserting control. "Or are you here to issue threats?"

"I want to see her."

"I'm sure you do. To take her back to London, perhaps? Claim Doctor Connor's gratitude?"

Malachi snorted. "What use have I for his gratitude. No, in thousands of years, this is the first such birth. I can help you. I can read her thoughts clearly, if I lay my hand on her."

"And why would I need your help?"

"If the doctor wakes up, you will be forewarned. I want to be part of it. Witness her growth. Nothing more."

Lars settled back in his chair. Although the sentinel said nothing, Malachi recognized the invitation to proceed.

"Learning what the child is thinking will add information that examinations and tests cannot provide. And understanding her will make controlling her an intriguing possibility."

Lars' continued stony silence did not deter Malachi. The sentinel's regard stirred with fervor. *Time to find out the worst. Seren's condition.* Connor's biggest concern was how his family fared. Rebekah, Malachi dared not mention. *Not yet.*

"Can I see her?"

Lars straightened in his seat. "I am afraid not. In a few hours, perhaps."

Malachi lifted a thin brow, his curiosity creasing his paper-thin forehead, and waited.

"Seren is in grave sleep."

Seren. Malachi smothered a smile. *If the child has registered as a person, it can only be a good thing.* His thoughts turned to the mechanics of grave sleep. "Where do you have her confined? Is she safe?" Malachi's hand flapped in apology when Lars shot him a sharp glance.

"You need not concern yourself. You're not her mother," Lars said coldly.

Amusement stirred inside Malachi. *So, Rebekah's giving him a hard time. Connor will not be surprised.* Thinking of the violent seizures of grave sleep, Malachi risked a question. "What was your solution? If you have not sealed Seren inside a stone box. Do you have a crypt?" *And where is it?*

"I have bound her, of course. Chains and an antelope-hide cocoon seemed appropriate. But I left her face uncovered. I don't want her to wake up disorientated and scared. She is half human. It might make her more vulnerable. Who knows?"

Malachi tilted his head, ranging his eyes upwards as if he could see into the chambers above. "I don't hear her?"

Lars grinned. "She is somewhere safe."

Malachi allowed hope to glow brighter. *It looks like the child's visions of a dungeon are still accurate. That is good for Connor.*

Talking about Seren appeared to trigger other thoughts in Lars and he sank into deep contemplation. Malachi happily let the minutes tick by. Every one that passed brought Connor closer, and the longer he could keep Lars in his sights the better.

The two vampires sat like stone adornments in the yawning chasm of the fireplace, unmoving for over an hour.

Finally, Malachi tapped one bony finger on the arm of his chair, and Osiris broke into distracting movement, designed to call Lars back from his trance.

Osiris absently rearranged his cloak and adjusted the serpent amulets on his biceps. As though the metal was cutting in, he grimaced.

Lars' head shot around, and his curiosity shifted to include Osiris. "And your pet? He will be a distraction to my men. I cannot guarantee his safety within these walls. Will he stay here with you?"

With beguiling nonchalance, Malachi said, "Perhaps the need of human pets is coming to an end. Has the child's blood been drawn? Can her blood unlock the vampire brainstem?"

Lars swallowed down saliva when Osiris moved again.

The Egyptian's heart rate accelerated with a masterful performance of nerves which Malachi knew to be false. *Controlling the biorhythms of his body is child's play to Osiris.*

Osiris' mellow tone surprised Lars' in its gentleness when he said, "Master. You need to feed."

Lars shot a glance at Malachi's knowing smile.

"He is right, of course. He too, has his gifts. I am in need of relaxation. Do you have somewhere I can take revival sleep?"

"You would feel safe doing that here?"

"I think we need to trust each other. It will give you time to consider my proposition. I hope you will welcome my help." Malachi shrugged. "And if not, then if I could just see her for myself. I will take the news back to Egypt that there is hope."

Lars stared long and hard.

Malachi sank into vampire stillness, absorbing the storm of indecision radiating from his host. *He will agree, and while he is speculating about Osiris, wondering what his blood tastes like, he will not be looking over his shoulder.*

In sudden agitation, Lars surged up from his seat, and, as though the words were torn from him, he said, "This *pet* of yours, he has no bite marks."

Amusement glimmered beneath Osiris' impassive features. The unblemished skin of his throat and broad chest were laid open to view. His narrow hips accentuated the rock-iron girdle of muscles that promised great strength.

"He does not look fed upon."

Malachi's clear crystal gaze clouded over, his bony fingers scraping at the arms of his chair as he said, reprovingly, "We all have our secrets. Let us reach an agreement before we share them."

Lars' curiosity glowed like embers, but he retreated, placed a boot on the hearth of the soot-lined fireplace, and nodded. "Very well. It makes things interesting."

Malachi rose smoothly to his feet. "I am at your mercy. If there is a safe place in which Osiris can recover after our meal and where I can sleep?"

As though Lars' thoughts conjured him, a tall vampire guard appeared from between the pillars.

"Erik will show you to a suite in the east turret." In another impressive feat of sleight of hand, an iron key appeared on Lars' extended palm. "You can lock yourselves in." His eyes darted to Osiris' quiet form, and he added, "It is probably better if you do."

"You are very generous. We will retire now." Malachi took the key from Lars.

All the while he and Osiris followed in Erik's wake, Malachi absorbed the noises within the castle walls and disappointment scuttled through him. He thought he detected a faint heartbeat somewhere on the other side of the great hall. *Has Lars separated Seren and Rebekah?* He could not be sure, but if it proved to be so, then it became another obstacle for Connor to overcome.

Lying on their stomachs in the long grass, Connor and Julian had watched Malachi and Osiris' progress. The intimidating tactics of the horsemen had set them on edge, and they were ready to step in. When deciding on the plan, the group were fully prepared for Sentinel Lars to make his uninvited visitors stand out in the gathering gloom for hours before letting on he had seen them. The speedy response of the first contact promised a willingness to listen, or curiosity, at least.

Of course, Connor *also* saw the pale gray ovals floating in the glistening black window panes. *They are watching. We know now, the castle is on alert.*

Minutes of silence ticked by into over an hour, before Julian glanced at Connor's intent profile and said, "Well?"

"Nothing yet. Malachi needs to concentrate."

"How will we know if something has happened to them? Malachi can't share his visions if Lars crushes his skull."

Connor turned a frown on Julian. "Cheerful, aren't we?"

Julian shrugged, but said nothing.

The setting sun bled into the sky, framing the fortress in a pink halo, and when Connor closed his eyes he could still see the outline of the hulking shape imprinted on his retina. Honing in on Seren's vision, in the near pitch-darkness, Connor stared at a crumbling stone ceiling and could smell the musty odor of wet moss. *So, they are in the dungeon, but why is she not moving?*

As the one in command, responsibility for others weighed heavily on Connor. *All Greg and Seth have to do is stay put.* He allowed himself a smile. *They aren't Rebekah, thank goodness.*

He could trust the combat hardened Marines to hunker down for the night in the foxhole they dug between the roots of a beech tree. The small wood made a good landmark. Home comforts did not feature on their list of requirements. *I don't have to worry about them.*

When, at last, Malachi let him see inside the fortress, lying in his prone position, Connor pushed his fingers into the dark damp soil, compressing the earth into rock-hard pellets. He lost himself in the visions that Malachi's more refined skills filtered into his mind.

The images became crystal clear. Malachi conveyed Lars as a controlling presence, emanating confidence. The great hall sat at the heart of the castle, and everything else stemmed from there.

He could see an upper gallery with a row of walnut doors, and dark apertures where stairwells led to unknown destinations on the other levels.

Connor hissed, "Malachi can't get a precise fix on them, but Seren is not in the upper levels of the castle." Satisfaction rattled through Connor as Malachi's words rose in his mind like frost on cold glass. "They got back to the dungeon."

Julian grunted.

Opening his eyes, Connor shot Julian a sharp look. "Now," he said, pushing himself up and taking off in a crouched run, heading towards the cliffs.

Julian hung on to his coattails, mimicking every turn Connor made.

The low rumble of the sea grew louder when they reached the top of the steep bank where broken rocks littered the slope downwards, becoming a pebbled skirt leading onto the beach.

Skimming down over the scree, disturbing barely a grain of dirt, Connor made it on to the sand. He shrugged out of his coat and slung it over a rock, and, rolling up his shirt sleeves, he waded into the surf. Connor's forging stride remained easy, the undercurrent dragging at his legs and the pebbles clattering against his shins barely registering.

Julian walked alongside him, and the water became steadily deeper. Connor turned to face the other side of the bay where the charcoal gray walls of the distant castle rose from the sea. Walking forward with his eyes open, when the water level crept up past his chin, he clamped his vocal chords shut, preventing his abdominal cavity and lungs filling with water.

Within seconds, both vampires were submerged beneath the waves.

Connor's world took on a green tint, the rays of weak sunlight creating peppermint-colored pools in the rippling surface overhead. Effortlessly negotiating a seabed slick with algae covered rocks, Connor and Julians' heavy tread fractured the barnacle-encrusted terrain. Amplified by the water, the cracking sounds had the explosive force of gunshots to Connor's ears. The thrill of going into battle ignited a furnace in his gut.

The murky waters in the shadow of the fortress darkened Connor's vision to dull jade. He placed both his hands against the slimy moss-covered walls of the castle. His hair billowed in a soot black cloud, obscuring the eager light in his gray eyes. He could almost taste victory.

Connor waited until Julian arrived at his side, and then burst into movement. Digging his fingers into the gaps between the huge stone blocks, Connor climbed the wall. After scaling twenty feet, his head broke the surface of the turbulent sea. The crashing waves tossed lace-white froth over the granite, and Connor began looking for weak spots in the centuries-old mortar.

A curved turret wall met another which was straight, and the joint between the two had been repaired many times over.

"Look for holes. Anything," muttered Connor.

Julian's stark white hands joined Connor's on the wall. Digging in between each stone, they searched for signs of where moisture had penetrated, and where, in winter, the expansion of water freezing to ice had caused fractures.

Julian's grunt of satisfaction brought Connor to his side. Their broad backs took a beating from the surf while they hung, anchored to the wall by their fingertips. Their footing on the slimy algae-coated wall was more precarious. Vampires do not float, so a fall would just mean another twenty- foot climb up from the rocks beneath the waves.

"This one." Julian tapped a hard finger on the polished surface and chunks of eroded stone fell away.

Both vampires pulled shards of granite from around the edges of the block they had chosen, and used them as ax heads to chip away at the mortar. Pausing every few minutes to grip the stone and wiggle it in its socket like a rotten tooth, both felt a surge of excitement when the grinding action released showers of gravel.

Positioning themselves on either side, they rocked the stone, easing it from its space until it began to tilt downwards. One final heave dislodged it, and they watched it plummet and disappear into the depths, where the onyx black currents obscured its final resting place.

Connor shoved his crude cutting tool into the waistband of his pants, heaved himself out of the water and crawled into the grit-lined aperture. He prayed it was not a dead end, and his prayers were answered, in part. As a sudden flood of seawater rushed into the channel, transforming grit and dirt into mud, and then somewhere up ahead, it drained away. Connor shunted his weight forward until he gripped the inner edge of the seawall and was faced with another. *Two walls, with a space in-between.* Connor guessed it acted as a crude form of temperature control. Stone conducts heat as well as cold.

A hefty knock on the sole of Connor's boot started him moving again. He squinted back over his shoulder, and Julian's irritated features streaming with a waterfall of sea water almost made him laugh.

"I'm hanging on by my fingertips here, literally," grumbled Julian.

Connor used his elbows to drag himself to the inside ledge. He swiveled in the tight space until he could drop feet-first to the ground and sidestep out of Julian's way, his chest grazing the rough inner wall.

Julian lowered himself into place beside Connor. The near pitch-black atmosphere turned their features into a landscape of coal black shadows.

Turning his head left and right, Connor decided that the darkness appeared less thick to his left. In a barely audible whisper, Connor suggested, "Let's try this way."

Julian's eyes glittered as he nodded.

Within moments of starting out, the wall hugging their backs began to curve and it became clear they were tracking the outline of a turret. Velvet-black gave way to smoke-gray where light spilled into the cavity somewhere up ahead, around the bend. Light coming in meant they could be heard, so the two vampires slowly picked their way along, straining to hear any noises. Although, the profound silence did not mean the turret was deserted.

Vampires at rest, with the human world no longer looking in on them, could stand without breathing, blinking, or fidgeting. Blending in was an abandoned state. Connor had been quietly amused when mannequins first appeared in shop windows in the 1900s. *They were a great way of hiding in plain sight.*

The light glowed brighter and the source turned out to be an iron grid set into the inner wall at floor level. *We're in luck.*

A few yards further along, the passageway widened, and Connor could walk normally. He wondered where the tunnel disappearing around the bend might lead, but the glowing light coming from the chamber within the turret beckoned. The detail he recalled of Seren's view from her dungeon window made this entry point the quickest way to find her.

Connor tapped Julian on the arm, indicating he should wait, and then he sank to his knees. Leaning sideways, he could see across the stone floor beyond the grill. Resting his shoulder on the ground gave him a clear view of the opposite wall and of rows of leather vests hanging on hooks.

Damn, the guardhouse. Not so lucky, after all.

With a grim expression, he pulled the shard of rock from the waistband of his pants and held the serrated ax blade edge at the ready. Easing back up to sitting, he braced his feet on the iron bars, pushed his back into the wall, and shoved with explosive force. Chunks of cement erupted, scattering over the floor. The dust cloud pelted his face, and Connor threw himself forward into the room.

Rolling swiftly up onto one knee, he scanned the circular chamber and found it empty. Surging to his feet, he took a moment to feel thankful. "Clear," muttered Connor.

Plumes of dust accompanied Julian's arrival. Connor circled the room, counting the sets of empty pegs and the vests still hanging up. He calculated the vampire garrison to be around a dozen.

Both vampires were damp and caked in cement dust. The ghostly gray cast to their faces now extended to cover their heads.

Scrubbing his hands through his hair, Connor restored some of the strands to their blue-black luster. Taking a leather tunic from a hook, Connor tilted his head at Julian and raised a what-are-you-waiting-for brow.

Julian grinned, and within minutes, both vampires had stripped off their wet shirts and pulled on metal-studded vests. The soft leather strained over Connor's chest as he moved, and the supple sleeves clinging to his biceps were too tight, but at least he looked the part.

Dropping to the ground in front of the square hole in the wall, Connor shoved their discarded shirts into the space behind. He quickly swept the lumps of stone into the cavity with his hands, and, releasing a blast of air, blew most of the gravel back through the hole before wedging the grill back in place.

Satisfied that it would take a close inspection to detect where they had broken through, with unspoken communication, both vampires moved to the door. Pressing an ear to the wood, Connor gave the thumbs up.

They stepped out into the gloomy corridor, the humidity in the air acting as a reminder that just the other side of the thick granite walls the rolling surf launched a perpetual assault, destined to conquer even the hardest rock, given enough centuries of time.

Connor scanned the passageway, punctuated on both sides by wrought iron sconces where naked flames burned brightly in terracotta bowls. The pools of light stretched far into the distance, but a deep shadow half way down suggested there might be an alcove. *Another tunnel? Or a stairwell, maybe?*

"The dungeon window Seren showed me looked out over the sea. We need to go up a level," mouthed Connor. With a jab of his thumb, he headed quickly along the slick flagstones.

The black hole in the wall framed the bottom step of a steep staircase. It ascended in a sharp turn around which Connor could not see. Aware time was ticking, he brazened it out. Squaring his shoulders, he marched up the stairwell as if he belonged there.

Another sharp bend at the top put the two vampires in another corridor running directly above the first. This one was different. Lit torches rested in holders along one wall only. Each was positioned opposite a door, and the iron nails set into the age-stained wood glowed in the flames like demons' eyes.

"This is it. Each door is a dungeon. We just need to find the right one."

"My guess is that one," whispered Julian. "The torch has not been set properly back into its frame. Put back in a hurry, perhaps?"

"Worth a try," murmured Connor, checking in both directions before he moved. Outside the door, the sight of a deep scar in the wood brought a smile to his face. *Seren saw this, too.* Seren's happiness seeped through the grains of the wood and filled him. His skin prickled with apprehension as he gripped the door handle and prepared to force his way through it. *This is going too well.* Doubts crept in when he could not detect a human heartbeat, or smell the familiar scent of Rebekah.

"Something must be restricting the movement of Seren's head," Connor hissed.

He already knew that much because all she could show him was the pitted, stained stone ceiling. Confirming his worst fears for Rebekah, he heard her thoughts. *I can't move, and it's too dark to be sure, Papa, but I think I'm alone.*

Alone? The 'storming the room and making a quick exit' scenario faltered. Connor met Julian's eye and shook his head.

Forcing his finger into the keyhole, Connor mangled the mechanism inside into iron filings without altering the outside appearance. The empty lock-chamber no longer pushed the metal tongue into the doorframe. Sliding open the bolts at the top and bottom took another nanosecond, and then, Connor stepped into the room.

His eyes darted immediately to the stone plinth upon which Seren's bound and gagged figure lay. 'Rebekah is not here,' were the words running inside his head, but he shoved them aside.

Julian wedged the door shut with a stone from the hearth and took stock of the surroundings, staying near the exit and listening out for approaching vampires.

Connor rushed forward, loomed over Seren, and peered down at her. In the pale glow of dusk, his face remained buried in shadow, but the metal studs in the leather vest he wore glinted in the gloom. Seren's body jerked to attention. *It's me. Sorry, Squirt. Just a disguise.*

Seren managed to smile, despite the pebble inside her mouth held in place by a leather gag. *Is all this necessary, Papa? For grave sleep?*

Connor's lips twisted as he studied the antelope hide cocoon bound around her body, squeezing her shoulders out of alignment. The gag covered the entire lower half of her face, and the pebble was a precaution in case her snapping jaws shattered her teeth. *This Lars appears to be thinking of her wellbeing.* Even though jealousy reared inside Connor, he reluctantly allowed words of approval to fill his head. *I think the sentinel is playing safe. Looking out for you.*

Seren's relief became concern. *Where is Mama?*

Connor crumbled the chains binding Seren and frowned. *You don't know?*

No.

"You two better be doing something other than just gazing into each other's eyes," hissed Julian from across the room.

A scowl from Connor was some reassurance.

"So, where did Seren say Rebekah is being held?" Julian muttered urgently.

"We don't know," replied Connor. Holding up a hand to silence Julian, he returned his attention to his daughter. *When did you see her last?*

Connor stared into the mid distance while Seren showed him the journey she had taken in Lars' arms to bring her here. Being carried had restricted her view, and her body swinging in time with the sentinel's driving stride had disrupted the pictures. Connor tamped down rage. Every second of her recollection increased his desire to kill the arrogant bastard.

She shared the vision of the great hall and the banquet table at the same moment that he pulled back the final layer of the animal skin cocoon, revealing Seren's silk finery. Rebekah's similar, but more revealing attire caused his gut to twist. Fear was a dim memory inside his human psyche, but his vampire senses felt an echo of it, now. Unbinding Seren, Connor helped her to stand. He spoke aloud for Julian's benefit. "Julian will look after you, take you to safety. I'm going to bring Mama home."

Connor's smile did not reach his eyes, and the calm he forced to the forefront of his mind did not fool his perceptive daughter.

Papa, be careful. Seren's dark eyes narrowed with a keen edge beyond her years. *There is an ugly old vampire here, too. He's plotting, I think.* Her jaw dropped open at Connor's amusement. *You know him?*

Connor nodded. *Malachi is my maker.*

"Sorry to interrupt, but if you have the-" Julian waved the impatient hand of someone feeling left out of the club. "-picture of where she is, then, shouldn't you go find Rebekah so we can get out of here?"

Connor crossed the dungeon, saying, "Go out through this window." He pulled out the bar already removed by Seren, and then dug out another four while he spoke. "Take Seren to Greg and Seth, leave her there and come back."

Julian joined him at the window. "You think you can take them all on?"

Connor knew his friend was reminding him of the dozen sets of uniform they found in the turret guardroom. "I have Malachi as backup. Just get Seren to safety. I don't need to be worrying about her, hmm?"

Julian nodded. "I'll be back as soon as I can." Turning to Seren, his face relaxed into a 'wicked uncle' grin and he said, "Your chariot awaits, climb aboard."

Connor gave Seren one last hug. *I'll bring Mama home. Promise me something?*

She met his eyes, her gray stare rock steady. *Anything.*

Stay out of my head. You use revival sleep if you have to, but stay out. You'll distract me.

They both knew he was holding back. He planned to do things he did not want her to see. Killing Lars was something he needed to do in private.

Yes, Papa, I promise.

Connor released her, and felt a measure of peace, watching Seren cross to where Julian waited.

Julian's penetrating look gave Connor reassurances he needed. "I'll be back," said Julian as he swung out of the window and held on to the ledge. Under Connor's watchful eye, Seren sprang up onto the ledge too, climbed out and settled into place on Julian's back.

Casting a sideways glance at Seren, where her cheek almost grazed his, Julian said, "You will have two Marines to look after. Do you think you can let Greg and Seth feel useful?"

Seren chuckled quietly. "Yes, Uncle Julian. I can do that."

"And you can hold your breath for fifteen minutes, right?"

She dug Julian in the ribs and, suddenly a child again, she poked out her tongue. She could stop her heart and hold her breath for a lot more than that, as well Julian knew.

The last sight Connor had of them was like a shot from a horror movie. Julian simply released his grip, and he and Seren plummeted into the sea below.

Their landing would, of course, cause a crater in the bedrock of the sea. But Julian would absorb most of the impact, and Seren's human softness was encased in a rock-hard shell, so Connor had no concerns about her safety.

Replacing the rods of iron in the window, Connor quickly tidied the room and covered the tracks of their hasty departure. Hardening his heart, he shelved all thoughts of Seren. *She's in safe hands.* Leaving the dungeon, he stepped back out into the passageway, closed the door and shot the bolts home. After a quick glance around, he set off to follow the path Seren had shown him.

Chapter 19

The great hall was larger than Connor had expected. The halo of burning candles lining the vast wooden hoop of a chandelier barely dented the shadows in the rafters. Tall candle sticks were essential to illuminate the space around the banquet table. An orange glow flickered between the pillars on the left side of the hall. The faint crackle of hungry flames and the smell of carbon told Connor that a fire blazed just out of view.

Advancing slowly, he sidestepped along the wall to an alcove and sank back into darkness. From this new vantage point, he calculated the distance to the open staircase which rose, seemingly to the heavens, to where a gallery ran the entire circumference of the hall. He inspected each wooden door ranging along the curving balcony and listened for clues.

Rebekah's scent wafting on the eddying currents teased him. *But how long ago was she here?* He reined in his compulsion to rampage through every room until he found her. Moving sideways, he could see further along the gallery and spotted the entrance to another passageway. *If she was behind one of these doors, I'd hear her heartbeat.* Making a decision, he took a step toward the ascending stairway.

A shadow moved up above and Connor darted back.

With a whisper like sand trickling through a funnel, an aperture opened in the wall near the top step, and a guardsman emerged onto the landing. The panel in the stone slid shut once more. Watching intently, Connor battled with the cocktail of disappointment and relief. The vampire blocking his path had not seen him.

Retiring behind a pillar, he reassessed his plan. *Fighting a guard now will blow my cover.* Connor diverted down another corridor where the pale gray atmosphere suggested the natural light of a window, and not the yellow hue of torch flames.

At the end of the hallway, he pushed open a window and, with his back to the sea, climbed out onto the stone ledge. His chin scraped against the masonry as the howling wind tore at his hair and tried to crush him into the wall. Blindly running his hand up over the rough stone, he dug his fingers into the mortar between the blocks, and pushed the window shut with his boot. He steadily scaled the sheer face of the fortress, and when he reached the battlements, he darted a quick glance over the parapet before swinging in through a notch in the crenellations and landing silently on the wooden boards of the ramparts.

The walkway filled the gap between two four-foot high walls, each crested by the familiar angular castellations of traditional medieval defenses. Connor scanned back and forth constantly as the gale force winds whistling in from the sea continued to shriek through his head, making even vampire hearing almost impossible.

Moving swiftly along the narrow walkway towards the large circular platform at the top of a turret, he experienced a jolt of triumph when, from somewhere beneath his feet, he detected Rebekah's agitated heartbeat

The setting sun's dying rays cast long shadows across the floor, and the black silhouette of the battlements looked like square-pegged teeth devouring Connor's legs up to his thighs. It took him only seconds to spot the iron ring handle on the hatchway in the pearl-gray weathered wooden boards.

Without warning, the heavy door flipped open.

Connor hit the deck, diving back into the dark shadow at the base of the wall and shielding his pale face from view with his sleeve as a vampire ascended the stairs and stepped out.

Waiting barely a nanosecond, Connor rolled into a crouch. As the guard turned, comical confusion crossed his face at one of his brethren being up on the roof, and acting like a lunatic. Using the element of surprise, keeping low, Connor rushed forward and grabbed the vampire around the thighs. He felt his ribs creak when the vampire landed a glancing punch, but he kept moving. He ran at the wall, shoving his opponent along the slick wood like a snowplow. The guard smashed backward into the rough stone, and Connor reared up, lifted, and flipped the vampire over the battlements and onto the rocks below.

Resting his hands on the wall and looking over the edge, Connor caught glimpses of the set white face as the body cartwheeled in descent. He had a passing regret that the fall would feel excruciatingly slow to the vampire's quick brain. His victim would relive the details of the lost fight a hundred times over before he reached the rocks.

When it hit the jagged boulders, the stone-like body shattered into several pieces. White spray erupting on the surface of the sea marked the final resting place of the dismembered parts, and Connor smiled grimly. For the vampire there was no coming back. *One down.*

Dismissing him in an instant, Connor gave thanks for the advantage wearing a guard's tunic had turned out to be, and descended through the open hatchway. He pulled the door shut behind him, making sure the sound did not echo along the dark passageway and raise the alarm.

Following the achingly familiar scent and sounds of Rebekah's blood pumping around her body, he descended a spiral staircase which led down to the bed chambers. He stopped on the bottom step when he heard Rebekah's voice, and Lars'.

At the end of the dim corridor, Connor spotted the chandelier hanging in the great hall – he was at the opposite end of the passageway he had seen from down below. The doors that had been hidden from view in the great hall ran along either side of this corridor. A distant shadow moving out on the gallery suggested the vampire who had appeared was on guard duty. *So, this is Sentinel Lars' private suite of rooms.*

Connor heard Rebekah's voice again. She sounded calm, but her thundering heartbeat told him differently. "When Seren wakes up you will take me to her," she said.

"We shall see." The male voice oozed charm, and Connor's hackles rose.

He took another step along the corridor, coming within thirty feet of the room from where the voices came.

"While I have you alone, I wonder, if we should negotiate?" the sentinel asked.

Connor heard Rebekah's breathing begin to race. She was agitated and her retreating footsteps took her away to the farthest side of the room.

"I don't think you found my attentions repulsive, hmm, min skat?"

'Attentions' was a word loaded with intent and Connor's body jerked.

"You're hurting me."

About to break his cover, the noise of her fingernail rapping on metal made Connor smile. He remembered Seren's vision of Lars, and the breastplate he wore blazing in the lamplight. It certainly lowered Connor's chances in a fight, and he instantly knew what Rebekah had in mind. *She's getting him to remove it. Don't push it, Rebekah.*

The rustle of fabric and the way her voice shook pushed him to the limit. *I'll give her just one more second.*

"You are right of course," Lars breathed. "This is not a battlefield. We both know I can take what I want."

Rage rattled inside Connor's chest but he forced himself to stay still.

Tuned to her body as he was, Connor sensed the moment Rebekah held her breath and her heart thudded louder. *She's scared.*

When she spoke again, Connor recognized the resignation in her tone. "I know the secret of Seren's conception." With an audible swallow, her voice became stronger. "I'll give you a hybrid child, but on condition that Seren's life is not threatened."

"Not pining for your doctor, min skat?" Lars seemed distracted by this enticement. "If we are to have a child together, I will protect Seren with my life. No one will ever get near her."

Rebekah's laughter was brittle. "Even Doctor Heinrik?"

"Especially the good doctor."

"I must see Seren. Make *sure* she is safe, before-"

"Komme, you can trust me."

Connor strained every sinew listening to a pause which stretched interminably, punctuated only by Rebekah's steady breathing.

"There," Lars said. "No metal breastplate between us, just this dress."

"I want to see Seren."

"And I want a child."

Rebekah's yelp was drowned out by the crash of something wooden falling over. Connor moved too late. The vampire out on the gallery rushed into the passageway up ahead, with another close on his heels. And like oil seeping from between the cracks, two others appeared out of the darkness, stepping from behind another concealed panel in the wall.

As the guards surrounded Connor, Rebekah screamed.

Bursting into action, he rammed one vampire against the wall and cracked his skull on the stone. Hands gripped his shoulder, and he shunted his elbow into the ribs of another attacker, and felt the knee cap of the guard directly behind shatter when he lashed back with his boot. He ricocheted their bodies from wall to wall until the noise was deafening.

The door, now only twenty yards away, jerked open, and Connor had the satisfaction of seeing Lars step out in time to witness Connor driving the heel of his hand up under a guard's chin – the tendons in his neck snapped before his spine crumbled.

Lars moved forward, and his bare chest and the loosened leather belt at his waist drew a snarl from Connor. Making full use of his knowledge of anatomy, Connor drove a vicious uppercut into the gut of another guard, rupturing the vampire's stomach and cracking his lower rib.

Another four vampires rushed into view, and Connor smiled. He had achieved his aim and drawn Lars away from Rebekah. *Even if it costs me my life, Julian will see Rebekah is safe, and Lars will pay.*

The reinforcements grabbed Connor and pinned his arms behind his back. Their solid bodies crowded his. The bones in his wrists creaked in their jittery grasp. *If there* were *twelve-* Connor ticked through the numbers in his head. *One shattered on the rocks, one with a detached skull, one without a stomach, and another with a useless leg. Julian and Malachi should have this sewn up.*

Silence fell when the sentinel stepped forward.

"So-" Lars tapped a long white finger on his thigh, and the vampires restraining Connor forced him down.

Connor's knees hit the flagstones with a crack. But, he held his body defiantly upright, even when the fingers clamped on the back of his neck bowed his head and fought to shove him facedown onto the floor. Clamping his jaw shut, Connor refused to budge, his tight sinews and muscles set like stone.

A pair of boots appeared in Connor's limited field of vision and a voice said conversationally, "We meet at last, no?"

The hands which held Connor's head slipped away. He jerked his chin up and stared into the glacier blue eyes of Sentinel Lars.

Connor was shocked at the accuracy of Seren's visions. He knew the face very well, even though he had never before set eyes on the sentinel.

Lars frowned as Connor glared up at him.

"Hvad hedder du? Your name?"

"Doctor Connor."

"So, Rebekah is your woman?"

The door down the hallway opened. Without moving his head, Connor knew Rebekah was looking out. Her heartbeat thundered through his chest, and, for a moment, the instinct to leap to his feet and ram Lars in the wall was hard to suppress. Instead, he turned and met her terrified eyes, his steady gaze begging her to trust him as his lip drew back in disgust.

"You are satisfied with another vampire's leftovers, Lars? You must be desperate." Connor spat on the floor. "You can have her, I just want my child."

Rebekah retreated and closed the door, and Connor fought down the anxiety in his gut. *She'll know I'm acting.* But doubt ate at him as Lars barked orders to his men. The heavy oak door was all that stood between Rebekah and a broken neck. Studying Lars' granite features, Connor saw the unveiled threat.

"I shall decide her fate. If you cooperate, I may let her live." Lars arrogantly walked to within easy reach for Connor. Gloating, he said, "You injure one more of my guards and-" At a jerk of Lars' head, a vampire moved to stand outside the door of Rebekah's prison. "Erik here, will be happy to end her life. We are clear, nej?"

"My daughter?"

Lars' eyes glittered. His intent glance shared communication with the vampires who held Connor still. "They will take you to see Seren now." The casual familiarity with which he used Seren's name stirred bile in Connor's stomach.

They both knew the sentinel was lying.

The guards jerked Connor to his feet, and Lars raised a hand to stop them. "Oh, one more thing. How long did the coma last?"

Bingo. He knows, Malachi, get out of here, now. Connor smiled, letting his thoughts hang there for his mentor to read.

Connor's narrowed glare remained pinned onto Lars' face while two guards yanked Connor to his feet. Behind his back, his hands were shoved into chainmail gloves and the shackles they clicked into place pressed the metal fabric into his wrists. The vampire escort swelled to six, and Connor grinned with satisfaction. *You do well to fear me. I'm going to rip your heart out.*

As he submitted to being shoved down the passageway towards the great hall, Connor heard the echo of Lars' voice. "Sergeant, go to the east turret. Stand guard until the others return. If the old vampire or his dark companion try to leave, sound the alarm."

The part of Lars' statement which gave the game away, for Connor, was 'until the others return'. *Malachi, they plan to kill me.* Connor's escort took him through the great hall and out of the main entrance, and then, they headed down a spiral staircase. Flexing his hands inside the metal gloves while he walked, Connor gradually stretched the chain of the shackles. Distorting the circular steel links into ovals added three inches to the chain between his wrists.

Connor recognized the route they marched him along, and, when they reached the dimly lit corridor where the row of dungeons lay, for a moment, he wondered if Seren's escape would be discovered. *Perhaps they* are *taking me to see her?*

Malachi, where are you? Connor continued to give the elder vampire every visual clue he could find. *Time is running out.*

He breathed easy when they passed by the door with the hollowed-out lock without pausing. *Game on, then. No touching father/daughter farewell, after all.*

An aperture further along the wall turned out to be a passageway which descended in a steep slope. The humidity increased as the ramp took them deep into the bowels of the castle. Scratches scored into the stone floor rang alarm bells in Connor's mind. *Prisoners come here already tied to a trolley?*

The moist air became harder to pull in and out through his throat, and the walls glistened with condensation. *We're going below sea level, why?* The series of iron grates set into the floor were rusted, and the glass lanterns hanging from metal brackets were frosted with dew. The surf battering the other side of the wall echoed like a low drumbeat, and everything began to feel terribly familiar.

The death chamber of the London hive's Storage Facility smells like this.

At the end of the corridor, Connor's world flipped on a surreal axis. The aged wooden door slid back to reveal a stainless-steel chamber. *Shit.* He stopped dead, and felt a hard shove in his back. But he did not need to enter to know what he would find. Metal examination tables fitted with restraints awaited each victim. He had performed the 'skull crushing' ritual himself when carrying out the sentences handed down in court by Julian.

A thick rubber seal ran all the way around the doorway to the chamber. Another shove forced Connor a step closer. Death chamber inmates were usually disabled with an injection of muscle relaxant before being strapped down. Two metal plates on a C-clamp vice would grip the prisoner's cranium at the temples. The metal arc of the clamp passing over the crown of the head gave the condemned an unobstructed view of the polished steel ceiling, and of their own reflection.

You don't miss a moment of your own death. Nicely done.

When the vampire executioner turned the screw with the flick of a wrist, the two plates would slam together – the victim's skull imploded, and a cloud of calcium dust obscured the final view of their death.

Okay, I'm not going in there.

At the next shove between his shoulder blades, Connor dropped into an explosive forward roll, passed the length of chain joining his wrists beneath his body, and regained his feet with his hands linked in front. Clenching his chainmail-encased fists, he whipped the chain in an arcing motion and demolished the face of the first of two vampires who rushed at him.

Go into the death chamber. The thoughts seeped into his head like smoke billowing from a fire and, without questioning it, he obeyed.

Unclamping his hands, Connor swung the loop of chain upward as the next attacker closed in fast. Triumph surged inside him when he dropped it around the vampire's neck, yanked the noose tight, and swung his victim in a flaring arc. The vampire's feet left the floor, the chain links gouged a trough into his neck, and then the chain snapped. His flailing body knocked two others off their feet as Connor backed into the steel-lined room.

The last pair of guards gathered like leather-clad crows. They oozed forward, filling the passageway and blocking the exit, and Connor began to wonder if his mind had played tricks on him. *What if the voice was not Malachi?* Going into the death chamber suddenly didn't seem to be such a great idea.

High tide raged just the other side of the wall. Rivulets of water seeped in around the edges of the guillotine-action sluice gate, which, when opened, would flood the room with rushing seawater and wash away the remains of executed vampires.

The red lever on the wall activated that process and Connor changed tack. If Malachi had not heard him, then sluicing the vampires into the sea would buy him time. *Not a lot, it will probably only take minutes for them to find their way back inside the castle.* Connor backed up, a 'worried frown' masking his plan of attack. *Come and get me, boys.*

Both vampires advanced to the ridge of rubber which ran along the threshold, but then came no further, blocking the doorway, shoulder to shoulder. The two who had been bowled over joined them, and four blank faces stared into space. *What are they waiting for?*

When the wall of solid bodies parted and a small weasel-faced vampire walked into the room, the atmosphere thickened with a chemical odor. Connor knew the aroma of a funeral parlor when he smelled it and the name Seren offered fitted the skittering nervous gaze of the intense face. *Doctor Heinrik.*

"Here to officiate my death? I see Lars is a coward to the last." Connor sneered at the company of vampires who, at last, filed in and ranged around the room. *Waiting for Heinrik's command?* While he spoke, Connor rolled the metal fabric of his gloves between his fingertips, crumbling it into holes that unsheathed his diamond hard nails. "How do you want me? Laid out on a table?"

"That would be perfect." Heinrik smiled. "But, I doubt you would give in so easily. Luckily, Lars gave me an inducement."

Bringing his hand out from behind his back, Heinrik opened his palm to reveal a hank of roughly cut hair.

Connor's body jerked as the blond-toned strands glinted in the light. Pretending relaxation, he shrugged. "Very macho. Hacking off her hair."

Glancing at his watch, Heinrik said, "I have seven minutes to report back to Sentinel Lars, before he sends a guard along with the woman's ear." The doctor's grin was hideous. "He thought you may be inclined to ignore the warning about injuring his guards, and-" Indicating the direction behind him where two felled vampires still lay, he added, "It seems he was correct."

Where the hell are you, Malachi? Seven minutes to kill four vampires, this rat of a doctor, and get back to Rebekah? Leaving her fate in the hands of others was alien to him, but he had no choice. Malachi could reach Rebekah within seven minutes. Connor used every ounce of concentration to plead with his mentor. *Malachi, get to Rebekah.*

Connor raised his hands in the time honored gesture of surrender, the broken chains still hanging from the manacles around his wrists.

With a flourish, the doctor tossed away the sample of hair and pulled a syringe from his pocket. Connor watched the silky, golden strands fluttering in the air, and anger boiled inside him. A snarl rumbled in Connor's throat, and unease rippled through the vampire guards. Fragments of metal rained down to the floor when he clenched his fists and the chainmail gloves broke apart.

Connor swung left, drove his hand into the stomach of the nearest guard and stared into the shocked features. He started towards his next target, when a wind tunnel effect of gushing air blew his hair back from his face.

GO. I have this. Malachi's command thundered through Connor's head mere seconds before Malachi rammed Heinrik in the back. The doctor skidded across the room and bounced from a wall, and Malachi rushed in through the door. Osiris appeared beside the elderly vampire, and Connor's confusion paralyzed him for an instant.

GO. GO. GO. Malachi glared.

Connor headed out of the chamber, and his last sight, before the metal-lined door swished into place behind him, was of Osiris opening the catheter on the feeding tube in his arm and letting his blood drip onto the steel floor. Snarls erupted from the vampires inside as the smell of human blood scattered their senses and they descended on Osiris in a mindless attack. Sacrificing Osiris was never part of the plan, and while Connor skimmed along the hallway, tuning into Rebekah's distant agitated heartbeat, sadness dragged him down. *Malachi has strength born of centuries of feeding, he will finish them while they are in a feeding frenzy, but Osiris? He won't stand a chance.*

On the final approach to the great hall, Connor bellowed loudly. "Laaars." The word exploded from deep inside him, driven out by desperation and rage.

Lars arrived on the gallery of the great hall at the same moment as Connor entered below. Looking up and sampling the air that clung to the sentinel, he felt relief when he could not smell Rebekah's blood. "She is unharmed?" Connor forced the words through a stiff smile. "I hope so, for your sake."

For a moment, Lars' state of undress crippled Connor. The Viking's bare chest registered as a good thing, even though the unfastened belt of his pants struck fear in his heart.

Lars tilted his head, his blue stare slicing across the fifty yards between them. "She? The leftovers you gave to me?"

Connor erupted into a run, his fingers itching to close around the sentinel's neck.

Lars' harsh laughter echoed in the rafters.

Before Connor reached the bottom of the staircase, the sentinel leapt the twenty feet from the walkway to the stone floor below, his crouched body absorbing the impact, but still cracking the paving slab beneath his boots.

Reaching up as he straightened, Lars grabbed an ax from a bracket on the wall behind him and advanced in powerful strides, swinging it around his head.

Shit, he's done this before, thought Connor.

Lars settled into a rapid figure-of-eight action which sent the blade whistling through the air. It skimmed past his solid shoulders with every driving stroke.

Connor backed away, looking for a break in the rhythm of the ax head slicing ever closer to his head. A metal disc mounted on the opposite wall glimmered in the light, and a snap decision exploded inside Connor's brain.

Diving under the wooden banquet table, he made it to the other side and yanked a manganese steel shield from its mount. Spinning around in time to see Lars leap up onto the table, Connor fended off an attack. The sentinel rained blows down, and the vibration of the ax smashing into the shield juddered through Connor's shoulder.

Connor was driven to his knees beneath the shield. He heard the heavy thud as Lars landed on the floor within striking distance, towering over Connor's folded body. The ax blows were accompanied by a triumphant snarl as Lars adjusted to a two-handed grip and used all his strength.

The shield fractured with the screech of buckling metal. Connor jerked to one side. The next blow of Lars' blade ripped through the leather sleeve of Connor's tunic and grazed along the flesh from his raised elbow down to his shoulder.

Connor threw aside the broken shield, and a shower of sparks accompanied the clatter of metal grinding on flagstone. Folding his arm over his stomach, Connor rocked on the floor, grimacing. He clutched the tattered sleeve together over his injury.

Staring up at Lars towering over him, Connor groaned, flexing his fingers to ward off the muscle-hardening vampires face when their blood network is destroyed.

Kicking the rattling shield aside, Lars planted his feet either side of Connor's body. He reached down, gripped the front of Connor's leather tunic, and hauled him to his feet. Smiling arrogantly into Connor's face, tapping the ax head against his boot, Lars said quietly, "I really shouldn't leave Rebekah waiting any longer. She will be getting cold." Lars' sneer as he uttered her name ignited a blaze of fury in Connor's brain, sweeping away the calculation of his plan and flooding him with visceral hunger.

Spitting the words into Connor's face, Lars added "After she bears me a child, I shall kill her slowly, breaking one bone at a time. And your child? She will be my own immortal blood supply, and maybe more." Lars tilted his head and leered.

"Over my dead body. Touching my daughter signed your death warrant." Connor grated the words out between clenched teeth. At the same moment, he drew back his fist and drove a hard punch forward. Crumbling the crazed bone of the sentinel's ribs with the explosive blow, he buried his fist inside the cavity of Lars' chest.

Lars bellowed, the sound bubbling in his throat as air rushed into his ruptured ribcage. His grip tightened on Connor's tunic and questions flooded his blue eyes with confusion.

Surging to his full height, Connor studied Lars' contorted features. "Never underestimate me and mine. Seren knew your weakness. Those battle scars you are so proud of? The broken ribs beneath the breastplate? They were your undoing." Connor clenched his fist around the vampire warrior's heart and wrenched it free of the arteries tethering it. "My Rebekah would never take you into her bed," he snarled, knowing Lars could still hear and see him. "My injury?" Connor delivered the final puzzle piece with a grin. "I faked it, it's just a scratch."

With his free hand, Connor landed an upper cut under Lars' chin, snapping his head back, and tearing the ligaments in his neck. Lars' broken body hit the floor, and Connor dropped the mangled heart back into the gaping hole in the sentinel's chest.

He took time to wipe his hands on a banner hanging on the wall, smearing brown blood over the intricately painted coat of arms, and then he was off and running.

He ascended the stairway to the gallery in a second and paused, scanning each door around the circumference of the vast hall and listening for Rebekah's clamoring heart. With each passing moment, he battled with the fear that it was no longer beating. *Unless he lied, and he turned her. Please God, don't let it be that.*

The notion of Lars turning Rebekah and staining her soul with his blood tortured Connor. Like the mythical vampire of popular fiction, if her 'maker' took a stake through the heart, Rebekah would feel the loss. Even though she would not want to care, Lars' dying would tear her apart.

Connor began walking fast when the whisper of her breathing drew him towards a door on the next stretch of walkway. He was so focused on the door, a blow on his shoulder sent him stumbling sideways. His foot slipped over the edge, his boot grating down over the coping stone as, with his back to the great hall far below, he began to fall.

Pushing off from the one foothold he still had, Connor leapt into the void, reaching for the wooden hoop of the chandelier. He caught it with one hand and dug his fingers into the intricate carvings, showering lumps of wood and candle-wax down onto the banquet table. Twisting in the air, he got both hands on the rail, swung his legs, and launched himself back across the space. The vibrations of the creaking chains tingled through his hands as, letting go, he crashed feet first into the vampire guard who had appeared from nowhere.

The vampire was flung backward, cracking his skull on the granite wall. Taking a step forward, Connor jeered as he buried his thumb and forefinger in the vampire's eye sockets. Pushing hard, he felt the orbs collapse as he gouged holes in the frontal lobe of the vampire's brain. He released his grip, and his victim staggered back. The stricken vampire dragged his shoulder along the wall until he suddenly disappeared sideways through an open panel.

Ah. A secret doorway. Stepping into the dark space, Connor dropped to his knees and peered at the prone figure. *Did this one escape Malachi? No. He's not one of my escorts.* He listened carefully. There were no tell-tale sounds of dislodged dirt settling, or leather brushing over stone or skin. Connor did not sense any other vampires. Satisfied, he rose to his feet, and, wiping his hands on his tunic as he walked, he honed in on the door again.

Turning the handle, he found it locked. Laying his palm and his cheek on the warm wood, he whispered, "Rebekah?"

The soft rustle of fabric brought a smile to his face. The scampering sound of bare feet reached the door, and she hissed, "It's locked."

Connor laughed gently. Gripping the iron doorknob, he turned it steadily until the spindle inside creaked and then snapped with an explosive pop. Pushing the door, it swung open, and he rocked back on his heels as Rebekah threw herself at him. She wrapped her arms in a choke hold around his neck and her thighs gripped his waist.

He smiled and buried his face in her hair.

He kicked the door shut behind them. His hands on her backside, he held her close and kissed her neck. His fingers entwined into her hair, and, with a relentless tug, he pulled her head back, lifting her chin and drowning in the heated currents stirring in her gaze.

His lips settled gently on hers, his tongue tasting her lips until she let him in and he drank in her scent. The scalding heat of her mouth ignited a lava flow that built into waves of relief and desire until his thigh muscles began to tremble.

Striding forward, he found the bed and laid her down carefully. His mouth devouring hers still, he knelt on the mattress. Settling his chest gently over her, he reveled in the feel of her heart thundering beneath him, and the heat of her skin burned through his tunic. His urge to touch her became overwhelming, but he stopped.

He lifted his chin and closed his eyes.

Staring up at him, Rebekah murmured, "What?" She wriggled, pulling the cotton neckline of her petticoat up higher. "Is someone coming?"

Connor fixed her flushed face in his gaze and stroked a finger down over her cheek. "No. No one is coming." His smile reflected his appetite and Rebekah's heart raced. Connor clenched his teeth at the enticing river of blood throbbing beneath his fingertips, and hunger sliced him open. *Malachi knows better than to visit my head now.* Connor would feel it, and, mentor or no, this was *his* time and the old vampire would live to regret it. Seren, too, had kept her word, so for now, there was nothing but him and Rebekah.

"We are alone, and *you* are at my mercy."

His hand stroking up her delicate ribcage drew a groan from her lips. An answering growl rumbled in his throat as, tugging the cotton bodice down, his hand covered her breast. The soft skin flushed beneath the delicate stroke of his thumb over her nipple. Running his hand up her thigh underneath the thin petticoats, his hand slid over her hip.

Rebekah winced, and Connor froze. Lifting his head, his gray eyes dark with his need, he frowned. "He hurt you?"

She didn't want his mind rushing into territory that would torture him, and to where he would battle the ghost of Lars touching her. She smiled, ruefully. "*I* hurt me. I've had a busy time throwing myself from horses and causing trouble as usual."

His expression serious, his throat worked as Connor said, "He wasn't wearing much."

Rebekah shared his pain. "I know. But, arrogance was his undoing. You were in time, and that's all that matters."

"Now, about those self-inflicted injuries." His relief made her heart ache as he murmured, "I'm a doctor. I don't know if I've mentioned that before?"

Connor's expression was tight with his longing to love her and to make her his. He eased back onto his knees, his fingers trailing down over the petticoats that skimmed her delicate form. He smiled and stared into her eyes. He tore the thin fabric, stroking back the lawn material and unveiling the satin skin of her breasts and ribcage. With an achingly delicate touch his cold fingertips traced the purple and deep red bruises before he gently kissed each one.

Rebekah closed her eyes and her sigh became a groan. She pushed her fingers into his hair, gripping the strands of black silk as he took her nipple into his cool mouth and played his tongue over it.

A chilled breeze wafting over her skin as Connor left her made her open her eyes again with a cry of protest. With vampire speed, he stripped the clothes from his body revealing the dirt streaked skin of his chest and the strong muscles framing his pelvis and thighs. He stood before her naked.

Connor moved to the foot of the bed, his eyes glowing like hot gray coals in the dim light as he felt the acceleration of her heartbeat thrumming through the atmosphere. The scent of her excitement wafted into his brain and pushed his control to the limit. He sought the refuge of revival sleep, the tension in his stomach and the knife blade in his gut fading to a mere ravenous ache when he found the gentle touch he needed.

Coming back to her, easing up the mattress, he trailed his fingertips up over the goose-bumps on her skin. His tongue traced up over her trembling stomach, teasing her breast until, at last, kissing her lips, he settled over her body. Their eyes met, and he stayed still, poised in the moment before he lost his sanity, nudging gently at the slick heat he yearned to bury his senses in.

"I love you, Rebekah. You drive me crazy, you make life hurt so much, but God, I love you."

She framed his face with her hands and pressed her lips to his. He clenched his jaw as the satin heat of her thighs closed around his hips and he grumbled, "Rebekah."

Smiling against his mouth, in the moment before he deepened the kiss, she whispered, "Love me, Connor."

He surged inside her, and feeling her melting heat close around him, he froze. "It's been too long. I'll hurt you."

He buried his hand in her soft blond hair, molding his fingers to her nape as he kissed her, and, without breaking the contact, he rolled slowly over onto his back and surrendered his body to her control.

Connor's fingertips dug into the mattress as she filled his vision and his heart with the perfection of her flushed heavy breasts. She arched her back, sitting up to take them both over the tumbling cliff edge. When the waves of pleasure trembling inside her engulfed him, he tore a fistful of wadding from the mattress with each hand. He locked her scent inside his chest as tension gripped his body in that final moment before the tide of release washed through him.

Savoring the drifting clouds of fading heat, his rolled up to sitting, enfolded Rebekah in his arms and held her to his silent chest. Her heart still thundered in her ribcage, and he enjoyed the vibration as if it was inside him too.

Lying back and taking her with him, he tucked Rebekah into his side, and took a deep vampire breath, finally feeling whole again.

His lips twitched as he said, "At least my bruises will not show. I can pretend I got it right at last."

"Oh, you always get it right," Rebekah murmured, tracing idly over the hard ridges of his abdomen. Suddenly pushing up onto her elbow, she leaned over to look at the groove in his chest her fingertips had discovered. "You have another war wound."

Connor grimaced while Rebekah examined his body, inspecting the crater in his arm made by Anthony's needle, the gouges left by his encounters with Viktor and Blake, and the freshest silver veined trough in his upper arm, the ax graze extending down from his shoulder. Lars had left his mark.

"It's been a tough day," he said lightly, and drew her back down, his arm creating a cage which trapped her. Using his free hand, he gathered the tumbled blankets and pulled them up over her body. "Sleep, hmm? I've missed that so much, feeling you sleeping beside me."

Even though she grumbled, Connor grinned when he felt her relax and her soft curves melted to fit his form. With a deep sigh, she settled her scalding cheek on his chest, murmuring that she loved him, and he replied that he loved her too.

Rebekah drifted off to sleep, and Connor invited Malachi's thoughts into his head. Expecting the worst, he heaved a sigh at the news that Osiris had survived. Malachi took great joy in playing out the highlights of the fight inside Connor's mind.

Gloating, Malachi? Connor's lips twitched as he teased his mentor.

He was rewarded with a front row seat of the action he had left behind. The plinking sound of blood hitting the stainless-steel floor of the death chamber had made every vampire's head whip around. Only two guards made it past Malachi as the old vampire executed an agile somersault, taking them by surprise. Grabbing hold of one vampire and using him as support, he landed a double-footed kick into the face of another. The force of the kick knocked the first guard in the line back into the one behind – the back of his companion's skull smashing into his snarling features with the force of a mallet strike shattered his nose and both cheekbones.

Malachi banged their heads together until one had nothing left of his face, and jelly thick brain tissue oozed out of the hole in the skull of the other.

Osiris was finely balanced, his powerful legs planted wide as he pressed the plug of wax back into the bamboo catheter tube, stopping the flow of blood. Reaching back, he grabbed a steel C-clamp lying on the trolley behind and swung it in an arc, tearing the hook of metal through the windpipe of a vampire who could see only the Egyptian's throbbing jugular.

The snarling muzzle of the one following on behind came to within inches of Osiris' neck, but his strong hands closed over the vampire's cranium and twisted hard. The sound of the vertebrae crumbling preceded the loud crack of exploding cartilage, and, with the motor function interrupted, he dropped to the ground.

Malachi finished off the distracted Doctor Heinrik who stared at Osiris, zeal glinting in his eyes as he realized the Egyptian was different.

A surge of curiosity burned through Connor, too. Lying completely still beside Rebekah's sleeping body, he resisted the urge to seek out Malachi and demand an explanation of Osiris' strength. *Malachi, you say he comes from a tribal people. Warriors?*

Who he is can wait. Malachi's next words drove everything else from his mind. *We have swept the castle, and we are alone. We should bring Seth and Greg into the fortress. They will be safer here.*

Connor nodded automatically, even though Malachi would not see. *Yes. Seren is with them by now, and Julian will be on his way back.* Connor smiled, knowing Julian would be sorry to have missed the battle. *Keep your eyes open for him, we are safer all in one place.*

Chapter 20

Winter in London arrived in an avalanche of frozen rain, somewhere between snow and hailstones. The chips of ice falling from the sky bounced from Marius' broad shoulders. Waiting on the top of the steps leading into the vampire council building, Alexander leaned forward, ignoring the elements and watching the darker vampire sweep into view. A wake of ice white spray pluming into the air marked Marius' progress until he finally joined Alexander in the sheltered embrace of the portico framing the doorway.

Marius appeared oblivious to the glittering shroud of hail sitting on his hair, skin and shoulders. His oil-black gaze was fathoms deep and enigmatic, prompting Alexander to ask. "Well?"

Turning an impassive look on the younger vampire, Marius said, "As we expected. Anthony has not heard anything."

Alexander bit his tongue. *No news is good news. If the rescue party arrives back too soon, I won't have time to deal with Matthew.* It had been two weeks, which was the mere blink of an eye in vampire hours, but for Alexander they seemed to have crawled by. He was feeling the strain. It would be better if Marius was easier to read. His companion's closed meetings with Captain Gerrard were unnerving. *Did Principal Julian suspect my involvement?* Not knowing was gnawing a hole in Alexander's gut.

Pushing open one of the twelve feet tall double doors, Alexander waved Marius through and fell into step beside him as they made their way to the courtroom.

"Is Anthony coping with hospital rounds?"

"Of course." Marius darted Alexander a reassuring look.

"And the humans?"

Marius' silence rattled Alexander. Finally, he replied, "You're better off not knowing. Neither of us can betray Doctor Connor if we do not know."

Alexander felt a little easier. Marius was not a liar, of that much he was certain. *If he says he does not know-*

Looking down the length of the hallway, Alexander spotted the waiting figure of Captain Gerrard. *Now him, I'm not so sure of.* He wore the purple garb of office declaring he was here on official business.

"Juror Marius, Juror Alexander," greeted Gerrard.

Marius nodded in reply and carried on into the anteroom. In silence both jurors donned their long black robes. Marius paused with his hand on the door handle and glanced at his companions. "Ready?"

Satisfied, he walked through the door and out onto the raised platform, and soberly scanned the full gallery of the courtroom.

The waiting vampire throng still only wore dark clothes, a habit borne of the hundreds of years spent blending in. Their frozen pale faces appeared dead, but the glitter of dark pupils could not disguise the hunger for news.

Marius took his place behind the polished wood of the jurors' bench in the central position of Julian's throne. The third seat remained vacant, although Captain Gerrard stood behind it with his gauntlet resting on the gilt-embellished chair back.

Alexander surveyed Julian's domain and, for the thousandth time, wished he could rewind the clock. The court seemed dull without the principal's dynamic presence. He fought to keep a frown off his face. The feeling of riding a runaway train had not abated. *Damn Serge.*

Marius opened the proceedings with a bang of the gavel on a wooden block and the sharp crack stiffened the spine of every vampire. Every eye settled expectantly on the door through which the accused should appear.

Under the keen gaze of the assembled court, the escorted vampire walked reluctantly across the courtroom and mounted the four steps to stand in the dock. He laid his hands carefully on the polished brass handrail, his posture tense, but he took care not to crush the metal. Although, Marius' authority was limited, the vampire had picked the wrong crime, on the wrong day, and Captain Gerrard was here to add the third vote.

Supervisor Matthew sat in the back row, but Alexander kept his eyes fixed on the defendant. He found ignoring Matthew difficult. *What the hell is he playing at? Keep a low profile. How hard is that? Idiot.*

Usually happy to play Devil's advocate, Alexander might have tried to sway Marius from his sentencing decision but, all of a sudden, he wanted the hearing over and done with.

Marius' tone of condemnation oozed through the court like an oil slick. "Explain yourself, Henry."

"I broke Charles' jaw," Henry said bluntly.

Even Alexander jolted upright in his seat.

"Blood dispensary Charles?" Marius snapped.

Henry nodded. His sinews and tendons creaked with the tell-tale sign of dehydration.

"And you did not collect your human blood vials?"

Henry nodded again.

"That is just as well, because you are destined for Storage Facility Eight." The jurors were on alert for any hint that allies of Doctor Connor were being targeted, and Charles, the small wiry vampire in the blood dispensary, fitted that description.

Alexander had visited the storage facility only once, as had all vampires. It was intended as a deterrent, seeing the rows of supine figures strapped into steel-lined coffin shells. Although each one stared at the ceiling, the shifting currents of their thoughts played out behind their pleading eyes, their active brains screaming while their bodies slowly hardened to granite. Eighty percent of the building lay underground. The polished quartz walls of each storage ward were bone dry – human respiration created condensation, however, vampires did not breathe – and years of infrequent movement made the air stagnant.

"You freely admit your crime." Marius' raised hand summoned two purple clad council guardsmen. "The jury will vote. Juror Alexander?"

"Guilty."

"Captain Gerrard?"

"Guilty."

Marius lifted the gavel. "The verdict is-"

Hearing someone call his name in the corridor outside whipped Marius' head around.

The door to the court flipped open and deposited a disheveled Anthony into the room. His attention flitting from the dock to the jurors, he said, "Marius, has the verdict been given?"

"Not yet." Marius raised a dark brow.

"Can I speak on Henry's behalf?"

"I don't see why not." Marius nodded. "Proceed."

"I should have spotted the symptoms. Henry was in revival sleep, sitting comatose for a minute and a half. Connor would have noticed it, he would have known the dehydration seizure would follow and injected Henry's ration of blood into his system via the carotid. I have to take some of the blame. Charles saw it, but he was too late, and he was too close to Henry when he flipped." Anthony paused, checking the jurors' expressions for clues. "Charles' jaw has been wired, and he'll regain full function, so no harm done, if the court pleases." Anthony glanced at Henry as he finished.

Marius' attention moved smoothly from Anthony to Henry and back again. "And how *is* Doctor Connor?"

Alexander played along, wearing an interested expression. Marius used every opportunity to add weight to Julian's pretense.

"He is still in a coma. No improvement as yet," said Anthony clearly.

"Henry, you're a valuable hive member, and I'm inclined to accept that your revival sleep meltdown could have been averted." Although Marius smiled, his probing look held a stern warning. "It looks like this is your lucky day. You are excused."

Matthew had glided smoothly to the edge of the gallery and slipped down the stairs at the mention of Connor, drawing every eye as he tried to make his escape. *Fool.* Alexander locked eyes with the supervisor and casually drew a long white finger along his cheek bone, baring his teeth in a smile. At the same moment Matthew disappeared out through the door, Gerrard shifted position on the dais. Alexander felt certain the captain would follow.

"Henry. You will report to Captain Gerrard in the guard room and wear a tagging device until further notice. You are on borrowed time, use it well."

Relief eased through Alexander. *Gerrard is busy, for now.*

The court adjourned, and Alexander joined Anthony and Marius in the jurors' chambers and took a seat.

Marius smiled, not something he did very often. "I am glad Charles is well."

Anthony grinned. "I guessed Henry would need my help. Imagining enemies lurking at every turn, that is a place I understand. But I don't believe he targeted Charles."

"He is tagged, so if he is part of a conspiracy against Connor, he is of no use now." The still air in the room weighed the vampires down. "When Connor and Julian return, the time will come to choose sides," Marius said slowly.

Anthony agreed. "The woods have been quiet. No one has yet set out to discover the tree dwellers' camp. But the longer Connor is in his coma, and Julian is in Scotland. Let's just say, someone will exploit the weakness."

Marius got to his feet and banged his hand on the table. "We will wait another week, and then I shall grill Matthew again. His nerves are crumbling, I could almost hear them jangling from across the courtroom."

The meeting broke up, the sense of resolve humming in the air putting Alexander on edge. Time had run out, that much was clear. *Where the hell is Matthew hiding?* He knew he would not have left the building. *Marius is right, Matthew will crack.* Slipping smoothly through the door, Alexander made his exit appear as casual as usual.

He sensed Matthew's presence before he saw him. "Not here," he said with a disarming smile – a smile meant for everyone except the supervisor, who absorbed the full force of Alexander's anger-laden glare. "The nest, in one hour." Striding away, he felt the daggers Matthew aimed at his back, and grinned.

Will anyone be surprised if Matthew goes missing? Marius has made it clear the noose is closing around his neck. That he has the guts to run would be the only real surprise. Alexander left the building and relaxed into his easy run. He had an hour to prepare things at the human eco-shelter. Only Serge called it 'the nest'. Matthew would be one of the few who would know what Alexander meant.

Inside the deserted eco-shelter, nature's sounds crept into Alexander's head like ghostly fingers drawing lines in fogged glass. There were three still, cold motorcycles standing on sturdy metal stands. The chemical odor of the gas in their tanks wreathed the air and burned Alexander's sinuses.

He walked along the main tunnel in what was pitch-black to human eyes, but Alexander saw a myriad of scuttling insect life glistening and lichen covered damp patches on the walls glowing in the darkness.

Flipping back the sackcloth curtain, the ash that had formed on the extinguished torches plumed in gray clouds when Alexander accelerated down the slick carved passageway and stirred a breeze.

He headed through the dining cavern and onwards into the kitchen. The buckled door of the panic room had been pushed closed even though the lock would never work again. Running his fingers over the ice cold stainless-steel worktops, he considered the assortment of dust covered knives and cooking utensils which hung from hooks on the walls.

He slid open drawers. He knew he would know it when he saw it, and then he smiled. A cleaver, the one Oscar used to butcher animal carcasses into chops and joints for roasting, lay in the bottom of the third drawer. But it was not that which drew him. A set of six-inch metal meat skewers glinted in the meager glow, and Alexander picked one out.

Weighing it in his hand, he closed his fist tightly around the steel and crimped it to fit his grip. He checked his watch. *Ten minutes.* He moved smoothly back out through the kitchen and slipped behind the curtain into the laundry and bathing area. The water in the abandoned Jacuzzi-sized pool had a thin scum over the top and a discarded basket of soiled laundry sat beside it. Evacuating their home and releasing Connor to start the search for Rebekah and Seren had pushed everyday chores to the bottom of the heap.

Matthew is my urgent chore. Where is he?

The privacy curtain covering the door swayed in the rush of air which signaled the arrival of a vampire, and Alexander wrestled with his plan of attack. *Should I jump him?* Suddenly, dread cramped in his stomach. But the vampire closing in was forceful and unfaltering. *It's not Matthew.* Of that much, Alexander felt sure.

Holding the skewer behind his back, Alexander peered through the gap in the curtain. The large bulk moved like an oozing ink blot across the width of the darkened chamber. Alexander recognized the silhouette, instantly. *Anthony. He cannot find me here.* There was no other exit, so the only option was to hide.

Pushing the skewer down into the waistband of his pants, Alexander upended the basket of laundry carefully into the pool, encouraging the garments to float out over the surface and then he, too, entered the water. Sinking to the bottom, he stared at the multi-colored iceberg of fabric settling above him and listened carefully. The water amplified Anthony's light tread, so Alexander knew when he entered the laundry room.

Why is he here? Does he know? Easing his weapon from his waistband, Alexander prepared to fight and lose. Anthony was a boxer when human, and his hardened vampire body packed a punch which would literally knock Alexander senseless. Fighting would be suicide. *But at least I'll escape a life sentence of storage.*

Another set of footsteps drew closer and Alexander cursed, the water flooding in between his gritted teeth. At the edge of the pool, Anthony dropped to his knees and the ice floe of fabric shifted and a bright red splash disappeared. Drops rained down onto the surface as he wrung the water from the blouse he had rescued and tucked it inside his shirt.

His footsteps returned to the doorway and then abruptly stopped. *Shit, he has heard Matthew.* Anthony left, and Alexander eased his head above water, waiting to hear what happened.

"Hey," Anthony shouted, and then started running.

Pushing the sopping clothes aside, Alexander leapt out onto the ceramic tiled floor. Ignoring the cloying grip of his waterlogged shirt and the waterfall streaming from his sodden pants, he set off in pursuit of Anthony at a safe distance.

At the entrance to the eco-shelter, Alexander hung back and watched Anthony crisscrossing over the greasy spiked grass of the moonlit meadow. The frustration etched on Anthony's features gave Alexander hope. For once, Matthew's yellow-bellied streak had done him a favor. The skittish supervisor had bolted, and Anthony had no clue in which direction the mysterious vampire went. In the end, Anthony headed east towards London and disappeared into the woods.

The red shirt Anthony took was for Leizle, Alexander guessed. *Talk about a lucky escape, but not for Matthew.* Alexander knew exactly which direction his rattled companion would have taken. *There's no telling what he'll do now. Anthony scared the shit out of him.*

Walking out into the moonlight and turning to face the tunnel entrance, Alexander grabbed a handful of the tree roots trailing down from overhead and pulled himself up onto the sloping hillside above. He set off across the rolling fields beneath which the excavated caverns were concealed. The human farm lay west of London, and Matthew would go to ground there. *I need to catch him before he gets away.*

Alexander caught sight of Matthew traveling at cruising speed, following the long wide ribbon of tarmac which eventually led to the delivery entrance of the human farm.

The road between the blood dispensary at the hospital and the farm facility was the most traveled in the hive. Matthew could easily have been on a routine visit to the human farm except for the agitated jerky rhythm to his stride.

Alexander hung back fifty yards, matching Matthew's pace. *Will he cut through the woods?* Staying on the road added twenty miles to the journey, which seemed a ridiculous option, so Alexander was hopeful the opportunity to ambush Matthew would come.

Matthew abruptly left the road, and headed into a derelict suburb. Alexander's curiosity made him bide his time. *Where is he going?*

Two miles further along the rural lanes, Matthew disappeared between tall hedgerows. Alexander reached the space in time to see his quarry disappear through the front door of a house. Its stone construction showed signs of being well kept, and the windows were spotlessly clean.

Stepping back into the cover of the over-hanging foliage, Alexander saw Matthew pass in front of a window and disappear as he sank down out of sight. *Is he taking rap-sleep there?* There was no other movement inside the rooms. *Perhaps Matthew has more sense than I thought.* Alexander knew the aggression of rap-sleep could make Matthew say something incriminating.

It never occurred to Alexander that Matthew could have a bolt hole outside the confines of the farm. *Vampires don't have homes.* Although some chose to escape and to get away from the brittle facade of pretending that living close to other vampires was anything other than repugnant. It was only the threat of being sentenced to 'skull crushing' which prevented vampires killing each other. *Might not be such a bad thing with the farm stock destined to decline.* Humans age and die, and there was no getting away from that. *Without Doctor Connor to solve the breeding difficulties-* Alexander felt a pang of guilt. *If Lars discovers the secret of Seren's hybrid biology, will he share it?* Alexander doubted it and being taken for a fool focused his mind. *Being a fool is one thing, being known as a traitor is entirely different.*

Swooping in through the gap between the ivy-strangled pillars flanking the driveway, Alexander surveyed the house. In his decades of experience, there were only three types of vampire who craved a home: the ones with something to hide, those who clung to the past, and those who coveted treasure. *As though money and jewels are of any use.*

Principal Julian's home in Richmond fulfilled a rare fourth category, protection from his enemies. *Or rather, a place where he did not have to smile at fools.*

Alexander paused at the top of the flight of six steps and boldly knocked on the door. Catching Matthew unawares played into Alexander's hands. The alarm of his secret being discovered would be replaced by relief, and then he would relax his guard.

He felt Matthew's presence behind the door, skulking.

"It's Juror Alexander," he said, his smile injecting reassurance into his tone.

There was a long pause, and then the door eased open. Three fingers gripped the edge and Matthew's blank face peered out.

Alexander turned to bathe his face in moonlight. "I saw Anthony at the eco-shelter, so I thought it would be wiser if I came to you."

Through tight lips Matthew said, "How did you know where to find me?"

Alexander's smile became indulgent. "You need to escape the relentless temptation of humans on the farm. I've always known where to find you, but I respect your privacy."

The suspicion in Matthew drained away. "I guess you'd better come in."

Alexander followed Matthew along the gloomy hallway and into a reception room. The windows looked out over the towering unkempt hedges which obscured the view of the road.

"It is a shame to spoil your view, but I guess cutting the shrubs back would be a dead giveaway," Alexander said idly.

"Does Juror Marius know?" Matthew turned to face his guest.

Distracting the supervisor by reaching out and squeezing his shoulder, Alexander stepped in close and shoved the metal skewer up into the space beneath his jaw.

Matthew's eyes snapped open in surprise.

"I *am* sorry, Matthew," whispered Alexander. He closed his hand around the back of Matthew's neck and pushed the spike home with the heel of his hand. The supervisor's throat gurgled as the skewer pierced his windpipe and severed the spinal cord before the tip buried itself in the brainstem.

The jolt of exhilaration Alexander felt dissipated quickly, leaving him under a landslide of guilt. *This is all my fault.* "I'm sorry, I should never have let Councilor Serge talk me into it."

Accusation shone in the jet pools of Matthew's blown pupils, and Alexander knew his partner in crime could still hear him. Death would come slowly as his brain dehydrated.

Switching to autopilot, Alexander guided Matthew's slack body to the floor. Gripping his ankles and avoiding looking down at what he had done, he dragged the body through to the back of the house. An explosive back kick fractured the lock on the rear door and within moments, Matthew's dead weight had flattened a tract of grass leading to the bottom of the garden.

The smell of crushed grass and disturbed soil clumped in Alexander's nostrils as he mindlessly dug a hole with his hands. And then, gripping the stricken vampire by his coat, Alexander guided the stiff lifeless form into the deep grave. The image of Matthew's crumpled body lying in the bottom of the pit would be etched into Alexander's mind for decades.

He replaced the earth wishing he had the guts to do what he should, and crush Matthew's skull. *I could've offered him a quick death.* But he failed, even in that.

Chapter 21

Connor scanned the group of adventurers gathered around the banquet table. Greg and Seth had only a few patches of clean skin left, but the ingrained mud and khaki paint was forgotten in the jubilation of triumph and the prospect of a decent meal.

"So, are all the vampires dead?" Seth asked through a mouthful of bread.

Connor nodded. "Julian and I swept the castle, including the secret passageways." The phrase 'no stone unturned' certainly applied in this case. They had help from Malachi and, surprisingly, Osiris. Connor bit back the questions Malachi's version of events raised. He really thought he had seen the last of the young Egyptian when the door of the death chamber closed. *Malachi has some explaining to do, but that time will come.*

Contentment filled the cavernous space of the great hall as the men relaxed for the first time since the group left the eco-shelter.

"Well, this is nice," said Greg, in the understatement of the year. He was too tired to smile, but his eyes shone as he spoke.

Connor sat back in his chair at the head of the table and took a mouthful of fresh rabbit blood, enjoying the heat tingling in his stomach. Lowering the glass, he watched Rebekah eating. She studiously ignored him, but the telltale flush traveling over her cheeks and the pulse thundering in her throat delighted him. Still gazing at Rebekah, Connor said, "I agree, it is very nice, Greg."

"What happens now?" asked Seren. "Are we going home?"

"Yes, Squirt, we are going home." Connor ruffled Seren's hair. "As soon as the guys have had a bath and grabbed a few hours sleep."

"Home sounds good," said Rebekah.

"Is that old vampire coming too?" asked Seren. *He seems nice, Papa. Who is he?*

Connor stared hard at his daughter. She was a young woman now, and the last few weeks had wiped away all traces of childhood. *The old vampire is Malachi, my maker.* Connor's lips twitched. *And the handsome young man is Osiris.*

Seren's innocent gaze gleamed with amusement. *You think he is handsome, Papa?*

Connor laughed out loud. "I'm sure you think he is handsome, too, Squirt," he said, drawing Rebekah into the conversation.

"Who?" asked Rebekah.

"Osiris, the Egyptian," Seren replied. "Why is he not eating with us, Papa?"

"He is Malachi's servant, Seren." Rebekah's lowered tone hummed with concern. "You know we may not see him again."

"But he has to eat. Papa?"

Connor saw again the door of the death chamber closing, and Osiris standing fearless with blood dripping from his arm onto the steel floor. "Yes, he has to eat," Connor said absently, shifting in his seat. "Your Mama is right, though, Seren. He is Malachi's servant. He probably ate in their room."

Seren shrugged and returned to her own meal.

Certain that Seren's concern stemmed from curiosity, Connor felt easier. *She has led a sheltered existence and Osiris is as far from an Englishman as you can get. Of course he will spark an interest.* His daughter's peaceful expression and steady hybrid-slow thick pulse seemed to back up that theory. Connor's own curiosity rose to the fore and he admitted to being preoccupied with having Rebekah back in his arms. *It's time I knew more about Osiris' miraculous escape.*

"I better go and see how Julian is getting along preparing the ship for the journey home," Connor said briskly. Rising from his chair, he dropped a kiss onto Rebekah's upturned lips and vanished from the room.

Malachi? Connor knew the ancient vampire would know he was on his way. *Meet me on the battlements.* Going up the stone stairwell and pushing open the wooden hatchway, Connor emerged on the circular platform of the east turret, the gales trying to tear the hatch door from his grip. The bracing surroundings, where there was no escaping the forces of nature, cleared Connor's mind. *And Seren will find it harder to listen in.* Or so he hoped.

As expected, he found Malachi waiting. Osiris stood beside him, his coal black hair whipping around his face, his dark regard steady and penetrating.

"I meant alone." Connor flicked a glance at Osiris, feeling irritated by the Egyptian's arrogant bearing. The younger man stood with his arms crossed over his bare chest, his muscular frame impervious to the gusting wind, his gilt armlets glinting in the sunset.

Connor's skin tingled when the weak rays of the dying sun broke through the clouds, but he lifted his chin and faced the young warrior, unflinching.

Malachi smiled as the air hummed with aggression. He looked at his young companion and nodded.

Osiris moved smoothly aside, planted his hand on the wall, and, in a fluid movement, vaulted over the top. He jogged along the ramparts to the turret at the south corner of the castle. Connor resisted the urge to look, but still caught sight of the young man's progress in the corner of his eye as Osiris swung up and over the far wall, and disappeared.

"He will wait in our rooms until I return," said Malachi.

"Is he human?"

Malachi's thin brows lifted and he chuckled.

"You trust him, I know, but I need the truth." Connor stopped beside Malachi and stared out over the gray rolling sea. He rubbed a hand over the hardened capillaries where the sun had burned his skin and laughed. "It is a long time since I had a young buck on my stamping ground. Should I be worried, Malachi?"

"Not on Osiris' account. But I don't think this is about him alone."

"No, it is about my family." Connor rested his hands on top of the wall. The wind snatched his words, but speaking out loud was only for his own benefit. Malachi was inside Connor's head where words were not needed.

I have known Osiris since his birth. You have no need to fear him.

Connor asked the question that intrigued him. *How did you protect him in the death chamber? His blood was flowing, and you could not have saved him from injury against all four vampires.*

I did not have to. Malachi's crystal-tinted gaze was unwavering. *He does not have a scratch on him. He is not human.*

Both vampires stood motionless as the exchange rattled between them, and Connor relaxed into the familiar sensation of having his head filled with images which were not his own. Malachi knew the words would not be enough.

He is a human-vampire hybrid.

As Malachi's memories thickened inside Connor's mind, the gray sheet of rippling ocean blurred and shifted until it became the mirror finish of polished quartz. The eyes he looked through were Malachi's, but how many years ago, he had no idea.

Malachi followed a line of vampires down the slick slope and into a chamber. *We are inside a pyramid?*

No, this is a sacrificial chamber, constructed by the Cairo hive beneath the desert sand.

Connor frowned. *You were part of the Cairo hive?*

Malachi's laughter rattled like phlegm in his throat. *When it suited me, I used my 'elder' status. Two thousand years of immortality carries with it respect. 'Know your enemy' is a creed not to be ignored.*

It was a peculiar feeling for Connor, sharing his consciousness with Malachi, but these were not his own thoughts.

The cavernous space had the gilt embellishments of an Egyptian tomb. The figures adorning the walls could be Osiris' brethren – each one was depicted bare to the waist, wearing gold skirts and jewels, and the crowning glory of glossy black hair.

The vampires entered the cavern in single file, circled the room, and found a place on a curved stone bench. The circular floor sloped away towards the center, where a stone altar drew Connor's attention and spawned a feeling of fatalistic dread. 'Sacrificial chamber', Malachi had said.

The white faces in the row were as individual as human faces always were. Vampirism enhanced those differences, if anything. The thoughts inside each head created a mesmerizing current. Every one assembled had but one thought. *Blood.*

The door the procession had passed through closed, and the sheet of steel covering the aperture was not what Connor had expected. The Egyptian illusion was shattered. Profound darkness descended and yet, he could still see the visceral glint in the eyes staring back at him, like revelers waiting for the performance to begin.

He realized that all eyes were focused on him. *Or on Malachi, at least.* And Connor felt expectation swell inside his own chest. *What are they waiting for?* He did not have to wait long.

Malachi's chest rumbled with the incantation he recited to the convened vampires. "Human blood lives in us as we release the soul into the waiting hands of God. Thirst is our cross to bear, and suffering for an eternity is our punishment for defying God's will. Our oath is to save our sacrifice from pain."

His words faded and eerie silence stretched into motionless minutes. *Malachi, what happens now?* The tension was palpable.

Wait, you will see.

The soft shuffle of bare feet grew louder until Connor turned to face the dark alcove he had thought was only a shadow. *A tunnel.*

Four figures appeared, walking carefully between the vampire attendants who guided them. Their heartbeats clattered with terror and the hessian sacks over their heads barely muted the ragged breathing.

Their grimy clothes declared them as prisoners. Their dirt-encrusted hands bore the cracked skin of hard labor. Connor recoiled when he realized that two of the unkempt figures were women, and one was heavily pregnant.

The four moved down the slope, mounted the step, and were guided to the stone dais. "Lie down, now." The kindly tone of the vampire directing the prisoners surprised Connor. The humans laid out, arranged like four arms of a human cross, and, while the escorts withdrew, Malachi recited again the incantation.

The chanting swelled as each vampire joined in. The tunnel entrance was sealed when another steel door grated across the space and, before Connor knew what to expect, the pack of vampires descended. Malachi remained seated, watching the vampires vying for position as each one sank their teeth into human flesh.

The screams reverberating around the room swelled into a wall of sound. The glimpses of thrashing limbs grew less frequent. The screaming faded and the humans sank into unconsciousness. The undulating mass of feeding vampires suddenly parted when a keening cry sliced through the air, and, this time, Malachi moved.

Malachi shoved vampires aside and took his place beside the pregnant female. Pulling the sack from over her head, he met her glassy stare. Blood poured from the torn flesh of her arms, pooling beneath her body. Without speaking, Malachi, laid his hands over her distended belly.

"Save my baby, please." Her face contorted with grief, not pain. She had no care for herself. The blood still inside her flooded into her face, her torso jerked into spasm and she screamed. Her grip on Malachi's arm broke her fingernails as her body arched and pink fluid gushed from between her thighs.

The sudden rush of watery blood snapped every vampires' head around. Like a pack of hounds on point, they sensed vulnerability. *And a tender morsel. I don't suppose many vampires have fed upon a newborn baby.* Even Connor experienced a moment of curiosity.

As the baby's head crowned, his mother died. Being the elder vampire in the coven, unchallenged, Malachi took control. The dead mother's belly slackened, leaving the baby still trapped inside her. Malachi pressed firmly on her stomach, and with the other hand he eased the infant's shoulders out. The birth happened in a rush, the slick scrawny body slipping into Malachi's hands. Without pausing to look at the baby, he knotted the umbilical cord, and sliced his fingernail through it. Picking up the child and wrapping it in his cloak, Malachi headed for the exit. He thumped three times on the steel door with a force that dislodged a shower of gravel.

Connor felt the tension rippling through Malachi's body as the rumbling growls of the pack closing in behind grew louder. The smell of blood still hung in the air but the vampires were intent on the infant. Malachi half turned, prepared to fight. But, as if the Gods smiled down on the baby, the placenta slipped from the mother's ruptured body with a wet slopping sound; an iron-rich clotted blood aroma plumed into the air. The pack reared, circling in confusion, the door opened, and Malachi slipped through it.

The scene faded and the sound of the waves crashing into the castle walls brought Connor back. Staring out over the pink dusk-streaked sky, Connor said, "And the baby is Osiris?"

Malachi roused himself to speak aloud. "Yes."

Connor scanned Malachi's wizened features. "So, why did you name him Osiris?" Connor knew Malachi well enough to know the old vampire would have a story to tell.

"The Legend of Osiris is an ancient religious myth in Egypt. Osiris was known as God of the Dead and Lord of the Underworld. It seemed fitting. But it was his father, Imhotep, who named him." Malachi smiled.

"You knew his father?"

Malachi nodded. "Although, I was unaware of it, until after. I took the child to the Earth Walker tribe, who I trusted."

"Earth Walker? What is so special about them?" Connor stopped breathing and waited – if Osiris was an example, then he was keen to know.

As if Connor had not interrupted, Malachi continued. "When I took the infant to them, I found out then about the kidnap of Imhotep's life partner, heavy with child." Malachi's sorrow thickened the air. "I couldn't save *her*, but it brought him some comfort that a part of her lives on in his son." Malachi straightened, shook off his regret, and said decisively, "Osiris understands he is a hybrid. Vampire venom traveled along the umbilical cord before the placenta detached."

"And that interrupted his transformation?"

"That is the only explanation. Osiris has the honed senses of a mature vampire, and his human bone marrow means his strength is at the perpetual peak which usually comes with vampire age. He no longer needs my protection."

Connor said, "But he likes you, after all, he is not in Egypt with his father. He knows that if humans die out, you may need *his* protection, his blood, to keep you alive."

"We have a bond, yes." Malachi assessed Connor's tight grip, where his fingers had burrowed holes into the battlement wall. "You can trust him. And I have a hankering to see London once more, to see what you have done to the old place in the last hundred years."

"You won't like it," Connor said bluntly. "The pandemic altered the face of the globe. The City of London is dead, only vampires exist there now. The human farm was built in a more rural and easily defended place, out to the west, where the crops we needed to farm were more easily transported."

"Rebekah lives there? On the farm?"

Connor's harsh laughter echoed through the dark. "Not at all. Rebekah's group of humans were refugees who escaped discovery for the first fifteen years of vampire domination. I kind of screwed that up and owed her my protection."

"But, you fell in love." Malachi smiled. "You forget, I have seen inside you. You owed her nothing, but you fell in love. Gives you hope, does it not, that we are not monsters, not through and through? I felt compelled to save Osiris, and you, Rebekah. We have some decency left inside us."

Not all of us.

"Sentinel Lars was not as impervious to emotion as he appeared."

No, but Rebekah and I have been through so much. I have killed to save her. I'll gladly rid the vampire race of those who deserve no mercy.

Curiosity got the better of Malachi. "And where does Principal Julian fit into all this?"

"Let's just say, he is my comrade in arms, and he, too, has discovered he still has a heart."

"Are you talking about me?" Julian said, as he emerged silently through the trapdoor. "The vessel is ready to set sail."

"And we have two more pairs of hands to help out."

Julian stared at Malachi and lifted a brow. "It will be easier to sail with six men on board. I'm guessing the Egyptian is coming, too?"

"We will set off in an hour. Greg and Seth will be keen to get started, and we can make it back to London by dawn," said Connor.

"Very well, I'll go and tell Osiris." Malachi left the two friends sharing a moment of peace.

"You know what you are doing? Taking Malachi to London?" said Julian.

"*Numu* was the evil twin, Julian, you know that. Malachi is a thorn in your side, but nothing more." Connor laughed. "He just wants to fill some time. He won't stay."

"And Osiris?"

"Of course," said Connor. "Where Malachi goes, Osiris goes, too." *At least, I hope so.* Seren's interest in the dark young man unsettled Connor, and even though he welcomed a chance to swap tales with his mentor, Malachi's exotic companion, he would rather not think about.

The climb up the rope ladder and onto Lars' ship was a different experience for Rebekah this time. The face of the vampire waiting on the deck, extending a hand to help her, reflected care and adoration that made her heart pound against her ribs.

Connor's mock leering smile made her blush, and levity melted from his keen gaze.

Rebekah gulped when he pulled her inexorably into his arms and kissed her. A growling sigh rattled inside him as his cool lips eased the tingle of desire in hers. He released her slowly, keeping hold of her hand while he cleared his throat and turned to face Seren.

The wind tore tendrils of Seren's black hair free of its braid, and the full moon lit up the delight in her gray gaze. Her moon-bleached complexion gave the illusion of a pure-bred vampire as she smiled and ran her tongue over her teeth.

Alarm bells rang for Rebekah. She had never seen such manic excitement in her daughter's expression before.

As though staying still was impossible, Seren grabbed Connor's free hand, and said, "Come, Papa, I'll show you where he kept us. With an insistent tug, Seren towed him away.

Rebekah only kept up because Connor set the pace. Shooting a glance back over his shoulder, their eyes met and Rebekah's suspicions were confirmed by his sharp nod.

The cabin remained the same. The handcuff hung from the pipe, the other bracelet bent out of shape from where Lars had unfastened it for the last time.

"Here, Mama can sleep in here. I'll keep her company." Seren's eyes shone. "Unless I can help you on deck."

Connor wanted to use handcuffs on his daughter, and know that she would be out of Osiris' orbit, but he had more urgent things on his mind.

"I think Mama will sleep here alone, Squirt."

"But, why?"

Connor smiled. Seren could barely stand still as the part of her vampire brain which regulated excitement and passion screamed out for refreshment.

"Seren, I think you have reached another milestone."

He had her attention, now.

"You remember the compartments in your brain you must learn to unlock, and rehydrate?" Connor took both Seren's hands in his and her fingers fluttered wildly, fighting against the confinement.

"You need rap-sleep, and when you do, your emotions will be out of control."

Seren looked at Rebekah, and understanding dawned in her eyes. "I might hurt Mama."

"It is better if you stay with us. Julian and I can help you through it."

Rebekah smiled. "It's okay, Seren." Looking around the familiar cabin, she said, "It's no longer a prison." Just seeing Connor in the same place where Lars had once stood wiped the nightmares from her mind.

"You'll be okay here. Greg and Seth will come and keep you company when we are underway," said Connor.

"Perhaps, I'll take a walk around the deck in a little while," Rebekah said demurely, veiling devilment beneath her lashes.

Connor laughed. "I'm sure you will be happy to distract me. Although, you may have trouble recognizing me after sun up, so don't go throwing your kisses away on the wrong vampire."

In the weak early dawn, Julian, Malachi, and Connor planned to wear the satin-thin leather hooded capes of Lars' guardsmen, and, if the sun became strong, the eerily terrifying leather face masks. *And perhaps Osiris, too?* Rebekah was not sure and, aware of Seren moving restlessly around in the cabin, she did not ask. She found, that right now, she did not want to draw attention to the imposing Egyptian warrior.

Rebekah placed a hand on Connor's arm, wondering again at the stark beauty of his strong features. "I won't have any trouble recognizing you."

His smile lit up her world as he gently lifted her chin and kissed her. "I'll be back soon, perhaps, I can keep you company."

"That would be nice," she said, releasing him. He stepped back and held out his hand to Seren who paced the room like the floor was covered in hot coals.

"Come, Seren," he called, and, with a final glance at Rebekah, they both vanished, the soft thud of the closing door vibrating through the air.

Retracing their steps along the gangway, Connor opened each door and got his bearings. As he expected, at the end of a sloping passage leading down into the bowels of the ship, he found a row of steel-lined cells. To enter one, he would have to turn sideways and, even then, his back and chest would be wedged against both walls. Each chamber resembled an upright cadaver drawer. The polished metal panels bore dents and scratches. *So, this is where the crew took grave-sleep.*

He glanced down at Seren's curious expression and decided he would rather hold her in his arms than lock her inside one of these cells.

The rolling motion of the ship told Connor that they had set sail.

"Let's go up on deck and find Uncle Julian," said Connor.

The moonlit deck glistened, and coal black shadows pooled in corners, looking like black holes which would swallow anyone who stepped into them. Malachi appeared from one such shadow, and Seren looked over the old vampire's shoulder to see if he was alone.

"Malachi," Connor said sharply.

The smile dancing in Malachi's eyes irritated Connor. "We've been waiting for you. Julian has us underway, but six rowers will be better than four if we're to cover some ground while it's dark."

Connor was torn. It looked as though Seren would be left alone after all.

"I'll be okay, Papa. I'll go and sit at the front of the ship, keep a look out for other vessels."

Connor had not given the super tanker another thought since escaping, but perhaps they should be cautious. More casually than he felt, he said, "Okay, Squirt. Go sit up front." Scooping a coil of rope from the deck, he added, "But I'm going to tie you in. Rap-sleep can make you hallucinate, and it's not as if you'd float if you decided to go for a swim. This is not a good time to test out how long you can hold your breath." Connor framed Seren's chin, fascinated as always by the slow thick pulse deep inside her dense tissue. "You are not quite indestructible."

Seren dutifully allowed Connor to secure the rope around her waist and anchor the other end to a steel ring bolted to the deck. His final glimpse of Seren was of her standing at the prow with the wind tearing at her jeans and shirt, and the tangled mass of her hair framing her delicate features. The smile on her face was both unsettling and reassuring at the same time.

"Just call out, I will hear you," said Connor, and he disappeared around the wooden structure of the cockpit which offered the pilot protection from the sun, and from where Lars would have taken command of his vessel.

The ship was moving fast, and the rhythmic splashing of two sets of oars cutting through the surf was a comforting sound. *We are going home.* Connor emerged onto the aft deck and watched the effortless motion of Julian and Seth on one side, and Osiris and Greg on the other. Seth and Greg were tiring already. The upright rowing position was awkward for humans. The sea was many yards down, and the oarsmen, even though they stood in what could only be described as a hole, still had to hold the oar at a thirty-degree angle. The oar passed through a hole punched in the side of the ship, and the task was more akin to paddling an enormous canoe.

Connor and Malachi took up places at the rear. Connor gave himself over to the repetitive action where every muscle in his body moved like a well-oiled machine, and it allowed him time to think. *Greg and Seth will need a rest soon.* Staring past Greg's solid sweat-stained back, Connor caught glimpses of Osiris.

His concerns over Seren becoming smitten overshadowed his clinical curiosity and he admitted that, under other circumstances, he would welcome the young man and be keen to find out how he balanced the needs of being both human and vampire. As things stood, he would be glad when Malachi and his consort departed.

Greg's grunting effort and the sizzling sound of his muscle fibers tearing focused Connor's attention. "Stop rowing," Barked Connor, loud enough for the humans to hear over the wind tunnel whipping past their ears.

When the current stirred by the oars faded to gentle waves slopping onto the hull, Connor said. "Greg, Seth, go below and eat. Go and have some down time with Rebekah. I'm sure she'll be glad of the company.

Greg grimaced. "I'm not sure sweaty men are great company."

Connor laughed. "There are barrels of water in the hold, you could always wash first."

"We'll have our moment when the sun comes up and your lot are skulking in shadows," grumbled Greg with a tired grin. He clambered out of the chest-deep hole looking ten years older than when he had jumped in.

Connor chose not to disillusion him. True, being well covered for extended periods softened vampire skin, and, in a world where all your peers were strong it left a vampire vulnerable to harm, but with the garb used by Lars' guardsmen, Connor and Julian could row through the glare of the midday sun, if they were careful.

The group of four rowed without pause for three hours. Connor listened for Seren's call and by this time, he would have been happier if she *had* called out. *Or talked to me telepathically. At least I'd know what was happening with her.*

Of course, her first experience of rap-sleep might creep up on her, instead of being the drop of a hammer which Connor could activate in himself.

Just when he was considering telling Malachi to stop so he could go and check on her, Rebekah emerged from below. A bitterly cold wind which scattered needles of icy spray over his back made this a bad time for her to be up on deck.

Connor forgot Seren for a moment and scowled at Rebekah.

Malachi's glance sharpened suddenly in the split second before Osiris dropped his oar, vaulted from his rowing station, and disappeared down the port side of the ship towards the prow.

Seren's thoughts shrieked inside Connor's head at the same time, and he, too, catapulted from his oaring point.

He sprinted the forty yards to the prow and found it deserted. The rope still anchored to the deck stretched like a tight rope across his path and disappeared over the wooden hand rail. Leaping the vibrating cord, Connor peered over the side into the black water. He easily picked out the hanging figures of Osiris and Seren and inhaled sharply.

The young Egyptian glanced up and shouted, "She is okay."

In an effortless vault, Connor threw himself over the side and immediately the creaking rope fibers began to tear. As quickly as he had left the deck, he pulled himself back up. Instead, he gripped the rope and began to haul the two figures up, winding the rope around his fists as he went.

The two faces staring up at Connor were cheek to cheek and again a father's jealousy tightened his gut.

Osiris reached up and grabbed the rail. Bracing her foot on the young warrior's thigh, Seren boosted herself up and over the side. The puddle of water gathering at Seren's feet oozed like an oil spill in the darkness. Connor cocked his brow, folded his arms, and waited. The questions stayed locked inside while he appeared to ignore Osiris climbing aboard and landing lightly beside Seren.

Concentrating on untying the wet rope from around her waist, Seren busied herself wringing out the fabric of her shirt as she muttered, "I wasn't sleeping. I saw a black seal."

"Well, you would. The North Sea has a lot of them." Connor suddenly realized that his daughter had only seen pictures of the aquatic life, and his attitude softened. "You know, curiosity killed the cat, and the young vampire, apparently. You didn't fall, so?"

Seren smiled apologetically, "I thought I could climb down the side and get a closer look, and *then* I fell."

Finally turning to Osiris who stood in his own puddle of seawater, Connor said grudgingly, "Thank you, Osiris."

They both knew he probably saved Seren's life. Even if she had stopped breathing, dropping like a stone to the seabed could have broken something and finding her could have been almost impossible.

Osiris nodded gravely. He appeared oblivious to the water running from his black hair, down over his naked torso, and turning to frost on his skin. "It was my honor." His soothing tones eased Connor's irritation.

Osiris' white teeth glinted in the gloom, and Connor realized it was the first time he had seen the youthful Egyptian smile. He suddenly acknowledged he owed Osiris respect. After all, he had put himself in the firing line by entering Lars' castle. *I'm being an arrogant jerk. And he will be gone soon.*

Seren watched her knight in shining armor walk away, and said, "I agree with the first part." She added wistfully, "But, does he have to go?"

Connor grimaced. *You were not supposed to hear that.* "I can't see him drinking tea in England. But we shall see." Meeting her serious gray gaze, Connor reached out to squeeze the water from her hair. Pulling the tangled wet strands of the braid apart, he draped an arm around her shoulders. "Go below and get yourself dry. You seem calmer now, perhaps the excitement of the seal was a useful distraction."

The next couple of hours passed smoothly. The wind direction turned to a chilly brisk southerly. Hoisting the mainsail, the ship made good progress, needing only a guiding hand on the tiller. Julian and Connor stood shoulder to shoulder inside the cockpit, gazing out from the elevated vantage point through sea-salt encrusted glass. The early morning sun cast an undulating carpet of gold over the sea and long purple-tinted shadows across the deck.

Both vampires wore the oil-slick thin leather capes, and gauntlets molded to their fists like molten tar. Their masks were tucked into their belts, neither wanting to wear them until the sun forced them into it.

"How does it feel, to be going back into the London hive? Back to running the hospital and looking over your shoulder?" asked Julian quietly.

"About the same as it must feel to be going back to presiding over petty squabbles in court, and fending off the zealots who mean Seren harm, I should imagine."

"We should keep this ship as spoils of war. You never know when we might need it again." Julian's probing glance surprised Connor. He felt an answering surge of unrest inside his own chest.

"I agree," said Connor.

The thick silence of co-conspirators had barely settled when Connor heard girlish laughter. He smiled while he concentrated on connecting his mind to Seren's, already imagining Rebekah's answering laughter lighting up her face.

The face he found staring back at Seren was male, alight with its own laughter, and the black pools of his dark eyes shone even from where he stood in the half shadows. *Osiris.* A tide of inexplicable anger flooded Connor and without a word, he swung around, leaving Julian staring open-mouthed after his receding figure.

It took three seconds for Connor to reach the wide deck at the stern of the ship. His muscles were strung tight and he battled with the heavy-handed paternal instincts which Rebekah tried to curb. He could almost hear her voice of reason, telling him to slow down and take it easy.

He stopped behind the stacked crates secured to the deck with steel cables which Greg and Seth had filled with artefacts from Lars' castle. More spoils of war, as Julian would say. But this time they reflected the magpie instincts of *human* nature. They were reminders of their adventure, mementoes to look back on.

Pulling his flowing cape around his thighs with clenched fists, Connor stood still and listened to the lighthearted exchange unfolding between his daughter and Osiris. He focused on the electrical activity of the synapses firing inside Seren's brain, and found one area going into overdrive. The temporal lobe. *She's practicing rap-sleep.*

Moving slightly, Connor could see Osiris' broad back clothed in a cape similar to his own. Beyond him, even though a hood shadowed her face, Connor zeroed in on the scowl marring Seren's features and the anxiety filling her eyes.

Osiris whispered gently, "It's okay, let it happen." His demeanor was reassuring as he said, "You can throw things at me. Let the anger out. You can't hurt me."

A snarl broke from Seren's throat and she threw herself at Osiris. His strong arms darted out and folded around her. Resting his cheek on the crown of her head, Osiris did exactly what Connor himself would have done, he held her in silence until the storm of emotions passed.

The two figures remained locked in an embrace which would appear peaceful to a human observer, but Connor knew better. Osiris' steady heartbeat thudded hard, and the flush creeping across his skin was mirrored in Seren's own body. Witnessing the attraction between the two hit Connor like a fist in the gut, and his convulsing grip tore holes in his leather cape.

Connor deliberately scuffed his boot over the wooden deck and stepped out into the open.

Both youngsters turned to face him.

Osiris' impassive expression was betrayed by the ruddy stain over his high cheekbones and the veiled excitement in his coal-back stare.

"Papa-" Seren's breathless exclamation stemmed from a cauldron of emotion. "I did it. I unlocked the door and took rap-sleep at my own will. Like you do, Papa. I chose it." Her smile detracted from the worry in her eyes as they darted from the tall Egyptian and back to Connor's stiff features. "I'll be safe around mama if I can control it."

Connor opened his arms and smiled. He tried not to notice Osiris' muscles flexing as he released his daughter's hand. "Well done, Sq- Seren." His usual nickname no longer seemed to fit the woman emerging like a butterfly from a chrysalis. He thought of his own collision of senses when he first met Rebekah. *There's no going back.*

Looking over Seren's head while he hugged her, Connor saw Osiris smile tightly when he noticed the tattered edges of Connor's cape and the pellets of crushed leather lying on the deck.

"I think," Connor said slowly, "That you should go and tell Mama." Giving her a final robust squeeze, he held her at arms' length. "And Uncle Julian."

Is everything okay? You don't mind that Osiris helped me? Connor's jaw clenched as he met Seren's frank appraisal. *I like him, Papa. Please be nice.*

I just want to talk to him. But Seren, alone, okay. No eavesdropping and I promise to be nice. He gripped her delicate looking chin, feeling the steel strength beneath his fingertips. *I know you like him. I do, too.* Surprise registered when Connor realized he was telling the truth. *I do like him.*

"I'll go and tell mama." Casting a smile back over her shoulder, Seren left the men alone.

Walking into deeper shadow, both vampires shed the constriction of the leather capes and faced each other. *Things were simpler in 1910, merely holding a girl's hand was a declaration of romantic intent.* Connor had no idea of Egyptian custom.

"Thank you for helping Seren." Connor forced a smile. "She has grave sleep to master, yet. That should be interesting."

Osiris inclined his head. "I like her, too."

"So, you can read her mind?"

Osiris shrugged. "Hers, yours, Malachi's. But nothing is clear, I just get fragments, like pieces of floating ice breaking the surface. A connection is made, and then it disappears again.

"We are all connected by Malachi's blood," said Connor. "Except Seren, but she's part of me."

After a lot of thought, Connor had arrived at a theory – he was a receiver. He could only put his thoughts out there. It appeared that Seren and Malachi could visit his mind and create a two-way connection. But he had to wait for it to happen. How Osiris fit into that framework, Connor couldn't be sure.

"I saw Seren's face before I met her." The smile slipped from the young man's features. "I knew she would be fascinating."

Feeling like an old-fashioned fool, Connor asked the only question he could. "What are your intentions, Osiris? If you are leaving with Malachi, don't make my daughter fall in love with you."

"It's too late."

Connor bristled and his sharp glance looked for arrogance.

"I would die for her. If my master will allow it, I shall stay to protect her." Dark currents stirred in Osiris' gaze. "I don't think this London hive will be a safe place."

Connor believed him. He had risked his life already, not just by leaping over the side of the ship, but by fighting off Lars' guardsmen before he had even set eyes on Seren.

"Let us get home first." Connor rested a heavy hand on the Egyptian's hard shoulder. "I know you would die for her. But more importantly, you are a hybrid and you can help her."

"What is it like, Connor, being a vampire?"

His own name on the young man's lips was a huge step in acceptance. "Being a vampire is like carrying a gnawing pit of hunger around in your belly that is never satisfied. I hope you have vampire strength, but not our suffering, otherwise, if you are not the best of both species, then what is the meaning of it all?"

Osiris lifted a curious brow. "Rebekah is still human. Why have you not changed her?"

Connor's amusement bubbled up inside. "It's a question which haunts me. There is no easy answer. Turning her and spending an eternity together is what I yearn for, but until I am sure she will not starve and die as a vampire, I can't do it."

"She would gladly die to be with you. Seren sees it."

Connor took a deep breath, gathered his cape, and swung it into place. "These are things that will become clear in time, once we are back home." As he stepped out into the sunshine, his eyes gleaming in the shadow of his hood, he said, "We will speak again. Welcome to the family, Osiris."

Chapter 22

Sailing into the Thames estuary and passing between the huge steel bonnet shapes of the infamous Thames barrier created a surreal moment, even for Connor. It settled a peculiar blend of foreboding and relief in his chest. *Home.* After all, it was all he had ever known, but it also loomed as the battlefield upon which he always needed to be at the ready.

Connor and Julian stood at the prow watching the black silk of the water slipping by, making ready to make the leap onto the quayside and guide the ship in safely.

"I wonder how Marius and Anthony have fared?"

"Perhaps it would be better if the hive continues to think I'm in a vampire coma? Until we are settled, at least."

"Settled where?" Julian frowned. "We're back to square one, unless..."

"Unless?"

"We could just turn around and sail into the sunset."

"And I thought I was the impulsive one. What about Leizle?"

"Think about it, Connor. You could hide out at Seth's camp for a while, but I think we have to say goodbye to London."

"We?"

Julian smiled. "You're not going anywhere without me. I want to see Seren grow up. Someone has to stop her turning out like her father."

"Looks like we have some plans to make. But let's get everyone home first. Time to go," Connor muttered. He pushed away from the wooden balustrade and launched himself over the side of the ship.

Connor embraced the exhilaration of working alongside Julian, Osiris, and Malachi, dragging chains thicker than his biceps across the dockside and winding them around the mooring points with ease.

He grinned spontaneously into the darkness at hearing the noise of a car being driven at a sedate pace. The engine stopped and, moments later, Marius and Anthony drifted into sight.

Anthony chuckled. The slick leather capes of Julian and Connor's rowing garb gave them the appearance of black crows. "You're certainly a sight for sore eyes." His gaze flicked over the wooden hull of the Viking ship. "Everyone is okay?" he asked casually.

"Yes, Anthony. I have a few more scars, but everything is perfect," grinned Connor.

Marius' inquiring glance took in the tall Egyptian and Malachi, and, never one for jumping to conclusions, he raised a brow.

Connor weighed his words carefully. "It's a long story."

Marius' nostrils flared and his black eyes latched onto Osiris' face.

"As I said, Marius, it's a long story. But we have a new addition to the group and, for now, he is best kept under wraps. He is a hybrid, like Seren." Connor held up a hand, sensing that even Marius was overcome with curiosity. "No, not *exactly* like Seren, but let's go home. Explanation will have to wait."

The journey back to London became a parody of a presidential parade. Malachi drove the limousine carrying all the humans, along with Seren and Osiris, and the remaining group of four vampires ran alongside.

While running, before they entered the City of London, and where there was less danger of being overheard, Marius and Anthony did much of the talking.

"Supervisor Matthew was certainly part of the plot to disable Connor, but he is merely a pawn, I'm sure of that," said Marius.

Julian nodded. "Now we are back, send Captain Gerrard out to arrest him. I'll call a closed session of the council. Matthew is a coward. I'm sure he will talk."

"Where is Alexander?" asked Connor.

"He thought it wiser to remain at the council building. He's playing good cop to the intern who jabbed Connor, in the hope he'll let something slip," Marius replied.

"Any problems with our human friends, Anthony?" asked Julian.

They all knew he was thinking of Leizle.

"All is good there." Anthony smiled. "She's beside herself with worry, but I'm sure seeing you will put her mind at rest."

"First. I want Matthew's head on a platter. We'll send a messenger to Principal Tavish at Loch Glascarnoch Hive and have Serge detained. His influence is all over this."

The smell of the ocean clung on as salt deposits on hair, skin, and clothes of the travelers, but the low rumble of the surf and its untiring efforts to grind away the rugged coastline quickly faded. The jagged skyline of a dead London rose on the dark horizon until even Rebekah, looking out through the window of the car, could pick out the individual derelict buildings.

"Nearly home, sweetheart," she murmured, squeezing Seren's hand.

Will you stay? Seren stared straight ahead, even though her other hand sought Osiris' relaxed fingers.

I will stay as long as your father allows it.

Osiris' thoughts filled Seren with a sense of wellbeing. *Good.*

The car jolted over the growing number of potholes which had turned the long-abandoned road into an obstacle course. Finally admitting defeat, Malachi pulled over to the grass verge.

Connor opened the car door and drew Rebekah out to stand beside him. Dropping a kiss on her lips he said, "It looks like I'll be carrying you from here."

"I can double time it with the men," she laughed. "I'm not an invalid."

"But why slum it, when your chariot awaits," said Connor, executing a Sir Walter Raleigh bow.

With everyone grouped on the side of the road, Connor quickly outlined the game plan.

Slapping his friend on the back, Julian said, "I'll meet with Gerrard and get the arrests underway. I'll see you at the council buildings when you get back." Traveling alone had a certain freedom, and Julian became a speck in the distance in seconds, and then he hit his top speed and vanished.

The remainder of the group traveled in formation with Rebekah at the nucleus. As the most precious cargo, to Connor's mind, the journey to the eco-town was accomplished efficiently with him getting his way and carrying Rebekah.

Even at a 'human friendly' vampire pace, Greg and Seth struggled to keep up. Both men looked thankful when they peeled off to visit Seth's camp and deliver the good news to Harry, Oscar, Leizle, and the others.

At the familiar expanse of pasture on the edge of the woods, Marius stopped abruptly.

Connor set Rebekah onto her feet and walked back to where Marius waited. "Are you coming inside?"

Marius said slowly, "I would like to, but if Matthew and Serge are to be dealt with, I think it should be now. Another time, perhaps."

"You're right of course. Tell Julian I'll follow on once they're settled in." Connor felt happier knowing Malachi and Osiris would be staying with his family. He could spare Anthony to patrol outside, for now, at least. *Being home is just as complicated as Julian said it would be.*

◇◇◇

After a smooth flight back into London, Julian hit the first snag. His complacency evaporated. Unusually, his outward appearance reflected the inner agitation – his hair remained uncombed and salt deposited by the sea spray still clouded his skin. His anger thrummed through the atmosphere and, even though he looked like he had slept in his clothes, every person in the principal's chambers snapped to attention.

"He cannot have just vanished," Julian snapped at Captain Gerrard.

"He's not at the farm, the blood dispensary, or at his house."

Alexander, sitting beside Julian, smothered his surprise. *I didn't know Gerrard knew about Matthew's house.* The supervisor's burial site was well disguised. He was beyond communicating by now. Even if he *was* exhumed, a blood infusion could not reanimate dried out flesh. But if it did happen, the hunt would be on for who wanted him out of the way. *I just have to hold my nerve. If Serge names me, I'll deny it.* Alexander made a promise to any deity who may care to listen. *I've learned my lesson. I just lost sight of whose side I was on, God forgive me.*

"And Councilor Serge?"

Captain Gerrard registered satisfaction. "Principal Tavish has Serge under guard."

"You haven't told them anything?"

Optimism sparked in Gerrard's eyes for a second. "I do not know the details myself, as yet."

Julian smiled for the first time since he had entered the council building. "It was quite an adventure. Once the dust has settled, I shall tell you all about it."

"If we cannot find Matthew, then let's get Councilor Serge down here," said Marius quietly.

"Already in hand," Gerrard replied. "Tavish is meeting my sergeant at Hadrian's Wall. Councilor Serge should be here within the hour."

"Put him in the morgue when he arrives. At least in a cadaver drawer there's no chance he can squirm his way out of this. Somehow, we know he *is* involved. In the meantime, keep searching for Supervisor Matthew." Julian rose to his feet. "Dismissed, Captain, we'll reconvene in one hour."

An hour gave Julian time to do as Anthony had suggested, and put Leizle's mind at rest. *I should catch them coming back through the woods if I leave now.* He knew Greg and Seth would not stay away, and commonsense told him that Leizle, Oscar, and the rest, would be dying to see Rebekah and Seren, too.

Ten minutes later, in the cool air beneath the green canopy, Julian scanned the woodlands for human activity, but he was also on alert for any vampires breaking the twenty-mile exclusion zone. Being caught red-handed by the hive principal would make a hearing redundant, and, the mood Julian was in, he would deliver a fifty-year sentence without a seconds' thought.

A vampire could cover twenty miles in mere minutes, but the percussive soundwave of one travelling at speed was a dead giveaway. *All is quiet.*

He detected the human tang of salty perspiration before he heard them. He stopped on the path he knew they were following and waited expectantly for Leizle to notice him. His ethereal complexion glowed dimly in the shadow, but the slick leather of the cape he wore flowed like a river of oil and he blended in with the trees.

Seth appeared first with his staff held tightly in his hand, his eyes alert. The tension in his face eased when he spotted Julian and waved in greeting.

Julian reached inside the hollowed-out compartment in the tree trunk beside him and held out the bundle of four twigs, stripped of bark. "Looks like it's all clear, and there are four humans in residence. If you count Osiris and Seren as human," he said.

"I think the vampire standing in the corner kind of told me that," Seth huffed.

"Spoilsport," Julian grumbled.

The huddle of trudging figures following Seth emerged in stages, each one reaching the beaten track and stepping out onto the flinty path. Seth lost Julian's attention as he looked for her.

When Leizle appeared, her flame-colored hair glowed like a beacon to Julian's preternatural sight. Her eyes shone like emeralds in the lucent white setting of her radiant complexion, and the pink flush of exertion tinting her cheekbone entranced him.

He locked every muscle still, pushing himself deep into revival sleep as his errant hand crumbled the clutch of sticks he still held to sawdust. The crack of splintering wood drew her startled gaze and, in that instant, she froze.

"Hey, Red," Julian murmured.

Leizle shrugged off her backpack and threw herself at him.

"Pleased to see me, hmm?" he chuckled as he caught her and lifted her to straddle his hips. His next words died in his throat as she framed his face and stared into his eyes. Kissing her and drowning in her scent was all he could think of.

Her heat laid fire over his chest, and his body tightened as he stole her breath, his lips closing over her soft mouth and drinking her in.

Greg, Oscar, Evie and Thomas were part of the group who followed Seth's lead and walked past without batting an eyelid.

"See you at the eco-shelter. Don't you kids get lost, now," Greg said as he disappeared between the trees.

Threading his fingers into her hair, Julian tilted her stubborn chin and absorbed the exhilaration glittering in her eyes. "Did you miss me?" he asked.

Lowering her lashes, Leizle mewed thoughtfully. "You've been away? I hadn't noticed."

Julian slipped his hand up inside her sweater, savoring the satin heat of her skin. He pressed her hips closer into his. "Minx, *I* missed *you.*"

Leizle smiled. "So, I see," she muttered, distracted as she unbuttoned his shirt and pulled it open, kissing his throat and down over his chest.

Julian's growl rumbled beneath her lips as he teased the side of her breast, grazing his thumb in a mesmerizing caress. Desire trickled through her, and the damp heat between her thighs tortured him as he buried his face in her neck.

"We should be getting back," he said gruffly, pushing away from the tree and lowering her gently down his body until her feet touched the ground.

He thrilled at the disappointment which cleared the haze of desire from her gaze. Smiling, he said, "But first-"

The woodlands whisked at the hurricane-swirl of air around her as Julian vanished, returning a second later without his coat and scooping her up into his arms. Leizle relaxed into him. His control was compelling.

The scenery became a haze of green and brown which kept spinning until he lowered her to the ground in a glade overgrown with bluebells where moonbeams danced through the canopy.

Her bedroll and pillow were laid out beneath her, and her backpack sat a few yards away. Nothing else registered as Julian reared up, pulled off his shirt, and thumbed open the button on his pants. His expression took her breath away. His eyes darkened and his smile unveiled male satisfaction. Leizle suddenly knew how his prey felt as, with the muscles of his naked torso rippling, he dropped to his knees. Moving slowly up her body, removing her clothes as he went, he trailed kissed over her skin, a feral growl purring in his throat.

"We should get back," she said weakly.

His kisses drifted over her throat, and he nipped her flesh with his teeth. Her heart rate thundered, and hunger tore through him. "Can I bite?"

Leizle arched her body beneath his and excitement skittered through her.

He had only bitten once before, and his body trembled while he fought for control.

"Yes."

Running his tongue over her carotid artery, Julian lifted her knee, biting into her soft flesh at the same moment he entered her. Fiery heat closed around him and he rode her wave of ecstasy as she shuddered with the overload of sensations.

The molten fire of her blood filling his mouth burned through his center. He stayed still. His vision clouded to red at her galloping heartbeat resonating through his chest. Her blood tingled through his tissue, sizzling along his nervous system and unleashing a storm in its wake. His jaws clamped down. He fought the urge to take every last drop of nectar, and drink his fill.

He clutched her thigh and rocked his hips into hers and, dragging his lips away, he whispered, "Hold tight, Red."

He took her with him as he rolled over onto his back, settled his hands on her waist, and pushed firmly up into her soft warmth. Leizle's hooded gaze drifted closed and she let his rhythm sweep through her, her breasts brushing his chest as she made love to him, knowing he was trying hard not to bruise her skin.

He clenched his jaw, his white face reflecting intense pleasure when he felt her release rippling through her. He growled gently and, with a final twitch of his hips, he joined her, holding her close when she collapsed onto his chest and her teeth playfully nipped at his neck.

"Welcome home," she murmured.

Smiling, Julian reached out a hand and dragged a blanket over them both.

◇◇◇

Julian buried his satisfaction at being with Leizle deep inside. Her love made him feel whole, and he embraced the feeling with fervor. But, right now, standing beside Connor in the morgue, he was Principal Julian, and he wanted answers. At his brisk nod, Anthony gripped the handle on the cadaver drawer.

"Well," said Connor. "Here goes nothing."

"His reaction to you being here should tell us all we need to know," Julian muttered.

Alexander, Marius, and Captain Gerrard stood on the other side of the door, and Connor wondered what Serge would make of his welcoming committee.

Julian nodded again, and Anthony pulled the steel bed out of the wall and looked expectantly down at Serge.

The old vampire's pupils flared as his eyes adjusted and the faces surrounding him snapped into focus. His body jolted, and he scrabbled away from Connor, leaping to his feet. His hip collided heavily with the metal edge of the bed. The empty sleeve of his coat flapped, but there was no arm there to save him.

"Careful, Councilor, I wouldn't want you to hurt yourself," said Julian.

"Is this a parole hearing? Am I leaving Principal Tavish and his delightful hospitality behind?"

"Sarcasm. Good one," said Connor on a wry laugh.

Serge's innocence was convincing.

"It seems you have been spreading rumors of the hybrid birth far and wide," said Marius quietly.

"There is no law against it. Although, it seems to me that Doctor Connor is above the law."

Alexander said, "None of us are above the law. You would be wise to keep your council about Doctor Connor, for fear of inciting others into action."

Serge cackled, making Alexander the focus of his attention. "Someone showed enough guts to make a stand, then? I would like to shake their hand."

Connor grinned. "Shaking hands is not so easy for you now, Councilor."

Serge's thin lips curled in scorn. "You are still standing Doctor Connor. I cannot imagine you would be so cocksure if harm had come to your human woman or your half-breed brat. Pity."

Connor ground his teeth and stepped forward, gripped Serge by the throat, and slammed him back down onto the cadaver drawer bed. The older vampire's thin bones crackled as he landed heavily. With a tight grin, Connor shoved the drawer shut and clicked the catch.

"I'll let you decide what to do with him, Julian, but I don't think he'll admit to anything we can use."

Knowing Serge could still hear them, Julian responded, "I'll leave him in there until Supervisor Matthew is found. Let's hope he fed before he left Scotland, or those words may well be his last."

"My feeling is that this Sentinel Lars used Matthew as a puppet. But with Lars dead, and Matthew gone, I guess we'll never-" Alexander's jaws snapped shut at Julian's abrupt throat cutting gesture.

Alexander's expression said 'sorry'.

Julian glanced pointedly at the steel wall of cadaver drawers. "We will keep looking, for now. Can you send Isaac back in, Captain?"

Captain Gerrard slipped from the room at Julian's nod.

When the morgue attendant re-entered, Julian said, "There's a guardsman outside the door if you need him. Only authorized personnel in here, got it?"

The four vampires left Serge in Isaac's charge and returned to Julian's chambers.

Alexander still looked shamefaced, "I'm sorry-" he began.

With a shake of the head, Marius pressed his lips together. "It is done, but think before you speak in future."

Alexander nodded. "I shall."

"I'm sure you will." Connor turned to Julian. "I'm going home. There's nothing I can do here, and Anthony is coping well with the hospital rounds. You know where to find me." Julian's satisfied demeanor suddenly registered, and Connor quirked an amused brow. "And it looks as though you already know how Leizle is faring?"

"I saw her safely home, that's true," Julian said innocently, but his smile slipped.

A short time later and twenty-five miles away, Connor walked into the small cavern his family called home and found Rebekah waiting for him.

He glanced around the room. "No Seren?"

"She has grown up in the last few weeks and, for some reason, Osiris' company is far more interesting, right now."

Connor swung around and Rebekah said darkly, "Oh no you don't."

He froze mid-stride. "She is still my little girl."

He waited the endless vampire seconds it took Rebekah to get up from her seat and cross the cavern. "She's a good girl, Connor. She knows that going too fast with Osiris would be a mistake." Rebekah smiled. "I'm also sure he would be in here asking permission before he would risk her father's wrath, so lighten up and let them be."

Connor's indecision rumbled in his chest. "Where is Malachi?"

"Out hunting. Anthony gave him a pass to get him into Dartmoor. He'll be hunting lions as we speak, and more importantly-" she reached up and tapped her finger on Connor's temple. "You are entirely alone, and all mine."

"Oh?"

"Now, those new battle scars you were telling Anthony about." Rebekah tugged on his hand and he let her lead him across the room. Pushing him down until he sat on the bed, she stood between his spread thighs and lifted his chin.

"Mmm, let me see." She ran her fingertips down the nape of his neck, feeling the line of fingernail gouges left by Captain Laurence when he had fought for his unborn child. Pushing his shirt away from his powerful shoulders, she found each groove carved into his taut abdomen by Sebastian's sword blows when he had fought a duel for her. Finally, she drifted her fingers down over the roughened texture where Lars' sword had scraped from his shoulder down to his elbow, tearing through the leather tunic he had been wearing.

Connor watched intently as her eyes burned a trail over his skin and finally, his hands on the back of her thighs drew her firmly in against his body. He took her with him when he laid back, and, lacing his fingers into her hair, devoured her mouth.

He growled gently against her lips. "It's been a while since I've seen *your* battle scars. It seems only fair."

Straddling his hips, Rebekah sat up and pulled her shirt slowly up and over her head.

His mouth dry, Connor muttered, "Wait, Wait."

She stared down into his gray eyes, watching the currents in them stirring from flint to soft mercury as he sank into revival sleep. The snarl frozen on his features melted slowly, and then his hands began to move.

One hand grazed down over her shivering belly, stroking along the line of her C-section scar. His fingers slipped beneath the loose elastic of her sweat pants and dipped tantalizingly lower for a moment.

He stroked his hand back up over her hip, and she moaned, "Connor..."

The tearing of fabric barely registered as his hands pushed down to cup her backside and he reared up to sitting. The smooth silk of her bare skin torturing him, he lifted her, freeing himself from the only barrier between them and, at last, lost himself in her warm damp heat.

Her breasts brushed his chest, and his hunger tightened his face as he buried it in her shoulder, muttering her name like a prayer. Mesmerized by the tension he felt building inside her, he closed his mouth over her flesh, and, feeling the blood pulsing beneath her skin, he sucked until he could almost taste it, and a bruise blossomed beneath his lips.

The molten core of her closed around him, and his teeth nipped hard. She jerked in his arms, the shudder of pleasure rampaging through her rippled through him too, and her body clung to his.

Connor groaned as his muscles locked tight and they both tumbled over the edge. Her heartbeat vibrated through his chest, and Connor felt alive. Laying back and holding her close, her molten heat warmed him as he stared up at the ceiling with glazed eyes.

"You know the clock is ticking?" she whispered, feathering kisses along his collarbone.

Connor molded his hands to the swell of her hips and hung onto his concentration. "Clock?" he muttered distractedly.

"Our third anniversary. We had a deal."

Rebekah eased up his body, delighting in the cool hard length of him and framed his beautiful face between her palms. His gray eyes, clouded with sated desire, drifted over her delicate features and a half smile put the barest of creases into the perfection of his skin.

"Turn me, Connor. It is time."

www.ingramcontent.com/pod-product-compliance
Lightning Source LLC
Chambersburg PA
CBHW051210190726
48288CB00006B/1900